QUADRUPLE BIRDIE

a historical novel

D1715699

R.N.A. Smith

To order additional copies of this book, contact:
Xlibris
844-714-8691
www.Xlibris.com
Orders@Xlibris.com
836212

Contents

For Mom, Dad, and Jay

For George, Bob,
And the two Nicks

For all the
Other fallen golfers
I've known.

INTRODUCTION

Texas Quartet

Y IPPEE KI-YAY, I did it. Or, it was done to me if you prefer. Yesterday, August 1st 2020, they celebrated my 100th birthday, and I even got to have 2 pieces of cake. How my 'sweet tooth' rejoiced.

Today, though, is a different matter. I face serious business upon which I am eager to begin, though my tummy is feeling a bit 'off' from all that sugar.

What I intend to do with my perhaps final breaths is to commence the publication process for a manuscript which I've penned and then polished over a period of many years. This book-to-be records the physical, emotional, and spiritual woes confided to me by a foursome of golfing greats 70 years back, when I was an unknown of 30.

Will their spirits censure me for breaking at last the pledge of confidentiality which was understood between us? I trust not, seeing that each of them is long buried. Yet, their impressive humanity should not be obscured, and that has been somewhat the case. It's a common irony: the champions of our world having their flesh-and-blood trials outshone by the ultimate record of their achievements.

So since I can add to the luster of these 4 golfers as mortals, why should I keep silent? My name is Robert Nickel Jefferson Shout. Or, "Dr. Shout" as Ben came to refer to me when he wasn't calling me, "kid."

My 4 'patients' that momentous year were fellow Texans Ben Hogan, Jimmy Demaret, Byron Nelson, and Lloyd Mangrum. Two of them are icons, of course, while the other pair has been forgotten by most golf fans. All of them have claim to Majors and more than 30 official wins on the PGA Tour. That's how damn good they were, a foursome that grew up in the same state while separated by only 4 years in birth. Rivals both early and late, rivaled only in reputation during 1950 by 'the outsider' Sam Snead. Not a 'shrinking violet,' that one. Sparks were bound to fly.

CHAPTER 1

October-December 1949

IT WAS A cool autumn day in Fort Worth on a late October afternoon when I, Bobby Shout, still recovering, still feeling a failure, 'clocked out.' I'd decided to take a late lunch and left work at 2 p.m. With a bagged bologna sandwich and soda pop in hand, I'd set out for my now customary lunch stroll, heading from the TCU campus northwest toward Colonial Country Club where I'd once played in a college tournament during better times.

Only on this occasion I didn't stop to eat at the bench on Mockingbird Lane where one was afforded a glimpse of the golfers. An impulse drove me instead to continue forward and over to Hulen Street, hard by the Clear Fork of the Trinity River. A water-view bench under the shade of a pecan tree sat unoccupied there, so I Bobby Shout sat to consume my humble feast, little knowing …

Musing between bites of baloney, my attention was grabbed soon thereafter by the sight of a thin little man wearing sunglasses and a fedora. The guy was winded obviously, and radiated pain in the halting way he walked. It seemed that he also had been conversing with his inner self, for as he neared my bench, the poor fellow pulled up, seemingly uncertain now whether to join me. Well, his fatigue won out. Mr. Fedora eased himself down as far from me as he could.

For the next 10 minutes he sat, saying nothing, while his breathing slowed. Then, without even a nod nor a glance, the guy rose and resumed his labored walk, heading back north up Hulen Street.

A nothing encounter, yes, but the impression he made on me was far from silence. My head was ringing with the realization that I'd just shared a seat with Ben Hogan, the world's greatest golfer as recently as 9 months back – 'til his car was crushed by a wayward bus in foggy West Texas. So sad that today he should appear as such a frail figure still, with no hope of a return to the game it appeared, certainly not to professional golf, let alone championship form. Mr. Hogan had been the most obsessed player on earth, demanding golf perfection. What would he do with himself now, I had wondered?

That night, I tossed in bed thinking again of Ben. It occurred to me that his home in the exclusive neighborhood of Westover Hills perched easily 3 maybe 4 miles from that bench we shared. Heck, I'd driven by his house on Valley Ridge Road just to ... well, to maybe get a glimpse of him. It *was* a few miles!

If he was pushing himself to walk all the way from there to the bench on Hulen -- and back again! – Ben was now covering more than the distance encompassed in going 18 holes. Then again, maybe he'd called his wife Valerie to come get him at a phone booth 100 yards away from the bench. How far could a man will himself? A personality like Ben Hogan, damn far, I knew from my studies, yet still – walking wasn't like swinging with the grace and violence he'd once possessed. No, no way.

The next morning, I did my job calmly counseling Texas Christian University students concerning their mental dilemmas, while my own mind was dithering about what to do at lunch. By 1 o'clock I'd had enough. I told myself, *Leave at 2 again and go to that bench. If he shows he shows. End of story.* So I did, and yes Ben Hogan did appear. Once more not a word was said by either of us while seated before he left. *Gutless*, I scolded myself, *you're gutless!*

Thursday was rainy, giving me my excuse for not lunching outside, i.e., at Hulen Street, but Friday presented us Fort Worthians with a deep blue sky and warmer air. I packed my lunch with Ben's bench in mind, honing my resolve to speak to him should he show.

After his awaited, dreaded arrival that day, it only took me 5 minutes and 3 puffs on a cigarette to finally stutter, "Good-od afternoon-on, Mister Hogan." (I was *never* a habitual stutterer!) Well Ben gave me that look with his grey-blue eyes that have melted the mettle of a thousand brawny men before pointing toward my mouth while saying, "Can you spare one of those, Mr. Shout."

Count me double-stunned. Hogan knew my name?! And, here was Ben, a renowned smoker on the course – so cool! – without a butt? I was to learn later that he was 'on vacation' from smoking just then, but only because his wife Val had pleaded with him to stop during his recovery.

Just then though, after he'd murmured thanks and lit up, it appeared that our conversation for the day was finished. Ben had recommended his silence and begun staring skyward, that was until he commented like it was nothing special, "For a college kid you had a damn nice swing. Thought I'd see your name in the papers at the Amateur these past few years." What?

I should explain that back in the spring of '45, my sophomore year at Southern Methodist University – that's over in Dallas, 30 miles east of Forth Worth for you non-Texans – I Bobby Shout, had been Ben's partner in an exhibition to sell war bonds. It had been him and me against Byron Nelson and the number 2 man on our college team, Tad Everston, at Dallas Country Club. We'd won, Ben 'carrying' our side naturally. And, with as little as he said to me that day, I never thought he'd remember me 5 minutes later, let alone after 5 years. But he had, obviously; a genius some people thought him.

No offense taken if you're wondering what we four were doing, golfing rather than fighting the war that fine May day. Mr. Nelson was a bleeder and therefore had been categorized as 4-F by the Selective Service Board. I also had received a deferment, the nature of which I'll get to later. Tad, he was the smart one, studying some sort of physics at an advanced level, so the draft board had been ordered to leave him alone.

Only Ben had a uniform among us. He was an Army training pilot based in Texas, and so available for the occasional round if it could help the war effort. In fact, he was relieved from duty just 2 months later.

Born in August of 1920, I would be turning 25 that summer, kind of old for a college kid – for reasons to be revealed. It was my thought that a lot of the returning vets were going to be pretty messed up in the head, and I wanted to help. So, psychology was becoming my major course of study. In fact, I was driven to leave SMU and my beloved Texas for the frigid north the very next fall on account of this desire ... but more on that in a minute.

You remember that Ben had commented on my golfing prospects. Well, it was then that I felt obliged to mention to him about moving to Chicago. Hogan being Hogan (i.e., golf-obsessed), his first response was about how there were *some* decent courses 'up there.' I think he mentioned Tam O'Shanter and Medinah among others. Still, Ben read my eyes soon enough, realizing that golf had nothing to do with my relocation, and said, "Okay, Mr. Shout, why the move?"

That answer was simple, the influence of a single man: The psychologist Carl Rogers. In the '40s he was the chief proponent of a more humanistic form of psychology. No cold authority figure prying out sexual secrets defined his profession. Instead, Rogers' recipe for helping those with mental disorders was to be a friendly therapist, one who recognized that each individual's perception of the world varied, and affected their behaviors in turn. "Listen, listen, listen, don't judge," he'd say. I've oversimplified here, but as we Texans describe super smart guys like him, "He learned his horse some geometry!"

So, when I found out in the weeks after teaming with Hogan that Carl Rogers had been hired by the University of Chicago, and his plan was to establish a counseling center there, I left my clubs behind like I was Mr. Noble. Nor did I have any regrets the next 2 years as one of his prize students, if I do say so.

But then, Chicago was too stuffy to hold onto him when the University of Wisconsin came a courting -- just as I was preparing to graduate with my B.S. in the spring of '47. Well, he moved on, and I Bobby Shout listened foolishly to the prognosis of other faculty who declared, "Now you must go to medical school. You won't be able to prescribe any drugs for vets in need, unless you have an M.D. I shook my head later; as if skillful talking wasn't powerful in its own right.

Anyways, I was homesick for the Lone Star State, so it was going to be a U. of Texas med school for me sure'nuff. And I chose the one in Galveston, far from family ties.

The only trouble was, all that memorizing in school about bodily functions that had nothing to do with the brain didn't seem worth the effort after my daddy died. At least, that was the excuse given by me when I dropped out during my 2nd med year, at Christmas break.

Not that money was a problem in 1949 for Bobby Shout, son of the deceased Big Tom Shout, wildcatter supreme. I could rejoin the family oil business whenever I liked. But, this cushion sat last on my list. I'd already 'served my time'; we'll get to that soon.

The point is that the job I took next at Texas Christian U. had me doing mental health work, yes, but only in a junior way. It was my job to judge which students should be shuttled on to my superior – a psychiatrist who did love to prescribe – rather than try to help them myself in the infirmary through psychotherapy.

Yes, at age 29 I was a failed flunky when I crossed paths with Ben Hogan on Hulen Street. But perhaps it was because he sensed my humbled aura that Ben went on to both treat me with an unusual softness for him, as well as taking the risk of 'opening up' to me. You see, I was fully honest with him in telling this life story of mine that day, but who knew that he would reciprocate?

And, as fate would have it, the fact that my dad had died young, suddenly, and moreover in a plane crash, proved a powerful touchpoint between Hogan and me. First because his father Chester had shot himself to death when Ben was just a boy; and secondly because Ben, golfer-turned-pilot, had barely escaped disaster in the air 3 years earlier, having had to crash-land fellow pro Johnny Bulla's plane, with friends and family on board!

After murmuring condolences for my early orphaning – the 1st anniversary of my dad's passing was still a month off – Hogan asked me a question that would prove to be the 'starting gun' for our run through the darker corners of the mind. "So, are you afraid to fly now," he asked adding, "Wouldn't blame you."

On the knee-jerk flight home from Galveston upon my father's death, the takeoff and landing were brutal, I told Ben. "I gripped the sides of my seat like I was breaking in a bronco, sure that my ass would be flying through the air any second. And, my mouth felt like I'd just swallowed a pound of Texas prairie dust. Since then though, I'm merely terrified on airplanes," I finished with a ghastly chuckle.

"Hmm," was all Hogan replied at first. Then a pause. "Before the war I was the same. Fact is I've always had to combat a fear of heights. Some folks said that I joined the Army Air Forces 'cause of a secret guarantee that they'd keep me in Texas – away from the fighting. It was claimed my service was cushy, playing golf with 'the brass' as much as flying.

"Well, kid, it was true that I was desperate to serve in a way that wouldn't separate me from golf for the duration, but there was more to my decision than that! My life has been all about overcoming my fears, on the course and off. I had to choose piloting in order to beat my fear of being up in a plane … of dying in a plane, which could happen even on a training run."

At that juncture, somehow I summoned the guts to respond to that formidable man's assertion by posing a tough though fair question. What I asked was, "And now, are you still comfortable with flying?" having recollected the crash landing he'd had to make.

Ben's icy stare back soon collapsed into a grunt of humor, much to my relief, followed by these words, "No. I won't be boarding any planes for a long time, but it's mostly Valerie's fault. She's always been more scared than me, and now my wife is petrified about planes on my behalf. So, I'm blaming my reluctance on her."

Later, a playful Hogan gave begrudging approval to my assessment that this revealing exchange between us was key to the relationship we developed. At the time, however, I wondered if I'd ever see him at 'our bench' again. And for the record, on the date of this conversation in October of '49 – when Ben switched for the first time to calling me "kid" – he was age 37; me, 29, only 8 years' difference. I have to confess though; I did feel like a kid or a younger brother at best, in his company. That was a testament to the monumental power of his personality, for generally I was no 'shrinking violet,' even when 'wounded.'

The next week Ben and I only crossed paths a couple of times. I'd had 2 afternoon meetings which couldn't be ducked, and he didn't show on the Friday afternoon when I Bobby Shout was able to be at 'our bench.' The following Monday, however, something seemingly minor yet psychologically momentous occurred.

I'd made it to Hulen Street a little past 2 p.m. and settled on the seat, uncertain yet hoping that Hogan would show. After 30 minutes of waiting, my heart began to sink. Maybe Ben had decided to try other training routes, maybe he'd had a setback that meant he couldn't make it this far … or perhaps, he's said the hell with it! But no, before I saw him, his voice called out --rather light for Ben -- "Good afternoon, kid."

Turning my head around to see him, "I responded, "Hello, Mr. Hogan." And then, surprise overcoming tact, I added, "Where have you been?"

He didn't look exhausted at all, but still eased himself onto the bench. "Oh, I decided to continue on to Colonial today. Stopped in at the shop. Said hello to some of the guys. Had 'em check on my clubs, just in case you know …"

In case? I smiled at this thought. Colonial Country Club was a full half mile east beyond our bench from the direction of Ben Hogan's home. He'd made it there walking, and still felt he might have some golf in him. I'd blurted, "Are you going to start hitting full shots?"

"Kid," the world's greatest golfer of the late '40s shot back with a tight-lipped smile. "You've lost too many balls in the high weeds." I knew that this was Texan for 'crazy.' But I knew I wasn't crazy.

My bench partner didn't rematerialize Tuesday through Thursday. *He's using his limited strength chipping and putting, I bet*, this thought making me feel somewhat happy, though I missed Ben's company. *Come Friday, he'll probably be elsewhere, too*, I guessed, seeing how that would be November 11, Veterans Day. Back then, that date of remembrance was a real holiday, so I was 'off' from work. What would I do with myself, to dull my survivor's guilt?

Maybe it was Hogan inspiring me; I don't know. But, on a whim I decided on Friday morning to drive over to the Meadowbrook muni to see whether I might 'get out' as a walk-on. It had been almost a year since I'd played, so Meadowbrook's short 6,300 yards from the tips would suit my rust. After nearly an hour's wait, I Bobby Shout, was paired up with 3 other singles, and off we went …

Things progressed at first pretty much as I expected. My older playing partners looked at wiry me with skepticism at my announcement that I'd be playing from the back tees, then with awe after witnessing my first drive which I 'nailed.' On the front 9, rusty me couldn't sink a medium birdie-try to save my life, or I'd have shot under par, having piled up a bunch of 'greens in regulation.'

Of course, I was only putting with 1 good eye; have I mentioned that? Yeah, my right one was damaged when I was caught in an explosion involving one of my daddy's oil rigs back in '41, me a 21-year-old, 3 years' into the promised 5 of servitude my old man had coaxed from me. He was sure I'd come to love the oil business, but after that accident, well, we both knew that I'd be going to college and studying anything else when my 5 years were up.

On the other hand, I had that bad eye to thank for avoiding military service and perhaps a quick death. It turned out that though the accident had crushed the little bones in my right ear, too, a hearing disability wasn't enough to keep me from non-combat duty. Nope, it was the eye that gave me 4-F status, and the chance to be a hotshot college golfer, what with so many of my peers away fighting. So, you can see why Veterans Days always troubled me to the point sometimes of anger at Fate. I was ready to murder that short Meadowbrook layout, I remember that!

However, while we were waiting on the 11ᵗʰ tee I got distracted and my play suffered after that. You see, one of my playing partners had asked, "Did you gents hear about Hogan?" My heart leaped at the way he said it.

The guy went on to share that his brother was an employee in the restaurant at Colonial Country Club and heard that Ben had visited the practice range yesterday. "Poor man. My brother has it from one of the groundskeepers who was watching when Hogan tried to hit some balls that he tumbled over a couple of times! Fell flat on his face. Well, if he can't keep his balance, I guess he really is finished."

Though the narrator of this gossip had reported his news with a tinge of regret, another member of our group seemed to enjoy 'the falling part.' "Serves the bastard right," he'd proclaimed. "Mr. Frosty never gave anybody the time of day when he was on top. Acted like he didn't owe us fans a thing. I say good riddance."

I let the other two debate whether Ben was a total jerk or not. There'd been plenty of press about how he'd been softened by the unexpected outpouring of good wishes after his car wreck the past February, but no one could deny that Ben Hogan had been plenty frosty through the years. Unlike these guys at Meadowbrook though, I was far from ready to believe that my bench-mate was done with golfing, notwithstanding face splats. It turned out that I was right, but also nearly wrong.

As the calendar marched 2 more weeks into November that 1949, the air turned quite cool, yet still Ben found me several more times at the Hulen Street bench, prior to Thanksgiving. He didn't mention practicing at Colonial, and I was wary of bringing it up, lest he had given up. I didn't want to make him feel any worse. One afternoon though, Bantam Ben did touch on the topic indirectly, and his words made my mouth nearly drop open before I caught myself.

"Dr. Shout," he started – he'd begun this friendly mocking by then – "I want to lay out a case to you, so listen carefully. Every day now -- and your colleagues have warned me that there will be no end to this -- in order to get up and about, I have to go through the following regimen before and after, to keep the pain at bay:

"It starts with an hour in a hot tub laced with Epsom salts, trying to take the ache out of my swollen legs. Dr. Ochsner had to tie off my major lower vein after I got blood clots, so I'm stuck with bad circulation down there. Well, I hate pills, but I do take 1 aspirin. Then, Val rubs my legs with liniment before wrapping them in elastic bandages from my ankles to my 'balls.' Later, after I exercise, we repeat. Oh, and sometimes I drink a ginger ale, too, 'cause it works against swelling. My point is ..."

What this uncommonly tough man went on to say was that he could handle the physical pain he was sure; no aches were going to keep him from golfing again. But, all the prep required for him to get mobile each day was draining, and Ben knew that tournament golf on top of these preliminaries would take about everything else he had in his debilitated condition. "So, you see, I can't afford any other energy leaks," he said. "My anxieties about traveling – they're draining -- somehow they've got to be reduced. And, I'm thinking, maybe you know some psychic tricks that could be useful."

Ben Hogan at that moment bore such an imploring look that my brain began to vibrate. Humble me Bobby Shout, helping 'the Hawk' back to victory? What could I say? But, I had to try, didn't I, even if failure were likely?

We'd already talked about Ben's air-flight fears. He'd mentioned taking trains instead as though problem solved. It had to be traveling on the road that was shaking him. After all, who wouldn't be wary of driving – or was it even being driven by someone else? – after having a bus come out of the fog and into your lane at breakneck speed to crush you?

But, in fact, Ben had suffered recently a reinforcing event so diabolically caustic that an evil psychologist could not have devised one more likely to mess with the Hawk's views in this regard. What irony. His upped distress had resulted from an honor, Hogan being appointed the captain of the American side for the '49 Ryder Cup, held in England the past September. So, what were his travel woes on that trip?

Well, there was minimal stress getting over there. Ben had the relative security of making his crossing of the Atlantic on a mighty luxury liner, the *Queen Elizabeth*. When the ship docked on England's coast at Southampton, alas, a dubious choice was made.

Hogan could surely have ridden a train from there to London, and then made another rail connection to travel to the Ganton course up in Yorkshire where his team awaited. Instead, he'd accepted a ride with a Brit golf writer who was also heading to the capitol.

I wondered, had Ben remembered that they drive 'on the wrong side of the road' over there? That is, with steering wheels on the right side of vehicles motoring along the LEFT half of the road. Had he been cognizant that 70 miles of increasing urban hubbub awaited him in that strange automobile piloted by Louis Stanley? Probably in the haze of disembarking, Hogan was distracted, yet it would have been just like him also to try to brazen out the squeamishness he'd been feeling.

'Dr. Bobby Shout' – me -- decided not to press him on this question, since after all, it was the result not the thought process which mattered most. And, the

Hawk was such a proud man, not one amenable to even mild second-guessing. It was enough for him to have conveyed to me that traveling in England had upset him

Only years later did I learn to what degree 'my patient' had found this setup a nightmarish turn of events. First when I read the driver's account that "every oncoming car so tensed [Ben's] nerves that we reduced our speed at times to a crawling pace." And secondly when Hogan's 'best buddy' Jimmy Demaret – more on him later – told me of his friend's near hysteria on the homeward voyage when the two of them happened to witness an at-sea burial during a rocky time on the boat.

"Let me mull this," I'd answered Ben, and after assuring him that I'd be consulting no one else, we agreed to meet again the Tuesday after Thanksgiving, the 29th of November, I believe it was.

That afternoon proved gloriously sunny. As usual, I'd chosen to sit with my good right ear closer to the center of the Hulen Street bench – to aid my hearing. Upon sitting down, the Hawk neither said "hello" nor commented on the sparkling Trinity River. Just "Well?" he uttered, his impatience palpable for an easing of his dread.

"Mr. Hogan, I want to lead you through an imaginary scenario. I ask that you suspend your stellar sense of logic -- as best you can," I Bobby Shout requested, punctuating that command with a nervous little laugh. "Please just respond, not with questions but with answers to whatever I ask you. Will you do that?" His eyes, though communicating some suspicion, bid me continue.

"Okay, here's the deal. Suppose you were playing in a tournament run by God? Seventy-one holes have been played and all you need to do to win is par the last.

"But, as you arrive on the 18th tee, the Almighty proclaims, 'Ben Hogan, you can finish this hole. That is, after someone else hits the drive for you. This is my command!'

"Whom then, I ask, would you select out of all the golfers in the world to strike that opening shot?"

There was no hesitation in the Hawk's reply. "Jimmy Demaret," he said.

"Not Sam Snead, the longest straight driver in the world?" I replied.

With a grim smile on his lips, Ben held forth, pointing out to me that if this were God's show, who could say whether he might choose to throw a whirlwind toward the tee … or from behind. "Jimmy can hit that driver of his quail-high if need be to skirt below a gust, or hit it plenty high to make use of a following wind. Besides, I can usually trust him."

Inside I was glowing. I'd counted on 'my patient' to respond with stubbornness, to use his logic in spite of my instruction, and lulled by the comfort of doing so, he'd let the core matter slip out!

"Trust Jimmy more than Sam?" I prompted

"Damn right," Hogan barked.

"In fact," I 'Dr. Shout' remarked with professional coolness, "apart from your wife Valerie, there are precious few people you do trust at all. Right, Ben?" I spoke this challenge knowing, how could it be otherwise for poor Hennie Bogan, as the man before me had dubbed himself since childhood, half-orphaned by a suicidal father. Trust issues? Fears of abandonment? In spades!!!

When he asked me what I was getting at, I proceeded to quiz Ben about the Brit driver Louis Stanley. The answers given were as I'd suspected. Hogan hardly knew the man. He'd certainly never been in a vehicle with him before, let alone had the chap drive him anywhere. No basis for trust there.

So, I continued, "However, Mr. Hogan, every city you've played golf in on Tour, you've come to know some important people, right? And, big shots are the folks who at times hire chauffeurs – professional drivers – to ferry them to this or that occasion. Now I bet you've got a dozen acquaintances in L.A. who not only have done this, but are friendly also with race car drivers, men who can negotiate tight traffic at high speeds safely.

"Think about it, Ben. Decide whom you'd trust the most to drive you around Los Angeles: a chauffeur with great references from a person of stature in the community, or a racing driver who has to possess superb reflexes and skill to avoid collisions on the track. Then, go about locating and hiring one … Well, what do you think," I finished, unable to read his poker face this time.

His expression remained grim, but the Hawk intoned, "You may have something there, 'Dr. Shout.' In fact, I know a hell of a driver here in Fort Worth. Think I'll call him up and have him ferry me around a few times. See how I feel then. Thanks."

With that whiff of gratitude cast my way, Hogan arose and began walking the several miles back to home. It was enough to lift my spirits a thousand-fold. I'd helped Ben Hogan!

For those of you who may be puzzled by my focus on L.A. with Ben, its Open was the first golf tournament of the year for the pros back in 1950. Played then on Riviera as now, that course was called 'Hogan's Alley,' so successful had he been in competition there, including his win in the '48 national open. So, I knew that he must be wishing that he could start his comeback at that site.

As for any skeptics concerning Hogan's reputation for toughness, now that you've been apprised of this particular mental demon of his, let me set you straight: This man who met me in the fall of '49 at the Hulen Bench was not only recovering from a well publicized broken ankle, pelvis, collarbone, and rib, along with the leg troubles he described. I later learned that Ben also had torn cartilage in his right knee –which he refused to have his doctors mess with – and felt a chronic ache along his left shoulder blade.

Oh yes, and like me, he'd lost most of the vision in one of his eyes – the left in his case -- due to the car crash. Yet, still Hogan was contemplating not only competing again against the best golfers in the world, but beating them!

You may recall that I golfed with Ben back in '45 at Colonial after the explosion that damaged my sight. I've wondered -- since I didn't have the gumption to ask him -- whether my ability to hit the ball well that day in spite of having only 1 good eye offered some comfort to him 5 years later when he was envisioning his improbable comeback. I'd like to think so, but Hogan probably didn't need my example.

A week-and-a-half after the professional-driver conversation, Bantam Ben couldn't wait any longer to give real golf a try. And, on that day, December 10, 1949, Hogan completed not 1 round but 2 at Colonial! Yes, as he pointed out to the press, he'd made use of a motorized scooter to get him a lot of the way around. Nor, according to Ben, had he finished every hole. Yet, when I read that he'd scored roughly a 71 and 72 on that tough track, I like many other Fort Worthians became early believers that our Hawk could reach a lofty perch in the golf world again after all.

An angry Ben Hogan met me at our bench a little after noon 5 days later, he having phoned me with the request that I take an early lunch for a change. It turned out that his morning mail delivery had included a letter from the folks running the L.A. Open. When the Hawk read aloud the portion of that note which he wished me to hear, the hairs on my neck stood up, so seething was his tone.

And, what sin had that tournament committee committed? They'd had the gall to assume that Ben would be happy just being their honorary starter when the event commenced on January 9th. Well, inside I thought it was a decent gesture on their part, but I didn't dare to provoke 'my patient' further. So, I tried to harness Ben's negative energy toward a more positive goal.

"Two choices, I guess; either you turn them down and stay home, Mr. Hogan, like they deserve, or shock the heck out of them by showing up to play."

At that moment, a mix of pleasure and doubt blossomed amidst the wrath on Ben's face. "Huh, that's what Ray said last week," 'Ray' being Ray Gafford, Hogan's one-time caddying mate who'd gone on to be the pro at nearby Ridglea Country Club. "Bobby Shout, it's time for me to go," Bantam Ben said, concluding our brief meeting before I even had time to ask a question.

But, I got my answer soon enough. The grapevine told me that Ben had continued on to Colonial and proceeded to play a full round 'on foot' that afternoon. Somehow, we all guessed, too, that it was his intention to let that presumptuous L.A. Open tournament committee know that they'd better save a place for him in 'the field,' in case he continued to progress …

What none of us knew though 'til years later was that he'd had Valerie pick him up after that December 15 first 'walking round,' and upon returning home, Ben had fallen into bed immediately – utterly discouraged -- so tired and sore was he. Yet, somehow this emaciated man had rebounded, daring the punishment of a 3-day train ride to L.A., and the real possibility of humiliation in the tournament there. You have to understand, Hogan had visions that he might fall again while swinging, this time in front of thousands. He and Val left for the West Coast as soon as Christmas Day was past, a highly credentialed chauffeur awaiting them.

Me, I couldn't wait to see the January 7th papers, to learn how Ben had fared in his first round at the L.A. Open. I Bobby Shout knew in advance, in spite of how coy Hogan might 'play it' with the writers out there, that he would indeed be in the field. And, if you're wondering whether all you've heard thus far is just the 'hindsight' ramblings of a senile 100-year-old, let me assure you that I did write detailed summaries of our talks afterwards, plus I've been blessed with a damn good memory. End of story!

CHAPTER 2

January 1950

B EING A BUDDING psychologist, my interest in how Ben would perform out in L.A. went far beyond his effectiveness as a golfer there. For this reason, the first press involving the Hawk that got back to us in Fort Worth was doubly intriguing for me.

You see, the news story had included that Hogan chose to golf on the afternoon of January 2, when he could have been with 'everybody else' at the Rose Bowl game between Cal and Ohio State. And by the way, back then folks showed more respect for the Sabbath. New Year's Day being on a Sunday that year, the bowl and Ben's first reported practice round took place on a Monday.

While the reporter who'd gotten Ben's caddie to talk post-round was more interested in Hogan's score than anything else, I saw reason to worry. Why? Well, not because his game was bad; he'd shot a 70 at Riviera that Monday, following a supposed 69 a couple of days earlier. Good enough golf to win the L.A. Open!

Nor was I Bobby Shout overly concerned that 'my man' had been using a little portable seat to rest on at times during these rounds. Heck, there was no rule in golf to prevent him from continuing that during the tournament. No, it was the fact that Ben had gone out that Monday with just a caddie – no playing partners, on a day when the sporting world's attention in California was sure to be on football rather than golf.

As I mentioned not long ago, among 'the baggage' that Hogan had with him out in L.A. was a dread of being humiliated in public by a malfunction of his brutalized body. This man's pride was monumental! So was his brain's ability to prick him with outsized doubts. That combination had cooked up the image in his mind of falling on his face literally while competing on the course. If he was looking to practice in isolation as had been published, this told me that Ben's confidence was still razor thin in spite of our talks about this issue back in Fort Worth.

I'd tried to help 'my patient' see beyond his traditional view of the caddy as merely a bag carrier and nothing more. "Think of him, Mr. Hogan, also as a bodyguard for you literally," was my pitch. "Keep him close to you on the course as much as possible, so you've got the comfort of knowing that he's there to grab onto – or to grasp you – if you should lose your balance."

Ben had uttered a none-too-satisfied grunt at that suggestion and I knew why. His main nightmare involved falling in the course of making a full swing, as he'd done at Colonial when first 'trying his wings' again. So, how could any caddy be quick enough to catch him, considering the required space around a swinging golfer? No, the Hawk would be a wounded bird alone on the ground before who knew how many spectators were casting pity his way. That image was anathema for Hogan! I had to reverse course.

"Mr. Hogan," I Bobby Shout had begun, "just for the sake of argument, let's say that you do fall at Riviera. Well, you've got a choice then. You can look humiliated and flash a face full of resentment at the crowd for witnessing your vulnerability. Or, you can rise with dignity and after getting on your feet, flash everyone that million-dollar smile of yours. They'll cheer in response, I guarantee it, and any tinge of pity will be vanquished." He kind of liked my logic there, I believe. However, I'd failed to take another aspect of a 'falling incident' into account. That is, photographers!

Think about it: A picture only catches a moment in time. 'My patient' could follow my recommendation to a tee – picking himself up with aplomb and smiling away – only to find a single photo of him in the papers the next day, one that captured Ben prone and face down on the ground, his club flung from him. Pity city!

So Hogan being Hogan, first day of the L.A. Open, he'd tried to bull his way—as if his steely eyes would be enough -- to prevent any such photographs from being taken, rather than charming the press while asking them as a courtesy to him to refrain from this sort of shooting. How do I know this occurred, though the Fort Worth papers did refrain from mentioning Ben's unfortunate approach? It was Jimmy Demaret whom I met later that month through Ben who 'spilled the beans.'

"Well now, Bobby, when you want a bull to chase after you, what do you do?" Jimmy had begun in response to my innocent question about Ben's behavior at the Los Angeles Open – beyond his stellar play. "Wave that ole red flag right in his face, right?"

When I nodded, he'd continued, "And, what's the biggest, brightest red stop sign you think somebody could shove in a press photographer's face? Yup. The Hawk had some little kid come out on the first tee prior to Ben's opening drive with a poster on a stick that read, 'NO CAMERAS PLEASE!!! PLAYER'S REQUEST."

"Oh, no," I'd groaned.

"First he'd had to back off on that tee when a spectator began filming him, and then – it gets worse – out in the first fairway, Ben starts yelling, 'Can't you read?' after some press guys started 'shooting,' not having noticed the kid with the sign.

"Okay, so those fans who are in our friend's corner start threatening these photographers, who were smart enough to retreat to the tournament director's office for a nice chat. Upshot was, the kid and his sign were made to disappear on the 8th tee, I think it was."

Mr. Demaret shook his head, "Pictures were taken and Ben didn't even seem to notice after that – from what I heard. He also made nice with the newspaper fellows after his round, assuring them that there'd be no more signs, that he knew they had a job to do, and no, he was not going to quit the tournament just 'cause of some pictures being shot. He can be kind of crazy though, *you* know," Jimmy concluded with a grin.

Having heard Demaret's version, I felt terrible. Why hadn't I seen ahead about photographers at these events? Ben had told me nothing of this trouble when he'd welcomed me to Phoenix at the new 'Ben Hogan Open' two-and-a-half weeks later.

Moreover, my use of a week's vacation brought my worn-down 'patient' little luck. He finished for a 2nd straight tournament 'back in the pack' before he, Valerie, and I caught a train back to Fort Worth on January 30.

We do need to return to the season's start though, to complete the tale of Hogan's improbable comeback in L.A. And, by the way, it was Jimmy Demaret who took the $2,000 first prize at Ben's namesake Open in Phoenix. He nipped Sam Snead by a stroke.

That opening session of the Los Angeles Open had taken place on Friday, January 6. In spite of the distraction Ben had caused himself with his no-photos policy on the front 9, he'd still managed to shoot a 73, good for 16th place that day. And people there, pros and spectators alike, were openly flabbergasted that the Hawk could play that well during his first stab at competition in almost a year -- especially after what he'd been through. But that was nothing!

Rounds 2 through 4, Hogan beat the combined score of every other player in the field by stringing together a trio of 69s. He'd done this with 1 major break, Sunday's 3rd round having been rained out, which also wiped out a hot round by the tournament's current leader Jerry Barber. Still ... And yes, the curtailed golf schedule that day did allow Ben to get more precious rest than he would have otherwise. But still ... When Bantam Ben posted his 280 score on Tuesday the 10th, it looked like he'd won again at Riviera. I remember cheering aloud back in Fort Worth when they reported his finish on the radio. "That amazing son of a bitch," I'd uttered. Only, Snead had other ideas.

He'd already made 3 late birdies when Sam, after making a 3 on the 1-shotter 16th, was reported to have said to the gallery, "Guess I've got to knock a couple in to catch the Little Man," like he was going to do it. Well, ole Samuel Jackson Snead got his 4 on the par-5 17th, and had managed to get his ball to within 15 feet of the hole for a tying birdie on the daunting last hole.

It was then that the golf gods, who seemed to like to mess with Snead's head, played yet another trick on him. To wit, as he was getting ready to stroke that try for a bird, suddenly there was an ungodly *crack*, caused by a tree limb collapsing under the weight of a spectator.

"Must be a Hogan fan," the Slammer cracked back to the delight of his followers. Then Sam made the putt, which meant a Wednesday playoff round would be in order.

Ben was bummed.

The quotes attributed to him in the Riviera locker room upon hearing how Snead finished showed the degree to which playing a tournament had drained the Hawk. "I wish Sam had won it out there ... I don't feel bad about Sam tying me ... I just don't want to play another round."

When I Bobby Shout read that in our paper on Wednesday morning the 11th, I'd thought, "Don't count him out yet, not with his fighting will," but it turned out there would be no playoff that day. The course had gotten deluged again, overnight, causing the *mano a mano* event between Ben and Sam to be rescheduled for 7 days later, following the Crosby pro-am and preceding that Ben Hogan Open of which I've spoken already.

Well this time the rain delay did not prove so helpful to Hogan, seeing how he 'came down' with a bad cold en route to Bing's tournament, and the lingering weakness from its effects left the Hawk a mere 'paper Tiger' by the time January 18 rolled around. He'd returned to Los Angeles after finishing 19th up 'north' at 'Crosby's Clambake' in Monterey and could only manage a 76 in the L.A. Open's anti-climatic playoff, losing to Snead by 4. "It was just bad golf," he intoned afterwards. "I've obviously got a lot of work to do yet."

The man who uttered these words of disappointment was the same soul who'd recently received a rich settlement from the Greyhound bus company for their part in Ben's car accident, as well as a big payment from Hollywood to film his life story. Hogan had given the scriptwriters a near perfect ending for that projected film by doing so well at the L.A. Open. Yet, I knew that Hennie Bogan was whipping himself inside right then for not being man enough to beat Sam for another win.

CHAPTER 3

February-March 1950

O N THE TRAIN trip back to Fort Worth, it was obvious that Ben didn't feel like talking about internal things. He and Valerie chatted on and off in their very personal way and I listened. As we were approaching our home station on February 1, however, Hogan gave me a rare smile and asked whether I thought I could meet him at our old bench during my lunchtime that Friday the 3rd. I said I'd let him know.

Yeah, yeah, I put him off. But, could I help it if I Bobby Shout too felt disappointed? Here I'd taken the trouble to get to Phoenix and while there, though I'd had dinner with the Hogans twice, Ben never came close to 'opening up' to me as he did at our bench. Gees, he could have at least 'let me into' his thinking about each day's round was my thought, but no, the Hawk was silent in that regard as well. I had to remind myself that with this man, any sharing was a real gift.

The next day – Thursday – I duly telephoned my acceptance of Ben's proposal to meet on Friday. And, when I did arrive at the Hulen bench, Hogan was already there. It stunned me a bit that although his sunglasses and fedora somewhat masked his identity, there was nothing he could do to hide the degree to which he'd become freshly emaciated. That trip west had kicked hell out of the Hawk.

For this reason, I wasn't shocked when Ben announced that he was going to skip the next 3 Tour events, though all of them were Texan affairs: First the

Texas Open, outside San Antonio, from February 9th to 12th that year; then the Rio Grande Open the following week; succeeded by the Houston Open toward the end of the month.

Ben's plan was to combine rest and relaxation in conjunction with a studied effort to add strength and weight to his frame during this layoff. When he saw my face, he felt obliged to add that he'd be practicing plenty at Colonial, too, along with playing an occasional round there. It sounded good to me.

But 2 weeks later, Snead having invaded San Antonio successfully for his third win of the young campaign, 'my patient' had become less sanguine about 'sitting back' awhile. "Kid," he barked to me, "the thing is I can't feel the club when it's not warm out. But, damn it, I can't count on Jimmy [Demaret] and Jackie Jr. [Burke] to stop Sam from gobbling up the whole Texas swing. Maybe I should play at Houston?"

Well, Demaret had not exactly disgraced himself in the state open at San Antonio, finishing second to Slammin' Sammy by a single stroke. And, though we didn't know it yet, Jackie Burke Jr. was about to defeat all comers at the Rio Grande as the tournament week progressed.

It looked to me like Ben was far from revitalized at that juncture, so I tried to say something that would tamp down his competitive zeal for the present. Big mistake.

You see, I figured that it would soothe 'my patient' perhaps if I reminded him of others being sidelined as well. Misery does love company, right? And, who would be a more effective choice than another star player from Texas? I thought. Wrong.

As soon as the words, "Lloyd Mangrum with his shoulder injury …" were out of my mouth, Hogan exploded at me. "Don't bring up that cocky bastard to me, that Texas traitor, that gamesman-playing son of a bitch! I don't want to hear his name out of you again."

"Oh, sorry," I Bobby Shout mumbled. We sat on the bench amidst an air of tense silence for maybe a minute before the Hawk continued his tirade.

"Let me tell you about ole Lloyd. ("Ole" Lloyd was 2 years younger than Ben in fact.) "I assume you know that I authored a book called POWER GOLF in '48. Well, late that year Mangrum comes to me and says that he's doing a book too and would I mind writing a foreword for it? Naturally I asked to see a draft of the thing first. I'm not going to put my stamp of approval on just anything for another player. So, he gives me a copy of his so-called GOLF: A NEW APPROACH. 'NEW' my ass!"

According to the Hawk, Lloyd's effort was just plain lazy, a bunch of pictures of him with hardly any words of explanation to guide the novice. But, what really incensed Ben was Mangrum's offensive defense of the book in its preface.

"He wrote, and I quote," grumbled Hogan, "'the golfer who reads many of these [instruction books] surely must be confused with the multitude of instruction points that are thrown at him almost at once.' That ape criticizes my book in his opening, and expects me to applaud? Then he tweaks me on the next page to boot. Says Lloyd, 'I patterned my swing after Sam Snead's.' Not Hogan's, Snead's! And, that's just 1 example of how slimy that guy can be."

I wasn't sure what to say after that. It was rare for Ben to waste more than a word or two on someone he disapproved, and his putdowns were uttered with cold disdain. Yet, here was 'my patient' burning with emotion, in no mood to hear anything positive about Mangrum.

Of course, I had bought Ben's book. In fact, I'd been working up my courage to have him autograph it. The fact that Lloyd Mangrum, whose own nickname eerily was 'Mr. Icicle" on Tour, had even produced a volume was new to me. So I Bobby Shout couldn't judge whether Hogan was being overly defensive or not.

What I had noticed was that the 2 men shared enough similarities – and Lloyd was playing good enough golf – to assume the role of a threatening little brother to Ben. For instance, when 'my patient' referred to Mangrum as an 'ape' the fact was that Ben had very hairy arms but Lloyd even more so, his hands blackened with hairs. Surely the Hawk had noticed that, along with the man's slim frame that mirrored Ben's. Yet, Lloyd was taller.

On this account, and so much more – I was to learn – Bantam Ben had zero sympathy for this fellow Texan having to miss the '50 L.A. Open, even though Mr. Icicle was the defending champion at Riviera, a layout – you'll recall -- which had been dubbed 'Hogan's Alley.' I decided to change the subject fast.

In response to my question about his March schedule leading up to the Masters on April 6, Ben grew sunnier. He said he and Val couldn't wait to head east to the warmth of Palm Beach, Florida, not to mention his love of the nearby Seminole Golf Club.

Hogan crowed that the course was generally 'wide open' in March – great for practicing! – up until the annual Pro-Amateur took place there. When I asked whether he'd be playing in that, the Hawk chuckled as he pronounced, "Kid, sometimes I think the porch light's on at your place but there's no one home." Texan again for saying somebody's crazy.

Yet he indeed attempted to compete there in mid-March. However, his tournament-rusty 220 in the 54-hole event wound up far behind Cary Middlecoff's winning 207 among the pros. At least Ben had finished on 'a high,' I noted, shooting a 70 the third day.

While Cary repeated his mastery of the field the next week in Jacksonville FL and Slammin' Sammy won as usual in Greensboro NC toward the end of March, Ben was reported to have gone back to a practice regimen for conquering Seminole's 'inverted-saucer' greens and Atlantic-driven breezes.

Back in Fort Worth, I'd been pondering an incident he'd shared with me a couple of days before heading to the east coast. It seemed that Ben had barked at a couple of reporters he actually liked on his way to the 1st tee for his L.A. playoff with Snead. Why? He'd said to them that it was because they were writing down "every damn word I say," though later he'd explained to one of them that "I had to get mad at something … I use anger to drive away fear."

I'd coupled this confession with the Hawk's uncustomary outburst about Lloyd Mangrum, and I had to wonder, *Is there some fear in Ben's outlook regarding Mr. Icicle?* I Bobby Shout decided that it might pay dividends to look more into Mangrum's character and life story.

That nickname of his, I soon learned, was 2-pronged: Lloyd's persona on the golf course came across as someone casually going about his business, especially on and around the greens, even when a tournament was 'on the line.' In other words, he appeared to have 'ice water in his veins' when competing.

But, everywhere else his coldness expressed itself in grim short responses, often rude or insensitive, when questioned by reporters or fans. He hated to shake hands, give autographs, or speak to the press. Huh. 'Hogan's little brother'?' Sure sounded like it in this regard.

Remember how Ben characterized Lloyd as a "Texas traitor" when I first brought his name up? It didn't take long to see what the Hawk was getting at. Mangrum's time on this earth did begin in Texas – he was born August 1, same as me, in 1914 in a little town called Trenton, north of Dallas and not far from the Oklahoma border – but he left the state to live out in Los Angeles at the age of 15.

By then he was committed to being a professional golfer and since his big brother Ray had accepted a club-pro job out in L.A. that year, why wouldn't it make sense for the younger sibling to go along? Lloyd didn't 'walk into' a cushy spot 'cause of his brother out there either.

I found it written that the younger Mangrum spent the rest of his teenage years doing a bunch of other jobs to feed himself when not caddying. Those included parking cars, driving a taxi, and acting as a bouncer at a nightclub when not engaged in singing for tips. Like Ben, Lloyd had grown up having to fight to make his way, but this didn't stop 'my patient' from seeing Mr. Icicle as someone who'd abandoned the great state of Texas for showy Tinseltown!

Perhaps, I thought, the Hawk's discomfort with Mangrum stemmed in large degree from yet another similarity between the 2 men: their press images. By 1950 if a reporter had cause to mention Lloyd Mangrum, it seemed *de rigueur* to characterize his aura as that of the legendarily cool riverboat gambler.

The natty clothes, the pencil-thin mustache, a cigarette forever dangling from his lips – even when putting – this man who rarely smiled but seemed 'at home' in any situation with his movie-star looks -- and better still, he was a player dubbed as "mysterious" by his peers.

Do you see a pattern here? The younger Lloyd could be seen to be 'horning in' on Hogan's 'public persona' prestige in nearly every way. But what about 'the smiling part,' some might argue? Well Ben did unleash a great smile for the cameras when winning called for it, but still, he showed his grin sparingly otherwise.

This 'you're stealing my thunder' theory of mine did explain why there might be utter coolness between these 2 golfing stars. However, the more powerful psychology triggering their absolute distaste for each other would not be revealed to me 'til June of that year.

It was Sam Snead who'd delivered one of the most severe encapsulations of Ben's personality, and about this time I thought of a way of assessing how accurate the Slammer's remarkable remark was that, "Hogan didn't like anyone, except maybe his wife." My idea was to go to the public library again as I had for my Mangrum research. There I planned to go through the sports pages of old newspapers for the past several years to see how things stood publicly between Ben and the reigning saint of golf at the time, John Byron Nelson.

No I wasn't so naive as to believe that their private feelings toward each other would definitely equate to what was said in print. However, I Bobby Shout also knew that it was possible to 'read between the lines' of press reports to glimpse the truth. If the Hawk hadn't been able to stay friends with the gentle, outgoing, honestly religious 'Lord Byron,' then I was going to have to agree with Sam that 'my patient' was a prickly gent indeed.

Four decades later, in his autobiography Nelson would conclude his capsule about Ben and their relationship with a dose of sugarcoating. The quote was something like "We've always gotten along fine and we've always liked each other very much. We're simply different personalities …"

When 'I dug' though, back in March of 1950, what I read was darker.

Take 1940 for a start, a sunny time when Ben and Byron in their late twenties were traveling the Tour with their buddy wives along. The other hardscrabble pros had lumped them together as slightly odd, a couple of non-drinkers who were tightly bound to their mates. Yet, the Hawk dug his talons good into Byron when interviewed on the eve of a playoff between them for that year's Texas Open. This one I'm sure I've got right!

"Byron's got a good game, but it'd be a lot better if he practiced. Byron's too lazy to practice." Ouch? I had to choose – had this been just an example of the dry humor which some said Ben possessed? Or, was he trying to "get into" his friend's head; a piece of gamesmanship that the Hawk professed to disdain? Or, had his cutting remark stemmed from a desperate frustration?

You gotta understand, from the time they were kid caddies together at the Glen Garden course in Fort Worth 'til the day of that radio interview, it always was Byron who'd come out on top, both on the scorecard and in the eyes of those watching them. As of that Texas Open, Ben had won exactly zero titles on his own, while Byron possessed a bunch including 2 Majors at that juncture. So, how could Hogan see fit to critique such a successful golfer – and friend – so mercilessly over the airwaves?

I found my reluctant answer by tracking 5 years forward, well past Ben's first great period. He'd garnered 15 Tour wins between 1940 and 1942, though still no Major, and then faced 3 years of renewed frustration. That is, during '44 and '45, he'd had to serve militarily while Byron was free to win at a greater clip than anyone had ever done, not to mention adding his 5th Major.

The fact that the media had dubbed Byron Nelson as "Mr. Golf" by war's end, along with hailing him as golf's greatest player ever, obviously galled Ben. This time read, 'little brother' jealous of 'big brother.'

And so in September of 1945, Bantam Ben couldn't help himself from saying aloud to Jimmy Demaret upon finally burying runner-up Byron in the Portland Open by 14 strokes, "I guess that takes care of this Mr. Golf business."

Yet unfortunately it didn't, since Nelson bounced back 2 weeks later to eclipse Ben's newly-minted 261 tournament scoring record with a 259 of his own in the process of winning the Seattle Open by 13 shots! Worse, after that win, Byron made it clear that he'd tried extra hard just because of Hogan's Portland victory. Obviously they stood friends no longer. I debated whether the primary fault lay with Ben? His colossal need to win: Was it too great – or the essence of his greatness?

CHAPTER 4

April 1950

A S APRIL DAWNED, Bantam Ben was already encamped in Augusta, Georgia, though the Masters didn't start 'til Thursday the 6th. I planned to be there for the 3rd and 4th round over the weekend, with tickets in hand courtesy of Hogan. Of course, back then there was no trouble purchasing an admission badge – plenty on sale around town – and they weren't expensive, but Ben had given me ones with access to that plantation-like clubhouse so I was extra excited.

I'd 'borrowed' a couple of tranquilizer pills from our TCU pharmaceutical supply to 'see me through' the plane flights from Dallas to Atlanta. Since my boss had only given me 'off' from Friday mid-afternoon through Monday morning, it was necessary to cover the nearly thousand-mile distance between Fort Worth and Augusta mostly through the air despite my anxieties.

When I got up late Saturday morning, it was already feeling pleasant outside with a forecast of near summer-like temperatures later in the day. I Bobby Shout rode a bus with a whole bunch of other folks out to the course, Ben having gone there from his Bon-Air hotel 'digs' a lot earlier than I arose after my trip the previous evening. But that was okay. With the much smaller field of players back then, most of the on-course action didn't occur until after noon.

For a while I flitted around the clubhouse eyeing the encased relics like any Augusta National tourist, a tad nervous that some Green Jacket would take offense and show me the door. Then, it was time to 'relieve myself' before stepping outside.

"The Gents" did not disappoint, classy in its appointments, but before I'd made it halfway to a urinal, some God-awful retching erupted from one of the stalls. This was followed by the classic roar of someone 'relieving himself' in a different way, and that sent me back outside the room, not wanting to embarrass the poor drunken soul with my presence when he emerged.

After counting to 100 in the hallway outside, I returned to the bathroom. Shockingly, it was saintly Byron Nelson who was drying his hands at the sink. Just as weird, before I'd taken 2 steps in, he was stepping forward to offer his hand while greeting me with, "Why Bobby Shout, it's good to see you again," this announcement delivered in his soft Southern drawl.

He remembers me, too, from the match at Dallas Country Club back in '45? Yes, he had chatted with me that day, and very cordially, but heck, I wouldn't remember a nobody golfer like me after five years! So as if to justify myself being there, I blurted, "Ben gave me clubhouse tickets."

Byron replied once again in an unexpected direction, "If I recall rightly, you're a Southern Methodist grad?"

Still in defensive mode, I replied, "Yes, I work at TCU now."

"You're a religious man then," he said with obvious pleasure.

On the spot, I came up with what I thought was a decent reply, "I'm in church every Sunday," omitting the fact that my current girl Betty Ann preferred it that way. I Bobby Shout cannot deny that my faith had been shaken by then, due to the seemingly random, cruel events in my past. Anyway, the former "Mr. Golf" continued to surprise me.

Smiling, he said in a most caring way, "That's fine. Ben needs a real friend or two, especially someone on good terms with God."

And, at that juncture I would have mouthed my thanks and marched to the urinals, but Byron, it suddenly became clear, was clamping down on an echo of his nausea. "Are you ill?" I blurted.

After a moment's delay to recover, the man managed to assure me that he was okay. "No, no. It's just pre-round jitters. I get them all the time," Byron Nelson told me in a dismissive tone meant to quell my worrying I could tell. Yet, there was a world of pain evident to this budding psychologist in that great man's eyes.

Having 'done my business' and exited the building, a question occurred to me. Why hadn't Byron been using the players' locker room for his pre-round 'ritual'? Then I slapped myself on the side of the head mentally. Why would he want to share that weakness with his peers-slash-opponents? Not to mention the dignity of the man …

After gawking at the pros on the practice green for a bit, I started walking at a rapid rate along the par-4 1st, thinking to catch up with Ben a few holes ahead. However, it turned out that a fateful encounter awaited me on that opening par-4.

It so happened that Byron's drive had wound up close to the fairway bunker on the right side near my route along that hole. Awaiting the group in front to finish up after an apparent delay, he saw me, smiled and beckoned. As I walked toward him, Mr. Golf met me halfway between.

"Bobby, I want to apologize," Byron had said. "I forgot to ask what kind of work you're doing now. Did you go back to oil?" he asked.

I couldn't believe that he'd want to talk to me at all while competing in the Masters, let alone give me the chance to explain my life choices. I Bobby Shout hastened to explain about my psychology degree and the University of Chicago, then my position at Texas Christian U., all the while 'keeping 1 eye out' for the 1st green to become clear.

Byron replied, "Well, that's very interesting," like he meant it. And, I guess he did 'cause he pulled out a pencil, tore off a little piece of his personal scorecard, and wrote a phone number. "Here. I'd like to have you out to the ranch sometime soon. Show you my new calves," he laughed. "Let me know when you'd like to come."

Of course, I said I'd be delighted to do that, all the while wondering what the heck Lord Byron could want with me. After he hit a lovely iron up onto the putting surface I clapped 'til Nelson started moving forward, then picked up my pace again. Would he be offended by my hasty exit? I hoped not, since he knew I'd come to follow Ben.

Hogan was waiting on the tee at the par-3 4th when I caught him. If he saw me then, or for the rest of the round, he never gave any indication. His focus, as usual, was absolute.

What I remember from that Saturday as far as his round goes are a couple of odd things. First off, though Ben toured the front side in 1-under – 35 was a good score -- the Texans in his gallery were not thrilled. I knew that Bantam Ben had done better the day before, a 32, but still ... And, there was another factor besides that stellar total which had kindled heightened expectations.

My ear caught wind of this surprising development as we Hoganites were walking along the 7th fairway. Someone said, "Ben predicted this morning that he's going to win this thing; he's never done that before!" Two others added that they'd gotten the same story from good sources. No one there disputed the account either.

Well this had me worried. The Hawk was the ultimate 'one shot at a time' guy. I pictured him grunting with disdain when other pros had 'come forward' with similar inklings. The psychologist in me saw a man who must be battling deep inner doubts about his ability to triumph. That stated premonition of his represented an attempt to pump up his will even higher than usual. In simple words, Ben was telling himself, *You do what you say, so say it and then you will do it.* Unfortunately, looking ahead equates with self-distraction in golf. Not a formula for ultimate success.

The second thing I recall during that round was my own disappointment with the now fabled par-3 12th. It wasn't the design of the hole though. What I found uninspiring was the flat, puny strip of planks and railing that crossed Rae's creek to the left of the green. No wonder the powers-that-be built those wonderful bridges dedicated to Ben and Byron in '58.

Then there was the Hawk's deceptive appearance. He looked so good, tanned from the Florida sun and radiating an air of greater fitness than I'd yet to see. It seemed impossible that he would do anything un-Hogan-like on the back 9 after birdying 11, 13, and 15 to pull within a stroke of Jim Ferrier's long-held lead.

When the Hawk didn't connect with 2 good birdie chances on 16 and 17, his gallery did not lose faith. Bantam Ben would get his tie on the final hole of the day making for all the better drama, many of us were thinking. But alas, after knocking his approach shot 20 feet beyond the cup, Ben not only failed to dunk his downhiller – certainly forgivable – he missed an uphill 3-footer for par – bizarre, given the steel will of this man! *Fatigue after all,* I reasoned.

And so, Hogan had gone from potentially tying his prey to winding up 2 shots behind, alone in 2nd place. His chasers? Two shots higher than Ben's 212 lurked his sometime friends and forever Texan rivals, Jimmy Demaret and … Byron Nelson.

Yup. Puking Byron, a supposedly ceremonial golfer by 1950, had thrown up a 3-under performance at the rest of the field on this Saturday's third round, bettered only by Cary Middlecoff's 68. In the hours following, I was so psyched to see Ben complete his golfing resurrection here, fittingly on an Easter Sunday. Perhaps then, the press would stop using the tag "Little Ben" in writing about this golfing giant's tournament play in 1950. He was not a "little man"!

No, not a little man – but certainly a drained one come Masters Sunday. I guessed that the steep climbs demanded by the terrain at Augusta National had 'caught up' with Ben's legs that last day. He'd had no portable stool to lean on there. Otherwise, how to explain so many sprayed tee shots and erratic ball flights by the Hawk, causing his approaches to go too long or too short too often?

By the time Ben recorded his fifth bogey of the round – on the gettable 13th – against a single bird, he was 'out of it.' Watching him sip some scotch whiskey that evening before dinner – he'd found alcohol more to his liking since the accident – I imagined that I could read Ben's mind and account for the grim look he bore:

His 76 that beautiful afternoon had dropped him into a 4th-place tie with Lord Byron. *Couldn't even beat Nelson when he hardly plays now,* the Hawk was no doubt brooding. *And, that cocky Mangrum shoots the 68 I should have had today? I would have won by three with that score! It brought 'sneaky Lloyd' all the way up to sixth place, just behind Byron and me. Even worse, my failures let Snead beat me by a stroke – with a lousy even-par round today for third alone in the tournament!*

To the press, Ben had blamed his on-course decision-making of all things for his bad final round. That explanation fooled no one except maybe the Hawk himself. Why would such a master craftsman like Hogan grasp at such a theory? I think because that worn-out man felt much more hope at the prospect of fixing something mental rather than physical in his game.

So who did win the 1950 Masters? The final combatants proved to be third-round leader Jim Ferrier and the crazy-dapper Jimmy Demaret.

As a budding psychologist, I Bobby Shout had applauded the mental fortitude displayed by Demaret well before I met him through Ben at Hogan's namesake Open back in Phoenix. You see, the fact was that fate had handed Jimmy a strange-looking physiognomy, one that would have crippled the personality of many a person, but the Houston native instead 'ran with it'!

What do I mean by that?

Well, let's consider that ole psychological term, "fight or flight." Some folks face a menace – take action against it – while others think only to run and hide from the threat. Jimmy Demaret was not only a fighter, but an absolute genius at using everything at his disposal to come out on top.

Here he was, given by God a freakishly short upper body – you talk about 'high-waisted' – combined with the kind of chunky thighs and wide ass that any sophomoric wag would relish as a target, and what did Jimmy do? He used his face, his voice, his demeanor, and to cap off his defense – clothing! – to make even the thought of taunting him seem worthless.

Moreover, talk about reverse psychology! Jimmy's approach dared you to examine him, like he didn't give a damn if you did. *Look at me, look at me* the man appeared to be crying out anywhere he went. Meet him up close, he'd be smiling like nothing could bring him down, cracking witty lines and grabbing drink after drink as though he hadn't a care in the world. This guy vulnerable? Ha, his style said!

Catch Jimmy in a crowd and he'd be the one crooning with the band or without one – no matter -- displaying a handsome tenor or baritone voice for you, a nice mouth, and a twinkle in his eye. Go find some photos of him with his fellow pros; no one showed more teeth.

But it was Demaret's fashion choices that allowed him to perform with confidence, I think, before thousands on the course. He'd realized early that outlandish outfits would grab people's attention away from the wearer's form itself. They'd be talking about clothes, not him! So, boy did Jimmy give them something to gab about.

I still recall an Associated Press reporter for Lord's sake getting a little article into print on that Master's Sunday, its sole focus being the bizarre color combinations worn by Jimmy the first 3 days of 1950's first Major. There was chartreuse – kind of a yellow green – combined with salmon pink on Thursday if I recall correctly. Friday's outfit included purple pants, red with purple shoes, and red piping framing a white shirt, the guy wrote. I saw for myself on Saturday the rose-colored ensemble that was reported.

Surprisingly though, none of the hats which Demaret favored received any mention in this article, even though they ranged from floppy, gangster-style things to oversized tam-o'-shanters to giant 'Dutch-boy caps' – his choice on Sunday. A green one naturally, along with his pants, sweater, and shoes that day.

And, in case you're wondering whether Jimmy was hiding something unseemly like a bald spot beneath his chosen headgear, there are plenty of photos of him 'outside the arena' that show him sporting a great head of hair. Nope, "The Wardrobe," as he was nicknamed, was trying to distract us viewers from other parts of him beside his noggin.

Pardon this aside, as we return to the '50 Masters. As I was saying, it ultimately came down to whether Ferrier could protect his lead against a late-charging Demaret, though no one would have predicted that earlier in the day. You see, Jim Ferrier had birdied both 6 and 7 to get to 8-under for the front side while the Wardrobe was bogeying number 14 to drop 5 shots behind.

Still Jimmy, thanks to some super driving, a 'hot putter' and 1 mighty chip, was not done. By birdying 15 and 16 before parring in, he gave the big Australian-born Ferrier 'something to think about,' the leader being only 3 shots ahead now with 6 to play. Poor Ferrier, he'd been fighting a thyroid condition which cost him 25 pounds pre-tournament, and some say also the Masters, due to simply 'running out of gas.'

After a 4-bogey stretch fueled by a ball in the creek, a lengthy 3-putt, an over-hit iron, and a weak trap shot, Jim still did have a chance to tie Demaret with a birdie try on the 18th, but after missing that attempt, he missed again, the heart all out of him.

Being a Demaret partisan, I always liked to point out something to those who said that Jimmy had 'backed into' this win. The fact was he not only shot the best Sunday score among the top-ten players following the third round. He recorded that 69 in spite of having participated in 2 tense 3-hour meetings on Friday and Saturday night, while helping to forge a new agreement between the Tour players and the PGA. So he too had to be drained!

Yet, Jimmy won again the very next week, finishing off the Atlanta Open Invitational on April 16 with a 4-shot cushion over Slammin' Sammy. That triumph gave him 3 wins and 2 seconds with 8 months of tourney golf still ahead. At this juncture, it appeared that the Wardrobe's 1950 campaign might rival his best year to date. That was 1947 when he won 6 times, captured the money title, and the scoring average as well.

Unfortunately, Jimmy's buried streak of hyper-sensitivity about himself at age 40 was just that: buried not defunct, despite his many successes. And, some pickaxe-like words from a Tour legend the very next month can be blamed for derailing Demaret's career for the rest of 1950 and beyond. There would be no more wins or even near misses for him this year.

Yes, I was asked to play the part of psychic counselor in this case, too. Jimmy needed help not only with re-boosting his ego, but also in coming to grips with the emotional fall-out from his decision to confront his perceived tormentor in the press.

For the 'always' friendly, witty, care-free Jimmy Demaret, that verbal battle was a dangerous business indeed, cracking the public perception he'd worked so hard to cement. Regarding this sorry development I'll offer more details in my May chapter, but first there's the matter of my visit to Byron Nelson's place during the last days of April.

When I contacted the former Mr. Golf, he insisted that I stay over on Saturday night the 29th, though his ranch was located only a twenty-mile drive north of Fort Worth. I Bobby Shout was willing to say yes, partly because I'd heard that his wife Louise was a lively character, very different from the rigid and reserved Valerie Hogan.

On the drive out to Roanoke that morning it was dry but gusty, or as we used to say in Texas, "The wind was blowing like perfume through a prom." I'd done some reading in advance of the visit so the size of Byron's place came as no surprise. He had 630 acres to raise cattle, turkeys, chickens, plus a couple of 'eating hogs,' and as he took me around for an introductory tour, it seemed according to him that he'd had to repair his fences in about 630 spots.

Well, no one could blame him for being proud of what he'd done with the place, though Byron being Byron he was barely bragging, you understand. I heard more about her husband's ranching accomplishments from Louise at dinner than from the 'boss man.'

This short, sparkling brunette seemed indeed a spunky Texarkana gal who laughed at herself out loud over all the doubts she'd had about whether Byron could really be a rancher. "I told him back in '46 that he better make plenty more on the Tour that year if he expected to retire then, 'cause we weren't about to cash in some of our investments in order to buy any ole ranch!"

After the dishes had been cleared and Louise left us, I expected Byron to let me know what was on his mind, but he instead led me out to the visitors' 'bunkhouse' on the property and wished me a good night's rest. We'd be leaving for the Roanoke Church of Christ at 9 a.m. sharp, he advised me, so Louise would have breakfast ready around 8.

It turned out that the service did not commence 'til 10:30. However, Byron never liked to miss a Bible study class if he could help it, and there was one starting at 9:30 that Sunday. I learned in passing that the pair also attended another class on Wednesday evenings.

One could see how the Sunday demands on Tour would have chaffed the Nelsons for the 14 years they traveled for Byron's golf career, not to mention the times of separation when he was a club pro in Pennsylvania, Ohio, and New Jersey while Louise was called down South for family matters. Now Byron and wife were happy Texas ranchers.

They also were leading a good, comfortable, spiritual life -- there could be no mistaking it -- so you can imagine my surprise at the turn our conversation took once Byron walked me out to the privacy of his barn after Sunday dinner that April 30th. Hypnotism?

He began to convey his difficulty by way of a spiraling path, I recall. The first thing Byron said was, "So how many tournaments has Ben played this year to date?" He knew quite well, reeling off the L.A. Open, the Ben Hogan Open in Phoenix, the Seminole Pro-Am in Florida, and the Masters – a total of 4. "And, Ben missed winning at Los Angeles by an eyelash, then almost tied for the lead at Augusta on Saturday."

Lord Byron gave a wry smile then. "If I wasn't a Christian, I'd wager you today that Hogan will finish 1st in an event if he plays as many as 3 more this season. Why? 'Cause the Hawk will keep practicing longer and harder than most healthy pros would think possible, every day between the upcoming tournaments. Ben's gonna get sharper and sharper, even though not being out on Tour. Well, what the heck -- he's got that freedom; I don't."

My host had given a wave of his arm to indicate the ranch as he'd uttered those words with a weary tone.

"On the other hand," Byron continued, "I reckon I'd need to show up at maybe 12 tournaments a year now to feel good about my chances for a win or two. You see, without steady practice or competition, I'd need to 'luck' into some good play – particularly putting -- for 4 straight days."

Right then I wasn't sure what he was saying. "You mean you want to win more events?" I Bobby Shout prodded, though the answer seemed obvious.

Again, Byron was not ready to speak to the point. "I see how the other pros look at me now at Augusta: *Byron Nelson, a darned fine golfer before, but retired, no stamina anymore for tournament play.* Do you know, Bobby Shout, that it hurts? Hurts for me to see the lack of fear in their eyes. God forgive me for my pride!"

And now, emotion flooded out of him. "Heck, people say – I said – that we were tired of the long car-drives, wanted to 'stay put,' settle down with a ranch and our religion for a more peaceful life. Well, that was true and mostly still is. But, I've been asking myself now for the past year-and-a-half, 'Why can't I be like Snead or Hogan, rivals my age? Do exactly what's needed to give the younger pros a real taste of my talent? I tell you I know that I could whip all of 'em a time or two if I could just get 'out there' more often."

It occurred to me at that moment that Nelson had something dark to say, because long-distance travel was surely not such a hurdle at this stage of his life. The man could afford to fly, and unlike Hogan, he had no scar tissue involving planes or automobiles. Moreover, Byron had a hired man who could 'look after the place' on tournament weeks; I'd met the guy already.

So, why was Byron competing so rarely? I thought of him retching at the Masters. And I recalled the story about Cliff Roberts telling Lord Byron early on that his constitution was ill-suited for the grind of tournament golf. That he better find another career before too long. Hadn't Bobby Jones suffered the same fate?

The former Mr. Golf seemed to read my mind: "You remember how I couldn't serve during World War II, Bobby? My blood doesn't clot well. Louise has had to see me 'tied up in knots' stomach-wise at events all these years and she's been scared to death that a bleeding ulcer could kill me. Well, she's not alone," he conceded.

"You caught me at Augusta paying my 'stomach price.' Those internal ailments have returned since last year, since I've felt the desire build again to win a Tour championship. Oddly, it was taking the Texas PGA. title in '48 that 'tipped the bucket' for me. A relaxed regional win was no longer truly satisfying, I found. And, it sure didn't get the full respect of the golf world!

"This is why I've wanted to talk to you, a person who's both religious and acquainted with psychological treatments – because I'm not sure which way to turn."

Once more, Byron had me scared like a sinner in a cyclone as to what was expected from me. Did he want medical advice, a proposal for some psychological counseling, or merely my blessing for his new state of mind? I figured a safe start would be to learn what his family doctor had prescribed for the stomach pains.

Well, it was what one would expect back in 1950. First, Papoid pills had been suggested – their magic ingredient, papaya extract. Then the product Milk of Magnesia was tried with no greater success. You may know of Alka-Seltzer? That remedy has 'hung around' on the 'indigestion market' for decades. But it wasn't the answer for my 'new patient,' nor was a similar fizzy product marketed by the Rexall Drug Stores at the time.

Poor Lord Byron! These relatively crude antacids were not bettered for another several years into the '50s. So, I had no new recommendation for him on that April afternoon concerning a chemical solution for his 'stomach knots.'

Actually though, he wanted my opinion regarding a more radical treatment, especially back in 1950. This was, as previously alluded to, the use of hypnosis in Nelson's case to reduce or eliminate physical pain! I could see his logic: If a trance could keep his stomach relaxed, he could play a ton of tournaments in the future without courting a fatal ulcer. Yet, Byron's Christian distrust of something which seemed halfway to a satanic spell was 'coming through' loud and clear to me. Oh dear.

I wasn't even sure myself whether the psychological establishment had given its approval to such a method, let alone how hypnotism 'stood' in the eyes of the Church. When I told him that I needed to research these matters, he seemed to understand. And later, Byron gave me a squeeze of the arm along with words of thanks as I loaded my car, having promised the former Mr. Golf that I'd be calling him soon.

Let me begin by noting that I'd had zero training or education related to hypnosis by 1950, though I Bobby Shout possessed an undergraduate degree in psychology and had attended medical school for a year-and-a-half. The simple reason for this lack was that the technique had yet to gain official approval from the ruling bodies of medicine.

It wasn't 'til a full 5 years later that the Brits medical association gave a nod to the use of hypnotism to reduce pain, and only in specific cases: childbirth and surgery. Our national medical association was less forthcoming, approving a report about some uses of hypnosis in 1958, while the American Psychological Association waited 2 more years before designating hypnotism as a legitimate branch of its discipline.

As for the religious viewpoint on 'putting someone under' by this method, mesmerism received no credence 'til several years after my talk with Byron. Perhaps surprisingly, it was the Pope who blessed the use of hypnosis back in 1956, whereas in the Church of Christ even today the practice is preached against.

Needless to say, when I telephoned Lord Byron 2 days later, there was no good news to relate on these fronts, though I suspect he already knew where 'his church' stood. Still, I thought that I'd stumbled onto something which might help the man with his golf desires, and so my tone rang hopeful while sketching out my suggestion. Before I get to those specifics however, let's consider what I chose not to share with him, an analysis of his character. Since it was Byron's very goodness that contributed to his stomach woes, I thought.

First off, there's something that Byron didn't tell me that day which he easily might have, but I think his Christian modesty kept him from relating this episode because it spoke to his courage. You may recall how I talked about the power of reinforcing events to heighten fear. There was the example earlier of Ben Hogan's experience with English-driving after his auto accident.

Well, Lord Byron had a whopper in his past that would have paralyzed many a man's urge to keep playing tournament golf at the potential cost of a fatal bleeding ulcer. Yet, he had conquered his dread for more than a decade. I'm speaking of the fact that John Byron Nelson Jr. already had seen what it was like to be at 'death's door,' as an impressionable child to boot!

At age 11 he'd had to undergo a 3-week regimen of rabies shots – in the stomach! – away from home. During that time he drank some 'bad water' and contracted typhoid fever. So ravaged was he that his weight dropped almost by half over the next several weeks! As Byron recalled in his 1990s autobiography, his hipbones were sticking up at that point like twin mountain peaks from his view as he lay in bed.

It gets worse. The kid's temperature climbed to 106 degrees, prompting the doctors to pack him in ice while intimating to Byron's folks that they should prepare for death. Obviously the lad survived. An interesting aspect of his recovery from a psychological standpoint was the key role played by a member of his family's Church of Christ congregation. Did that intervention 'glue' Byron's faith for ever after? One might speculate, but let's return to my story.

Many a golfer has to fight the nightmarish vision of humiliating oneself on the course through horrid play, and it's natural, too, to have to combat the fear of failure when one is playing well yet does not 'close the deal' to win a match or tournament or championship. These scenarios equate to a feeling of pressure in golf before and during the round; dejection or elation afterwards.

However -- mercifully for most of us -- the additional burden of fearing to 'let others down' if we don't prevail is of minor importance in our psyches. It's a matter of being self-centered for mental survival, one might conclude.

Whereas the exceptional person, known as 'very good' in general, cannot help himself from caring strongly about the tender feelings of family, fans, town, state, country, *ad nauseam*. For him, this syndrome applies even when golfing, the unfortunate result of which is that this rare individual generates such great pressure within himself that the suffering of major bodily ills during important competitions follows -- win or lose! (Pardon my bloated medical prose.)

I classify Bobby Jones, retired from tournament golf at age 28 with trembling hands, to be just such a person, and Byron as his chief successor at this juncture in the history of golf. Lord Byron's sterling essence could not be changed by any psychologist. So, I needed to 'come up' with some way for him to get himself 'tournament ready' without resorting to a stomach-killing string of Tour appearances closely packed. When I called my 'new patient' back, I had a compromise solution in mind.

After I'd given him the bad news about hypnotism as a possible cure, I Bobby Shout followed with a question, "I was remembering last night, Byron, about that exhibition match 5 years back when you and I and Hogan and my teammate at SMU were raising money for the war. On the course that day you seemed to me to be totally relaxed. Were there pre-round jitters you'd gotten over, or were exhibitions not so hard on your stomach?"

"No and yes, for sure – is my answer," he drawled. "I've always been as fine as cream gravy when it came to playing those things.

"Heck, there ain't no question about making more or less money to worry about. You're already paid. And, the folks watching are much more interested in seeing you pull off a great shot now and then than whether you're grinding out a score. In fact, the fans are just as happy when you're talking to them, whether it's a pre-round clinic or a banquet in the clubhouse. What I'm saying is that exhibition scores mean nothing in your record book. There's no news in them for the media. They're just for fun."

This was exactly the perspective I'd hoped to hear and I Bobby Shout responded, "I guess though that playing in front of lots of people in an arranged match is a little more like a tournament round than going out for 18 privately with some friends, or staying on the ranch and beating balls by yourself?"

He replied, "Oh, sure. You've been paid good money to entertain. I've always wanted to give folks a decent show, of course. So, practicing and playing some around Fort Worth and Dallas has always been the deal before I head out for one of those dates. Still, the local pro or whoever I'm paired with just isn't 'in my league' most times. *They're* the nervous ones in front of all the locals *plus me*, though I do my best to calm them down."

Thinking to continue his contemplation of the positives stemming from doing exhibitions, I threw out another rigged question. "I read that you did a whole bunch of such matches in the Midwest the summer of '47, and you were quoted as saying that they'd tuned you up well for the Ryder Cup in Portland that year. Is that right, even though the Cup wasn't played 'til the start of November?"

Lord Byron gave me a chuckle in response. "I did 35 of them darn things over a 2-month period on that tour, so yes, my game did stay 'grooved' that fall."

In response to this vote of confidence, I pounced. "So, what's to keep you from taking on smaller exhibition tours from here on, timed to get you sharp for a Major while not over-taxing your stomach in advance?" Having declaimed this gem, I Bobby Shout hoped to see a 'light bulb' go 'on' in 'my patient's' head at last. Instead, his sheepish look disappointed me.

"Well, that would be a nice idea, and I appreciate your thinking of it, 'cept the exhibition offers have 'dried up' over the past year. It seems, according to my rep at MacGregor – they still pay me some yah know – that I'm kinda 'old news' now as a golfer, and I can't blame folks for having that notion, seeing how it's nearly 4 years since I last won on Tour."

I remember being flabbergasted. Who wouldn't want to see Byron Nelson hit a golf ball? Heck, he'd finished tied for 4th at the Masters just 3 weeks earlier. In response to my blurted suggestion that it had to be a matter of someone at the company not trying hard enough to book him these types of matches, the former Mr. Golf replied that he'd look into it. But, I could tell that Byron was saying this more to ease my disappointment than to help himself.

During the fall of this year, and more tellingly, early in 1951 there would be a 'sea change' in this regard benefitting that oh-so-decent man. More on that in subsequent chapters. It's time now to skip to May and back to the amazing Ben Hogan.

CHAPTER 5

May 1950

BACK IN MARCH, one of Ben's friends at Seminole having come up with the idea of a new tournament called "the Spring Festival of Golf," asked him if he would play. Ole softie Hogan had given his okay, anything to help a buddy, right?

Not quite, I realized soon enough. First off, the Hawk knew that he would benefit from a tournament tune-up before his beloved Colonial Invitational which was set for the last week in May. However, there were only 2 other national PGA events scheduled for that month, the 'Spring Festival' – the first week in May – and the more revered Western Open, to be contested the week before Colonial.

The problem for Bantam Ben was that 'the Western' was being played in 1950 about as far west as one could go, the site being the Brentwood Country Club in Los Angeles. Well, you'll recall that getting to L.A. by train back then required a 3-day trip. There thus was no way that the Hawk could compete there and return by train in time to tee it up in Fort Worth without half-killing his fragile self. So, by default the 'Spring Festival' made sense schedule-wise.

Moreover, the location of this new 'Festival' had to make Ben smack his grim lips. Hogan's Seminole pal who had an interest in getting the famous Greenbrier Resort some renewed recognition had chosen that hotel's premier layout, the "Old White Course" for this event.

And it so happened that this was where Slammin' Sammy had 'cut his teeth' as a club pro. A victory there by Ben would amount to a slap-down of the high-riding Snead – Sam beaten at what amounted to a 'home game' for him. Hogan relished such opportunities, I knew by now.

So was it the Hawk or poor Hennie Bogan who made his presence known on the 'Old White'? Starting with a brace of 6-under 64s, Ben stayed 'hot' and tied Byron Nelson's 4-day tournament record of 259 from 4 years earlier, in the process besting 2nd-place Sam by 10 strokes!

Then to 'punch' Snead in his other eye, 'my patient' pooh-poohed this accomplishment as part of his post-win remarks while intimating how much better he'd have to play to score well at the upcoming stiffer tests like Merion … or Colonial. After reading Ben's words, I imagined that Sam would be after a 'knock-out punch' of his own

Hence I could hardly wait 'til May 25th to watch those two 'battle it out' in Fort Worth. My plan was to be at Colonial each day Thursday through Sunday and I'd gotten the afternoons 'off' from work. The disturbing thing though was that I Bobby Shout felt no longer sure which man I wanted to win.

As a budding psychologist, I could understand why Ben might be ungracious toward any other player who rose now to prominence as a rival for the golfing supremacy he'd attained before his accident. In the Hawk's perpetually fatigued state, it probably did help him to paint those potential usurpers as unworthy characters, his iron will sparked all the more to keep fighting … to not give in.

Yet when Hogan upon his return crowed to me about how he'd humiliated that West Virginian son of an ape, referring I assumed to Snead's exaggerated flexibility in his joints, it sounded mean and ugly. Fortunately, a more positive development related to Ben's psyche was 'taking flight' at that time, a new interest for which I felt able to take some credit.

To simplify my analysis, during the winter and spring of 1950 I'd discovered through talks with Ben that 'my patient' saw his father Chester's suicide to be akin to that of a martyr. A kind, hardworking, competent blacksmith had seen his trade 'run over' by the rise of the Model T which needed no horseshoeing.

Worse he was a depressive whose wife Clara had served as his fatal persecutor, at a key moment fanning the bipolar anguish he bore over his mental health and value as a human being. She'd done this ultimate disservice by refusing to show faith in him when after much effort he finally felt ready to reunite with her and their 3 children.

In response, Clara Hogan had been adamant during the late afternoon of February 13, 1922. She did not believe that her husband was 'cured' of the depression that had led them to Fort Worth for its Sanitarium in the first place, and told him so.

The family would stay on without him, Clara stated, in the rented house in Fort Worth – and she would remain a seamstress in that city – though Chester had spent the previous 2 months resuscitating his blacksmith trade back in their former hometown of Dublin, Texas, hoping to lure them all back. Sadly, Mrs. Hogan was right.

Crushed, Chester's response had been to shoot himself at dusk in that rental house's front parlor with 9-year-old Ben alone a witness, although some disputed this account. One thing was clear though to me: Somehow Bennie Hogan had always blamed his mother more than his dad for leaving him a half orphan in his childhood.

And this being so, there was a gnawing need in the child alter-ego Hennie Bogan to do something that would commemorate his blacksmith father to the world – and himself! – as something other than an utterly defeated soul. After a couple of masked discussions regarding this desire on Ben's part, the kernel of an inspiration did come to me in the form of the expression, "forged golf clubs."

Before explaining further, I should note that the Hawk's take on his mother's role in Chester's death did not preclude him from maintaining a loving admiration for her strength and drive in raising the family afterwards. Still, from time to time, he would manifest bouts of coldness toward her during that year I 'had his ear.' No 'my patient' never talked to me about the specifics of Chester's death, nor did I have 'the balls' to inquire. I gathered the above details from other sources.

In any case, my most fortuitous line-of-thought for Ben in the spring of 1950 had begun when the term "forged golf clubs" rang in my head. Soon thereafter, I asked him if he knew much about how the heads of golf irons were made, particularly how the 'forged' part fit in? This approach was a risk because 'my patient' could 'close his mind' in a flash if he thought a response beneath him, but I wanted 'the discovery' to seem to be his.

As the Hawk began to describe how the metal was super- heated in an iron forge before being stamped with a clubhead shape prior to being hammered, grinded and polished, the far-off look of memory in his eyes was exactly what I had sought. *He's recalling his father's blacksmith forge; he's seeing his dad wielding a hammer, pounding the metal into better shape, then using a grinding wheel to smooth things.* I was so excited inside, it took all my will power to stay bland, to let the connection play out in his mind.

But Ben, as I've mentioned, had plenty of horsepower in that brain of his. He'd leapt all the way to, "Are you suggesting that I get in the club-making business, kid? That I set up shop against Wilson, Spalding, and my own sponsor MacGregor? That the 'Ben Hogan Company' could honor my blacksmithing father as the source of the urge born in me to make great clubs? That we'd actually include him as part of our P.R. and advertising campaigns for 'Ben Hogan'?"

What could I say but, "Yup," hoping for the best.

"That would need a lot more thought," he'd growled, obviously dismissing the topic that day. However now, here he was in May telling me how he'd broached the club-making idea to his most powerful local friend Marvin Leonard between martinis at the Hogan home earlier in the week and that Leonard had shown some healthy skepticism. "I answered him, Dr. Shout, that I could make it work because I'd be making better clubs than those big established firms. 'For anybody who wants to play golf the way it ought to be played.' How's that for advertising copy?!"

The rest as they say is history -- to borrow a tired old 'saw.' Within 2 years Ben would open his company, with production of clubs in Fort Worth beginning in 1954. It's a pity what happened to the business later, however that's beyond the scope of my account at this juncture.

My point is that Ben Hogan was feeling especially good in mid-May, having committed to the idea of becoming his own club manufacturer. On top of that, his ego was getting a major massage at that point by the masters of such endearments, those Hollywood folks who would be 'shooting' the biopic about him starting that summer. *Follow The Sun* was to be its title, the Hawk revealed to me – I think before the public knew, though I'm not so sure about this.

Regardless, during this 'honeymoon period' prior to the actual film production, Ben being Ben, though 'riding high,' was dour as an old Scot in his preparation for 'pinning Sam Snead's ears back' at the upcoming Colonial National Invitation Tournament. That's what my restaurant friend at the course reported to me anyway.

Whereas Jimmy Demaret was to look back on this same month of May in 1950 as not only the beginning of a career-changing 'blow' to his ability to focus confidently on the course, but worse, a severe puncturing of his well-tended yet fragile ego. The ruckus that caused this fallout began with the publishing of yet another golf book, this one by a feisty pro no longer winning 'the big ones.'

Gene Sarazen at age 48 had the hot new golf volume in America at the time. THIRTY YEARS OF CHAMPIONSHIP GOLF was a first-class autobiographical effort, ghostwritten by the renowned golfing journalist Herbert Warren Wind and published by a division of one of the 'big boy' firms, Simon & Schuster.

Never shy of courting controversy, Gene had included a penultimate chapter headed "The Masters of Modern Golf" in which he'd ranked Bobby Jones and Walter Hagen, his contemporaries, as the top players of the century, with a second tier made up of 2 additional 'old timers' – Jim Barnes and Tommy Armour – along with the Brit Henry Cotton, plus Hogan, Nelson, and Snead. Canny Sarazen had left it to the reader to decide whether the first man to win the professional slam – him -- should also be part of a top triumvirate. But what about Demaret, the only man with 3 Masters to his credit?

Jimmy had been lumped in among an alphabetical listing of a dozen players less accomplished than the above. Worse – surely from Demaret's viewpoint -- Gene's commentary accompanying his rankings included several pages devoted to analyzing the greatness of Hogan, Nelson, and Snead, while he had spared a paltry 3 sentences for the Wardrobe, which boiled down to Jimmy being too nice a golfer for his own good.

Well, happy-go-lucky Jimmy must've either just gotten wind of Sarazen's words from someone else, or read 'em for himself between the first and second rounds at Colonial, because when he met with the writers before teeing off there on Friday, May 26, he was hotter than a burning stump.

I remember feeling my jaw drop at the vehemence and emotionally-driven hyperbole on Demaret's part -- so unlike him! -- when I read his vitriol in the Saturday paper. No wonder he'd followed an opening 69 with a score-killing 75 on Friday! Nor did he recover his competitive composure, shooting a 73 and 72 to finish well back of his rivals Hogan and Snead. And I feared that sudden mediocrity could be the start of a long, long 'tournament drought' for this likable Houstonian.

All due to Sarazen's opinions? I thought so after several days of digesting and analyzing what Jimmy said that Friday and beyond.

First off, the miffed Wardrobe had 'gone after' Sarazen for "never saying anything good about golf," and more specifically, "forever running the game and its players down." Note the "never" and "forever"; these were patent exaggerations, the sort of illogical assertions that deeply angry people are apt to make, and the 'normal Jimmy' had always tried to *never* appear angry.

There was only 1 previous occasion to my knowledge when Demaret's poise had supposedly slipped on Tour, back in '48 when he walked off the course at the New Orleans Open in the second round. But, it was later clarified by the tournament chairman that Jimmy's action had nothing to do with a competitor's grooves controversy that had erupted after the first round. The Wardrobe, it turned out, was simply tournament-tired and playing badly.

A second sign of the extreme discomfort caused in Jimmy's mind by Sarazen's book came in the form of his accusing Gene of 'sour grapes' with a final twist that got to the 'heart of the matter.' Demaret was quoted on that Friday morning as claiming that the Squire was playing the best golf of his life yet could not compete with the best on Tour. (Sarazen was past 48 years of age then for heaven's sake!) And therefore, Jimmy continued, "There's no reason he shouldn't be winning today, if the old-timers were so much better, as he persists in saying, than the players today."

This sorry outburst smacked of being a veiled reference to the ranking chart in THIRTY YEARS OF CHAMPIONSHIP GOLF that placed Jimmy well below several "old-timers." Moreover, Demaret even pointed to the relatively high scores shot in the past by these "old-timers" as numbers which 'proved' the superiority of his ilk, though the Joneses and Hagens had played on far more primitive tracks – with feeble hickory rather than modern steel shafts. Jimmy Demaret knew better; he'd caddied as a boy on those terribly maintained courses and swung hickory clubs, but he was 'out for bear.'

One final excerpt: Jimmy surely was also aware that Sarazen was a fellow veteran of the caddie yards and a birthright American, having been born in Westchester County, New York. Yet Demaret could not stop himself from hurling a personal, cockeyed insult before that Friday round, proclaiming "Heck, if it wasn't for golf, Sarazen would have been on a banana boat between Naples and Sicily."

Oh how I wished I could have reasoned with him before Mr. Wardrobe 'blew his top.' Did he consider that Gene's player rankings in THIRTY YEARS were formulated *before* Jimmy's third Masters win the previous month? There's always been a big time-lag in book-publishing. Perhaps the poorly-schooled Demaret was 'in the dark' about such matters. In fact, a second edition of the book might well have placed him higher in the golfing pantheon. Nor would it have been surprising for Sarazen to make mention of this due revision, if only Jimmy had 'taken the high ground' that May morning in 1950.

Instead, having been attacked, the Squire responded in the press with cool disdain 3 days later. He parried Demaret's various charges, feeling "unperturbed," and concluded by defending his old-time buddies by waxing philosophical: "An outstanding athlete in any era would be outstanding in any other era." That was and is an arguable premise, but it's far more defendable than Jimmy's emotional outbursts were.

Of course, this confrontation between 2 former friends was playing 'second fiddle' for most of the golf writers. The main story was always going to be Hogan versus Snead at Colonial. Would the Hawk be again triumphant or would Slammin' Sammy exact sweet revenge? And that's how it did turn out – with one of them the champion.

But before I focus on that final round, May 28, 1950, let me add a footnote. Byron Nelson was also in the field. He totaled 298, 21 shots behind the winner. I Bobby Shout could feel his pain, knowing that the competitive fire was back in his belly. The man needed a good exhibition tour 'under his belt.' 'His day' would come again, but not for quite some time.

The last round in that tournament began on May 28 with Snead comfortably in front, his 204 total through 54 holes leading Porky Oliver by 5, and two other un-elite pros (Alexander and Harrison) by 6 and 7 respectively. Only Ben, trailing by 8, had the stuff to still make it a tournament, in the eyes of us locals.

Sam proceeded to putt like he was using a rattlesnake, taking 36 swipes on Colonial's putting surfaces, to shoot a gettable 3-over round. Unfortunately, our Hawk could manage only an even-par 70, which was good enough to tie for 3rd, seeing how none of the top 10 leaders did any better! I remember heading home that Sunday, being bummed by the anti-climatic finale, and angry at the tournament officials who'd decreed such difficult pin locations on a gusty day when they should have been promoting 'a charge.'

I got a call from Ben that very night after his loss asking if we could meet the following day. I Bobby Shout assumed he'd want me to join him on the practice ground at Colonial or in the grill, but no, he said our Hulen Street bench would be fine.

At that time, Hogan was representing the Hershey Country Club on Tour. He was one of the first to get that sort of sweetheart deal. Hershey asked little of him in terms of a traditional club pro's duties. There was no lesson-giving or shop-tending, of course. Ben merely practiced on site from time to time, taking out a lucky member or two along with him when he decided to play some. It was the publicity of being connected with his wins that the club was paying for.

He'd mentioned wanting to put in an appearance there for a couple of days before being chauffeured down the Pennsylvania Turnpike for a week of prep at Merion for the U.S. Open, so this explained the need for a Monday May 29th get-together, seeing how the 'big show' began on June 8th. However, his choice of our old bench was puzzling.

The 29th was expected to be on the hot side. Was the Hawk intending to walk all that way from his home again, after the drain of competing at Colonial? I thought about it. Was this his way of punishing himself for failing to win that tournament against Snead? Or, was he feeling the need to keep pushing his stamina with Merion's hilly layout in mind? Or both?

Either way, it would be a testament to this thin, physically devastated man's iron will to overcome everything in his path. I was glad once more that my rooting interest in him had returned at Colonial. I'd been against Snead wholeheartedly after watching Ben limp through his first holes at the tournament. No one else wanted victory as badly as the Hawk!

When Ben did show at the Hulen Street bench on Monday afternoon, his clothes were sweated through but he was grinning. Maybe even he'd had doubts as to whether he'd survive the walk. As the Hawk eased himself down, my eyes were drawn to his sweat-stained pants. Ben Hogan, I suddenly realized, would probably never wear a pair of shorts again, regardless of the temperature. His harsh pride, the pitiful elastic bandages he had to wear … no, none of us would see his 'bare legs' again if he could help it. Suddenly, my eyes were stinging, but I made damn sure to hide it from 'my patient.'

It turned out that Bantam Ben had a favor to ask, not something that came to him easily – to say the least. He'd begun by talking about my summer. He assumed that things 'slowed down' quite a bit at the TCU infirmary. Were any classes held in July and August, he'd asked. When I confirmed that the summer was supposed to be a 'light' time on the blazing campus with generous vacation absences granted, Hogan beamed as much as Hogan could.

"After the Open," he said, "I like to play in the Palm Beach Round Robin outside New York City, then it will be home for a week at least, though I may head to Detroit for the Motor City Open through July 4th. After that, normally Val and I would return here for a good rest …" At this point, the Hawk paused, as though expecting me to 'connect the dots' and finish his line of thought for him. In a flash, I knew – the movie!

I Bobby Shout commented, "I guess you need to head out to Hollywood for a while to advise them on the set, huh?"

Ben replied with evident frustration about how they'd cast Glenn Ford to be him – "a gardener, not a golfer for Christ's sake!" He went on venting for another minute, sprinkling in several of the oaths he'd acquired in the military, about how he could tell that the director and crew were far from perfectionists and that they'd do a sloppy job of recreating his life if he didn't 'hold them to the fire.'

The Hawk continued, "I don't want Valerie to be involved too much in all of that …"

Bantam Ben meant that he didn't want to subject his wife to all of the negative energy he anticipated would emerge in him because of this project. And, that was where I might come in. Hogan knew I didn't need my current job to 'make ends meet.'

There were plenty of oil-stock funds at my disposal from Shout Petroleum Company should a change of plans warrant my taking a hiatus from work. What the Hawk could not see was that I had my own motive for considering a departure from TCU at the end of the upcoming fiscal year on June 30th. It involved what seemed to be imminent far from the U.S.A. at that moment. I told him I would be interested in coming out to see how movie-making worked, but gave no hint on the duration of my visit.

We went on to discuss what Ben expected at Merion. Well, he talked mostly and I listened. This included a prediction that he expected the scores to be unusually high. I was marveling at how the Hawk could diagnose a course like that before even seeing it in its current state, when Bantam Ben let out what could only be described as rare for him: an approximation of a giggle!

He'd been 'pulling my leg.' "No, Bobby, I don't really know what will be needed score-wise to win there yet, but it never hurts to get the other guys thinking that the course is gonna play damned hard."

Later, to my total non-surprise, it was reported in the papers on the eve of the Open that Hogan thought the winning total would be "unusually high." He would be proved painfully right, but I could never get up the gumption to ask him whether that had been his honest assessment this time or a playing out of the stratagem he'd shared on the Hulen Street bench. The suffering which that championship cost Ben was epic.

CHAPTER 6

June 1950

I'D FLOWN (FEELING my usual duress) from Dallas to Philadelphia on late Friday afternoon, June 9th, the first 2 rounds of the 1950 U.S. Open 'in the books.' It pleased me to read in the evening paper that Ben had followed his opening 72 with a 1-under 69 to climb to 5th place, but this positive reaction was momentary. Farther down in the article it was reported that Hogan had obviously suffered cramping in his legs upon finishing the 11th hole.

The description of Bantam Ben requiring his caddy's shoulder for support while limping to number 12 was an ominous sign, as was his weak finish to the round. Instead of tying for the lead with Dutch Harrison, 'my patient' had first 3-putted the uphill 16th for bogey then recorded another with a loose tee shot on the par-3 17th over the infamous quarry.

Ben would begin the 36-hole marathon on Saturday 2 shots behind and with 4 men ahead of him: Harrison; Jim Ferrier, the big Australian whose thyroid had perhaps cost him the Masters; Julius Boros, an Open rookie that year but good enough to win 2 in his career; and Johnny Bulla, he the owner of the plane that Ben had had to crash-land 4 years earlier.

Could the Hawk conquer more cramping and far greater fatigue than he'd yet to bear, in order to best the entire field on the morrow? Or would he 'crash and burn'?

I didn't try to contact him that night, knowing that he'd probably retired quite early, as I also needed to do to get to the course well before Ben's 9:30 tee time. He'd be there by eight. I Bobby Shout hoped to be on the range at 8:30 when Ben, as was his rigid custom, would be beginning his warm-up – 1 hour exactly prior to the start of his round.

Hogan's day had started at 5:30 a.m. on that Saturday, June 10th. The 2 hours before departure for the course had been spent typically. There'd been a tub soak, the rubbing of his legs with liniment, and then a wrapping of those throbbing limbs of his with elastic bandages, followed by a breakfast of bacon and eggs.

Half an hour later, having been chauffeured from the Barclay Hotel to Merion, Ben was in the locker room for his usual 20 minutes making sure his appearance was immaculate before proceeding to the course's practice area aside of the 18th fairway. I was there waiting, grateful that the weather was warm enough to stretch his muscles gently, but not too hot a forecast. There was sunshine with light winds, a beautiful day for golf.

Still, the lovely air could not save the Hawk from the torments of his body. The agony of cramping grabbed him this time 2 holes later than the previous day. Having putted out on the short sand-surrounded 13th a bit after noon, Ben felt such pain that he muttered to his caddy, "That's it. I just can't make it," intending to walk off.

What his boy caddy replied was unheard by me, standing in the gallery close by, but some said afterwards that the kid, whoever he was, had gushed, "No, Mr. Hogan, you can't quit because I don't work for quitters." And Ben somehow chose to continue on, rather than staring that youngster to death.

You probably are wondering what 'my patient' had to say about that incident. Well, days later when we were both back in Fort Worth, Ben's response to my query was, "Dr. Shout, wasn't that about the most ridiculous cornpone you'd ever heard? A kid lecturing me? I'm surprised at you, Bobby." But, the way he uttered this rebuke, his eyes gleaming with a trace of wonder, left me wondering.

Anyway, whether it was due to this "cornpone" inspiration or to the fact that a certain competitor had emerged from the pack at the Open by that time – more on this gent soon – the Hawk gritted his way through the final 5 morning holes to record a 2-over 72. His 3-round total of 213 was good enough to tie Johnny Palmer and Cary Middlecoff for 2nd place, but left him 2 strokes shy of the new leader, a 'hot golfer' who'd just 'cleaned up' the previous week on Tour in Indiana at the Fort Wayne Open.

70 years later, this may be hard to believe, but during the interval between his rounds that Saturday, Ben had adjourned to the outdoor terrace of Merion's clubhouse – which practically borders the course's 1st tee – to sip a bowl of chicken broth with Valerie at his side. The 1950 press corps, fans, and other players all

had the decency to grant him privacy during this meal in that very public setting. No questions asked. Can you imagine such an act of respect and courtesy in the athletic arena now?!

However, among the Hoganites who had migrated to that first tee, waiting for their hero to begin his final round, there were plenty of speculations being bandied about. Many of them were of the gloom-and-doom variety. Far fewer were laced with cautious optimism regarding Ben's chances – of finishing, that is, not winning. Only a small minority of the Hawk's supporters were daring to speak of a triumph for him then.

I Bobby Shout like to think that I was surer than any of those other fans as to how things would go. I believed that Hogan would win, even if he had to crawl between shots. Why?

The reason for my certainty was that hatred can be an amazing motivator. And, the pro who'd started that final round of the 1950 National Open as its leader was in Bantam Ben's mind an absolutely despicable man. To whom do I refer? To none other than 'sneaky' Lloyd Mangrum, a.k.a. "Mr. Icicle."

You remember the Hawk's rant regarding Mangrum back on the Hulen Street Bench? According to Ben, Lloyd's move from Texas to California in his youth constituted desertion. Who'd ever want to leave the Lone Star State unless they had to, which spoke to an unsavory character! And, what kind of jackass asks a fellow pro to endorse his instruction book when its viewpoint contradicts the earlier author's own volume?

Worse still, the most heartfelt charge against Lloyd Mangrum that I had noted from Hogan on that February day was cockiness!

Well hadn't the Hawk traveled a long and difficult path to reach the pinnacle as a player in the late 1940s? Hadn't he through an ungodly amount of intelligent effort on the range become nearly a supernatural ball-striker by then, though lacking the physical advantages of his rivals like Demaret or Snead?

If so, and the answer was resoundingly a yes, then Ben believed that he had earned from everyone connected to the Tour a show of deference each round, out of respect for this accomplishment. Ah, but "Mr. Icicle" like a snotty little brother would have none of that game. Whether in the locker-room, on the practice field, or during play, Lloyd Mangrum acted like he didn't give a damn what anyone else thought, including Mr. Hogan!

Let's begin by reviewing the ways that Lloyd displeased Ben. First off, there was the younger man's 'mouth.' Whereas Hogan could swear like a soldier when not in polite company, he still expected decorum to be maintained in public. Not so, Mangrum! He churned out 4-letter-words regardless of the setting. Nor did the Texas traitor desist-- even when he won – from reminding reporters how his rivals' failures had played a part in the story.

Then there was the man's style of play. The press had latched onto the image of a riverboat gambler as suitable for Lloyd not merely because of his dashing appearance. He also maintained the best 'poker face' on Tour!

While it was obvious that Ben grinded on every shot, mulling over this and that and dying to win, Mangrum even at the most key moments always gave off the air of a gent who could care less, as he 'got down to business' briskly. Hence that moniker given to him, "Mr. Icicle" – well before Ben was dubbed the "Wee Ice Mon."

It took multiple readings of Lloyd's own oft-repeated explanation for his seemingly nonchalant attitude in competition, however, before my understanding of the psychic relationship between Hogan and this 'little brother figure' finally crystallized. And, to be honest, I felt pretty dense on that June 10th that I'd missed the 'big picture' for so long.

You see, Lloyd was fond of saying that any soldier who'd been in combat instinctively knew that the outcome of any golf tournament, no matter how big, was hardly a life-and-death affair. So, why shouldn't he be relaxed on the course?

A trite oversimplification to 'put off' the press? No. Rather, a major 'dig'! 'Cause with this speech, former Corporal Mangrum meant to remind Snead, Demaret, and Hogan, along with the other top pros who'd found a way to stay stateside during WWII, that guys like him who'd fought and bled on 'the front' were their superiors. *My competitive calm was hard-earned* was Lloyd's message. Though ironically, there was a hell of a lot of anger and resentment on his part tied to that stance.

Out of fairness to "Mr. Icicle," I must report that he'd had a perfect chance to avoid the frontlines, too, in the form of an invitation back in the spring of 1944 to become the golf instructor at Fort Meade in Maryland. To his credit he'd turned that offer down.

Instead, the riverboat gambler had wound up a Corporal in the 90th infantry over in Europe doing reconnaissance work. In the fall of that year he'd suffered his first injuries while in France when the jeep he was in flipped over during a blackout. That accident cost Lloyd a double break in his left arm along with a chipped shoulder bone. It was the break that shook him as he recuperated in a U.S. military hospital in England. The word from the doctor was that Mangrum might not be able to lift his arm above his head after the cast was removed.

Lloyd liked to quip during interviews later about overcoming that problem. "Imagine a golfer who couldn't do anything but swing like a hockey player." But, who could blame him at the time if he was scared to death that his golfing career might be over?

Two additional occasions before war's end saw him flirting with other debilitating injuries: The enemy nicked his knee with a bullet while he was rescuing a fellow soldier, and a hunk of shrapnel took off a piece of Lloyd's chin – all of which earned him 2 purple hearts to go along with 2 silver and 2 bronze combat stars. In other words, he'd been a 'real soldier' in the war, risking his life repeatedly, while guys like Ben were playing golf exhibitions back home, as far as 'Mr. Icicle' could tell.

No wonder he'd come back to America late in '45, proud of his wins in several recent golf competitions over other servicemen in Europe, but resentful, too, of the Tour time he'd lost to his rivals. Lloyd didn't just stride around looking superior to the other non-combat pros post-war, he felt superior! And Ben, who had photos of himself posing with generals at golf exhibitions on display at home, must have hated sensing that aura of superiority which Mangrum projected – toward him as much as toward others.

As I've said, I wasn't at Merion for the practice days nor rounds 1 and 2, but I can imagine how puffed up Mr. Icicle probably appeared, both fresh off a win, and perhaps even more tellingly, with talk swirling everywhere regarding a potential new war in Korea. No, to say that Ben didn't want to lose that Open to Lloyd – the two of them tied with 1 each at that point – would be a gigantic understatement. So I bet on the Hawk's magnificent willpower.

To recap, as the final round began on that Saturday afternoon, those barely trailing Lloyd's 211 were Dutch Harrison with 212, then Ben, Cary Middlecoff, and Johnny Palmer – all at 213. I expected the less heralded Harrison and Palmer to fade, leaving Mangrum, Hogan, and Middlecoff to decide the winner. Well the 2 'outsiders' did cooperate with my prediction, both of them shooting a 5-over 41 on the front, but so did Mr. Not-Such-An Icicle!

We Hoganites were thrilled to see that Ben now held the lead as he teed off on number 1 at 3-over for the championship, and things got better and better on the front 9. While the Hawk was playing his mechanically perfect golf over that stretch, his sole blemish a 3-putt bogey from 40 feet on the par-3 3rd, Middlecoff was acting like he was 10 shots behind. His several daring gambles cost him big time on the way to a closing 79.

What that meant was that after 11 holes Ben 'merely' needed to match the back-9 par of 34 to beat those in front of him by 3, a 71 giving him a 4-round total of 284, while George Fazio was the best in the clubhouse with a 287 – along with alas Lloyd Mangrum. If it had been the pre-accident Hogan playing that back side, our confidence would have been unshakable. But already on the front side there had been signs that the Hawk's legs might yet 'do him in.' Merion's steep hills were causing him to halt; would they prematurely force him to stop 'for good'?

By the 12th tee which is somewhat secluded, it appeared to those few of us who were permitted up close to see Ben drive that we'd been given our answer, a disastrous one. As he ripped into his shot on that uphill par-4, suddenly he was stumbling on the follow-through and needed to grab onto a friend to keep upright. Then I heard him murmur, "My God, I don't think I can finish." My mind flashed back to his first return swings at Colonial, when he *had* 'fallen on his face.'

Were more leg cramps the culprit? Had his footing slid due to fresh sod on that site? Some thought his knee had given way, but what did the specific cause matter, if Ben could not complete the round? One thing we did know from thereon was that something was really wrong. Our Hawk couldn't bend to the ground! The caddies were both teeing his ball up and pulling it from the cup for him, and Cary Middlecoff was doing the marking of Ben's ball when required. No wonder his score started to slip as well.

When the Hawk launched his next shot on that hole, it landed and bounced un-Hogan-like to 12 feet above the pin. Ben was unable to exert the right 'weight' as he struck his putt and it wandered 5 feet beyond the cup. Our fatigued hero failed to sink the come-backer, raising his tournament total to 5-over. Now, he could afford only 1 more bogey to win this Open outright.

A good chance to 'get that stroke back' went a-begging when Ben missed a 10-footer for bird on the tiny 13th. After another par, the Hawk messed up on 15 in agonizing fashion for us fans.

One of Merion's true 'bears,' that steeply tilted dogleg-right hole aims the player's drive at a road where the traffic seems to scream "Out of bounds." Fortunately, for the Hawk's natural fade this was no big deal. Safely in play, he'd sent an iron up toward that hole's pear-shaped putting surface, its pinching bunkers perched higher than we could see. His 'line' looked good; the roar from the folks up there, even better.

He had an 8-footer for birdie we eventually saw, but missed that, then 'blew' a tap-in. His cushion was gone, with the course's infamous quarry finish ahead!

Such a good chip to 4 feet and a solid putt saved his par on 16, but Ben couldn't repeat that stroke after blasting his 2nd shot from sand to 10 feet on the long par-3 17th. Now, he had to par the wicked final hole just to make a playoff with Fazio and Mangrum. If you've seen the iconic photo of the Hawk's completed follow-through after he lasered his longest iron onto the green, you probably know that Hogan did get his needed 4.

That left us in his gallery with 1 giant question? Did Ben Hogan have anything left for Sunday's playoff, or would he stumble through it the way he had with Snead back at the Los Angeles Open in January?

Jimmy Demaret on Saturday night told me of a telling exchange that had occurred in Merion's locker room a few hours earlier. An ashen-faced Ben was sipping ice water after his 6-hour afternoon round before a record-breaking gallery that numbered between 13- and 15-thousand folks. The reporters of course asked him how his legs were. The Hawk responded in his typically laconic fashion: "Fine."

When the press guys continued to circle back with questions about 'my patient's' physical condition, he'd responded by getting Hogan-testy rather than showing his 'new' more cooperative-with-the-media self. To paraphrase Ben, he said that he was tired of reading stuff in the papers about his body and he was sure that everyone else was tired of the subject, too!

That response seemed like good news to me: Hogan showing that he still had 'some fight' in him even after 9 miles of grueling effort and championship pressure that day. This wasn't the portion of Jimmy's report that excited me the most, however. Leave it to sneaky Lloyd Mangrum to 'goose' Ben on to his best efforts.

Late during the interview phase, Mr. Icicle had popped his head around the corner of the locker room where Hogan sat and inquired, "Hey boy, how do you feel?" Can you imagine? Calling Ben Hogan "boy" even back then. Whether Lloyd had used this term with conscious intent or not, I knew that it would rile Ben.

Eyes blazing (Jimmy said) the Hawk had given his one-word response again. "Fine."

"Okay. See you in the morning," was Mangrum's retort before retreating. Poor Lloyd though was unaware apparently of Pennsylvania's 'blue laws' which dictated among other things that no sporting events could be held before church services were finished on the Sabbath. Ben would have all morning to regain his strength before the playoff round set to begin at 2. A huge potential advantage for Fazio and Mangrum had been negated by fate.

The weather for the Sunday playoff on June 11th did Ben another good turn. Cooler air had arrived and the thermometer was not expected to exceed 75 degrees on this dry day. As I began to make my way through the clubhouse, heading for its rear exit in order to observe the Hawk hitting on the informal range beside number 18, I was surprised by the touch of a woman's hand on my arm.

Equally unexpected was the look of warmth on Valerie Hogan's lovely but normally reserved face – at least in my company. She said in a rushed voice, "Oh Bobby, I wish you could have been there for the scene in the hotel this morning." I had no inkling what she was talking about.

Val continued, "They, the gentlemen of the press, were gathered in the lobby waiting for Ben. These men who have been so harsh about him at times, nearly every one of them it seemed stepped up to shake his hand and wish him good luck today. The group clapped for him as we left! I know you're aware how the public sentiment has softened, how Ben still receives so much support from well-wishers since the accident, but to have the writers now so openly on his side, well, I know it heartened him whatever may happen today."

There was a wobble in her tone while completing her thought. I assumed that Mrs. Hogan was doubtful still that her husband could play winning golf this afternoon. However, that was not exactly the case.

In response to my voicing this doubt, she laughed almost gaily. "Oh Bobby, when we got back to our room last night I was only hoping that he'd be alive this morning." Val chuckled again at her maudlin exaggeration. "He actually downed several martinis after his bath," she said, "in spite of my protests." Yes, I could imagine that.

"But then Ben slept wonderfully all night in spite of a racket outside which woke me. When he did get up, I was so grateful – he looked fresh as a daisy. And, first thing he had to say, was, 'Isn't it a wonderful day, Val?' Can you imagine?"

What could I do but shake my head at the toughness of this remarkable man? "Going outside to watch him hit now," I said by way of parting, anxious to see Hogan for myself. Valerie would not ask to come with me, I knew. When Ben played, her role was to 'keep the home fires burning' in the clubhouse. Any other place and she would have gotten too wound up.

On the front 9, Ben Hogan played the way we all expected him to, with 1 exception. After birdying number 7 to get to 1-under, he lined his subsequent drive into a penal bunker on the drive-and-pitch 8th costing him a bogey. This mistake put him back into a tie with Mangrum whose only non-par holes had been a 4 on the long 2nd followed by a 3-putt bogey from the back fringe on the 1-shotter 3rd. Fazio, meanwhile, was making ball-striking mistakes but compensating with good putting for a 37, leaving him 1 back of the other two.

Ironically, it was George Fazio – not Ben – who seemed 'to run out of gas' on the back side. His 4 bogeys over the final 5 holes left him out of the late-round drama. The Philly pro's 5-over 75 became an afterthought in this Open.

I felt for him. George's swing was sweet but he'd only won on Tour 2 times, his 2nd win coming at the Crosby 3 years earlier. I Bobby Shout could taste the extra pressure he was under as the 'hometown hero.' He had to be playing 'on fumes' in a 5th round of a Major championship.

While Fazio was 3-putting the 14th to begin his downfall, Lloyd also messed up the hole to fall 2 strokes behind our even-par Ben. But Mr. Icicle came right back with a bird on the next hole to halve the future 'Wee Ice Mon's' lead. We Fort Worthians were now worried, considering how our man had faded toward the end on the previous day.

And yet, it was 'sneaky Lloyd' with the honor who failed to get his drive in the fairway on the uphill, over-the-quarry par-4 16th. When he had to hack from thick rough to a point barely beyond his 2 competitors' tee balls, and Ben's 2nd got him to reasonable birdie length yet again, all of us were able to heave a sigh of relief, unaware of the twists and turns immediately ahead.

First we had to wait on Fazio to putt out. Then the Hawk again missed his, one that would have put him at least 2 ahead with 2 to play. Still, there was the prospect of Mangrum failing to hole his 9-footer which would give us all the chance to 'breathe a bit.' The last thing we Fort Worthians wanted was an extra delay as we waited -- hearts pumping -- but that is what we got, when Lloyd, having replaced his ball down on the green and begun to settle in his stance, noticed something and straightened back up.

Using the end of his putter this time, rather than a coin, to note the ball's position, Mr. Icicle provoked titters from some in the crowd as he showed us that there was a ladybug on the damn thing. Ole Lloyd blew it off like he was at a picnic then rolled his ball right into the cup with just as little fuss, saving par and foiling our hopes that he'd fall 2 shots behind.

The next hole awaiting us was the daunting 230-yard par-3 17th, where Ben had found sand the previous day and failed to get up-and-down. *If Mangrum gets his shot on the green, I'll be really worried*, I was thinking, because even the great Hogan might have a 'bad feeling' on this tee.

It was at this moment that the odd ways of the USGA intervened in our hero's favor. One of their officials stopped Lloyd from teeing off though we all thought it was still his honor. Turned out that Mr. Icicle had broken not 1 but 2 of their rules on the previous putting surface. Though the PGA allowed a 2nd marking of one's ball on the green as well as the cleaning of same, the USGA forbid both apparently.

Hearing this over-the-top explanation, we spectators could not blame even Sneaky Lloyd for reacting with grim anger. "What if it had been a snake there and no fucking insect?" he'd spit out.

This official, to his credit -- though a bit 'put off' by Mangrum's language obviously -- continued on to the good news: The USGA didn't believe in double jeopardy, so the bug-cleaning had cost Lloyd nothing; the only penalty he had to take was 2 strokes for marking his ball a 2nd time on 16th's green.

I wondered whether Mr. Icicle was going to 'deck him.' After all, Mangrum and fighting were hardly strangers I'd heard. In fact, Lloyd's shoulder injury that had cost him the 1st few months of the 1950 season was rumored by some to have been received during a bar brawl rather than the publicized car accident.

However, that straight-whiskey drinker surprised me, reverting to the cool grace of his riverboat gambler side with an aside to the gallery. "Well I guess we'll all eat tomorrow," he grumbled, well knowing that 'the game was up' for his Open chances.

And, to Ben's credit, he 'slammed the door shut," following his own shot safely onto the front of the putting surface with a dunk-shot bird from nearly 50 feet to stretch his lead to 4. A ho-hum par on the final hole finished the job, making Ben a 2-time U.S. Open champ.

Did I say "ho-hum"?! The Hawk holed a near 10-footer for his 69th and final stroke of the day and when he did, the crowd swarmed him. He was totally mobbed in a few seconds. I was afraid they'd try to lift him on their shoulders and wreck some part of his frail body sure'nuff.

During the interlude when Jimmy D., Cary M., and the other guys in the locker room were toasting Ben's triumph with cocktails, the winner disappeared for so long that his name had to be called over the clubhouse loudspeaker to come forward for the trophy ceremony. Naturally, the Wardrobe later repeated to me the quip he'd made at that point which 'cracked up' his cronies. Demaret had crowed, "Hell, the Hawk's already up at Oakland Hills practicing for next year's Open!"

Meanwhile the man who'd been dealt a 'bad hand' by fate that day eventually was cornered by the press in that same locker room. And what Lloyd Mangrum said convinced me that he like many a man had an intriguing personality. As I read the following day in the paper, Mr. Icicle – who could have bitched lengthily – 'moved on' and accepted his blame for not knowing the USGA's rules well enough. The guy had even waxed philosophical after that in his rough lexicon, concluding, "Anyway it ain't my life, and I'll still win a lot of golf tournaments." Well, ole Lloyd was right – right away.

The very next week he blasted the opposition – including Ben – in the so-called Palm Beach round-robin golf tournament, a points affair. This event, which was played not in Florida but rather on the outskirts of New York City, at the Wykagyl course in New Rochelle to be exact, saw Lloyd beat par every day by so much that he nearly doubled the point total of the 2nd-place professional, Lawson Little. Mangrum had now gone 1st-2nd-1st on Tour in June with the PGA Championship on deck, a match-play marathon too grueling for 'my patient' Ben to even consider entering.

Hogan never told me but I had a guess as to why he ultimately decided to head out to Hollywood by way of Detroit in late June to be on hand for the start of the Motor City Open. After all it wasn't a title he lacked; he'd won there in '48. And yes the event was being played at a different layout in 1950, but still, it was only a minor Tour stop 1 week after the PGA Major. No I believed that the Hawk's driving interest in Detroit that year was to derail 'sneaky' Lloyd's stroke-play success streak.

Speaking of that PGA, which was contested over 6 days back then – from June 21st through the 27th – my chief rooting interest was for Jimmy Demaret to rebound from his Sarazen-induced slump. Unhappily, his tie for twentieth in the recent U.S. Open spoke only of fading glory: He'd finished 2nd in '48; 6th in '46.

However, Jimmy held an even stronger record in PGA Championship play, having made it 3 times to the semi-finals (most recently in '48) along with a quarter-final appearance during the most recent playing of the event. Obviously, the Wardrobe had 'the right stuff' for hole-by-hole competitions! Hence I 'Dr.

Shout' was still hopeful on his behalf as the PGA began upon the Scioto course in Columbus, Ohio.

At the same time, I had to admit that there was something about Mangrum triumphing yet again in June that appealed to me. The guy did have an anti-hero charisma about him that was only a bit ahead of his time. Consider James Dean and Marlon Brando on the 'big screen.'

Both Jimmy Demaret and Lloyd Mangrum did manage to make it into the quarterfinals of this PGA's match-play event, me following their progress through radio and newspaper accounts. It was Mr. Icicle who fell 1st, though not without a fight. He'd been 4-down to the Virginian Chandler Harper after 21 holes in their double-round contest, but by the 30th, Lloyd was dead-even again with his rival.

On the next-to-last scheduled hole, Harper not only blocked Mangrum's ball stymie-style by the placement of their tee shots on the par-3; the Virginian holed his out when it was his turn, for a birdie and a 1-up lead. Chandler's 7-foot birdie-make on the 36th preserved his advantage for the win, Lloyd having already made his 4 on that par-5.

Though Mangrum had been favored to win, he certainly didn't 'give the match away,' having shot 7-under for the 36 holes. Yet, Lloyd had forfeited 'the high ground' to his opponent over the opening 9 of the day by not making a birdie 'til the 8th and shooting even-par for that side, leaving him 3-down, just as he'd been through 6.

Early that Sunday, June 25th – the 1950 PGA competition had begun the previous Wednesday and would stretch to Tuesday the 27th – a momentous event across the world was 'in the works' overshadowing any golf. Specifically, North Korea was reported to have finally invaded South Korea. Some folks were not shy about saying this would be the start of WWIII. And why not, with our communist foes China and Russia possibly willing to back the North against the Western-allied South?

I remember wondering whether Mr. Icicle could have been particularly shaken by this news, accounting for his slow start? After all, at age 36 it would not be improbable for him to be called back into the Service, should an all-out war explode. And even if Lloyd were not sent again to 'the front,' it would still constitute a 2nd career-shattering interruption of his golf, when he had to think that he – for one! – had already done 'his part.' Of course it made me chuckle grimly, too, knowing I'd never get to talk to Mangrum about such matters. But what did I know?

Unfortunately, the "laughing boy of the links" as Demaret was termed in that same news account which covered Lloyd's quarter-final loss had nothing to laugh about after he took on Chandler Harper in the succeeding double-round on Monday.

Time and again during their semi-final, the balding Harper, though only 36 years' of age – to Jimmy's 40 – combined pinpoint iron-play with solid putting to retain a lead which the Wardrobe could never quite overcome. During the opening 9, when Demaret rallied from 3-down to get back to even on number 8, Chandler had answered with a 25-footer for bird on 9 to go ahead again.

Then they traded wins on the back side, leaving the Virginian still 1-up at lunch. Through the next 6 holes, Chandler again managed to build his lead back up to 3 with 2 birds, but Jimmy responded with back-to back wins to leave himself only 1 behind with 10 holes possibly ahead.

Alas it was all pars from there on in for both players except for 1 birdie-make from 18 feet by Jimmy's foe on the 33rd hole, resulting in a 2-and-1 vanquishing of my chief rooting interest. For the record, Harper did take the title on Tuesday.

However, I was more concerned about Jimmy Demaret's psyche after this, his 4th defeat in the semi-finals of this event! Would he be taking a glass-half-full or glass-half-empty perspective concerning his performance, or was that renowned tippler leaving a flurry of alcoholic beverage bottles in his wake to blot out any sort of thinking?

'Dr. Shout' was hoping to speak with friend Jim sooner rather than later as I was fearful for his current state of mind. Of course he like Ben was headed presumably to Detroit and the next Tour stop at that point while I was 'stuck' working in Fort Worth. So what could I do besides worrying about him and me? A major decision of mine was about to change all that.

My supervisor at the T.C.U. infirmary was 'long gone' late in the afternoon on the last Friday of June 1950. I remember that the temperature had reached 85 degrees in Fort Worth and a strong breeze was blowing west on that dry June 30th. Come Monday morning he would find an envelope from me on his desk.

The single sheet within that receptacle said simply that I was giving 2 weeks' notice, making my last day on the job July 14th. Should you feel that such a departure was too abrupt on my part, please recall that our campus was rather 'dead' at that time of year and so there was little 'live business' at our facility. I Bobby Shout was merely 'ducking out' on a summer of mostly make-work projects. Moreover, back in 1950 a resignation letter 2 weeks prior to a desired employment end-date was not unusual.

As I locked the door to our office suite, I remember singing out to myself inside, *Hollywood, here we come!* Then, having gone directly home, I phoned my mother at the Shout Petroleum company headquarters. It was no surprise to me to find her there. She was what would later be called "a workaholic," I suppose, though back then it was simply considered a virtue to be "hardworking."

There was no friction between her and me openly, though for the past year-and-a-half – since her husband/my dad died --Margaret Edwinson Shout had been hinting that she'd welcome my return to the company to lead things along with my older brother Leroy. Well, maybe I had some good news for her or maybe I didn't. All I established during our call was that I'd appreciate a private meeting in her Dallas office 2 weeks hence, around 6 p.m. on July 14th.

My mother Margo responded that she'd be happy to oblige as well as staking me to a fine dinner at our favorite old steakhouse afterwards. I said that sounded swell to me.

CHAPTER 7

July 1950

FITTINGLY THE MOTOR City Open opened the second half of the year with a hint of fireworks between the Tour's 2 biggest winners. Tuesday July 4th, Sam Snead had teed it up on his 72nd hole at Red Run Golf Club's par-5 finisher needing only a birdie to tie Lloyd Mangrum for first place while Ben Hogan had limped in, 9 shots worse at 283 leaving him tied for eleventh in this Detroit suburban event. The Hawk had failed to stop 'sneaky' Lloyd, and I felt bad for Valerie having to share the long train trip to L.A. with her no doubt silently furious husband.

The papers said that Slammin' Sammy had gotten up by the green on that final hole in 2, then made a good chip to 4 feet but "flubbed" the tying putt. Rubbing salt into his wound was the fact that Snead had held a 3-shot lead over Lloyd beginning the final 9. So, when Mr. Icicle chose to include in his victory speech a note of thanks to Sam for his failure on the final green, who could blame the 2nd-place winner from getting the hell out of there at that moment?

And why was Lloyd such a bastard this way? As I've mentioned already, I Bobby Shout thought his resentment was monumental toward his fellow pros like Snead who'd 'had it easy' during the war!

Of course, by the next day Sam Snead was touting a less wimpy reason for his sudden departure at Red Run. Supposedly, he'd had 'to catch a plane.' To where? An airport in southwest Virginia from where he'd trained to his home, because he had to … No answer was supplied. The next Tour event was a full nine days away, thanks to the consecutive Tuesday finishes at the PGA Championship and Motor City. And then? The Slammer would get his chance at revenge.

That July the Tour's next event was being held in Ohio upon the Inverness Club's distinguished course where a teenaged Bobby Jones had failed to impress an aging Harry Vardon in 1920. The title at stake there had been a U.S. Open, and Vardon almost won it, surrendering a big lead through shaky putting toward the end of the final round.

Inverness's tournament format this time consisted of a 4-ball invitational, requiring each 2-man team to play a round against the other 7 pairings in the field. That meant completing seven full 18s – that's 126 holes – over only 4 days, well beyond the current stamina of one Ben Hogan. Thus, I knew that the Hawk had given little thought to delaying his trip west any longer, Mangrum or no Mangrum!

Well Mangrum was on hand in Ohio, with fellow Open champion Cary Middlecoff as his partner, a formidable duo set to play Sam Snead and Jim Ferrier on the morning of the final day of the invitational, Sunday July 16th. Naturally, Snead's 'thirst for revenge' was an open secret, causing that match to be followed by thousands, and what they saw pleased the Slammer's rooters.

Not only did Snead's team blow away Lloyd and Cary 4 up before crushing their afternoon opponents 5 up, Sam and Jim Ferrier recorded the 3rd highest holes-won total in the event's history – plus18. Besides cashing the winners' checks of $2,000 each, the Snead Twosome got $125 each for making the most sub-par scores in the event, 48 birdies and an eagle. And, on top of that, the Slammer had netted another $200 for winning the long-drive contest.

More of interest to me reading the tournament account was a mention of my 'patient' Jimmy Demaret. I was relieved to see that he was seemingly in bounce-back mode, having tied Snead for the most birdies made at Inverness, an impressive total of 30. Yet, the team of Demaret and Jack Burke Jr. had gone 1-and-6 in the matches. Had the Wardrobe been playing like Dr. Jekyll and Mr. Hyde there? Or, had Burke 'stunk up the place'? I was still worried then. Maybe Jimmy somehow was blaming himself for his partner's poor play? I wanted to see him soon, but how?

After my final day of work at T.C.U. on July 14, I'd figured to need about ten days to 'square away things' in Fort Worth before following Hogan out to Hollywood. So, I'd made a plane reservation for Tuesday, July 25. However, something ominous happened at the Tour's next stop, the St. Paul Open, which made me push back my reservation to Friday of that week.

The headline stuff relating to that tournament was not what delayed my departure. The fact was that it was only moderately interesting to me that Snead and Ferrier, who'd just triumphed as teammates the previous week, were now battling each other for the win at St. Paul. Nor was their being tied after both the initial 72 holes plus a Monday play-off the turn-of-events that made me rethink my schedule. (Ferrier proved the winner with a bird on the third 'sudden death' play-off hole, for the record.)

No my change of plans stemmed from what was included at the very bottom of the coverage of Saturday's round, where it was noted in the paper that Jimmy Demaret after a front-side 40 had withdrawn from the event on the grounds that he was "too tired to go on."

Well what was I Bobby Shout to think? This quitting a tournament was not a first for the Wardrobe I knew. But, pros when they 'wanted out' could always claim an injury was forcing them to retire. Jimmy had just cited fatigue. And hell yes, he had undergone 7 rounds of competitive golf the previous week, but so had many in the field now at St. Paul.

My fears about Jim's mental state concerning his place in golf were goosed by this incident. I felt he could benefit from our talking face-to-face again. Would Demaret travel on to July's final PGA event in cosmopolitan Sioux City, Iowa? Probably not, I figured. He would be returning to his home in Houston no doubt 'to lick his wounds' – or douse them in alcohol. So I hoped to travel from Fort Worth to Houston on either Monday or Tuesday to visit him, the 24th or 25th.

On the phone, Jimmy sounded okay. Yet, when I offered to come, he responded with a whoosh of breath followed by the words, "Sure. Why not? Can't hurt. That's kind of you, Bobby Shout." I told him to expect me on Tuesday, then having hung up, I exhaled to myself. Did I have the slightest idea how to help this man now? Really?

The drive from Fort Worth to Houston, being near 5 hours back in those days, gave me plenty of time to reconsider the potential mental dilemmas that might be preying on Demaret. However I hardly expected the first words that came out of his mouth when he met me at the door.

"Hey, Bobby," Jimmy began. "I heard from the Hawk that you're flying to California on Friday to help him straighten out those golf-blind movie guys. That's a shame."

"Why is that?" I'd replied somewhat alarmed.

Breaking into his customary grin, the Wardrobe continued, "Because you needn't have driven way down here for a confab, seeing how I'm winging it on Saturday to my post at Ojai for a ten- day stint, and hell that's only an hour-and-a-half from L.A. I'll be bound to breeze into the big city for some of that time to take money off the celebrities (he winked). So you'll be seeing me around for sure.

Jimmy, like Ben who was playing on Tour for Hershey, and Lloyd Mangrum who had a similar 'sweetheart deal' with the Tam O' Shanter Club outside Chicago, represented a country club when playing with the 'big boys.' In his case, it's what's called the Ojai Valley Inn resort, east of Santa Barbara and North of Los Angeles. The attached 'track' had been designed by the great George Thomas back in '23 and was said to be on a par with the likes of Riviera!

Putting one of his meaty hands on my shoulder, Jimmy had crooned, "Anyway, thanks for coming. Idella has little Peggy at my sister Jane's, so it's just you and me. Now, let's get some drinks in us, 'Dr. Shout,' to enhance the therapy session."

While we were getting well lubricated, Demaret couldn't resist returning to the subject of his Ojai gig and celebrity golf. "You know," he'd said, "sometimes they come to me, that is, some of Hollywood's best golfers. Like Randolph Scott, he actually owns a piece of Ojai. It doesn't matter where. I always enjoy their company," Jimmy crowed with a conspiratorial grin.

It was my turn to say something positive. I knew that Jimmy's golfing image of himself at age 40 was hardly a matter of how many amateur pigeons he could fleece. And then there was the ironic downside of being "The Wardrobe," in regard to the man's golfing skills being fully appreciated.

A month earlier the *Saturday Evening Post* had featured Jimmy, but ... that article's title I'm certain was not what 'my patient' would have chosen. Its title blared "Golf's Gorgeous Jester." Though its author was a revered golf journalist who'd competed on Tour, Charles Price had focused on highlighting the 'sunny face' of Jimmy Demaret, commenting on all the "hand-shaking, backslapping and stroking children's heads" that transpired in between Jimmy playing his tournament shots – those almost as an afterthought, it was implied.

Along with commentary about the Wardrobe's "Gorgeous" clothes, Price did provide an analysis of Jimmy's golfing style. However, that description contained uncomfortable content for Demaret's psyche, I reckoned. To wit, Charley Price wrote, "*Because of his odd physique*, Jimmy addresses the ball with his feet very close together and a pronounced sitting down effect and hits full drives with a stance that most golfers employ on niblick pitches."

Ouch! I was sure that 'my patient' wouldn't have approved of that copy.

As far as glorifying the Wardrobe's golfing results as opposed to his methods and manners, there was this: "Demaret's build gives him a low center of gravity, making it very easy for him to keep his balance even in the highest of winds. Many experts say he is the greatest foul weather player on record ..."

Again with a reference to Jimmy's unusual body – he probably hated that – and a tone which made it sound so simple for Demaret to do what he did so well, just because of this peculiarity. Does foul-weather golf not require a ton of proper calculating and resilient perseverance, too!?

On top of those irritations to be found in the article from Jimmy's perspective, I knew that just as chafing for him was the fact that while Hogan got his face on magazine covers, the June *Post* issue didn't even include Demaret's name 'out front.' So I had to ponder quickly. Should I bring up this article, his recent PGA defeat, or the withdrawal in St. Paul first?

Surprising me, the Wardrobe 'got down to brass tacks' by beginning with his April Masters win. "You know, 'Dr. Shout,' I gave the press a bunch of hooey after that final round. Telling them that I knew I had a chance to win if I played a hot back 9. Not true; I always thought I was playing for second. In fact, Jim Ferrier was said to be looking so good as he finished number 12 that I was ready to 'ship off' from the locker room. Hit the road, Jack!

"Guess who convinced me to wait around for the finish. Gene Sarazen, 'The Squire.' And, you know why I did – hang around? Because I know that Gene's a smart cookie, smarter than me! Hell, I'd always admired his ingenious 'take' on things golf-wise. He saved us all a bunch of strokes by inventing the sand iron."

Jimmy paused then, as if to gather strength. "So when Mr. Sarazen writes that you're an also-ran among the great players, guess what? He's right. I never should have insulted him with those silly things I said back to the press in May."

I tried to interrupt his morose rant, repeating, "Jim you're a 3-time Masters winner. A 3-time Masters winner. No one else can say that!"

But 'my patient' would not be consoled. "For now the only one yeah. So what? Hogan and Snead – one or both of them will surpass me, I'm telling you … and who knows who else will win even more Masters. Bobby, what's worse though is how I got those 3 wins. I've heard it whispered that I lucked into each of them and there's some truth in that."

He went on to 'pick apart' his triumphs at Augusta in '40, '47, and '50, life-long insecurities lighting his way. "It's been ten years since my first Masters win, but folks still talk more about how Lloyd Mangrum shot that record 64 in wet conditions the first day than how I played overall."

Following this opening shot, the Wardrobe got really heated, ranting how some people had proposed that either Craig Wood or Snead might have caught him in the final round if they hadn't had to finish the last several holes in heavy rain. Jimmy spit out that he'd beaten those two by 8 strokes for Christ's sake, though yes he'd been lucky to finish just as the rain began and his closest pursuer Mangrum did not.

And the greater meaning of that Major win in Demaret's eyes? He cursed himself in front of me that day for being too easily satisfied by a certain level of golf success. "You know, that Augusta title in '40 was my 6th win of the season and pushed me past Ben for 1st place in winnings. So, what did I do afterwards? Didn't notch a single damn title the rest of the way.

"That's been a pattern for me. The other year I got 6 firsts was '47 – all of them early 'cept one in December -- including two as Hogan's partner, so they don't even count much. Yup, I won the Masters that year, too, only to over-relax into mediocrity again. Plenty of night life and lots of 'picking up the checks.' This year, 3 wins and 2 seconds by April; nothing since. Gene's right: I basically 'backed into' this year's green jacket and I 'lack the fire' to be one of the all-time greats. Or, as he put it in his book, I'm too 'civilized'."

"Oh," Jimmy went on unable to help himself, "and my 3rd round at Augusta in '47, I was the luckiest son of a bitch in all git-out, driving lots of balls into the pines only to find an opening and a 1 putt to save me ..."

"Stop," I practically shouted at Laughing Boy as he also had been dubbed by the press. "Jim, you've still got several years to improve your record and at age 40 already have 29 titles including 3 Majors to your credit. No one believes you're a lucky bum, for heaven's sake – except maybe you. But, let's talk about who James Newton Demaret wants to be from here on."

Jimmy got up from the couch and walked around for a bit saying nothing. This conversational lull was unusual in Demaret's company but I was heartened that he'd taken my question to heart. Having sat down again, 'my patient' flooded me with ideas in rapid succession.

"First off, since I'm known as such a 'clothes horse' – sometimes overshadowing my golf as you know – I'd like to make that pay by partnering with some company that's in the sports fashion business. You know, be part of the design process and then model those outfits. I'm already invested in a local company here that manufactures uniforms, but you know me – it's flashy I'm after, and that's not what people expect nurses or bus drivers and such to wear." He stopped then to refill his glass.

"Secondly, I know that Ben's planning on starting a golf-club manufacturing outfit of his own. Well, I'm not one for the nitty-gritty of controlling every detail like him. I would like to consult in the design of drivers and wedges though, more than MacGregor has asked of me since I joined them as a supposed adviser more than a decade ago. So, maybe I invest now in a smaller club-maker?"

I Bobby Shout was nodding and smiling, encouraging Jimmy to continue on, while my mind was applauding the man's practicality. These were things he could make happen!

The Wardrobe paused before saying, "And speaking of Hogan" – here Jimmy flashed his world-famous grin – "I'd like to avoid meeting a Greyhound bus head-on. What I mean is, any one of us out on Tour is 'playing with fire' driving long distance so many times each season. So, not only do I think it's time to 'cut back' on my golfing schedule, I'd also like to take more flying lessons so getting to tournaments by plane rather than car becomes my norm."

"Any urge to design golf courses yourself?" I ventured.

"Hell yes," he crooned back. "And, I know just the sort of project I'm looking for. It's gonna involve an established, classy resort like Ojai Valley is, but one that has plenty of additional acreage and the bucks to build a 2nd course better than the existing one, or a 3rd to surpass the previous two. You get my idea.

"Still, like I said about golf clubs, I'll leave the details to a pro architect; it's the vision where I can help, I reckon. Oh yeah, and they have to want me to do some singing for the guests each night I'm around. Performing is like another glass of good liquor to me. By the way, I'm a pretty fine emcee, too, if I do say so. So who knows -- maybe there's movies or television in my future?"

His excitement at this point seemed so genuine that it was me who brought the session to a close. Jimmy did have a ten-gallon mouth, you know, and I really was hungrier than a crippled fox – while he'd become 'tighter' than bark on a log, so I urged him to 'throw' our steaks on the grill right there and then and he happily obliged.

It wasn't until I was driving home the next day, July 26, that I Bobby Shout let myself worry about the implication of the path I'd led Jimmy so merrily along. If he did get himself involved in these various ventures beyond the Tour, how was his golf going to be affected? Improved? Probably not. Was he really ready to accept the role of being a less than great player on Tour over the next few years? We'd have to talk about that.

And then there was a golf-related project he'd described which I'd merely nodded to at his house. Laughing Boy's idea for making some dough as an instructor did not involve producing another golf book. Not surprising, for Demaret was no reader, notwithstanding his later volume MY PARTNER, BEN HOGAN.

Instead, he'd described to me a course of lessons delivered through the medium of 45-rpm records mainly, including narration by him and music to practice by, not to mention a title song for Jimmy to sing, *The Swing's The Thing*. As I didn't know of any driving ranges that provided power plugs for record players, this product's chances seemed dubious to me. But hey, not everything the Wardrobe tried had to be successful. At least, he'd no longer be judging his worth largely in terms of his golfing status.

CHAPTER 8

August 1950

T HERE WAS A lot of cash to be had on Tour during the first half of August that year. Back-to-back tournaments funded by business titan George S. May and hosted at his Tam O'Shanter Golf Club offered both the typical purse of the day -- $15,000 for the field – at the humbly named All American Open, followed by a whopping $50,000 event which May had christened the "World Championship."

So, you can imagine how eager most of the pros were to be on hand outside Chicago from Saturday, August 5, through Sunday, August 13, to 'take their shot' at these pots of loot. Ole 'sneaky' Lloyd of course was there competing, with perhaps more incentive than the rest, seeing how he was Tam O'Shanter's 'face' on Tour, not to mention arguably the hottest golfer in the world that summer.

On the other hand, I reckoned that perhaps he faced more pressure than any other player to do well, considering his 'home course advantage' and the fact that George May expected returns on his 'investments.' (During my time in Chicago as a grad student back in '46, I'd gotten a close-up look at the brash May's style of golf promotion.)

Speaking of Mr. May, though I'd seen lots of smart ideas at work in his attempt to grow an audience for professional golf, Ben Hogan felt differently. The Hawk had pronounced the carnival atmosphere he felt May encouraged to be deplorable, and thus, even if Ben hadn't had his movie biography to keep him in Hollywood, he still meant to scorn any invitation to compete at the Tam O'Shanter jamborees – ever again.

Whereas I knew that Jimmy Demaret had no such compunction. The Wardrobe had told me that it was his plan to 'hightail it' to Chicago from California in time for the second, far richer May extravaganza that year, and I wished him good pickings!

By all rights, Lloyd Mangrum had the first of the 2 tourneys 'sewed up' when he walked off the 18ᵗʰ green after a final round of 67, highlighted by a 31 on the back. Given an early starting time, and thus avoiding the worst of the heat and storm potential on that Tuesday August 8, Mr. Icicle's 282 looked impregnable as his closest pursuer Bobby Locke stood 4 behind with 5 to play later in the afternoon.

Reading the newspaper account, I Bobby Shout wondered whether Lloyd gave "Muffin Face" – as the jowly South African Locke had been unlovingly nicknamed – any chance at that juncture. Or, did the home pro respect the fact that Bobby had won so much when he came over to the States in 1948 that the PGA had found a way to ban him from the Tour in '49.

It seemed to me that Mangrum was not to be caught off guard, partly because it was Locke who'd finished second to him at this event back in '48, but more so on account of Locke's repeated proof of his putting wizardry. Hogan with utter disdain (yet a touch of wonder) had described both Bobby's equipment and technique on the greens during one of our dinner occasions. According to Ben, Locke's blade was so rusted it looked like the thing was left outside after every round. And, Muffin Face's putting technique?

"I'd say it's not worth spit!" the Hawk had sneered to me. "The guy spends 5 minutes figuring out every long putt, even 50-footers, like only some imperfection on the green is going to keep him from sinking them! Then, he hits down on the ball with his putterface tilted toward the hole like he enjoys making divots! Says that gives the ball perfect overspin. Christ, Locke hooks some of them 'in,' and claims he'll sometimes slice a putt on purpose. The man's a lucky S.O.B. as much as he's a great putter!"

Be that as it may, I counted up the number of feet of putts made by ole Muffin Face on holes 14 through 17 in registering 4 consecutive birds on that August 8, 1950, and if you believe the papers, his total was 96 feet, good enough to tie him with 'sneaky' Lloyd with 1 hole left to play in that year's All American Open.

Fortunately for Mr. Icicle, Bobby Locke had merely parred the last hole but still matched Lloyd's 67 that day as well as his 282 total. They would play off for the title 24 hours later on Wednesday the 9ᵗʰ.

Thursday's paper told a tale of yet another anti-climatic playoff, reminiscent of Hogan versus Snead at the first tournament of the year. Locke birdied number

2 and 2 subsequent double bogies by Mangrum on par-4s left him 5 behind with 4 to play. Could he match Muffin Face's miracle finish from the day before? No. Lloyd did birdie the par-5 15ᵗʰ but only managed to match pars with Locke the final 3 holes.

When I met Ben at the 20ᵗʰ Century Fox movie studio that afternoon to watch the previous day's film rushes with the director Sidney Lanfield and his assistants, a grinning Hawk looked as fine as cream gravy. My guess was that he was finally getting the actor Glenn Ford to swing more like him – they'd had a practice session that morning.

However, Ben's first words to me were "Did you see how Locke stole that tournament from Lloyd? In the future, I'm fixing to be more respectful of Moon Face," (another of Bobby's nicknames, and the one favored by 'my patient'). "In fact, I'm even going to forgive him for that big loopy hook he gets away with."

I should note that Bobby Locke's style clashed with Ben's mantra that only faders of the ball could be a consistent force on Tour. The South African did hit lots of fairways and greens 'over here' in spite of his "loopy hooks." Of course, anytime any player beat out Lloyd Mangrum, it was apt to put the Hawk in a more mellow mood, so strong was his aversion toward 'the riverboat gambler.'

Alas the grim side of Ben returned soon enough that day, not long after the film projector began to run. His perfectionist side hated the film folks' grudging attempts to placate his stance that the golfing sequences in the film be technically right. Otherwise, Ben did not hesitate to repeat, he'd as soon 'junk' the whole project, a threat which did command the studio's attention, seeing how the Hawk had made sure to make his final approval part of the film deal.

In this instance, What got Bantam Ben's ire up were the clubs they'd given Glenn Ford to use in a certain sequence of shots. "Those aren't the MacGregor model I was using that year!" he'd yelped. And, Hogan demanded that the scene be re-filmed with the proper equipment.

Valerie had hinted to me that I should try to 'talk him down' – not support him as Ben had asked me to – when the accuracy of the film involving obscure details became an issue, but neither I nor Sidney the director could change the Hawk's mind. At the cost of many thousands of dollars, the correct clubs used by Hogan during that stage of his career do appear in *Follow The Sun*.

On the other hand, 'my patient's drive for realism in the film did have a positive side. Seeing how even Ben's tutelage could not develop Glenn Ford's swing into an athletic effort resembling the master's, the real Ben consented to wearing a partial face mask at times so when he was being filmed swinging from afar, the viewer saw a man with facial features echoing Ford's – more than Ben's!

Unfortunately, there was also an aspect of the movie script which I feared might be 'bad medicine' for Jimmy Demaret.

To wit, Ben's closest buddy in the film is pictured as a big drinker with a secret fear of being 'washed up.' Yikes! Remember that the Hawk had full right of approval regarding the content of *Follow The Sun*. So, though Hogan claimed that "Chuck Williams" – Jimmy's seemingly fictional counterpart – was a made-up man, what was Demaret to think?!

It was 4 days earlier, on Sunday August 6 – the fifth anniversary of the Hiroshima bombing – that Jimmy did rumble into Hollywood, having come back from Ojai, with a flight scheduled out of L.A. the following day for Chicago and the World Golf Championship later in the week. And, by this time, he'd recently gotten wind of the sad role being played by this "Chuck Williams."

Jimmy called me late that afternoon, already 'in his cups' I could tell, wanting to get together for a "nice private dinner." While it seemed that something in his voice was 'off,' what could I do but agree? However, before I relate the details of that baffling encounter, let me mention a fact about the film which does put Ben Hogan's character choices in a better light.

That is, if you've seen that rather mawkish movie, you probably recall that Jimmy does appear as himself in it, too -- the sunny Demaret who stops by Hogan's – Glenn Ford's – hospital room along with Cary Middlecoff to ask 'Ben' to captain the 1949 Ryder Cup team.

This scene had been filmed around mid-May, I think, when there'd been a gap in the PGA tour schedule. Those were 'early days' in the filming process though, when Demaret still had some Masters glow in his psyche and the Sarazen fiasco had yet to happen. By August, he was a different, prone-to-wild-swings-of mood personality, ready to believe his 'close friend' Ben was willing to shame him for the sake of a spicier movie. But it was me that Jimmy 'went after.'

The Wardrobe did have the good grace to wait 'til we'd ordered our food before making his attack. Yet, then again, the way it turned out, maybe he had meant for me to get 'stuck' with the bill for both our meals.

"Dr. Shout," he'd begun. "Would you like to share with me this time the instructions that Hogan has given you?"

I know that I must have looked at him with astonishment because that's what I felt, but it seems to me that my mind was also chanting *Stay calm, stay calm* like a mental health professional should. I tried to manufacture a sympathetic smile, too.

Asked what he was talking about, Jimmy had begun a sneering diatribe. "Oh, you're good, you're real good. Looking as innocent as a new born calf. Well you ain't fooling me no more! All that talk at my place about what else I'd like to be doing besides playing tournaments – I figured that out soon enough: Hogan … He's busted up and can't play regular on Tour now, so he don't want his old rivals getting more chances than him to pile up the victories. What's the matter? Ben afraid I just might 'buckle down' and 'live up' to my talent? And you, acting like my friend, like a real doctor prescribing for a patient's ills. Well doc, I don't feel so good right now. Looking at you here I've lost my appetite. I'll see you around, Bobby – messenger boy!"

And, having delivered this final rebuke while rising from our table and flinging his napkin down, Demaret had stalked out of the restaurant. Who had gotten Jimmy to see things in such a paranoid way, I wondered? His wife Idella? We hadn't even met. Another of the Tour professionals? Maybe Sam Snead? He and the Wardrobe were chummy at times, plus Slammin' Sammy always believed the worst about Ben I'd heard from Ben himself.

More to the point, how could I repair my relationship with Jimmy now? I Bobby Shout honestly believed that he did need counsel like mine to help him transition to a multi-purpose life, which was the best course for his future happiness, I was sure.

Fast forward ahead 5 days to Friday August 11th – 2 days after Locke's playoff win over Lloyd and 1 day after the World Golf Championship's opening round, and there was Jimmy Demaret in the sports pages doing something again that expressed an inner tumult over whether he belonged on Tour or not. At least that's how I saw it ...

In Friday's papers, Demaret was not the 'lead figure' in the coverage of the Championship's Thursday round. None of the pros were. Rather, it was Mother Nature who had starred, unleashing a deluge of rain with 4 of the 32 pros still out on the course. George S. May, who had every right to, declared that day's scores null and void. The tournament was to remain a 72-hole event still, with 4 rounds squeezed into the next 3 days.

Only 2 souls were cited by the press as having complained passionately about May's decision, in fact even threatening to quit the event. One of them was an amateur who'd had the round of his life, having shot a 68 which bested the best pro scores by 2! The other man who felt like quitting? Jimmy Demaret.

And why? Had he too been shooting the round of the day amongst his peers only to have his effort 'washed out?' No not at all. In addition to 3 professionals who were 'in' with a 2-under 70, another 3 had shot 71s. Then, there were 4 other guys who'd finished at even par out of the 28 pros who were done. Having played 15 holes, Jimmy along with Middlecoff were on pace for merely another even-par round if they could handle the wet.

It was only Bobby Locke among the foursome still competing who did have something to gripe about if he cared to, as Muffin Face had needed just a par on the final hole to secure his own share of the 1st-round lead. Yet, the Wardrobe alone was the pro who couldn't contain himself about the 'washout.'

I Bobby Shout tried to get in touch with him by phone the next 3 evenings, hoping to help him see that his inner turmoil about the Tour was real, not some idea I'd implanted in him. But he didn't return my calls.

When that event was finally over on Monday August 14th, with a playoff round once more needed, a journeyman pro had become $11,000 dollars richer and Jimmy had not won a dime. 'Dr. Shout' decided he'd better give 'his patient' some time before trying to contact him again, so that's what I did, making no further attempt 'til September.

Later that week, my attention was drawn again to 'sneaky' Lloyd Mangrum who was competing in Baltimore at the first major pro event held there in 20 years. Jimmy Demaret meanwhile had declined to enter this "Eastern Open."

On the hilly par-72 Mount Pleasant layout, Mr. Icicle had 'laid in the weeds' the first 2 rounds, compiling a 1-under total through Thursday and Friday, well back of "man-mountain" Clayton Heafner who'd scorched the course with a 65 the first day.

However, my morning Sunday paper on August 20th told a different tale. There was Lloyd climbing into contention on Saturday with the day's best score, a 67, good for third place, in spite of continued muggy weather a third straight day. It was reported that substantial rain was expected that Saturday night, which would make the course 'play long' the final round. Since 'length' was not Mangrum's strong suit and I Bobby Shout certainly wasn't rooting for him, I took this for a good omen.

Wrong. Tam O'Shanter's Tour pro beat all the leaders again on Sunday – by at least 3 shots! – with his 3-under 69 good for a 9-under tournament total and a 2-shot victory. I knew without looking it up that this was Mr. Icicle's 4th win of the summer along with two 2nd places. One had to admire the quality of golf he was playing, especially since Lloyd's shoulder injury had prevented him from competing in the early months of the year.

Still, he continued to be a tough man to 'get behind,' for reasons made evident again in the press coverage of Lloyd's post-triumph remarks. To quote, "The others just faltered and I came on," followed by a declaration that there was nothing special about his final round. This 'dig' at his peers was preceded by a similar sentiment in Mr. Icicle's trophy-presentation remarks to the crowd: "My heartiest congratulations to the rest of the pros for taking as many strokes as they did."

Lord, I thought, *why couldn't the man just win with class? Why did he have to slap the other fellows in the face?* Well, there would come a time when I'd come to understand the twisted Mangrum better – surprisingly soon.

At least on this occasion he spoke kindly to the local folks who hadn't hosted the pros in so long. As well as commending both the spectators and those who'd run the tournament, Lloyd had declared the Mount Pleasant layout to be the "finest public course I've ever seen or played on." Now, what was I to make of that? Had he meant to impart a simple flattery, or a mocking hyperbole with such praise? I Bobby Shout certainly couldn't 'take' his words at face value – not where 'sneaky' Lloyd was involved.

Oh, and the paper had also mentioned that with this win, Mangrum had passed Demaret for 4th place on the Tour's 1950 money list. I had no reason to think that Mr. Icicle would not continue to climb, nor that Jimmy's earnings rank would keep falling. Damn!

Back in Hollywood, I was continuing to try to keep Ben from 'walking out' on his movie when I got a call at the studio in the afternoon on yet another of L.A.'s endlessly beautiful golf days. It was a Wednesday August 23rd. When the voice barking at me on the line identified himself as Lloyd Mangrum -- "Hey boy, this is ole Lloyd calling. I'm home." – I was sure some jokester was at work.

After all, the Tour pros had headed to Montreal that week to compete in the Canadian Open. I figured that Lloyd, on his hot streak, would surely be among them, piloting his fancy emerald-green Cadillac due north from Baltimore for the 500-plus miles needed to reach the course. Well in response to my stating these facts he soon disabused me of this suspicion.

"Fucking Christ," Lloyd had begun, "why would I want to go play in a national open where they can't even 'cough up' a standard Tour purse?" (It was true. That Open only had a $10,000 pot rather than the $15,000 the pros were used to.) "Besides, with the event after that not starting 'til Friday -- with the Labor Day finish -- that gives me a week-plus to relax out here. I fly back to Baltimore next Tuesday. I'll pick up my car and motor on up to Albany for 2 practice rounds before the Empire Open starts."

I was stunned, and not only by the mere fact that Mr. Icicle had knowledge of my existence, not to mention his being interested in contacting me. The weak utterance of mine that followed stemmed more so from having heard that Mangrum didn't talk much, yet here he was having spoken a whole paragraph to me a stranger! "Out here? You mean California?" I'd stuttered.

What was up? This guy was anti-social enough that he avoided shaking hands, and rarely gave a decent interview unless it was when he'd won. So, what kind of sucker bet did the 'riverboat gambler' want to offer Bobby Shout over the phone? It didn't take long to find out ... and yet it did.

"Listen, Bud," Lloyd continued. "Like I said, I'm in L.A. for the week. How 'bout we play a round on Friday at my brother Ray's club. It's a mostly Jewish joint so the course will clear out by mid-afternoon. You've heard of Brentwood, right? That's where Snead won the Western this past spring. Nice track. Do you have your clubs along? I heard you were a decent player once, but maybe Hogan's messed up your game? Heh heh." His laugh was rough like the rest of him.

Of course, my first impulse was to hang up on that S.O.B. But, somehow he'd hit me where it hurt. Specifically, the fact that Ben had not once asked me to play with him since that day we first met on the Hulen bench. Now from a psychological standpoint I could see a reason for the Hawk being reluctant to have me golfing with him. I mean, his persona on the course was that of an unknowable, invincible force of nature. The tender moments he'd shared with me in conversation ran counter to such a state of mind.

Yet still, when his name had appeared in the L.A. papers over the past 3 weeks linked to Hollywood stars and other big-shots enjoying morning rounds at places like Riviera, Lakeside and Bel-Air, I would have appreciated at least a couple of words from him later about their games or foibles or … something!

And it wouldn't have killed him to throw me 'a bone' – fib or not – by saying he was sorry that he couldn't bring me along. But that wasn't Hogan.

So, channeling my anger elsewhere, I'd responded to Mangrum with, "Yeah, me and my clubs can make it then. I can be there at 2 for a 3 p.m. tee off. That work?"

He said just 1 word before hanging up. "Yup."

Okay, I told myself. *Why shouldn't I play with 'sneaky' Lloyd? And, Ben has no reason to 'beef.' Well, we'll see,* my less emotional side had countered.

The next morning, Thursday, I returned to one of the scruffy L.A. muni's that I had already played a few times since coming out to California. My plan was to do at least 27 holes as preparation for my round with Mr. Icicle the following day. And, I figured that if Ben was interested enough in my absence from the studio that afternoon to ask me about it on Friday morning, well … I would tell him the truth. That I needed some practice prior to tackling Brentwood with Mangrum. There would be no hint of apology in my voice, I told myself.

At the muni, both my swing and putting were good the first 18. I considered stopping to save my energy for Brentwood, but my insecure side whispered that my 'touch' with the wedges needed more reps, so I joined up with a couple of new strangers on number 1 to 'scratch that itch' for the planned extra 9 holes.

Big mistake. 'Dr.' Bobby Shout's game 'went south' playing the opening 9 over. Worse, the meaty pad just below the thumb on my right hand had begun to blister by my 23rd hole that Thursday and I had no band-aids with me. The puffed-up piece of skin was stinging by the time I finished, as were my eyes and ego.

Naturally, this made me even angrier with the Hawk. Illogically I swore that if Hogan were a better golfing friend I wouldn't be wrecking my hand the day before a match! Deep inside though, I knew that the double insecurity of not trusting 'sneaky' Lloyd's hospitality along with fearing that my golf might embarrass me in front of him were the real emotional levers tipping my usual sympathies away from broken Ben.

Somehow I slept surprisingly well that night. My optimism about my game in turn felt renewed as I drove to the studio for Friday morning's work, a box of bodily and mental band-aids now in my bag.

Well Hogan being Hogan, he didn't quiz me at all on the set regarding my whereabouts the previous day. Instead the Hawk surprised me by bringing up something we'd talked about but which I'd assumed he'd forgotten. That is, the fact that we both were born in August – I on the 1st; he, on the 13th – and so could share a celebratory dinner during the month.

"I'll get Val to make us a reservation at the Brown Derby for tomorrow night," he'd said, not bothering to inquire whether I had any other choice in mind. "I mean the one on North Vine, close to here, not over on Wilshire Boulevard. You'll get to see plenty of celebrities there." Ben then 'broke off' our chat to wave at poor Glenn Ford who was passing by. It was time for another chipping lesson for the man who had to look like Hogan, golf-wise. When I slipped out of the studio at 1:30, Ben was still tutoring Glenn in his hectoring way.

The drive to Brentwood Country Club from Hollywood was easy enough. I just had to follow Santa Monica Boulevard west most of the way, then veer north to the clubhouse on South Burlingame Avenue. When they took my clubs out of the rental car, the 'bag boy' told me that Mr. Mangrum was in the pro shop awaiting my arrival. My face probably said that I hadn't been here before. As I tipped him, the young man motioned, saying "You'll find the shop right around there, Sir."

Ole Lloyd couldn't have been sweeter when I stepped into his older brother Ray's domain. After inquiring about my trip over, Mr. Icicle introduced me warmly around – billing me as one of Ben's closest friends and advisors. Then 'little brother' proceeded to hand me a fancy club towel from a display of them on sale, joking that Ray could charge it to his account.

After a trip to the locker room for me to 'use the head' and put on my spikes, Lloyd led me out to where 2 ultra-fit teens were awaiting us. One of them seemed to be smirking at my unprepossessing bag of clubs while a bigger boy was rubbing a towel with care over Mangrum's already lustrous irons, housed along with his woods in a leather golf bag as big as all hell and half of Texas.

Well at this juncture you may be reckoning that I was as nervous as a whore in church, but it just wasn't so. The golf gods had somehow put me on a pillow of peacefulness, and I was neither in awe of Lloyd's game or his fame, let alone whatever machinations he might try to pull on the course. When Mr. Icicle started to lead us toward the practice area beyond the tennis courts, I sang out, "No need; I'm ready." And though he kept his 'poker face' on, I was betting that this declaration might have unsettled him.

You haven't heard me wax philosophical much in this memoir, but I can't resist musing on my calm state of mind that day. Had Bobby Shout's brain sensed that his body was 'on target' to cooperate fully and therefore felt serene; or was it my quiet state of mind which led me to swing so smoothly right from the start? Don't know, but I've been fixing ever since to capture that combination again. Alas, it comes rarely.

In any case, after I'd pounded my opening tee ball right down the fairway, Lloyd hooked his into the left rough. This was a slight 'bail out' on Brentwood's opening par-4, a hole which paralleled a parking lot on the right, separated in the driving area by only a skinny line of trees.

Playing second, I lofted a wedge onto the center of number 1's putting surface for the 1ˢᵗ of my 16 – count 'em! – 16 greens-in-regulation. Hell, Lloyd only 'hit' 13 by my count. And I can forgive myself for a less than stellar putting day, since those surfaces were running far quicker than on the public courses I'd been enjoying. Still, but for several lip-outs I might have shot even par or better, which was needed to match Lloyd's 68, his magnificent 'short game' on full display.

Over drinks in the grill, Mr. Icicle had been as warm as chicken fried steak in his praise of my ball-striking. I think he really meant it, too. How could he not?! Yet it's not my golfing performance on that Friday, August 25ᵗʰ 1950, that's the important thing here. I'm sure you're much more interested in what the 'riverboat gambler' had in mind to say to me as we traversed Brentwood's amiable fairways and greens.

To begin with on the course, Lloyd seemed to be alternating questions involving Ben with others about me which indicated that he'd bothered to 'get my story.' Did Ben plan to play again this year after his Hollywood stint? Did his doctors think his knee was going to need surgery eventually? Was the Hawk really afraid to drive on the 'tournament trail' anymore? My responses were steadfastly vague, bordering on "no comment," in every case.

But regarding myself, I felt free to respond as honestly as I felt prudent. When after 9 holes Mr. Icicle complimented me for my level of play despite having eye and ear problems, I explained to him the adjustments I'd made involving my 'dominant eye' and sense of balance. (I said nothing about Hogan's damaged sight.)

Lloyd had responded by remarking, "So, you really did get fucking blown up on one of your daddy's oil rigs. Damn. Were you thrown far?"

I said, "Fifteen feet. Cost me a couple of broken ribs and 'did a number' on my left shoulder but those things have healed, not like the eye and ear."

At this point, I witnessed the slightest tremble shaking the shoulders of the supposed Mr. Icicle. Simultaneously, he'd spoken softly, "That's some feeling, isn't it, flying through the air helpless? I know from the jeep accident I was in during the war. What scared hell out of me afterwards though was thinking that I might not be able to do this again," Lloyd laughed as he flicked a hand toward the course.

And, so it went … Him satisfied that I was no blabbermouth; me finding my way to the core of this tortured man who put on such a show of nonchalant toughness in public. We really 'got down to it,' I recall, when he asked me between shots on the long 12th whether I ever had dreams about the explosion on that rig. I'd replied "hardly ever now," which seemed to disappoint him.

Then Lloyd muttered, "Not me, I can't get rid of the damn things, and it's funny: The more I win, the more often they come and the worse they get."

"What do you mean?" I Bobby Shout asked, though being pretty sure I already knew, based on my conversations with ex-soldiers over the past year at the TCU mental health clinic. It was called "combat fatigue" or "shell shock" in the world of psychotherapy back then. We were still 30 years away from having enough knowledge about the condition to officially term it "Post Traumatic Stress Disorder" or "PTSD."

Yet we did know of a couple of ways to improve things for some guys, even though a 'good drug' for the condition had yet to be found. So, after Mangrum had finished describing to me the horrible visions he suffered in his sleep, leaving him soaked in sweat and scared to death that his racing heart was going to burst as he awoke, I asked first whether he'd seen a doctor about the problem.

His response was vicious. "Them god-damn medical men know nothing. The son-of-a-bitch quack I saw put me on tranquilizers like that would 'do the trick.' Messed up my golfing good; did nothing to stop the bloody dreams! No way I'm going to another doc, Shout," he railed at me.

Fortunately, my training – and a piece of good fortune – allowed me to point him in another direction to lessen his suffering potentially. I told Mr. Icicle about it on Brentwood's short but demanding par-4 13th.

After he'd struck a beautiful little 'cut' 8-iron to about 5 feet from the cup, I Bobby Shout went to work. "You know what helped me, Lloyd, to chase the bad dreams away I think? Pretty simple really. For a month or so several years back, I made myself sit down daily and write every new detail about the rig accident that came into my head.

"Some days, that meant ten minutes of my time and nothing useful. But, on others, by the time I stopped, my notebook was ten pages fuller and a clearer vision of what was tormenting me started to form."

With skepticism barely contained in his harshly nasal voice, Mr. Icicle grumbled, "Like what?" before blowing a bit of smoke toward my face, courtesy of his omnipresent cig.

I paused for effect before looking him dead in the eye.

"Well, for instance, that explosion didn't just mess me up. Two of my co-workers, guys I liked – family men! -- died from it. And boy, in my dream state they often seemed to be 'pointing fingers' at me.

There was a blink of recognition in his eyes as I railed on. "It was my fault! I should have told Rick to double-check the pressure balance when I first sensed a 'kick.' I should have warned Pete sooner to get away. Why hadn't I realized that the blowout preventers weren't going to work?! All of these charges were pretty much nonsense, but that didn't matter in dreamland because there's a powerful force in us called 'survivor's guilt.'"

"You're telling *me*, brother," was the hoped-for response I got back from Lloyd. With the war casualties he'd had to have seen over in France, his own guilt at still living probably dwarfed mine.

Having given him a sympathetic nod, I tried my best to convince him in layman's terms how one could teach one's own brain to stop 'making up' harmful stuff by bombarding it with the real facts in the calm 'light of day.'

From the fact that he let me continue on, even while maintaining his Mangrum 'poker face,' gave me hope that I was making sense. However, Lloyd followed my remarks with, "Shit I'm no writer. Could never do that like you. So I guess it's 'tough titty' for me, huh?"

My spontaneous response to him – which gave Mr. Icicle a good shock, so seemingly irrelevant was its direction – I count as one of the few genius moments of my life. What I'd said to him was, "You probably know Bing Crosby, don't you Lloyd?" in a perfectly neutral tone of voice. (Of course I knew he did, since it was Bing not Ben who'd provided a foreword for Mangrum's instruction book.)

Well, it was darned impressive, how lightning quick he was in resuming his mask of 'cool' in spite of the surprise I'd provided. Lloyd gave his bark of a laugh before telling me, "Oh yeah, Der Bingle and me – one of Bing's nicknames – have done plenty of business on the golf course, at the card table, and over those nags he raises for racing. Hell, I couldn't dress as well as I do without my yearly payouts from Crosby ... But so what, Shout? His groaning records may put me to sleep, but they don't cure nightmares."

After chuckling for show at Lloyd's wit, I explained how Crosby had been making a habit of coming over from his movie set to ours to chat with Ben, giving me the chance to hear what Bing was 'up to.' "Lloyd," I'd asked, "did you know that Der Bingle tape-records nearly all his radio shows now, rather than performing them 'live?' In fact, he's bought a big share in the company that makes the best reel-to-reel sound recorders out there. They use magnetic tape, I'm told."

This extra bit of detail meant possibly boring Lloyd and I feared that by choosing to talk about technology at all I was in danger of losing his interest. However, it turned out that he was more a 'fan' of engineering than I ever would have thought. His time as an advance scout for our troops overseas had given him plenty of respect for gizmos.

So, when I proposed that he see Bing about getting one of those newfangled recorders that Crosby's outfit was starting to market for home-use, Mr. Icicle was at least willing to listen to me -- though he ultimately proved a 'hard sell.' First off, he mistook my drift in encouraging him to get one. Lloyd's initial thought was "Oh shit, will Maw get a kick singing into that!" ("Maw" being his 'pet name' for Eleta, an older woman he'd married back in 1934 at the raw age of 20, though she, a widow, already had 3 kids.)

That's right. The riverboat gambler had not grasped the therapeutic potential that lay in getting his hands on such a recorder, picturing it instead as simply an entertainment.

It took me a while to lay out what such an instrument could mean to him: Not only could he use it in lieu of a pen to efficiently 'set down' that multitude of conscious memories from his war years – not to mention the content of his current dreams. Lloyd could send me a copy of any of his taped reels to study and comment back to him; or, we could talk on the phone about his self-discoveries, with relevant bits of his recordings being played for me 'Dr. Shout' right over the telephone.

Although, Mr. Icicle did 'come around' about how getting a recorder was thus worth a chance, there was 1 sticky point that remained. He wasn't 'hot' on the idea of mailing something so revealing to me, fearing that the tapes might get in the 'wrong hands' through postal failure or worse. At the same time, Lloyd squawked big time at the costs he could incur by talking for hours long-distance.

Fortunately, due to my new employment status – to be revealed shortly – I was able to soothe Mangrum with a cheery reply that I'd take his calls at any time and he could 'reverse the charges' so the bills would be mine. Naturally, this did lead to 1 further dilemma: my getting away from Brentwood's grill before the riverboat gambler, sensing Bobby's new financial status, 'picked my pocket' playing gin rummy at which I'd heard he was a master.

I'd been told to meet the Hogans outside the Brown Derby on Saturday (August 26th) at 7:30, so I made sure to be at the restaurant's entrance at 7:20, knowing that 'my patient' was a stickler for punctuality. Five minutes later, Ben and Valerie joined me on the sidewalk, though neither of them seemed very festive about our birthday bash. *Then again*, I thought, *how often did this couple look relaxed in public, away from the winner's circle?*

Ben had said with a whiff of pride that we would be seated in the "Academy Room" along with whatever 'stars' were in attendance. His words hardly registered with me as I had other things on my mind.

However, it turned out that we were in for quite a show. More than half a dozen of Hollywood's most game golfers – including Randolph Scott, Dean Martin, and Fred Astaire – found their way to our table during the evening. It was almost comical to see the near reverence they showed toward Ben, each in turn waving him down as Hogan started to rise as they approached. The chit-chat each made was of a nervous type, asking after the Hawk's health, expressing wonderment and pleasure at his come-back, and begging our pardon for taking Ben's time away from his meal.

Even some starlets got into the act. And, though they too showered Mr. Hogan with 'love,' not surprisingly they were both more composed and more sensitive to both my and Valerie's presence. The divine Ava Gardner even offered me her hand – to shake, not in marriage!

Well the upshot of this acclaim from the famous did wonders in improving the mood at our table. Not even Ben Hogan could stay grim and silent as he had been early on. By the time we'd finished our desserts, he'd been smiling broadly for over an hour.

It made me wonder … but no, the true Hawk took flight as we were sipping the last of our drinks. Without any prologue, Ben had growled at me. "What did you shoot … at Brentwood?"

Huh. I'd heard that 'word traveled fast' in L.A. "Seventy-four," I replied.

He didn't compliment my score. As Val put her hand on her husband's forearm as if to make a last-ditch effort at softening him, Hogan said, "Bobby, thanks for your time on the film." And it was clear from his commanding tone that he was dismissing me from Hollywood, and maybe his life. I'd consorted with an enemy. That was treason for the Hawk.

When I was able to shoot back at him that I already had a flight booked to Dallas on Monday, it brought me at least a touch of gratification in seeing the tiny trace of surprise and – was it hurt? – on Hogan's mug. Anyway, I got up, pulling my wallet out. He waved that away but didn't offer me his hand. At the same time, Valerie did rise and gave me a full hug while whispering "Thank you." It was my turn to be thrown off balance. I hadn't even thought she liked me, so stiff was her usual demeanor when I'd been around.

Oh yes, these were Ben's last words to me. "See you around then."

I doubted it but nodded. California had seemingly cost me 2 'patients' while perhaps initiating another counseling role – this one long distance -- with the also prickly Mr. Icicle. I Bobby Shout was darn ready to get back home and 'get on' with my life.

CHAPTER 9

September 1950

A S THE 9TH month of the year began, my perhaps new 'patient' Lloyd Mangrum might as well have stayed out in L.A. rather than returning to the East Coast for New York's Empire State Open in Albany. Mr. Icicle had a 'cold' putter and lagged behind leader Ky Laffoon by 11 strokes after 54 holes. He proved a non-factor the final 18 as did Jimmy Demaret – stewing at home.

Meanwhile, I was initiating a new effort which might prove profitable for both men's psyches and pocketbooks. In order to explain what I was 'up to,' allow me to delve into my own world for a bit.

You know, here in the Lone Star State we've got a saying, "There's two theories to arguin' with a woman. Neither one works." So, when I first reported to the Shout Petroleum Company's main office in Dallas on Friday September 1st – after a couple of days of R&R following my flight back from L.A. – I Bobby Shout felt a certain degree of anxiety despite the fact that it was my mother Margo who reigned as the company's chief executive and thus my new boss.

Oh, don't get me wrong. Mom was thrilled to have me back in 'the fold.' And, she couldn't have been nicer when I'd explained at dinner back in mid-July about the kind of work which would interest me, though there was some confusion at first.

When I'd stated that I wanted to work in personnel, she'd felt obliged to protest on my behalf. "Dear, do you really want to get involved with all that dreary payroll and insurance stuff? I know that the drilling operations are not for you, but I – the company – could really use someone personable and educated like Mr. Bobby Shout to represent us, both industry-wide and especially in Austin!" (She meant government lobbying, we'd say today.)

Well, hell no, I wanted nothing to do with politics back then. Fortunately, I just needed to be more specific with my mother about my career vision in order to get her initial approval. "Mom, what I meant was that I would like to be in charge of hiring from now on; whoever watches out for staff salaries and benefits can keep doing it. I'm not looking to nose anybody out."

That last sentiment seemed to cheer her and Mrs. Shout had raised her glass of bubbly to me without hesitation and spoke in a queenly way, "Here then to our new Vice President for Position Management. Does that sound all right, honey?"

So far so good. As we were enjoying the finest beef that Dallas had to offer at the restaurant that evening, I had dared to outline 'step 2' of my employment vision.

There were so many men and women who'd served nobly in the Second World War and been scarred by it. And now – with talk of communist China maybe getting involved on the Korean peninsula -- a huge new wave of Texan ex-soldiers could be coming home from Korea with mental and/or physical troubles. Why shouldn't we at Shout Petroleum 'go out of our way' to recruit these folks for jobs with us during these booming times for oil companies?

I knew from my counseling work that some vets needed quiet employment while others felt safest laboring amidst a steady stream of noise. We already were engaged in a wide variety of work environments which would most likely continue to grow as we expanded our work force as needed. War veterans could be found who'd been given all sorts of technical or practical training, courtesy of 'Uncle Sam,' as well as having strong discipline instilled in them ... And so I preached that night, and the C.E.O. of Shout Petroleum had responded positively.

However, on this, my 1st day actually at work, there was more to my plan – involving a substantial amount of funding – which I needed to 'run by' the boss, and Mrs. Margo Shout would be wearing more of a 'hard hat' then, I imagined. Hence, my anxiety was jelling beyond 'first day jitters.'

My mother had scheduled us for a face-to-face in her no-nonsense office as the final item on her agenda that first day. Margo's desk was large but clean of any paper piles. Behind it were small models of drilling rigs mingled amidst neat stacks of technical manuals on cheaply-hung shelves. She did own a spacious window but its view was unspectacular – typical Dallas.

I assumed she'd figured on just quizzing me a bit about my fresh impressions of the company headquarters before our going out to eat afterwards. I hoped she would indeed still want to 'share bread' together after I, her beloved Robert Nickel

Jefferson Shout, laid out my unexpected initiative. It had seemed a 50-50 bet at best, one that Lloyd Mangrum would surely have passed on.

So what happened? After letting mom 'pump' me with the usual "How was your first day" type questions, I got right to the point. I had to hurry, as you'll see, because there was little time to spare for organizing a first-time event on the scale which I had in mind, taking Texas's uncertain fall weather into full account.

"Mother," I'd begun, having sat down. "You know that I reckon we at Shout Petroleum are in a position to both reward ex-service folks while benefitting the company as well." She'd nodded.

"However, 1 oil company alone starting this kind of effort will hardly make an impact on many of those in need of a good job. It's going to take a concerted effort from the Texas oil industry to better a considerable number of deserving Texan lives. For this reason, I want us to take the lead in getting our competitors to rally around the idea of an industry-inaugurated golf tournament of a special kind, to be held this October on the weekend of the 21st and 22nd, with the 28th and 29th as a 'rain date.'"

Wow. I'd 'thrown' a lot at her in a hurry. Thus, it was no surprise that Margo was somewhat puzzled at this juncture, but to her credit, she still seemed ready to listen. "Okay ..." my mother had uttered, her voice trailing as she remained seated.

"First off," I continued. "We will combine this 2-day golf event with a 'job fair' plus publicity regarding training-opportunities for attending veterans. Naturally, vets will be admitted for free. Funding for this aspect of the weekend will come from the public, who will have to pay to see our star golfers." When I look back at these exclusionary terms I'd proposed, vis-à-vis today's labor discrimination laws, well ... I'm glad it was 1950 and not 2020!

Mom, an enthusiastic golfer herself, could not resist interrupting. "But, Bobby, what *is* this golf tournament you're touting?"

With a hammy flourish I announced, "The First Annual Texas Sharpshooters Invitational, that's what. I'm pretty sure that pros like Hogan, Nelson, Demaret, and even Mangrum can be convinced to compete for that title, especially since we'll be offering a $10,000 purse: $5,000 to the winner, $2,500 for second, $1,500 for third, and even the last-place man out of our recruited foursome will get $1,000."

Please note that back then, fields of 50 men or more played for only $15,000 generally on Tour, with a $2,600 top prize, so we'd be offering major cash at far better odds than 'my patients' usually faced, not to mention giving them a unique opportunity of one-upping each other *mano a mano*.

"That's a lot of money for 2-day's work," my old-fashioned mother mused upon moving to her window – she a wary survivor of the Depression. Margo and Dad had been plenty poor like most folks 'til he'd struck oil big time. Still, I knew

I had a dynamite idea for a tournament format to 'spring' on her now, and so I 'kept my chin up' as I proceeded with my 'pitch.'

"Here's how the Sharpshooters Invitational will work, Boss. Spectators will be treated to a modified closest-to-the-pin contest. Each of our 4 players will get to hit 3 balls toward each putting green on our host course, which will have informal teeing grounds set up on its 18 holes varying from driver to wedge range from the cups.

"Out of the 12 shots launched to each hole, the Texan whose ball finishes closest to the pin gets a point. 1st-through-4th-place prizes will be awarded according to the players' ultimate point totals, 18 holes having been contested on Saturday with a second 18 to follow on Sunday."

My enthusiasm was in full swing by now. "Won't it be riveting to see how close those stars can come to holing out? And if we leave the current closest ball on the putting surface through all 3 rounds of their shotmaking, the added suspense of watching whether a 'tight shot' gets knocked away by a later effort will be in play! Our spectators will be asking, 'Was it luck that Ben's ball hit Byron's ... or amazing skill?' We'd be sure to attract a large audience of golfing veterans and paying customers to such an event, don't you think, Mom?"

I know, I know! This initial approach to my mother/boss was about as naïve as Mickey Rooney in an Andy Hardy movie saying, "Come on, kids, let's put on a show." That concept of mine was a good one, if I do say so, but I was woefully shy of having given proper consideration to the slew of logistics any golf tournament requires.

Over the next hour before we left to dine, the C.E.O. of Shout Petroleum Company 'grilled' me good on matters ranging from player security to food service to work-force issues to event publicity. "What about bathroom facilities for so many folks?" she'd posed. "And, Bobby, don't expect our work force to just volunteer their time for this weekend event. There will be cost involved! In fact, I think the sum total of expenses to 'put this on' would dwarf the ten-thousand-dollar purse you mentioned ..."

Had I 'lost' her, I wondered? Was my tournament idea 'dead'? The next few moments felt agonizing. Then though, my mother gave me a new spark of hope through the tone of determination in her voice. "We'd want to enlist support from Quintana and Placid or Southern Union" -- other big oil outfits in the state who'd been friendly with Dad. "Maybe one of the juniors, either Howard Hughes – he's keen on golf – or Jim West – he likes throwing money around – would 'sign on' to pay some bills. Yes, I think they might, especially if your tournament title included the phrase 'In honor of Big Tom Shout.'"

My father had been merely a 'hacker,' no match for my mother in golf. But, we'd all shared good times playing the game, so I was only half startled to see a tiny tear or two trying to escape from her eyes. Margo was no crier! My eyes were far wetter as I gulped for air to voice my approval. "Perhaps it's time we went to dinner then," she uttered, and I'd nodded in return.

It must be said that if there was a more popular figure among Texas oil men of that era than my late dad, I'm dumber than a watermelon. Even his rivals in the oil fields liked to 'hang out' with Big Tom Shout, so full of positive energy and decency was the man. By contrast, plenty of workers who found their way to employment at Shout Petroleum during my doomed apprenticeship in the '40s had less than stellar things to say about the other oil 'giants' in the state.

At this juncture, please accept my apology if it appears that I've been stoking my own ego over the past several pages. I realize that it may seem as though I've strayed like a too proud calf from the primary purpose of this memoir – to recount the triumph of a quartet of great Texan golfers over serious physical and psychic ills – but as the Tour season wound down in the fall that year, this Sharpshooters exhibition did come to mean a lot to each of those 4 men -- for various reasons to be detailed ahead.

I won't delay our return to the 1950 Tour action by describing the further discussions between my mom and me over dinner that evening. That is, except for this 1 exchange that provided an answer to a key tournament question:

C.E.O. Shout, a.k.a. mom, had put her fork down suddenly in the midst of dessert to ask, "Bobby, won't it be confusing to keep track of whose ball actually is sitting there closest, when so many shots are being 'fired' to each given green? I mean, the officials will be sure, but the rooting spectators may not know how 'their man" really stands, which will be frustrating."

I'm happy to report that I'd at least thought through this aspect of things in advance. With barely a pause, giddy me was able to respond, "Well, we could use a megaphone announcement at each green to keep the spectators posted, but even then, I agree that some in the crowd might not hear correctly and get mixed up.

Trying to keep my smile modest, I'd conjectured instead, "No, a better approach I think will be to have each pro hit balls that have a distinct band of color on them. For example, Byron Nelson's could be red-banded while Demaret's are bright green. With color-codes posted at various spots on each hole as well as within the spectator programs, then everyone should stay clear about whose ball is where, don't you think?"

Margo Shout, my dear mother but a hell of a businesswoman at the same time, had rewarded me with a nod of her head and the words, "If you can come up with answers that satisfactory for every angle, you should have no trouble getting some other oil companies to 'come on board.' Then, it was her who was smiling. Yikes, I'd been hoping my mother would 'run point' on the 'convincing side' of things. After all, she knew and was respected by the H.L. Hunt's and Murchisons of our world. Whereas I, Bobby Shout, was the kid who'd left the business in favor of academia, now 'back' with big ideas. I sure as hell didn't sleep well that night …

During the second week of September the Tour had sped from New York to Pennsylvania for the Reading Open. To that point, Lloyd and Sam Snead were tied with 4 wins each following Mangrum's return in March after recovering from his late 1949 'accident.'

At Reading, however, the Slammer had his game in high gear, setting a record for that event with a 268 score, while Mr. Icicle remained cold, trailing Sam by 12 shots at the end. I still had received no word from Lloyd as to whether he had gotten a recorder through Bing, or had used it for therapeutic purposes. Of course, I Bobby Shout had plenty 'on my mind' anyway, trying to make the Sharpshooters Invitational a reality.

Making 'cold calls' to the titans of our Texas oil world had proved just as nerve-racking as I'd feared it would be. That is, until I got inside their offices and began to talk. Each and every one of them seemed determined to be agreeable, and several times I was helped along in my train of thought by these eminent listeners.

After my third successful 'pitch' for support of both the tournament and its goal of adding more veterans to our industry, I'd walked directly into my mother's office upon returning to our building.

She looked tired but threw me a tender smile as she asked, "So, how did it go?"

I returned her pleasantness with a grin of my own, "You tell me."

Mom nodded to herself before responding, "I thought you'd 'catch on,' but remember, I only paved the way for you. They'd agreed to nothing based on what I said."

Well many a son might have seethed at having a mother's undercover assistance, but not this one. I said simply, "Thanks, Mom. You helped a lot," before retreating to my own lair down the hall.

The first inaugural Texas Sharpshooters Invitational was now definitely 'a go' funding-wise. It was up to me still to determine where the event would be held. In 1 sense, any old course would do, considering that our foursome would not actually be playing the layout, only trying to 'knock down' its pins from the artificial teeing spots we chose.

Yet the aura of the proceedings would benefit no doubt if our stars were presented with a greater challenge due to the sort of green complexes only to be found on a first-class layout. In fact the pros I hoped most to recruit might consider this factor essential in their deliberations as to whether to compete. Thus, I had to 'shoot high' for the site.

Now you may not know it, but even back then there were a bunch of quality courses within the great state of Texas. However, it seemed to me that I need look no further than Dallas, seeing how our home locale offered important advantages.

First off, neither Hogan, Nelson, Mangrum, or Demaret were based here, while all had some familiarity with the city's clubs. In other words, a Dallas course 'checked the box' for not giving any of the players an unfair 'home court' advantage. On the other hand, each of the oil companies to be involved in the event had their headquarters or a major office in town, which would eliminate a lot of travel time for those helping 'on site' or simply attending the event.

After a brief shower subsided on Monday morning, September 11th, I drove around to the city's 3 finest municipal courses: Steven's Park, Cedar Crest, and Tenison Park. Cedar had hosted a PGA Championship; Tenison a UGSA Pub Links. Their layouts offered plenty of challenge in regard to green complexes, and it didn't matter that they were a bit short by the Tour's standards.

Not surprisingly, though the head pros at each place showed enthusiasm over hosting the kind of event I had in mind, none of them had the authority to give me a 'green light.' So, it was on to the city offices to speak to the director of parks and recreation.

I won't name him but the guy was a pompous bureaucrat. That is, until my 'pitch' identified the players I expected to attract. Then, he practically drooled while repeating, "Hogan here, Demaret, maybe Nelson and Mangrum? Lordy yes! I can assure you that we'll make one of our best courses available whenever you say, if those are the gentlemen competing."

Mission accomplished, I Bobby Shout left his office in a better state of mind. Yet, there was the toughest 'sell' still to come, so my brain was churning like the legs of a roadrunner in 'heat.'

Which of my 4 targets was most likely to say 'yes' without any assurance about the other 3? Who out of that quartet would lean toward 'no' unless I had his 3 rivals already in tow? Would riverboat Mangrum deign to come back to Texas from Chicago or L.A.? And if not, who could 'make up' the 4th if we really couldn't 'get by' with 3 contestants instead?

Fortunately there was 1 perfect substitute out on Tour, a player in fact whom the 'big four' might well wish to beat in our event, along with a Texan-born Tour retiree who'd once been on top of the golf world. *Him* dusting off his clubs for our event – like Byron Nelson – would make for a riveting storyline. For now though, I'll hold back on those names.

The Tour's two 1950 titans, Snead and Mangrum, failed to best each other the following week on Tour, I observed while reading my Monday morning paper on the 18th. At St. Louis it was Cary Middlecoff and Ed Oliver who were to face-off that day in a playoff – Cary won – while Sam and Lloyd had tied for 4th place.

However the very next week at the Kansas City Open, there was Lloyd again in the winner's circle having nipped Jackie Burke Jr. and Ed Oliver by a stroke. This meant that Slammin' Sammy and Mr. Icicle were again in a 'dead heat' for tournament wins at 5 after Mangrum joined the Tour in March.

I Bobby Shout thought it a shame that this hot twosome now had to weather a 5-week pause in the Tour calendar, no events being scheduled 'til the North and South Open commenced at the end of October. On the other hand, how would we ever entice the field I wanted for our Invitational during that last clement month of the Texas year if Lloyd had to face 'losing ground' to Snead by choosing our event over a Tour stop? After all, the prestige and extra loot from winning 'player of the year' honors were at stake!

So back on Tuesday September 12th, I had begun my toughest task to date, trying to assemble a reunion of my 4 Tour 'patients' here in Dallas at the inaugural Texas Sharpshooters Invitational – with no mommy help. No, it wasn't easy!

Of course, I didn't tell anyone back then that part of my vision for this tournament had been to help Byron specifically. He was the one who was most in need of doing exhibitions for cash at the time, and it seemed a lot more probable that MacGregor would be able to set up a whole string of one-day affairs for him the following spring if the former 'Mr. Golf' showed himself at our event to still be a master shot-maker.

After driving northwest out of Dallas on that Tuesday September 12th, I'd reached Byron's Roanoke ranch around ten in the morning. His wife Louise directed me to the henhouse where Byron said he'd be happy to listen to 'my surprise' while continuing to do his chores. Well I laid out the plans for the inaugural Texas Sharpshooters Invitational and hinted about the exhibitions that could follow. MacGregor had scrapped a planned tour for him back in August due to lack of interest, he'd admitted to me earlier.

To my surprise at first I got little warmth from him over this new proposal. When Byron asked about who was already 'in' I had to admit he was the first I'd asked. "So, you're asking me to act like the female bird staked out to attract the tom turkeys?" he'd drawled. "But, maybe I'm not such an attractive lure anymore," Nelson continued, a rare trace of self-pity showing. "Bobby, you might get Jimmy – he's looking half 'out to pasture' – but Ben? Lloyd? I don't know … and it could be downright embarrassing for me if I wind up matched with some run-of-the-mill pros from our state and don't 'lick' 'em!"

"True," I'd countered, "but I think you're underestimating how much pleasure it would give the Hawk and Mr. Icicle to 'show you up,' not to mention how much those 2 enemies would like the opportunity to go head-to-head against each other – anytime anywhere that Hogan can drag himself there.

"Plus you know that Jimmy feels vastly underappreciated compared to you and Ben! Heck" – I avoided saying 'Hell' in front of that good Christian man – "the Wardrobe will be dying to 'set the record straight' by topping you all in such a shootout."

Still, Nelson remained unconvinced I could tell. Having halted his broom work, the former 'Mr. Golf' had sat down on a bale with a sigh. So then I knew it was time to reveal my potential 'mystery guest.'

"Look, even if one of those gents won't do it, there are other viable candidates."

"Oh. Who?" the chicken man had challenged me.

And then I closed the trap. "Ralph Guldahl for one," was my silky reply. "I mean, the guy won back-to-back Opens in his day, a Masters, and 3 Westerns. I reckon he'd get the other three's attention all right, if you decide not to compete. Should I call him at Medinah? Ralph's probably bored to death with being a club pro by now. Say, you've known him a long time, right? Could I 'use your name' at least, Byron? Him showing up for this would be on a par with yours as a comeback story ..."

"Let's reckon not!" my rancher-friend shot back, with as much acid as I'd ever heard in Byron's voice. "You can wait to contact that dumb Swede if Ben or Lloyd turn you down!"

"So, you mean you're 'in'?

"You know darn well I am – now," he spit at me before collecting himself enough to flash a grim smile. "And I'll be practicing extra hard if he winds up in the foursome."

Fact was that Guldahl had given Nelson some bad beatings in match play during their teenage years in the Dallas area, and eclipsed him at the '39 Masters. On top of that, the "dumb Swede" had been about the slowest player on earth, even taking time to re-comb his thick hair between shots, which I knew had to have bugged Byron. It had shocked me to find that Ralph was only a year older than Nelson, considering that the man had left the Tour – his 'game' mysteriously collapsed – nearly a decade earlier.

Ah, but no boy forgets the humiliation of an early lopsided defeat. That's what I'd counted on with Byron when I had sprung Guldahl as a possibility for the Invitational.

Heading home that afternoon, I'd tried to cheer myself with the chant *One down, three to go!* However, having found that even Byron wasn't an 'easy sell,' I found myself feeling lower than a tailless rattlesnake as I contemplated which of my now frosty 'patients' to approach next: Demaret or Hogan?

It seemed to me that if I got Ben, Jimmy would be sure to follow, so subservient was the Wardrobe under the Hawk's spell. Yet there was danger that if Hogan declined first, Demaret might learn of his refusal and not even 'hear me out.' No, I needed to focus my attack on Houston next, trying to 'lock up' Texan number 2 before I dealt with Mr. Hogan. But what was I going to say?!

Although the prize money we were offering was darn good, I knew for sure that emphasizing this aspect would get me nowhere. Both men had turned down opportunities to win big cash before on Tour, in favor of their principles – or dislikes – I knew. So somehow I Bobby Shout had to unthaw our relationships first. Yes, that was a start …

However, I must confess that flipping a coin to decide whether to approach Demaret or Hogan did tempt me, because 'Dr. Shout' had no sure prescription for success with either man. Should I begin by confronting Jimmy, whose drunken paranoia had labeled me Hogan's stooge? Or, would it be better to beg for a meeting with that supposed Svengali, Ben, who'd classified me as a traitor back in L.A. for my dalliance with Mangrum?

Happily, the quarter I tossed did land head-ups, which I'd decreed in advance would mean tackling Mr. Wardrobe before Ben. And -- dare I say – with Fate backing my first impulse at this juncture, an ounce more of confidence propelled me forward.

That very night I phoned Jimmy. Then called another 2 times with no answer. At least back then, without caller I.D. or message machines and such, this initial lack of success could do nothing to 'cow' me. I simply continued to contact him the next day and the Wardrobe did 'pick up' around mid-afternoon.

"Hello, Jimmy." I began. "It's Bobby Shout. I hope you're not still thinking …"

To my vast relief, he interrupted me sounding like his usual good-natured self, having 'broken in' to apologize for his suspicions and rude behavior at the restaurant in L.A. "That was the liquor talking," he admitted. "As soon as I got to Chicago for May's tournament I knew that you were right. My 'heart's not in it' on Tour nearly as much as it once was, and I do need to move this big rear of mine in new directions. So, thanks."

With that opening, I was able to 'seal the deal' on his being part of our Sharpshooters exhibition faster than I could have hoped. Jimmy whistled at the prize money and didn't even pin me down on who else would be competing. He just said, "Count me in, partner. And, if the likes of Hogan or Mangrum won't budge, consider my little buddy Jackie (Burke Jr.) for a spot in the foursome. He's an up-and-comer, you know – won I think 4 events this year. Not big ones, but they all count."

I had to laugh inside. I'd planned to 'bring up' Jimmy's fellow Houstonian Jackie if need be in just the way I'd needled Nelson with Guldahl. You know, how it would look good to have some 'younger blood' in the contest if Demaret declined my offer. Having hung up, I howled with joy like a coyote communicating an impressive kill, so thrilled was I to have 2 great Texan golfers 'on board' now, with Burke and Guldahl still to spare. I Bobby Shout called my mother with the good news.

It was she who convinced me to try Mangrum next rather than Hogan. Mom called Ben "a master of grudges" and "more stubborn than a 3-horned steer." In other words, Margo Shout was saying that I needed every possible lure to get Hogan to 'forget my sin,' thus allowing him to accept a berth in the Sharpshooters Invitational. And, the prospect of humbling that uppity veteran Lloyd Mangrum might just be the strongest 'draw' we could offer to tempt the Hawk.

On Friday night September 15th, I finally 'caught up' with Mr. Icicle by phone at the hotel where he was staying for the "St. Louis Open." Within 18 seconds of saying "Hello" I was regretting having made the effort. Although Lloyd was in contention after the first 2 rounds, he sounded grumpier than Hogan at his worst. Moreover, Mangrum's wrath was being directed squarely at me.

Who the hell did I think I was – calling him when he was in tournament mode? What kind of ninny did I judge him to be, to suggest purchasing a damn expensive recorder that hadn't done a bit of good? And, now I wanted him to travel halfway across the country to entertain some oil barons with 3 other pros like trained monkeys?! "Boy, you got a hell of a nerve," he'd roared to complete his opening tirade.

Well I was reduced to a shocked silence. Not just by the vehemence of his attack, but also because I'd yet to mention the Texas Sharpshooters Invitational to him. How in heaven's name had he already heard about it? From Jimmy Demaret? Certainly not from Byron, seeing how Lloyd's profane nature could not possibly appeal to Nelson. Plus, was Mr. Icicle saying that he'd followed my advice to 'journal' his daily thoughts on tape about the war and had found no easing of his shell shock symptoms? Had Lloyd really given it a full try? If so, I was sorry, but ...

My racing thoughts were interrupted by Mangrum firing another question at me, but in a playful voice, "So Dr. Shout, cat got your tongue? I really got you going, didn't I?" After another second I realized that Mr. Icicle was not really mad at me. He'd just been kidding, another sort of 'poker face' play by the 'riverboat gambler.'

"Damn you, Lloyd," I'd thundered back. "You trying to give me a heart attack?" He'd chuckled in reply. Oh, how I recalled those words later.

At this moment however, everything stood rosy. It turned out that Mangrum was in quite the affable mood, especially for him. Lucky me! Yeah, he crowed, his sources had clued him in that I'd probably be calling, and Lloyd was ready to bet me a thousand bucks that he'd be the winner of that $5,000 we were offering to the best Texas Sharpshooter of them all. Heck, I hadn't even asked him if he'd play yet.

I knew better though than to take umbrage at Lloyd's 'cheek.' That man's demeanor was never far from ornery according to most sources. So, instead of challenging his assumption, I moved right on to the matter of his proposed wager. We settled on $500 as the bet, and that was that.

And no, I Bobby Shout didn't worry for a second about anyone calling my neutrality about the Invitational into question after that. In those days down in Texas a man's honor was worth more than any wager – we all thought that way, until a no-good cheat proved otherwise.

Before hanging up, Mangrum offered me another satisfaction, deeper than his desire to play. That is, he added, "Brother, I'm sleeping much better thanks to you and that recorder idea. God damn it, the little woman says I'm barely screaming at all most nights, not to mention I ain't sweat-soaking the sheets no more – saving her lots of washing. Mark my words, you'd be wise to bet on me to 'take' next week's tourney in K.C. 'cause I'm feeling real strong right now. Got to go. Bye."

Left holding a suddenly dead receiver, what could I do but smile? Tricky Lloyd Mangrum had morphed into my true buddy. For how long, who knew? But, I felt a lot better about approaching the Hawk now about the Invitational. For the rest of the night, I did my best Jimmy Demaret imitation, drinking and singing along with the radio 'til bedtime.

Back at work on Monday the 18th, I had my secretary Lucy phone the Hogan residence. If Ben still wasn't in the mood to talk to me, it would hurt less to hear his snub secondhand. Also, my hope was that Hogan might take my call just to sass me about being a 'big-shot' now with flunkies to do my bidding. I'd gladly give him that 'opening' if it meant we'd get the chance to dialogue.

He and Valerie had returned to Fort Worth about ten days earlier, according to what I'd read in the paper. And, the Hawk was probably practicing daily over at Colonial to get his perfect edge back after all that "wasted time" out in Hollywood. Still, I prayed to St. Andrew that Ben and I might connect sooner rather than later.

When my girl Lucy buzzed me then intoned "Mr. Hogan on the line," my heart jumped like an ant about to be gobbled up by a horny toad. It took me a few seconds to slow my breathing before I could press the right button on my phone.

I tried not to stutter while beginning, "Ben? Hello. Thanks for taking my call." His turn ...

"Don't know why I did, except Val said it would be unnecessarily rude not to. Well I don't know about that, Bobby, considering where we stand."

Heck, where do we stand – exactly? "I'm sorry you think ... Well anyway, I only need to take a couple of minutes of your time. It's the Sharpshooters Invitational I'm calling about ...

"Am I supposed to know what the hell you're referring to," broke in the Hawk, his voice sharp enough to slice glass.

Could that be true? I asked myself, stunned – when word had even reached Mangrum out in L.A.? *Or, was Ben just being Ben, super difficult when he felt like it!*

There was no choice but to 'play his game.' "Oh, well, several of us oil companies have gotten together to sponsor an exhibition tournament. We're calling it the Texas Sharpshooters Invitational. The purse is fat: $5,000 to the winner and even the 4th-place guy gets $1,000. Did I say it's a 4-man field? Anyway – I've lined up Jimmy, Byron, and Lloyd to compete, so it seemed natural that you would be the 4th?" My voice trailed off, "In late-October if you're free …"

Silence, several beats, then Hogan snarling, "Before I'd ever get involved with you again, Shout, I'd have to see your eyes while you made any 'pitch.' 1:30. Meet me tomorrow at the Hulen Street bench along with your baloney sandwich." Another second of time, then *click*, he was gone.

After a minute of panting, I Bobby Shout was able to get beyond wondering whether the "baloney" mention was meant to be a 'crack' at my integrity. In fact I was a bit angry. That bench was a few miles from his home; it meant more than a 30-mile drive each way for me from Dallas. And then, the Hawk was probably going to spit in my face, rhetorically speaking. But what could I do? I'd be there in Fort Worth just as he said.

At least it was a pleasant day for a drive on that Tuesday, September 19th. The sun was shining with an expected high of 82 degrees in Ben's town and the breeze felt good. I was able to park close to our rendezvous spot on Hulen and reached the bench with 15 minutes to spare before our 1:30 date. Hogan didn't show 'til 2:10, no doubt wanting to 'bust my chops' some more.

My time waiting for him though had not proved unpleasant. Rather, I'd felt nostalgic about the beginning of my friendship with the Hawk, which had started right there. If he no longer felt like being kind to me ever again, well … I'd had a 'good run' at getting a true sense of a remarkable human being.

"Kid, quit daydreaming and let's get this over with," said Ben in his gruffest voice, suddenly at the bench amidst my reverie. I saw with disappointment that he had brought nothing to eat as though he intended to stay hardly any time.

"Sure, Ben," I replied, my tone subdued. "Okay, like I told you on the phone there's to be an exhibition match held the weekend of October 21st and 22nd – with a week-later rain date – involving 4 Texan pros trying to outdo each other in a closest-to-the-pin competition. As I also said, the prize money is excellent: $5,000 to the winner, then $2,500, $1,500, and $1,000 to the 4th-place winner …"

"You mean a grand to the last-place loser," he shot back.

"If you prefer." What else could I say? This was not going well!

Ben snarled, "And we wouldn't be playing real golf! How's that supposed to work?"

I did my best not to get rattled while explaining how one of the finest public courses in Dallas would be set up with tees placed from wedge to driver distance on the layout's 18 holes. Then, we'd change those teeing areas for the second 18 on Sunday. The Hawk seemed about to interrupt again, so I hurried on to the part about each guy having color-coded balls and getting 3 attempts each hole, the ultimately closest ball to the pin netting its player a point, with the cumulative number of points for each competitor over the 36 'holes' deciding the final place standings.

"Christ! And Jimmy, Byron, and Mangrum have all signed on to participate in this circus, you say?"

"They're hoping to see you there, too, Ben," I'd countered. "Each of them wants this Sharpshooters Invitational to seem totally legit to everyone in the state." Yeah, this was 'a stretch.' Neither Nelson, Demaret, nor Mangrum had uttered exactly that sentiment. But, I really did believe that they wanted to face Hogan.

Shockingly – to me anyway -- the Hawk evinced no desire to meet their challenge. I remember him saying, "Well my money's gonna be on Byron to beat that fucker Lloyd." And having delivered this terse judgment, he was gone. I watched Ben retreat with that now halting stride of his, me all the while wondering what to do next while he no doubt headed for Colonial. Ralph Guldahl or Jackie Burke Jr. … Should I flip a coin?

Having driven back to my office, I asked Lucy whether I'd received any calls in my absence, still insanely praying that Hogan had had a change of heart. Five minutes later, I was fixing to go play some golf when Lucy did buzz me. "It's Mr. Hogan," she whispered as if he had super-hero hearing.

"Okay, put him on," I answered, caught between dread and hope.

He lit into me like I was a claim-jumper. "Hell's bells, Shout, I reckon you're either trying to make me look bad, or you're just an idiot salesman. Demaret just took my call and he set me straight."

This sounded promising! "Hello to you, too, Ben," I replied.

With a snort of disgust, the Hawk had continued, "Why didn't you tell me right off that this tournament was to support training programs for vets? Ben Hogan doesn't decline to help veterans, for God's sake. You had to know that!"

At this juncture, I Bobby Shout felt like lashing back by telling him that if he'd given me half a chance I would have got to the 'veterans part.' But, it was just so good to hear Hogan essentially say that he'd be playing, my response was to give his pride what it wanted. "Yeah, I'm not much of a salesmen. Sorry for my obtuseness" – knowing with some satisfaction that the Hawk might not know the meaning of that word.

In any case, now you've been told how it came to be that the inaugural Texas Sharpshooters Invitational was graced by the 4 greatest golfers in the history of our state. I got heaps of credit for making this happen. Yet really, it was a case of lucky circumstances and the event 'selling itself.'

Later on, it occurred to me how this day was evidence of a major change in Hogan's persona between the first and last time I met him at the Hulen Street bench. Most folks have heard how Ben received loads of well-wishing cards and such during his months of recovery after the early 1949 car accident. However I think it took all the in-person goodwill toward the Hawk during his 1950 tournament travels to 'seal the deal.' That is, to turn him into someone who did care what the heck others thought of him. Otherwise, he'd never have uttered that jab at me about trying to make him look bad. The 'old' William Ben Hogan would simply not have cared.

Two days later, the PGA Tour pros were about to compete in the final event on their September calendar – the Kansas City Open, as previously mentioned. And, as I've also previewed, this was the last official tourney scheduled for the pros prior to the North & South Open in late October.

You remember that Lloyd had told me he was feeling good with the extra rest he was getting? Well he went into that final round in Kansas City only a stroke behind the leader 'Porky' Oliver. Nearly as important to Mr. Icicle, I imagined, was 'the cushion' he had over Sam Snead whose 213 total at the start of Sunday's play put him 11 strokes behind Mangrum.

Well, the riverboat gambler brought in a winning hand again, shooting a 3-under 69 for a 17-under total. To match him Oliver needed to sink a 45-foot birdie putt on the 18th. He left his try a sinful 2 feet short!

This win at the Milburn Country Club course put Lloyd once again in a tie for tournament wins with Snead (now 5 each) during the 6-month span they'd both been able to compete during 1950, though of course, the Slammer *had* amassed an additional 4 victories during the first months of the season while Lloyd was rehabbing. One of them would go on to break this logjam by winning October's only event, but I'll leave the details about that tourney 'til the close of the following monthly chapter.

CHAPTER 10

October 1950

B Y THE TIME the first day of 1950's tenth month dawned, we not only had superb sponsorship for the Sharpshooter's Invitational – along with a stellar foursome of combatants – we also had a signed contract from the city of Dallas containing all the 'ins and outs' of having their municipal course Cedar Crest serve as the host layout for our event. Seeing how that 'track' had been my first choice from a design standpoint for challenging our quartet of stars, I was feeling pretty darn good on my way into work that Monday, October 2nd.

For one thing, the city had only purchased Cedar Crest from its private owners 4 years earlier. So the gussying up of the layout that followed naturally in '46-'47 was still in evidence. Its fairways and bunkers along with its tees and greens were surely 'on a par' with what 'the boys' were used to out on the Tour's lesser stops – better than some of the courses they competed on.

Then there were the 'bones' of this particular muni: Back during the late teens of the century, Albert Tillinghast had laid the course out amidst the hills south of downtown Dallas, crafting it to be the hub of a country club. Thus, that lofty designer hadn't 'messed around' challenge-wise.

His greens there were elusively small with several positioned up on the acreage's 'table tops.' Also, some of these putting surfaces as well as others at Cedar Crest flowed downwards toward their sides, further shrinking the size of the area which would 'hold' an incoming shot. This was just what was wanted, a stern test of accuracy to inspire our Sharpshooters!

On top of these pluses, the unusual routing produced by the great Tillinghast would work to our practical advantage as well, I believed. That is, Cedar Crest included 6 par-3s amongst its holes. Oh, and they were a stout bunch, ranging from 178 yards to 210 yards when played from the championship tees.

This design feature meant that we would already have close-cropped, good level turf at hand on a third of Cedar Crest's holes for both days without needing to hunt out and prep suitable ground in advance. Moreover, since each of these '3s' was long enough to provide teeing grounds of distinctly different lengths, we would not be trapped into offering the players nearly duplicate shots on Saturday and Sunday at any of these holes.

Naturally I was 'chomping at the bit' to get consulting with the home pro about selecting sites for impromptu teeing grounds on Cedar's twelve '4s' and '5s,' but before there was time for that, some other big jobs had precedence. Namely, the rest of that first week in October, I Bobby Shout was coordinating with the others on our Tournament Publicity Committee to make sure that both vets looking for work and the general golf public would have ample notice about the Sharpshooters Invitational and its related activities.

We of course were including newspaper ads, radio 'spots,' and billboards in our strategy to announce the events taking place on October 21st-22nd. However, someone on the Publicity Committee also had a brainstorm involving the staffs at each of Dallas's 6 municipal courses 'spreading the word.'

To wit, a competition was set up with prizes to be awarded to the employees of the muni who handed out the most 'dummy tickets.' The folks who received them could then 'cash in' those coupons for a discounted real admission pass at the Invitational's entrance gate. I recollect that more than 1,500 spectators both days 'turned in' those dummies for reduced-priced tickets, so this ploy did prove a success.

I won't bore you with a lot more details about the pre-event preparations that needed doing, but there is 1 aspect of that work which still makes me proud. That is, we who were the top reps for each of the 3 oil companies involved with 'putting on' the Invitational agreed that the 'veterans side' of that weekend would receive just as much care as we were putting into the golf exhibition. And, we stood by that pledge!

The best of our field foremen were recruited to demo jobs related to our rigs. Only employees on the accounting side who were expert with words as well as figures were allowed to represent us at the job fair. This same standard was applied in choosing folks tapped to explain other employment opportunities relating to areas ranging from health and safety positions to geological exploration.

Moreover, the group chosen to 'sign up' veterans for appropriate training programs were top-notch interviewers pre-trained (in some cases by us!) to appreciate the mental challenges that many returning veterans faced in relation to resuming a career.

Is there any wonder then that more than 180 men and women ultimately found work within our oil companies after attending the inaugural Sharpshooters Invitational? Good people, too, who went on to enjoy long careers in the business!

As the final-week countdown to October 21st began, everything – even the weather forecasted for our event – was looking under control, with 1 major exception. None of us involved with the Invitational had foreseen just how 'betting mad' the citizens of Texas would be in regard to what was after all merely an exhibition.

I must confess that our tournament committee did consider a proposal to run a Calcutta auction on Friday night the 20th. The basis of a Calcutta is that each player in an event can be 'bought' by the highest bidder, and if 'his man' wins, that lucky bidder gets the entire 'pot' generated by the auction. In our case, the guy who was 'talking up' such a scheme reckoned we could claim twenty per cent of that 'pot' for our training programs. But, we voted him down.

Why? First off, at the Sharpshooters Invitational --unlike most tournaments -- there were few players to be 'bought.' We figured that Hogan would draw the highest amount by far and no doubt was likely to win, meaning his 'owner' would not take kindly to having any portion of the pot beyond his major investment taken away – let alone 20 percent!

And secondly, whether the wagering winner was gracious or not about their required contribution to the training program fund, he or she would be a big part of the media story involving the exhibition's result. We didn't want that – the sleazy aura of gambling to be interlocked with our noble intentions concerning war vets. So, it turned out that we probably missed out on a whole lot of money for training them, by declining a Calcutta.

Heck, the wagering denizens around Houston were so 'hot' to back their local boy Demaret that by 'game time' the odds on him were nearly the same as on Ben. It was rumored that likewise, many luminaries from the Hollywood scene were backing Lloyd, dropping his odds among the bookies. When the 21st finally rolled along, only the name Byron Nelson could get you 'long shot' betting odds to make a 'killing.'

All this 'action' unfortunately led to an unforeseen development that we should have been better prepared for, but weren't. I have been forever guilt-ridden over our oversight. Still, the damage was done, as you shall hear.

Friday, October 20ᵗʰ, was a dry day around Dallas with highs in the 80s. A couple of showers had occurred early on Thursday but the rest of the day had been free of precipitation. Thus, Cedar Crest was in perfect condition to test our players – its greens firm yet by no means rock hard.

The forecast for Saturday afternoon said that we would continue to enjoy dry conditions, though a couple of showers could arrive after 5 p.m. That would be fine as our guess was that our 4 players, even hitting 3 tee shots each hole, would 'finish their round' in about 3 hours, having started at 1 p.m. Remember, each weekend morning was to be devoted to our employment fair for vets, though it was assumed that church-going would 'cut' into the attendance on Sunday before noon.

When I arose on that Saturday and looked at the morning paper, the weather news remained positive: No showers 'til late afternoon; temperatures starting in the mid-70s though falling to the mid-60s by 4 p.m.; and, a typical Texas breeze, ranging from 10 to 15 mph during our quartet's time on the course.

Of course, I Bobby Shout was fixing to get over to Cedar's clubhouse 'bright and early' in case any last-minute mix-ups surfaced among our job-fair staff. However, when I arrived there soon after dawn there was nothing amiss. In fact throughout the morning hours it shocked me how well run our veteran-related activities were going. A couple of times I even teared up a tad upon hearing ex-military men exclaiming about how efficiently the whole shebang had been set up – along with how enthusiastic they were feeling about getting trained for our industry.

My recollection is that Demaret, Hogan, Mangrum, and Nelson were absent from my mind 'til about 11:30 a.m. that day. Then I began to imagine again how these 4 greats might have chosen to prep for the Sharpshooters Invitational in distinctly different ways.

None of them had been permitted to step foot on the Cedar Crest property since signing up for our event, and yet … I could see Ben taking the trouble to inquire both about the topography of each of the Crest's putting surfaces as well as their orientation to the prevailing winds. Had he identified similarly designed greens at other courses in our area? And then arranged to 'have each to himself' for an afternoon hour so as to 'run through his bag' hitting various shapes and trajectories toward multiple possible pin placements? If this sounds like overkill, you didn't know Hogan! And, I was betting that he had the utter gall, too, to shoo other players past his target holes.

'Iron Byron' on the other hand – I pictured him giving nary a thought of wasting chore time to get to a golf course to warm up for the Invitational. My visits to his ranch had included the opportunity to try out his primitive driving range there, and believe me the turf was no thing of beauty. Yet, Mr. Golf's upright swing and continually flexed knees allowed him to bring a club through the hitting area so often with perfect 'squareness' that he could hit a hook or fade, high ball or low, whatever you wanted, on his weedy range.

Actually, the only tooling his swing needed was to 'lock in' proper timing. That is, he needed to avoid rushing his transition from the top. So I imagined that Byron had focused on this nuance.

As for Jimmy Demaret, I couldn't see him employing any special practice regimens for our upcoming competition either. He, like Nelson, had 'all the shots.' In fact, no one could hit 'em super low on command like Jimmy, what with his jackhammer forearms and hands powering into the ball while his trunk barely shifted in its narrow stance.

No, for him the question these days was confidence. I hoped that Jimmy had found some again, maybe by 'plucking some pigeons' down in Houston? Did I suppose he'd gone 'into training' for this event, some might ask? The thought of the Wardrobe 'cutting down' on his drinking and nightlife to clear his head – well that wasn't Demaret.

By contrast, I had little confidence in predicting how Lloyd Mangrum had reckoned to get ready for our event. If Hogan were a genius as some folks said, it seemed to me that Mr. Icicle didn't rank far behind in the intelligence department.

Just think about that $500 bet he made with me about winning the Sharpshooters: Soon thereafter I realized that by making me a direct beneficiary of the possibility of him losing, Mangrum had made me that much less likely to 'stack the deck' against him, e.g., like placing the majority of the pins in places that favored Hogan's fade over Lloyd's customary 'draw'. Yeah, he'd 'read' me right then upped the ante for my native integrity. Smart guy.

Yet still, his greatest strength as a player was his chipping and putting, not ball striking. As far as hitting a target consistently from tee or turf, Mr. Icicle was simply not in the same class as his 3 opponents. So, what could Lloyd do to somewhat 'even the odds' at the Sharpshooters Invitational, I pondered?

Well, unhappily the only equalizer I could 'come up with' was Mangrum's mouth. He had to diminish the performances of the others if he could, by 'getting in their heads' with his words. Would the riverboat gambler resort to such gamesmanship, I wondered? And if so, who would he be able to rattle? Hogan? I reckoned not. Nelson? Maybe … by attacking the faith of that good Christian man? Or Demaret? Yes, yes, yes. I feared for Jimmy the most.

The honor of acting as 'master of ceremonies' for this 2-day event had been given to me, so I Bobby Shout was waiting on the 1ˢᵗ tee as that Texas Quartet approached us from the practice field. (Have I mentioned that God gifted your narrator with a full, sonorous voice – part of the reason I got to 'run the show' so to speak?)

Well it was obvious that Jimmy and Lloyd were having a nice chat as they approached which didn't surprise me, considering that the Wardrobe even in his mid-life crisis these days was still a heck of a likable guy and never shy with a friendly word.

On the other hand, though Hogan and Nelson were striding together a few paces behind the first two, there was no evidence that they'd shared a single sentence. Could that be accounted for by Ben's myopic intensity in conjunction with Byron's usual pre-round nausea? No one could be sure but I did know that the 2 men, once openly buddies on Tour in their early days, had long soured on each other over the question of who was really 'Mr. Golf.'

This awesome foursome had been surrounded, of course, by a bevy of excited fans all the way from practice ground to tee box, yet there'd been no need for any of our 'security people' to help make way for the golfers to reach me. Such were the good manners of the time that the spectators had parted like the Red Sea to provide their idols with access to me. Nor had a single folk bothered the players with requests for autographs, handshakes, or any other sort of off-putting attention during their stroll 'into the arena' – such a contrast to what one sees at tournaments today!

When Jimmy got to me, he slapped me on the shoulder. Lloyd gave a grin while reminding me to remember our bet. From Ben I got only a cold nod which hurt. However, Byron grasped my hand and shook it while thanking me for including him, which brought a real smile back to my nervous face.

I proceeded to go through the unnecessary but crowd-pumping exercise of introducing each player while mentioning their Major resumes, then moved on to explaining how the contest would be conducted. You've already heard how each player had balls for his use with an identifying color band on them: Blue for Hogan; red for Jimmy; gold for Mangrum; and purple for Byron. I also let the crowd know before everyone began ambling down the 1st fairway that the order of play on each 'hole' would be determined by a 'draw of straws' at the designated tees.

For starters, we'd set up tee markers at about 7-iron distance from the green on that long, opening par-5 which bent twice to the right. Back then, its putting surface was intersected by a diagonal hump from back right running to front left. We'd placed the pin about 15 feet left of that ridge and centered in terms of the depth of the green. In other words, it was a pin the players 'could get at,' whether they chose to hit a draw and spin it down the ridge or play a fade to the cup.

It was Byron who picked the 'short straw' and so would lead off, followed by Ben, Lloyd, and Jimmy; then Byron first again for the second set of balls, and the third. I was happy for the former Mr. Golf that he could get his opening strike 'out of the way' as soon as possible, since he did look a bit 'green around the gills.'

However, when Byron hit a lovely little left-to-right shot at a medium trajectory, rolling it up to 5 feet from the cup, I shouldn't have been surprised. This man had always been a supreme competitor!

His effort in fact 'held up' through the first 2 rounds and his third shot died 8 feet shy, so that left it to the other 3's final tries. Ben being Ben, he didn't hesitate to change his strategy, having seen his classic fades 'bite' a bit too much to challenge Nelson previously. Instead, the Hawk played a tiny draw that landed 2 feet from the left edge of the ridge, then slide down the slope, stopping a mere 2 feet from the hole. My bad ear hurt, so raucous was the crowd response to the man's mastery.

Lloyd executed his final try in typical Mangrum fashion – having said nothing in acknowledgement of his opponent's feat. He just stepped up like he was on the range and hit. The ball couldn't have landed more than a pace beyond where Hogan's had, yet the result was a roller, ten feet past the cup. That left it to Jimmy Demaret to determine who was going to take the first point of the day.

Taking his time to settle into an address position, the Wardrobe was simultaneously 'egging on' the gallery by acting as though he were a radio commentator reporting on his own shot. The line I remember was, "And Demaret is looking very confident, very confident indeed and now he's 'broken' into song," at which point Jimmy's fine tenor warbled, "Luck be a lady tonight." Most of us had never heard this tune, but the Wardrobe with his musical connections had 'gotten wind of it' – part of the score for a show called "Guys and Dolls" which had had its pre-Broadway tryout the week before.

It turned out that the crooner needed some luck, seeing how he 'caught' the ball a groove low on his club, sending that 7-iron shot somewhat weakly on a sub-par height toward the green. We chuckled along with Jimmy, then watched. 'The line' at least was great. Demaret's ball hit a hard spot on its second bounce, sufficient to send it skipping ahead onto the putting surface, and his effort at last caromed gently into Ben's ball taking its place as the closest shot to the cup.

Jimmy responded by tossing his iron to the caddy then bowing to the crowd on all 3 sides before sashaying off, having resumed his singing of the "Guys and Dolls" tune. I looked at Ben and there was the devil in his eyes, though he'd said nothing. *Look out guys,* I remember thinking. *The Hawk's out for blood now!*

And indeed, he played a perfect faded 9-iron on his first try at the pin on number 2, though we'd placed the flag on a down slope back-right and treacherously close to a starboard bunker -- making Lloyd none too happy I was sure. With Hogan 6 inches from the hole the others couldn't help but 'press,' leading to a procession of mediocre tries. Thus ultimately I called out "Demaret '1'; Hogan '1' after two."

Cedar Crest's 3rd hole was a demanding par-3. We'd decided to really test the boys on this one, placing the flag in the back left corner of the putting surface and using the championship tee box, stretching the hole to about 220 yards. For a fader that meant 'taking on' a small but deep bunker in line with the cup, not to mention a concrete-basin pond just to the left of that trap, seeing how the shape of its green resembled a boomerang curving left.

Natty Jimmy had drawn the first crack, to be followed by Hogan, Nelson, and then Mangrum. The Wardrobe's first attempt was boldly aimed but didn't fade. Splash! Ben took a conservative approach for his first try, fading his 4-wood to the right of the hole by some twenty feet but pin high.

Mr. Golf appeared to me to be aiming no farther left than the flag – just as Hogan had. However, Byron's arching wood shot went arrow straight over the little bunker and settled 8 feet past the hole. With Mr. Icicle 'over-cooking' his 'draw' into the sand, that result left Nelson 'in the lead' after round 1. And though the other 3 each bettered their first attempts with their next 2 balls, none of them was able to inch inside Byron's 1st effort. Thus, after 3 holes, only Lloyd was still 'shut out.'

When I recollect that sunny day, it's hardly fair of me to characterize Demaret as the most "natty" as though he'd out-dressed the others. Yes, Jimmy's outfit was the 'loudest' by far, with his strawberry-colored shirt and vermillion slacks, but both Hogan and Mangrum were renowned for the razor-sharp creases of their expensive trousers as well as the pristine shirts and sweaters they favored to give the impression of an ultra-cool customer.

Top that with Ben's signature cap and tall Lloyd's bare-headed majesty -- his dark locks center-parted and luxurious; his thin mustache Errol-Flynnish – and each man would have been courted by Nike. Only humble Nelson trailed in this pack, his no-nonsense browns and less-tailored clothes not particularly eye-catching. Nor could his recessive eyes or shy smile compete with the 'movie-star looks' of his 3 rivals. Yet when it came to striking a golf ball I'd have put Byron up – even after 5 years of ranching – against any other naked man …

As though to reward my faith in him, Mr. Golf 'went on a tear' the next 3 holes (4,5,6). He won them all with shots respectively 3 feet, 17 inches, and finally 2 inches from the cup on number 6. His winner on number 4 was another straight dart – this time with a 5-iron to a front-left pin placement. The shot seemed other worldly the way Byron made that middle iron stop dead' after a single bounce and dribble, the ball played to one of Cedar Crest's tabletop greens!

And on the 5th hole, normally a drive-and-pitch-4, Nelson's driver-play from the 260-yard tees we'd set up not only finished inside 2 feet, it lipped out of the cup. So, naturally he had to better that effort when faced with 'only' a 185-yard carry from real tee boxes on the par-3 6th.

Uh-huh. But hitting that 3-iron to 2 inches – with him doing so on his first try. Yikes! His rivals had seen about enough of this Mr. Golfing, while the fans who didn't have money on the other 3 were screaming for more.

During the Texas Quartet's walk toward the green, I heard Lloyd gripe at him, and it was hard to tell whether Mr. Icicle was trying to be comical or not. "Christ, Nelson, you've got to stop begging that God of yours for help every shot. It's not sporting!"

It was hard to know whether Mr. Icicle's profane jibe had 'gotten to' Byron, but on the next hole the frontrunner did slice his first 4-iron almost onto Southerland Avenue, and his second and third attempts stayed well left of the center-cut pin. That left the fight to Ben and Lloyd, Jimmy continuing to have trouble with his distance control.

Hogan, playing second did carve a fade to 6 feet from the cup on his final try, using the northern breeze to make his ball stop quickly. It was a lovely shot. But Lloyd, following immediately thereafter, reckoned to get close by instead floating with the wind. He hit his customary draw but one aimed actually right of the putting surface and played with a 5-iron instead of a 4-. His ball landed front-right and scooted along the green, not stopping 'til it lay inside 3 feet from the hole … a masterful play. That success made the score: Nelson 4; the others 1 apiece.

The rest of round 1 was tightly contested – by 3 of the 4 competitors, with most winning blows settling close to the cups. Meanwhile, poor Jimmy was barely 'finding' some of the greens though given 3 tries. They must have looked like thumbtacks to him by then.

Having 1 hole left to play that Saturday, Byron had won 4 more to raise his total to 8 points, while Ben and Lloyd had matched each other in accumulating four closest-to-the-pins of their own, Demaret still stuck on 1. And so, as we approached the last temporary tee box, there was a palpable air of desperation among players – and bettors both – that Mr. Golf should not be allowed to pull 5 points ahead!

Thus, I Bobby Shout was hardly shocked to hear an audible groan when the picking of straws left Byron Nelson again with the last try at the target, in this case an 8-iron away to the raised last green, featuring a pin practically off the rear center of the sizable putting surface.

Of course, these guys could 'nail' an '8' on line all day but the uncertainty facing them was whether a lofted shot would 'spin back' down that putting surface's slick slope, or stick? And some of us hoped that Jimmy Demaret's skill at skipping a low-trajectory shot – no matter the club's loft – the required distance might stand him in good stead here. Since the Wardrobe had 'the honor' on the 18th, we would soon see.

However, on his first try Jimmy elected to send his red-striped ball as skyward as he could, testing to see whether such a shot could prevail. The answer proved "no."

Even his ultra-high iron which 'bit' a yard from the cup only stayed there momentarily before sliding almost twenty feet below the hole. When the 'herald' at the green called out the official distance as 19' 7" I recorded that number on my score sheet as I'd done for the previous potential winning shots that afternoon. You didn't reckon I was just remembering all the distances I've been citing, did you?

Ben, I saw, chose a 7-iron instead, and declined to use a peg. His ultra-smooth, gripped-down swing this time produced a lower shot. Though we couldn't see where it ended up, the crowd's excitement declared that Hogan had succeeded in skipping his ball close: "Six feet two inches" was the call. And, though Lloyd on his second try – and Byron on his last – gave the Hawk's backers a scare, that 6' 2" 'held up.'

That left Ben 3 points behind Mr. Golf, while Lloyd was 4 back; poor humiliated Jimmy 7 down and seemingly 'out of it.' I imagined that the Wardrobe would be 'the life of the party' at the banquet that night for sure now. Would he 'tie one on' to the point of embarrassment? I prayed not.

The Saturday night affair was held at the old Steerman's Club. Fortunately, it was not my chore to act as master of ceremonies there as well, though I did get to sit at the 'head table' along with our Texas Quartet and the other oil bigwigs. In fact, my momma was sitting up there beside me which added appreciably to the pleasure of the occasion.

Among the notes which I Bobby Shout penned on an extra cocktail napkin – the eating napkins were fine linen and so 'out of bounds' – were my ratings of the food. Both the steak and Gulf shrimp proved first rate, but the pecan pie was a bit gummy for my taste. I should add that the banquet committee had placed Byron Nelson on my other side, so I got to quiz him a bit about the match thus far. And yes, that cocktail napkin has stayed in my possession, the ink still legible though the paper has yellowed.

It had been decided that each of our famous foursome would 'get to say a few words' to the elite Texan audience in attendance, their little speeches to be made between the dinner and dessert courses. And, for this mini event, we had reckoned that the most loquacious and entertaining speaker Jimmy Demaret should go last so as not to leave any of his 'drier' rivals -- in every way! -- having to follow him at the podium.

Byron had been selected to go first, as he figured to speak with grace no matter how his day had gone. He wasn't apt to say anything memorable, but nothing off-key either. It was our hope that both Lloyd and Ben, at times waspish public speakers, then might follow Mr. Golf's cue.

As a sample of Byron's tone, I did manage to scribble this from his opening remarks: "And, I want to thank the organizers for giving me the chance to compete again against 3 such great golfers. Today was good to me, but I'm sure one of those boys will put on a winning show tomorrow …" There was no false humility in what he said. Nelson saw the world realistically – ego in check -- and those words he uttered encompassed his true assessment of things. He wasn't figuring to outlast both Hogan and Mangrum.

However, I could tell that Mr. Icicle was hardly so sanguine about Mr. Golfer's 'rust' making him an easy target on the morrow. Looking at times toward our end of the head table, ole Lloyd had joked, "Well, partners, I'm not generally a betting man" – loud guffaws followed.

"Still, if anybody's willing to give me decent odds that a certain broken-down rancher's not gonna win this thing, I'll be meeting yah in the men's room after the dessert. Or better yet, at the bar, drinks on me" – more laughs. I was just grateful that the riverboat gambler hadn't 'let out' a string of oaths nor baited Byron further with any "God's help" talk. *Okay, Ben,* I'd urged inside. *Play nice …*

The Hawk's side of the table wasn't visible from my perch, but I would have bet that he rose stiffly to his feet after that extended sit, before limping over to the center podium. It was good of him to be here, I'd realized. His body no doubt was aching and he was surely 'dying' to get into a hot bath. Instead, he'd shown up here, probably for the most part because the audience included invited military brass. Ben did have a sterling streak of patriotism in his fiber.

"I'm hurting a bit tonight," he'd begun – a startling confession from that man. "But let's be clear. Anybody who can still play golf has suffered nothing compared with many of the vets we're fixing to aid through this exhibition. It don't matter a bit which of us four comes out on top tomorrow, so long as the money we're raising helps a lot of war veterans to win back their lives. So, every one of you 'big shots' here – be generous in adding to the kitty. Thank you."

Hogan had worked his magic again. In spite of his blunt tone, the Hawk's words would probably be responsible for our collecting thousands of dollars more this weekend. I'll admit I clapped and hooted just as hard as the rest of the folks in the house when he'd finished. Where he and I stood was 'small potatoes' by contrast. I got that now. However, I Bobby Shout knew damn well that "this exhibition" did matter plenty to Ben as much as to his 3 rivals.

At this juncture, I suppose a lot of folks were thinking, *What is there left for Jimmy Demaret to say?* It occurred to me that he might just sing us a song and leave it there. But no, the Wardrobe had already had 'a few too many' for that.

Seeing Jimmy lurch toward the center podium, twice having to steady himself with a hand on others' shoulders below him, I really began to fear the worst. The man was definitely 'the worse for wear.' Well, he did make it there and then stood saying nothing, giving the audience only a drunken grin. They couldn't help but laugh.

Finally, Jimmy held up his hand for quiet, his listeners already 'in his hands.' "Speaking of aches and pains," he began. "You-all know that I'm older than these other guys, right?" At forty he was a mere 2 years more ancient than Ben or Byron. "Why, when I was young Lloyd's age, I was on top of the heap out on Tour, too." Not quite true: The Wardrobe's last big year had been 1947 when he'd turned 37 in May; Mangrum was 36 as Jimmy spoke.

"These days my left shoulder feels like it's about to fall off at times. One-armed golf is hard, man!" An uneasy buzz had started in the crowd. "In fact, I wasn't gonna come up to Dallas, except I thought they said I could hit from the ladies tees. Well maybe they will tomorrow." Jimmy had gotten a laugh, but there was an undercurrent of shock, too, at his excuse-making. A Texan just didn't do that!

He must have sensed this ambivalence 'cause the Wardrobe changed direction masterfully. "Before I put my big butt back in a chair, I'd like to share this song with you. Yeah, uh dedicating it to all of our military veterans in the great Lone Star State."

In his best crooner's voice, Demaret began the old spiritual updated by the Swing Band leader Harry James a few years earlier. *"Nobody knows the trouble I've seen ... Nobody knows my sorrow ... Nobody knows the trouble I've seen ... Glory hallelujah. / Sometimes I'm up, sometimes I'm down ... Oh yes Lord ... Sometimes I'm almost to the ground ... Oh yes Lord."*

When Jimmy jumped back to *"Nobody knows the trouble I've seen ..."* it seemed like half the crowd joined him in that verse. And upon the song ending, when he added, "Let's help every vet in this state to feel 'up' again," the cheers that erupted were obviously heartfelt. I actually felt my eyes water, grateful that this man who'd been a friend to so many had found a way to hold onto their admiration this night, in spite of his current mawkish mood.

Well I reckoned right then that the evening's emotional 'highs' had played out, and this was fine because our speakers' collective effect was bound to inspire greater gift-giving for our vets. It turned out though that I Bobby Shout was as wrong as a 2-headed chicken in 1 respect ...

With the crowd gone and my duties as one of the banquet's organizers done, I'd headed out the door ready for bed. Only there in the parking lot perched Lloyd Mangrum leaning against my new car. The first thing he called out to me was "Whoa, boy, you better 'hold your horses' with this beast. Oil business must be real good, huh?"

His words embarrassed me a bit, but I was proud of my 1950 Pontiac Super Deluxe Catalina coupe with its gleaming green body, white hardtop and matching whitewall tires. Trying to sound as folksy cool as him, I answered. "Hell, Lloyd,

I've got 2 other cars as fine as this, back in my garage." But he only chuckled not believing my tale for a second.

As fatigued as I was, it was with mild dread that I awaited his next words, praying that he wasn't going to drag me off to some big-time card game. This scenario though was far from what he had in mind.

"Listen, Bobby," he began in a joking tone, "I know you're not as young as me" – when actually he was 6 years my senior -- "and late nights ain't your thing. I can respect that. So I'm only here to take up a few minutes of your time. Then you can head right home to that pillow of yours…"

The note of unease beneath his bantering speech was not lost on me and I spoke quickly to help him uncoil. "No, ah it's fine. What can I do for you?"

Mr. Icicle's shoulders relaxed a tad as he motioned back toward the restaurant and said, "Well, my humble chariot's right over there. I'd like you to listen to something."

Dense me was puzzling over what could be so important on the radio that night, when we reached his rented vehicle and I saw one of the new fancy tape recorders sitting on the front passenger seat. Of course! He was fixing to have me hear 'him' – his recorded thoughts.

Lloyd grabbed the equipment, explaining that he'd arranged for one of the small private rooms inside the club. *Oh yeah*, I reminded myself. *We do need an electrical receptacle to power the machine.* It was both scary and stimulating – wondering what I was going to hear, with him listening right there too. Would Dr. Shout be up to the challenge? We'd find out soon enough.

Having gotten the recorder ready to go, Lloyd seemed uncertain what to say first, then mumbled "What the hell," and briefed me about a haunting episode that happened to him during the Battle of the Bulge, World War II's biggest European contest.

"Well boy," he'd begun. "After recovering from a smashed-up shoulder courtesy of a flipped jeep, I was serving under 'Old Blood and Guts' – that was General Patton – in his 3rd Army's 90th Infantry regiment during December of '44. And let me tell you, that man was a maniac when it came to wanting to get in the fight. He pushed us hard up through France and into southern Belgium where the action had started a week earlier in this dense, snow-clogged forest they called Ardenne."

Lloyd explained that their first order had been to beat back the Germans who had the town of Bastogne under siege. "Well, we took care of that in day. If anybody had told me then that we'd be fighting in that frozen hell for nearly a month more, I would have punched him in his goddamn nose."

He told me to picture endless sharp hills and ravines, every one packed with snowy evergreens forcing frequent detours … all the time white stuff coming down most days, mixed with deadly fire from the air – such was Ardenne. His harsh voice softening, Mr. Icicle had concluded, "That's where they decided I earned my first Purple Heart and Battle Stars, but you judge from this part I've cued up." Then he pressed the 'on' button.

As I'd instructed him, Lloyd started his recorded thoughts on that day by giving the date. It was September 13th. Mr. Icicle's voice sounded a bit shaky, even at the start of the episode he was about to recount.

"At one-five-zero-nine hours on December 30 1944, I was out on recon with a corporal named Mike Riley. He was driving the jeep; I was telling him where to go, using a compass. Our maps were pretty useless in that forest." At this point a small sigh erupted on the tape. Then Staff Sergeant Mangrum – his rank at the time – continued his narration.

"It was then that we heard the cries of wounded men – ours – off to the right through the trees. I ordered Mike to stay with the vehicle – it needed defending – and I made my way through some drifting snowflakes toward the sounds, my heart pounding like a big bass drum."

I looked up at Mr. Icicle at this moment. His mind was definitely locked in on that memory, both fists clenched, the tape recorder still rolling.

"The first guy I came to was bleeding bad from his neck. As I was hefting him onto my back, a rifle-shot rang out and I felt a stinging in my knee. I laughed if you can believe it. What do they call it? Gallows humor? Some sniper! – barely gave me a flesh wound with that first shot, though I reckoned he'd make up for it with his second. Still, the blood was pouring out of me … Why the hell he didn't keep firing – who knows?

"So, I'm fighting a case of shock, and luckily I had my own footprints in the snow to get me going back in the right direction. But just as I began to move, there's another wounded man close to us who lifts his arm while croaking out a call for help. I grabbed him with my free hand and began half-dragging him while still carrying the first soldier. Then, I let go of the second guy after about twenty feet. Couldn't do it. My hand was freezing, the rest of me losing all oomph fast. "I'll be back for you, buddy," I told him.

"After it seemed like an hour I was able to dump the first guy in the jeep.

"Right away Mike shouts 'What are you doing?' as I start to retrace my steps.

"When I answered 'There are other wounded,' he said that hell, we had to go back pronto just to get the first guy to the medics or he'd never make it. I was pretty wobbly by then … Still, I was the ranking officer. We heard a tank coming. Didn't wait around to see whose. Back at camp, I gave my captain the best directions I could about getting to the others. By then it was snowing harder. He sent out a patrol. They didn't find any of them though. Another day of shitty war luck …"

My nerves jumped like a chased jackrabbit when Sergeant Mangrum jabbed the 'off' button on the recorder at that point. But, I demanded to myself to be strong for him.

He began, now with that sarcastic grin of his, "Okay, Dr. Shout, here's the deal: I don't know why but something about you seems trustworthy. So, I want you to tell me the real truth, you hear? Was ole Lloyd a lowdown varmint for taking those medals after fuckin' leaving his brother soldiers behind? Couldn't I have helped that second guy somehow to our jeep … if I'd been tougher, or smarter, or something, dammit! In my sleep I see his eyes at the moment I dumped him and it's horrible – for him! Oh shit, all right I'm gonna stop jabbering. Speak."

I'd never seen the riverboat gambler anything like this. The humility and angst was so palpable it moved me to do something I'd never have imagined; I put my hand on his shoulder – and just as surprising – he let it stay.

To tell the truth I was struggling not to cry by then --he wasn't – as I mumbled how I'd met quite a few soldiers suffering similar guiltiness when in fact each one had tried harder than anyone could rightfully ask. "Oh Jesus, Lloyd, I bet that second guy in his heart thanked you for at least clutching onto him as best you could for as long as you could. You were the last kindness in his life. So, no, those medals were properly earned by you, along with as much peace of mind as you can muster. I'm honored to be your friend …"

Leaning away from me then, back in his tough shell, Mr. Icicle had answered. "Okay, Bobby, playtime is over. Thanks a lot, bud."

No, it was not a stellar end to the emotional pitch we'd reached just seconds before. Lloyd was hard to read. But I had to trust that I'd given this hard-bitten man perhaps a little gleam of self-healing. He did treat me well whenever we crossed paths thereafter, which had to mean something, right? Well onto the next day and the climax of the Sharpshooters Invitational …

On Sunday it was already over 80 degrees when I left my church following the early service which ended at 10:30. With the temperature expected to reach 90 by 3 p.m. I was glad that the breeze was supposed to also reach its maximum of around 15 miles-per-hour around then.

Over at Cedar Crest, I found all to be in order for the players to begin their warm-up around noon with a tee-off time of 1 p.m. One question which nagged me though was whether Jimmy Demaret would show up at all. There was no telling when he'd gotten to bed after no doubt making the rounds of the hottest night spots the Big-D had to offer. Had he gotten back to his hotel before or after dawn?

So who was it who slapped me on the back from behind not long after these musings in Cedar's clubhouse – Mr. Wardrobe himself! Though bleary-eyed, Jimmy still greeted me with a hale and hearty smile. And as if he needed to explain his early appearance, Jimmy gushed, "If anyone needs some extra practice this morning it's me, partner."

I was proud of him. He could certainly make good use of the $1,000 4th-place check but Demaret was hardly desperate for such a sum. Some pros would have slunk out of town after claiming a new injury, if having performed as badly as Jimmy had the previous day. But here he was, willing to risk further humiliation for a good cause. "Thanks, Jimmy," I knew was all I should say, and did. He nodded, then hurried off to his task after another of his witty self-barbs. *Please let him do well today,* I Bobby Shout prayed again.

After observing some of the day's employment demos and workshops we had going in the large rented tents from 11 a.m. to noon, I reckoned it was time to get out to the practice area myself after 'hitting the head.' However, a surprising development caused me to delay a bit longer.

In Cedar Crest's clubhouse at the time there was a small 'cards room' off the corridor that ran from the cramped men's locker room to the building's rear exit. As I started to pass its open door, my attention was jolted bringing me to a quick stop. There arising from the only table occupied in the room was – of all people -- Ben Hogan. I say "of all people" because I knew the Hawk to be more religious about his pre-round routine than he'd ever been about going to church. Hogan always – always – had himself on the practice range by 1 hour prior to his tee-off time. And, today that was 1 o'clock, but here it was already 12:10 and there he was, giving a nod goodbye to 3 men at the table, each somewhat younger than me.

When his eyes met mine, the Hawk's blue-gray orbs uncharacteristically seemed to convey some slight guilt in fact, and he even gave me (who was chained 'in his doghouse') a weak wave before striding stone-faced out of the room. As Ben's golf spikes told of his departure down the hallway and into the daylight, I spent that time introducing myself and getting the threesome's names back in turn. Then I could wait no more.

"Looks like you guys were having a nice chat with Mr. Hogan," I stated, hoping that they'd 'open up' to me, so curious was I as to what the heck the Hawk was thinking, departing from his routine this way. They grinned back with enthusiasm, but none said anything at first, so I prodded some more. "You're vets, right? Did he ask about your experiences?"

"Oh, no," one of them replied, baby-faced. "It was awkward at first – him standing there silently watching us play gin -- but Mr. Hogan wanted to give us something."

Yes, yes, I prompted the guy without speaking. *What?!*

Another of the threesome – this one a handsome son-of-a-gun – 'took up the story' relating how Ben had finally asked whether any of them were golfers. "I play some, but as Rick here told him, the equipment ain't cheap and we're all busy trying to make a buck in civilian life."

Baby-face resumed his narration at that point, saying with some awe in his voice, "Then, Mr. Hogan sat right there and pulled out some golf tees from his pocket. He borrowed my pen and wrote on the head of each peg his initials. While handing a tee to each of us, he said that he was fixing to start up a golf-club factory right in Fort Worth – probably within a year or two – and if we brought him back our tees he'd set us up with a full set for free! Ain't that something?"

What could I do but agree? Ben had trumped my limited expectations of him again. Before leaving the room at least I was able to make myself feel a bit better by answering their puzzlement about the letters "WBH" which the Hawk had written upon their tees. "His actual name is William Benjamin Hogan," I informed them. And, they seemed to treat this intel with all the seriousness that they might a military secret. Nearing the practice area, I had to chuckle.

Still, years later I could not cease debating the relevant impact of the fact that our event required no putting practice. Did that lack of need provide Ben with some peace of mind as he arrived 'late' at the practice ground that Sunday? Or did he feel like he'd sinned? I Bobby Shout of course could no longer ask him, following our 'break.'

That second 18 of the Sharpshooters Invitational began smoothly enough, though it would degenerate into outrageous commotion later. When Demaret hit a 3-iron from the pushed-back Sunday tee and won the 1st hole again – this time with a legitimately good shot – my hopes leapt for him to make a respectable showing. However, though Jimmy did hit some 'darts' fairly close to the cups several times afterwards, it happened that one of his rivals always hit one tighter, with the exception of Cedar Crest's par-3 9th where they were all 'firing wedges in' that day.

Thus the Wardrobe, swathed in shades of purple for Sunday, remained a non-factor in the match, while the other 3 seemed to be winning holes in a regular rotation. On the front 9, Ben had upped his total from 5 to 8 points; Byron, from 8 to 10; and Lloyd, from 4 to only 6, leaving Mr. Icicle in dire need of a 'hot streak.' He did not disappoint.

At the Crest', the back side started with its number 1 handicap hole, a long '4' crossing a creek to be carried just shy of the raised, kidney-bean green. We on the 'greens committee' had decided to make this the toughest shot of the day for our Texas Quartet as well. They needed to hit driver, and somehow strike their balls high and soft enough to 'hold' a firm putting surface. Only Lloyd Mangrum managed this challenge twice, and his second success, though 32 feet beyond the cup took the prize.

Then he followed that win by 'drilling' a 4-wood into a hostile breeze so well on the 200-plus par-3 11th that his gold-striped ball settled a mere 4 feet away.

Having gained a 2ⁿᵈ straight point, Mr. Icicle had now tied Hogan at 8 – just 2 behind Nelson with 7 left to play.

Alas for Lloyd, on the 12ᵗʰ hole where we'd asked the guys to hit a 6-iron to a narrow front portion of the putting surface -- threatened by twin bunkers -- his best effort was excellent, but not good enough. Byron came through with another perfect strike, his ball 'sucking back' downhill to 4 inches from the cup, easily besting Mangrum's shot to a foot-and-a-half.

It was shortly thereafter that I saw Mr. Icicle again 'getting in the ear' of Mr. Golf as the two trailed Hogan and Demaret toward the 13ᵗʰ tee. But when I asked Byron a couple of minutes later as to what was said, he just shook his head at me. Not good!

This next par-4 featured a rather featureless green, a bit narrow but protected by only a single bunker. We'd decided to give the crowd a real thrill, expecting that the guys would 'stuff' several shots real close if given a tee at only a 9-iron's length from the cup. Perhaps they'd even produce an ace!

After Hogan and Mangrum 'warmed up' with first attempts slightly inside 10 feet, the former Mr. Golf once again electrified the folks in attendance with another shot that 'never left the pin.' His ball in fact landed 2 inches to the right of the hole and stopped dead, right in its pitch mark somehow.

When the hoots had 'died down' and while Jimmy was still waving a towel of surrender in Byron's face, Lloyd suddenly could be heard by us around the tee speaking in a 'stage whisper' to Mrs. Louise Nelson. And, his words were also electrifying.

"Damn," he cussed. "Will you kindly remind that husband of yours that this is a goddamned exhibition and he should be a sport. The crowd don't want to see a shitty runaway; they want it tight right down to the end!"

Louise of course didn't know what to say. She just stared at him aghast 'til Byron broke the spell, grabbing Mr. Icicle by the arm while growling, "That filthy mouth of yours is gonna get you into trouble, Lloyd." After a strained pause, that good Christian man added in a more conciliatory tone, "Please, it's Sunday."

Ever cool, the man who'd fought at the Battle of the Bulge patted Nelson's reddened face in response, real gentle pats, replying, "Sorry. No offense meant, partner. Just stating the obvious." Then he'd strolled back to the center of the tee.

Two attempts later, Ben Hogan made his own statement the way he knew best. The Hawk's 3ʳᵈ shot went into the hole on the fly and stayed there, putting him once again only 2 points back of Nelson – now with 5 holes left. Or, so we thought ...

On Cedar Crest's next hole, normally the longest '5' on the course, Lloyd did get his wish about giving the fans a tighter match, though it came at his expense. You see, Mr. Icicle looked to be 'a lock' with his gold-striped ball sitting 5 feet from the rear pin on that 14th where the guys were hitting 1-irons in, and only Hogan had another shot coming.

Apologies to my fellow Texan Lee Trevino, but I knew someone who was great with a 1-iron, even if 'God couldn't hit that club.' When Ben swung his, I had a feeling it would be special. His blue-striped ball faded ever so lightly on its way to a roll-up nearly in the hole. Only 6 inches shy of the cup, the Hawk's win there put him at 10 points now, only a single point behind Byron. And Lloyd? This 'robbery' meant he needed to 'run the table' over the final 4 holes to guarantee a win.

Alas, it was not to be for Mr. Icicle. His best again was second best when Nelson's 5-iron into the breeze beat him out by a foot on the 15th, leaving the former Mr. Golf 4 points ahead of Lloyd with 3 to play. Still, competitive frustration could NOT excuse what happened next.

Completely uncharacteristic of the usually stoic Mangrum in competition, Lloyd once again resorted to some unwelcome theatrics with his mouth. I Bobby Shout was shocked along with many others around the tee box upon hearing that debonair riverboat gambler turned-sore-loser vent after he grabbed my megaphone away. "My fellow vets," he'd boomed. "I'm sorry. We tried to get Byron to 'ease up' so you'd get a thrilling finish, but you know how it is with those fucking 4-F-ers; they never serve."

Oh my gosh! I looked then at Byron, his face as agonized as if a fatal bleeding ulcer *had* begun. The megaphone back in my grasp, I offered it to him figuring he'd want to reply to the crowd. But no, instead the former Mr. Golf hissed at me, "That's as much profaning of the Sabbath as I can stand for 1 day, Bobby. I'm leaving – withdrawing … Louise, we're going home."

Hey, what was I to do? Reckoning that the mass of spectators needed to know what was going on – though I could have, probably should have – waited 'til Byron and Louise and his caddy had left before giving my explanation, I broadcast that Mr. Nelson could no longer continue in the competition and by rule would be awarded the 4th-place prize.

This announcement did not go down well of course with those who'd bet on the former Mr. Golf. There were scattered boos in Byron's direction and he was jostled by 1 disappointed gambler who shouted, "Get back there!" before our security guys intervened.

Still on the tee box, we watched this play out, each of us stunned I think. It did get my attention that Jimmy with his massive forearms had a firm grip on Lloyd. If Mr. Icicle had had any inclination to go after Nelson and urge him back – or to join in his mistreatment – Demaret wasn't taking any chances, I guessed.

Leave it to Ben to be the first to get back to business. He growled to me, "Are we moving on to 16 or not?"

I Bobby Shout could only nod at first, then suddenly I was shouting into the megaphone that the match would now continue. We moved, the fans moved, and a chaotic buzz continued around the central players in this drama right up to the moment I called for quiet when Jimmy with the first shot stepped forward to hit.

A 9-iron in hand, Demaret faced a flag placed near the very front of the wide, shallow, raised putting surface. Again it was a matter of getting just the right amount of backspin: too little and the ball would bound above the hole; too much, and the shot would tumble down off the green.

That Jimmy's head was not 'back in the game' yet became apparent soon enough. His first attempt was 'fatted' and reached only halfway up the fronting slope. Each of the Wardrobe's second and third attempts were long compensations for his first miss.

In between Demaret's tries, Lloyd too seemed off,' though he gave no indication of hearing the smattering of boos each time he teed up. Only Hogan 'stuck' his shots as close as one would expect, winning the point twice over. The crowd applauded his efforts, but with hardly the fervor we'd felt before Byron's departure.

The 17th, where the committee had chosen to use this par-3's back tee on Sunday, played out no differently. Ben hit his 3-irons 'tight'; the other two, sprayed them. Though it was now academic, Hogan had in fact tied Nelson's point total at 12. Would he surpass the former Mr. Golf on the final hole? I could hear impromptu bets being made as we walked. The gamblers who thought that the Hawk was 'a lock' to get that 13th point were forced to give steep odds. I wondered about that.

You see, we'd placed the pin halfway back but well left on the putting surface so that the cup was in line with a deep front bunker. And, with a driver needed to 'carry' this hazard on any shot directed toward the target, the incoming trajectories would be too low to 'bite' sufficiently. That is, any shot hit straight at the hole had no chance of stopping 'til reaching the back edge of the green or beyond!

Thus, the player who could 'craft' a draw to land short of the right front of the green and spin leftward toward the flag stood the best chance of getting close. This was Lloyd's 'baby' not Ben's, but we'd just have to see. One thing was for sure – I knew that Hogan being Hogan would want that win badly – exhibition or not! While Mangrum would get a great deal of satisfaction in thwarting him, their relationship being stone cold! As for Jimmy, he was friends with both – no surprise. Was he hungry for at least *one* good showing on this back 9? I was dubious, considering his body language.

By lot, it would be Ben hitting first, followed by Lloyd, then Jimmy each round. On his first try, Hogan did try his classic fade shot, but by having to start his drive left of the green, the Hawk paid a price. When his curved shot failed to move enough, the ball struck on the left side-bank of the putting surface and bounced farther leftward, heading downhill.

Whereas Lloyd, as I'd anticipated, had an easier time, sending his shot toward the generous, right side of the large green. Only the fact that he'd made too pure a hooking strike foiled him, his ball winding up almost directly behind the cup but 30 feet past it.

And Jimmy? He hit maybe the highest drive I'd ever seen him execute – and right at the flag – but it lacked the oomph to carry over the front bunker. He'd have to try another approach.

On round 2, the Hawk still stuck with his fade and managed to land it on the cropped surface left of the hole as needed. However, the combination of fade spin and a downward slope from the mounded spot where we'd placed the pin sent his ball about 40 feet right of the cup. Not a winner. Meanwhile, Mr. Icicle was homing in, placing his second drawn shot to 15 feet. And Jimmy, 'out of the blue,' managed a low hook that followed Mangrum's path but did not stop 'til his ball expired inside 10 feet. I was thrilled. He needed this victory for his psyche, far more than his rivals did.

Trying to 'pump up' the crowd 1 final time, I broadcast these words: "Now then, will that red-striped ball on the green withstand the coming assault by his blue- and gold-striped foes, or not? Let's see." I know, a bit corny yet the crowd did cry out in response.

Then Ben said in effect, "Enough of this," and switched to a draw as well, executing it so masterfully that his effort made it all the way to 3 feet from the cup. His fans were ecstatic; the other factions subdued – until a voice rang out as Lloyd prepared to hit, "Go back to L.A., you damn traitor!" (Of course, he meant a traitor to Texas, by settling elsewhere.) The upshot of this rudeness was a whole range of insults passed back and forth between the fans, with not a few scuffles 'breaking out' as well. It took ten full minutes before order was restored and Mr. Icicle could take his turn, yet what a turn it was!

Lloyd swung with his usual elegant rhythm, his motion an intentional mimicry of Snead's, right down to the squatting downswing. His ball once again was 'drawing,' its landing spot the required turf short-right of the putting surface. Then Lloyd's driver-shot spun sideways and began a leftward curve toward the pin.

As one, we spectators seemed to be holding our breath 'til – as it became apparent the ball might go in – a roar of anticipation sprung from the crowd. What could be crueler, what happened next?

The L.A. traitor's ball, seemingly like a putt, 'caught' the high edge of the hole and did what was later to be termed 'a power lip-out.' Though Lloyd's shot had been slowing the last few feet to the cup, nevertheless it was slung, partly by gravity, a full 4 feet below the hole, leaving Mr. Icicle with a great shot but no winner. Ben's effort to 3 feet still ruled!

Could Jimmy, having the last shot of the Sharpshooter's Invitational, produce even more drama? I pictured his red-striper striking Ben's ball and shoving it outside both his and Lloyd's efforts, but it did not happen. In fact, the Wardrobe's attempt at a hooking shot this time was 'over-cooked,' his ball winding up a sad thing in the front bunker.

Thus, strictly speaking, Ben Hogan had won the competition outright, his final total being 13 points to Byron's aborted 12, with 8 for Lloyd, and Jimmy a measly 3 -- accounting for all 36 points available. Still, who could say whether or not Byron might have bettered the Hawk's total if the former Mr. Golf had competed fully? It was obvious that the crowd had this in mind, judging from the hollow atmosphere in the air as we commenced the awards ceremony.

I hoped that our spectators 'might warm up' upon seeing the giant cardboard checks that were being brought out at this moment. It turned out though that Lone Star sportsmanship at its finest was about to 'save the day'!

This surprising turn-of-events commenced as soon as I'd handed Jimmy his 3rd-place check for $1,500. Lloyd put a hand on the cardboard thing and said, "Sorry, pard, I think that's mine. Ben and Byron beat my number. That makes me 3rd."

It took the Wardrobe only a second to grasp what Mangrum was getting at. "Well, Lloyd, if you're willing to drop from 2nd to 3rd money, I guess I'm 'game.' Bobby, hustle me up that 4th-place check before I change my mind." Laughter all around.

Wow, had they caught me off guard. But the sounds of approval growing in our gallery had me thinking, *the heck with that silly forfeit rule we'd concocted!* I glanced at the other committee folks and could tell that we were 'on the same page.'

So, Jimmy got his last-place money and Mr. Icicle 3rd, but what about Hogan? He could claim to have beaten Byron. Was he expecting the $5,000 1st prize and no guff?

William Benjamin Hogan took the megaphone from me at that moment. "Folks, if I can't beat a man face-to-face, then I didn't win. Byron Nelson deserves the trophy and the biggest check, and I don't want to see a single sign of discord out there among you because of this. Is that clear?"

The respectful silence that met what was not really a question but rather a command from the one-and-only Hawk gave me chills. He stepped over to where the 2nd-place check for $2,500 was leaning against a chair and took it. Then he motioned to his caddy – Valerie absent on the course as usual – and that twosome started for the clubhouse.

"Ben," I cried. "We need you for a photograph!" You know, the 3 winners with their checks. He just gave a slight wave with the back of his hand, never turning around nor stopping. I Bobby Shout improvised. "Okay guys – golfers and media – we'll get those shots inside." And, off we all hustled, trying to get to Ben in the locker room before he changed his shoes.

Meanwhile, ahead of us in the crowd, Hogan was receiving nothing but calls of adulation as he made his way. It was a lesson to me again that Ben was like a golfing god to most people connected with our game. And currently, I could count on nothing from that deity but the 'evil eye.'

That night, back in my lonely home with a drink in hand, I tried to shake my dazed self into making a phone call. But, who should I telephone?

I was aching to know whether Lloyd Mangrum felt any remorse by now over his cruel remarks to and about Byron. And, if Mr. Icicle was feeling repentant, perhaps I could help him see a way to resolve the bitterness he'd expressed. But alas, perhaps Lloyd, with his money-oriented gambler persona, felt that he had already made things right with Nelson by starting the momentum that led to the former Mr. Golf getting the fattest prize? If so, I didn't reckon I'd have the energy to oppose this viewpoint in a constructive manner.

Then there was Jimmy Demaret. How much boosting was he in need of tonight after his dismal 2 days? Well heck, how would I even find him by phone? He was no doubt at some party place, and moreover probably not nearly sober enough to have a real conversation. No the Wardrobe would have to wait.

Calling Ben Hogan seemed to me the most foolhardy thought of all. Even if I praised him to the skies for his generous gesture to Byron, I knew that the Hawk's response would be cold, rigid, and brusque to me, being Bobby Shout, 'Lloyd's lackey' in his eyes.

Thus, I reached for my address book to find Byron's number. However, I'm sorry to say, that was as far as I got. My weary mind came up with a couple of excuses: First off, it wasn't necessary for me to tell him what had transpired after he'd left, seeing how someone else had most likely informed him already by word of mouth. On top of that, the Nelsons probably got an evening paper at the ranch and certainly a morning one.

Wouldn't it be better to let Byron recover from the day's shocks and the news of his strange win before approaching him about the check I had to deliver? Well, that's what I told myself before finishing the scotch and dropping off to sleep in my living-room lounger, too tired to find my bed.

At noon on Monday, October 23rd – the birthday of my future wife-to-be – I was still dozing, stalling about calling Byron Nelson for some reason. Being MIA from the office, I also needed to call work first to let them know when I'd be in. That chore done, I had my cereal and juice before dialing the ranch.

It was Louise who picked up. My heart fluttered for an instant, hopeful that Byron was out, but she responded that he was close by and went to get him. Waiting, I told myself to sound bright. After all, he had won five grand in the end.

The former Mr. Golf sounded far from chipper, however, when he greeted me with, "Yeah, Bobby, I thought you'd call."

Did he know what had transpired? That his rivals had crowned him the big winner? I asked that good Christian man and he'd responded, again in a flat voice, how he had heard. I asked Byron next whether Lloyd's shenanigans had spoiled the whole thing for him, hoping in my heart that he'd answer me in the negative, since his sterling performance was bound to lead to some exhibitions in '51, I figured.

He said instead in his high-pitched drawl, "Well, some pigs aren't very pretty, no matter how much they're worth at market."

What do I say to that?! I Bobby Shout asked myself in a panic. My counseling skills seemed dried up at that moment. So, I inquired whether he'd like me to mail his check or deliver it to him.

Nelson paused, like he was looking for a polite way to tell me to shove it, but then inquired, "It's probably already made out to me for the $5,000, huh?"

When I responded "Yes" – though I actually wasn't sure – he asked whether I'd mind dropping it off the next day, and I answered that I certainly would be happy to – really relieved that Byron would take the check. Also on my mind was that this trip would give me the chance perhaps to ease his mind on the 4-F front; remember I too had wound up with that draft status and so was fully aware of the self-guilt and occasional reproaches from others which our reprieves from military service had provoked.

On Tuesday, I left the office at lunch time, heading out to his Roanoke ranch and arrived there around 1 o'clock. Byron met me at the farmhouse's screen door and motioned me to take a seat on his covered porch. "I'd rather Louise didn't hear about this," he whispered as though we were co-conspirators. And, there was a twinkle back in his kind eyes. What was going on?!

When I handed him the big check he made no fuss, just reached for the wallet in his back pocket to deposit it there. But no, that wasn't his real reason for the wallet. The former Mr. Golf pulled out a check of his own and handed it to me.

My eyes bulged as I saw that Byron's was inscribed to me in the amount of $4,000. He said right away. "Bobby, that's for the Sharpshooter's Invitational fund. It will help you get more vets trained to join the oil business." Although that was true – and a wonderful gesture – I couldn't help but protest.

We must have wrangled over what he was doing for at least 10 minutes, but I got nowhere. Byron's 1 condition was that his donation be anonymous. "That's why I made it out to you," he said at one point. "So you can see that it gets in the fund with no link to me. Listen, I don't want anyone thinking that Byron Nelson gave that sum to the vets' cause on account of me feeling guilty about my war record. Fact is I don't and I don't mean to have anybody concluding otherwise!"

I tried 1 last tactic. "Byron you earned that money. You could put it to good use here expanding your ranch's operation, get more livestock and bring on more 'hands.' You could hire vets for those jobs; not every returning soldier is cut out for oil."

At that moment, the iron in 'iron Byron' came to the fore. "Since you brung that up," he said with burning eyes, "let me just say that them other fellows were wrong to award me first place. I've always believed that the Lord expects us to play by the rules. Period. And, your event's rules said clearly that a competitor who failed to finish was only eligible for the last-place prize, $1,000, so that's what I'm keeping and nothing you can say is gonna change my mind."

Reaching with my free hand, I shook his. The man was inspirational. Still, I left Byron's porch feeling unsettled. His firm denial of feeling any guilt about his 4-F war years had left me 'no opening,' when I would have liked to unburden myself some in that regard. More on this later …

After work that evening and for much of the next day my attention was occupied by matters connected with 'moving on' from the Invitational itself. This phase included starting the process of harnessing the exciting amount of funds our event had generated.

Our Sharpshooters non-profit effort was again feeling good, like I'd gotten to shower after being muddied by the conflicts at Cedar Crest. However, the world stepped in on Wednesday the 25th and engulfed America like a giant mudslide.

Specifically the headlines that day concerned the Korean War. Up 'til September, the first 2 months of response by the U.N. forces – 90 percent of which were our boys – against the North Korean invaders of the South had not gone well. But then, there'd been a breakthrough for our side and we'd taken the fight all the way back into their country during October to the point where it looked like 'mop-up' time and a looming end to the conflict.

That is, until 200,000 Chinese soldiers who'd begun pouring into the North secretly on October 19th started to join the fight on October 25th. With the Koreas being 13 hours ahead of us time-zone-wise, our Texas papers had time to report this disastrous development on the same calendar date.

As I viewed the *Morning News* that day, my heart went out to the many thousands more American soldiers who seemed destined now to have to join the battle over there. And it chilled me to reckon how many of them would return home needing help beyond what the Sharpshooters Invitational had been born to provide. Would we need to 'come up' with similar fundraisers for the next 5 years? I mean, who knew with the Chinese involved how long this Korean conflict would drag out?

Though re-depressed, I vowed to 'fight the good fight' here at home, giving all I could to getting our current Texan vet population more job opportunities. And thus I started working like a maniac for this cause through the rest of the month and beyond.

There is though 1 more golf note before we turn the calendar to November. On Tuesday, October 31st, the pros were gathered down in Pinehurst to play the first round of the North and South Open, long considered one of the more illustrious events of the tournament year.

However, Pinehurst's patriarch Richard Tufts was no longer offering the pros the kind of prize money that was standard on tour. In 1950, the second-to-last year this event would be held, the boys were being given the chance to compete for merely a $1,500 first prize – a grand less than most elsewhere – though Tufts had received a formal complaint from the players.

I suppose this was why none of my Texas Quartet were in on the action, leaving Carolina-cozy Sammy Snead to march away from the competition with a third-round 66 following his opening 68. Yet I also wondered whether perhaps Lloyd, if not for his 'bad press' following the Invitational, might have headed east to try to beat out the Slammer for that 6th tournament win since March. Well there was no way for me to know, since Mr. Icicle had chosen not to return any of my calls over the previous 10 days.

At the same time, while Sam would go on to win the North and South – giving him 'bragging rights' over his buddy Lloyd – Snead's victory must have felt bittersweet. Why? Because there was an announcement in the papers which stunned much of the golf world bright and early on Wednesday, November 1st – before the Slammer had even begun his 2nd round. And you can count me among those who were shocked by the news!

CHAPTER 11

November 1950

T O TELL THE truth, the frightful tale of which I just spoke had probably found its way to Sam by Halloween eve, but I Bobby Shout – having not had time to listen to the radio that Tuesday night – knew nothing about the PGA's "Golfer of the Year" vote 'til I read my *Dallas Morning News* on November 1st. There was the headline, "Sportswriters name Ben Hogan …," and I thought *How could they do that? When Snead has won 7 more tournaments than Ben this year?*

More unbelievable was the fact that the voting hadn't even been close! The Hawk had eclipsed the Slammer by 43 votes, the former getting the nod from 112 writers while Sam polled a mere 69 – with Lloyd and half a dozen others trailing miles behind.

Wow. The urge to call Ben to congratulate him did follow, though I still thought his victory was 'highway robbery.' However, it was unlikely he'd take the phone from Valerie if it was me, I knew, and should we somehow connect, I doubted he'd be gracious. That was Hogan in 1950, so that was that.

Yet, I was itchy to talk with someone who'd know how the rest of the professional pack was feeling about this misplaced homage. *Should I start with Jimmy? No, Demaret's too loyal to Hogan to pass on any critical views about the award. Lloyd then? He certainly wouldn't 'pull any punches' about his buddy Sam being robbed.* But, I suspected he'd also exaggerate the discontent of his peers about the Hawk's mystique with the media. So, I decided to phone the calmest voice of reason I knew among the pros, the former Mr. Golf himself. Byron didn't disappoint, though in an unexpected way.

Having received the message I gave to Louise, he called me back after his noontime meal. And, I was pleased that it was the gentle, relaxed Byron Nelson who spoke again – not the Invitational's tense target from the previous week. "Howdy Bobby," he'd begun. "So, you reckon we oughta both call poor Sam to cheer him up?" I laughed. There was very little malice in this Mr. Golf but considering that Snead's language was often as 'blue' as Lloyd's, and the Slammer was unfaithful in his marriage to boot, he had to rub a serious Christian like Byron the wrong way.

"No, no, I think he'll survive" was my joking reply. "I'm more interested in whether you've heard complaints from other guys about Ben being chosen, and how you feel about it?"

"Well, now that you mention it, Bobby, a couple of our local sportswriters who didn't have a vote called me this morning at the crack of dawn. They must think we ranchers are farmers," he chuckled again. It was good to hear Byron's mirth, though I was pretty darn sure that he was already up when those calls came.

"And, what was their angle?" I quizzed.

With a bit less cheer, the former Mr. Golf drawled, "Oh, you know – trying to stir up something as usual. They wanted me to say that Ben didn't deserve it – that their voting peers had committed a disgraceful bit of favoritism – but, I reckon I surprised those callers."

He went on to remind me that Sam had won the same award just last year -- him being a Masters and PGA winner -- when Ben couldn't even play. So, it wasn't as if these newspaper and radio folks hadn't ever shown Snead any appreciation. "But, what them writers do appreciate is a good story, and who gave them a better bunch of headlines this year?" Nelson posed. "Ben with his all-time great comeback going from the edge of death to becoming U.S. Open champion again; or Sam, winning a bunch of run-of-the-mill tournaments but no majors this year?"

By the time Byron finished speaking, I had to admit that the vote had not been so crazy, considering who the voters were. I Bobby Shout thanked him for his wisdom before hanging up.

That evening, it was me who was on the receiving end of a jangling telephone, just about before I was ready to retire. After hesitating, I decided to 'pick up.' On the other end of the line at last was Mr. Icicle, calling from the West Coast.

In response to his "Howdy, Bobby," I'd answered, "Hey, Lloyd, thanks for getting back to me so soon." He ignored my sarcasm, so ready it seemed to 'state his piece.'

"About Byron, I ain't 'taking back' what I said. During my hitch fighting in Belgium we were lucky to even see an American newspaper most weeks. I'll never forget the article glorifying Nelson for all the damn Red Cross and USO exhibitions he'd golfed in. Poor guy had to play 9 holes a fuckin' hundred times across the country with McSpaden and civilians like Crosby and Hope – all of them so smug that they was raising money for the war effort!

"Oh, and man was I sorry to hear how this duty 'cut into' Mr. Golf's time to play tournaments back home during the war. Good thing that when he did win one – like in Kentucky – there was Alvin York on hand, a real fighting legend, to hand over the purse."

Like a locomotive behind schedule, Lloyd kept steaming on at full speed. "Christ, they made it sound like Nelson was a saint to visit the lesser-wounded vets who could take a lesson from him in putt-putting or hitting a wedge! Yeah, I know he was a bleeder and didn't belong on the front lines, but what Byron was asked to do, compared with what us combat soldiers faced, well – he sure didn't deserve any goddamn medals ... or publicity! So hell, you bet I'm 'pissed off' and plenty bitter about his 4-F war experience. What you got to say to that?"

Whew. I Bobby Shout was nearly 'blown away' by Mr. Icicle's renewed wrath. Scrambling in my head for a response, I blurted, "What you've just said, Lloyd, have you recorded it so you can listen to how you sound?"

"I would but I ran out of tapes," he said sullenly. "Somebody told me to just record over the ones I already done and the old stuff will get erased ..."

"No, no," I cried. "Don't do that. It's important for you to have a record of everything you've felt! Okay? Ask Bing – I'm sure he'd be fine about getting you more reels."

Remember, the two of them were quite friendly. In Lloyd's lone book the front photo showed him and Crosby out playing, and it was Bing who 'wrote' the foreword for GOLF A NEW APPROACH. So, Mr. Icicle seemed to warm to my suggestion.

With his emotional temperature down a few degrees, I was able to begin reasoning with Lloyd about Byron and the war. My first point was to ask him about his own experiences with newspaper reporters. "Do you," I asked him, "always control the tone of what they write? I mean, sometimes what they produce can be just the opposite of what you intended, right?"

Then, I reminded him of Byron Nelson's well-known humility. "Do you honestly think that he was craving attention, being stateside while his peers like you were fighting the war?"

Though the riverboat gambler was still 'holding his cards close to his vest,' it encouraged me that he wasn't disagreeing out loud. I continued, "Those places you mentioned in the article – the golf courses and outdoor rehab facilities – were just that: in open view. But, that piece which incensed you said nothing about what Byron also was doing in private. I was told that he went out of his way to visit the more seriously wounded vets in hospitals. And part of his message to them was always how much he appreciated their service. Obviously, Nelson didn't mention this to reporters."

"How the hell do you know?" blurted Lloyd. "Who told you?"

I answered without hesitation. "Ben." And this reply stopped Mr. Icicle 'in his tracks.'

He remained silent for a few seconds, maybe looking off in the distance. Then in a quiet voice my 'patient' uttered, "Shit. That son of a bitch never lies ..."

We talked on for a few more minutes in a lighter vein. He informed me that in 4 days' time he was going to play an exhibition at one of the L.A. suburban courses with guess who? Ben Hogan and Sam Snead. Lloyd explained that they were doing it to benefit poor Leo Diegel, a talented but zany pro who at age 51 had already been battling multiple cancers for 3 years.

Leo'd been best known to the golfing public for the crazy-looking, elbows-out putting style he'd adopted to fix his 'yips.' Few knew that he'd had to leave the Tour back in '34 after a freak accident in Australia caused nerve damage to his right shoulder. Not a lucky man, Diegel. He had 28 tour wins including 2 PGAs when forced to retire. At age 35 Leo might have been 'a force' for several more campaigns, might have claimed more Majors, instead of being just another California club pro in his late 30s and 40s.

It was a sign of the gap that had developed between Ben Hogan and me that I wasn't aware that he'd gone back out to Hollywood to work on his bio-picture. But, Snead – I did know where he was, in North Carolina working to win another championship in 2 more days. "So he'll be jumping on a plane on Saturday the 4th, flying across the country, and teeing it up with you guys on Sunday? That's big of him."

Lloyd concurred. "Yeah, Leo was nice to him, coming out." My phone pal went on to mention that this was something most folks didn't get about Sam. They heard he was cheap, but didn't know how often the Slammer forked over money to anyone in need, on the sly.

Our conversation ended with 1 more memorable expression. Mr. Icicle told me to tell Byron the next time I saw him that Lloyd Mangrum didn't know about the hospital visits and thanks him for doing that. I said, "Sure."

That November in 1950 was light on PGA tournament play. Six days after the North and South concluded, there was a minor event held in Savannah. Willie Goggin, whose best finish in a major had been way back in 1933, took the top prize, beating out Tommy Bolt by 2 on Sunday, November 12th. Then the boys had to wait 'til the end of the month to tee it up in the Miami Open. More on that event soon …

It had occurred to me that during my heated call with Lloyd Mangrum I'd never brought up the subject of Hogan winning Golfer of the Year. Then there was his relationship with Sam Snead.

They were thought to be buddy-buddy and had played as partners in the fall '49 Ryder Cup, proof of their amiability as recently as then. Yet, as you may recall, this year Mr. Icicle had gone out of his way on Independence Day in Detroit to give a victory speech that included tweaking the Slammer's nose. Why *had* Lloyd insulted his friend in public about missing a 4-footer to lose on the final green at that July tournament?

Though I'd gotten to know Mangrum from the inside out since that time, it was still a puzzle to me – how his war-time resentment could flare so hot still against his fellow pros who'd happened to draw stateside duties. After all, Lloyd had *volunteered* for combat when given the chance for a cozy assignment back home. He'd made that choice! Obviously, he needed more counseling to obtain a decent level of peace in this regard.

At the same time, I Bobby Shout was not so serene on the subject of Ben Hogan. My being in the Hawk's 'doghouse' gnawed at me. Why couldn't he accept my role as confidential counselor to multiple golfers – not just him? If things were not set right soon, I feared that the Hawk would place me permanently in his 'enemy camp.' It was time to do something!

Having thought about this challenge for 2 more days, I sat in my den on Saturday the 4th trying to pen what I considered might be the most important letter of my life to date. That epistle began easily enough: "Dear Ben:" But how should I word the rest? It seemed to me that a single false note in what followed would result in failure; that scared the heck out of me.

What you'll read below is based on the carbon copy I kept after typing up at the office what I'd handwritten at home. Back then, few men were 'up' on typing. It took me nearly an hour to carefully 'henpeck' the text of my short note so there would be no errors. And I don't mind admitting that when I'd finished, my hands began to shake like a rookie about to ride his first big bull. (I'd already cursed myself for my crappy handwriting which had necessitated the use of a typewriter.)

So here then is the body of that note:

> *Dear Ben,*
>
> *I want to congratulate you on being named the PGA's 'Golfer of the Year.' It is my belief that no other player on earth could have willed such a magnificent comeback.*
>
> *If truth be told, when I met you in the fall of '49 on that Hulen Street bench and saw your physical condition, I never thought you'd*

play professional golf again. How you proved me and the rest of the world wrong!

Discussing travel issues and other concerns that stood in your way of performing again at PGA events was a privilege for me that I'll never forget. Thank you for your confidence then in nicknaming me "Dr. Shout" -- which I took as an indication that you both trusted me to be competent and confidential about your affairs.

Perhaps I have not always been as competent as a licensed psychological professional but I am certain that I have been one hundred percent discreet about every sensitive conversation we've had!

It's the rare 'doctor' who has only one patient. Yet doctors do treat a multitude of individuals without compromising the privacy of any of them. I, too, have been capable of that and shall never change!

You didn't seem to mind when Byron or Jimmy made use of my counseling skills. I cannot say too emphatically that you needn't worry about my working with Lloyd either.

Finally, please know that I'll always be your friend and admirer whether we come together again or not.

Sincerely yours,
Bobby Shout

After exiting the Shout Petroleum building I dropped that letter into the nearest mailbox before I had the chance to think twice about sending it. Would I ever hear back from Ben Hogan? I wasn't ready to bet on it.

Following the several days during which I could assume the Hawk had yet to receive my note, anticipation of a response from him made me very flighty. He might phone me at any time; I had to be ready to 'plead my case' further perhaps.

It turned out that Ben chose to respond by mail. His letter consisted of 6 words: "Okay. See you during the holidays." I was elated despite his taut brevity. There was hope for us yet! The date was Monday November 15th 1950. I have his little letter still and have instructed my children to place it in my coffin, figuring that a blessing from Hogan -- even such a tepid one -- might just do the trick with St. Peter.

On Wednesday night, the 4th member of my Texas Quartet 'checked in' on the telephone. "Howdy, Jimmy," I'd replied to his greeting. "What can I do for you?" This query had been motivated by my worry that the Wardrobe had been facing a lot of abuse from his disappointed backers back in Houston.

However, he responded in a cheery way to my betting-concern. "Nah. Once I'd spread the word that I'd pay back half of any Houstonian's betting slip from the Invitational and 'made good' with a bunch of folks, I got a lot of nice press. Surprised you haven't heard."

"Are you joking about paying?" I said, not able to tell from his straightforward tone. But it turned out he wasn't. And furthermore, Demaret seemed to be in a very calm place for him that evening.

I decided to test his mask of even ego by asking, "So how's everything else going for you, Jimmy?"

He answered, "Before we get to me, did you hear how the Diegel exhibition went?" No, I hadn't. A 1-day golf affair out in California was hardly national news.

Jimmy snorted, "I reckon ole Sam wanted to make a point about just who was Golfer of the Year. He tied the Inglewood course record – 65 – while Ben shot 72. It was closer than that sounds though. The Hawk 'hung' with him on the front 9, shooting a 33. I suspect Ben's legs 'gave out' on him on the back, him being more in movie shape than golfing shape," the Wardrobe cackled.

It occurred to me that since I'd sent out my note to Ben on Saturday the 4th, of course he couldn't have replied to me before the Leo Diegel exhibition on Sunday the 5th. I can't say why I hadn't 'picked up' on this timing before. It was good news. There was Hogan, probably still stinging from the drubbing Sam had administered, yet Ben had been civil in response to my letter.

Glowing a bit with this thought in mind, I turned my focus back to the state of Jimmy Demaret's psyche. "What are your plans for the rest of the year?" seemed like a good opening question. If he spoke in a vague way, that would be a warning sign about his mental health. Fortunately, the Wardrobe was able to charge right into a full-throated reply.

"Well, looks like I'm still a wanted man, after all. Idella, Peggy [their daughter], and I have been invited by the owner Ray Parker to spend the Christmas holidays at his Concord Resort Hotel in upstate New York. Bobby, I think he's going to propose," Jimmy chuckled. "That is, they're gonna ask me to be their touring pro, I reckon. Ray's already mentioned how they have a sweet apartment right above the pro shop waiting for a new Director of Golf."

After a moment of consideration, I had to ask, "You know that the Concord is primarily a vacation spot for Jews, right? It might be a ghost house there over Christmas."

The Wardrobe laughed out loud. "Bobby Shout, you got something against those folks? I don't. I've met plenty of their tribe while representing the Ojai Valley Inn -- Hollywood people, a lot of them." In a mock whisper, he added, "They run Tinsel Town, you know."

Embarrassed now, I stuttered, "No, no – I mean, I mentioned the Jewish angle 'cause I know you like nightlife ..."

My boisterous friend interrupted me. "Don't you worry yourself about that! The Concord is huge; plenty of room for everybody – and classy. They've got a 200-foot-long bar, I'm told." He laughed then at his own joke. "Oodles of top entertainment acts get booked to perform there, year-round. And anyway, there's a ski place close by, so most of their thousand-plus rooms will be booked – Christmas or not. We're really looking forward to getting away."

This excitement on Jimmy's part was a relief to hear. I hoped that he indeed found the Concord to be the sociable beehive he'd been led to believe, and if so, that he did snag the gig as their new touring pro and golf director.

The second half of November was dominated by Thanksgiving week naturally. Although Ben and Lloyd were presumably both in the L.A. area for that holiday time, I doubted they'd be sharing any turkey. Not only did those 2 men-folk have their issues, I couldn't image 2 women less alike in their experience and outlooks than Mrs. Hogan and Mrs. Mangrum.

As I've written, Valerie (born "Fox") Hogan was raised elegant, a reserved, childless woman, a good match for her man. They had met in their early teens, (some said through church), and didn't marry 'til 1935 when she was still 23 and Ben 22.

Whereas, Eleta P. Mangrum had already experienced matrimony, the birth of 3 children, and her husband's death before she came into Lloyd's orbit. Though he was barely a man at age 20, Lloyd was 'hot' to marry the 30-year-old L.A. widow in 1934 and did so. His not-exactly-lovey-dovey 'handle' for her was "Maw."

One strange note I collected about Mrs. Mangrum's given name was that Lloyd refers to her as "Aleta" in the dedication to his book, but she is "Eleta" on the bronze plaque at their gravesite. It was my guess that a 'ghostwriter' was necessary for Mr. Icicle's instruction manual GOLF: A NEW APPROACH and it was the hired hand who heard Eleta's name as "Aleta."

Proofreading was probably not something which interested the supposed author. I don't mean to be snide in saying so, seeing how Lloyd never got as far as high school – full-time labor during his older teenage years being necessary for him to 'scrape by' in that Great Depression age out in L.A.

I've gotten off on this tangent probably because that 1950 Thanksgiving Day involved some friction between the 2 most prominent women in my life at the time. There was my mother, of course, Margaret Edwinson Shout, whom I've mentioned was better known as Margo. She, the current head of Shout Petroleum, wanted what was best for me, naturally.

Then there was Cheryl Lynn Highsome, one of the secretaries at our company, a lively honey-blonde who happened to be a young woman 'getting under my skin' at the time. In fact, we were on the edge of being pretty 'serious,' much to my mom's dismay.

Well I suppose it hadn't helped that Cheryl had garnered the nickname among some Shout employees as "The Double-Y Ranch." I'll leave it to you to ponder its meaning, but I took that slur to be no more than malicious, unfounded sexual gossip, and for heaven's sake, she'd acted perfectly properly with me through a succession of dates that autumn.

Anyway, Cheryl Lynn had invited me around the middle of November to join her family for their turkey feast on Thursday the 23rd. And let me tell you, there was nothing disreputable about her folks, Mr. Highsome being one of the distinguished bankers in Dallas. "It will be a way for them to get to know you better, Snookums," she'd cooed to me, and that sounded fine.

However, my mother Margo just about 'raised the roof' when she heard that I'd be elsewhere on Thanksgiving afternoon. I won't repeat here the unkind things she implied about Cheryl in the heat of the moment, but let me just say that I did join the Highsomes at their table on that day and the world didn't end!

On the following Thursday, November 30th, Snead and company were down in Miami starting their competition for that city's title Open, as previously mentioned. It wasn't much of a contest after day 2, with poor Ole Sam having shot the first of his 3 consecutive 66s for the event.

Trailing his 13-under total at the end by 5 strokes were 2 players tied for 2nd, one of them being a Houstonian, but it wasn't Jimmy. Instead it was Demaret's 'little brother,' Jackie Burke Jr. who took home the 2nd-best prize of $1,200 along with Dick Mayer.

This year 1950 marked Jackie's first run of success on tour, the 27-year-old having won 3 minor PGA events during the 1st quarter of the campaign. Unfortunately, for the fire-cracker-personality Burke, he was a very hot-and-cold performer, winning zero tournaments the next year, only to follow that with 5 victories in 1952, then a 3-year slump before 'hitting the jackpot with 2 Majors (the Masters and PGA Championship) in '56.

The Wardrobe had told me a couple of times how much he owed to Jack Burke Senior, who'd recently taken over the River Oaks professional job in Houston when Jimmy applied to caddy there at age 16. Not only had Burke Senior made Jimmy both the caddy master and starter in short order at that elite course. Jack Senior also – in Jimmy's eyes – taught him everything he needed to know to be a successful pro, before ultimately promoting Demaret to assistant professional – all before the Wardrobe moved on at age 22 to become the pro at Galveston's municipal course.

And, when I characterized Jackie Burke above as Jimmy's 'little brother,' I wasn't kidding. No, they weren't blood-related, but during his teen years at River Oaks, Demaret's duties included plenty of babysitting for the little boy Jackie, I'd heard.

On top of that, considering young Jimmy's deep vein of insecurity over his bodily oddities, I suspect that he especially welcomed the 'hero worship' given to him by his young charge, in contrast with the teasing he got from his brothers and others. Anyway, I'll have more to say about the later interweaving of these 2 golfers' lives in the chapter dedicated to Jimmy.

CHAPTER 12

December 1950

DECEMBER WEATHER IN Dallas started unseasonably warm that year. By 3 p.m. on the 1st it was 80 degrees, and though the wind was gusting near 30 mph, it hardly felt fresher.

Alas, the day's news from North Korea indicated that things were getting 'too hot' as well for thousands of our marines, those poor 'boys' who'd been told just a week earlier by General McArthur that they'd be home for Christmas. Instead, the ordered push to the Yalu River had resulted in a huge ambush leaving thousands of our troops surrounded at a place called the Chosin Reservoir.

For 3 weeks, I followed the reports of how our boys were fighting in an organized retreat 'back to the sea.' Thank God that many of them made it. Perhaps even some of them were back in the U.S. by the 25th, though the circumstances of their departure from Korea must have stung!

On the home front, I continued to fight a battle of my own with mom over Cheryl Highsome, but this of course meant little 'in the big picture.' There's more to tell of my interactions with the Texas Quartet during this final month of the year, starting with another intriguing telephone call from Mr. Icicle. It was 10 p.m. our Central time when Lloyd rang me on Thursday, December 7th.

When I 'picked up' and heard it was him, my thought was, *Oh this is probably to do with Pearl Harbor Day – his wartime demons stirred up by that signpost of*

American military misery. Well, I was right but I was wrong, like the wildcatter who declares he's struck oil only there isn't hardly any in that well of his.

"Hey there, 'Dr. Shout,' this is Lloyd on the line. I've been meaning to call you but things are being pretty hectic out here."

"Can I help?" I'd replied.

He proceeded to explain how he had gotten more reels of tape from Bing and had been continuing to record his war recollections along with his subsequent reactions. The problem was, according to Mr. Icicle, that his nighttimes were once again being besieged by horrific dreams, night sweats, and a pounding heart. "Damn, you got any more 'tricks' you've been saving for me?" Mangrum had asked.

The simple answer was "No," but I knew better than to say that to him. It was time to probe. "Lloyd, you said you've been very busy lately. Are there some family matters that are keeping you hopping?"

"Hell no," he'd responded. "Eleta's fine and the kids and their kin are doing well, too. I just meant I've been playing me lots of golf the past few weeks."

Well, that didn't sound like a problem. I mentioned that I'd heard about the exhibition with Sam and Ben, then asked if he was doing more of them or just playing some friendly games at his brother's club.

In reply to this question, Mr. Icicle let out a big chuckle. "Shit, Bobby, I don't know what your definition of a fucking friendly game is, but out here when you're playing for $10,000 – winners take all – I wouldn't say the vibe is a whole lot of friendly."

"What?" was all I could manage to say at first; remember – back then the PGA tournaments only paid $2,500 to the 'top dog' each week. My mind screamed *Lloyd's been playing for much bigger pots lately than out on Tour? And how much of his own cash is he putting up?*

That rogue's reply was classic gambler-cool. "Listen, I treat myself and my family to nice houses, nice cars, nice clothes. You name it. And goddammit, I ain't apologizing. The PGA purses are well enough for a man's basic expenses, but if we Mangrums and Griewanks are gonna live in style, I've got to close out each year winning me some L.A. money off the Hollywood folks and their bunch. Call it my bloody Christmas fund as the Brits would say. You need not to trouble yourself though, Bobby. Ole Lloyd does all right …"

I had to 'dig out' first who the Griewanks were. Then it came back to me that "Griewank" was Eleta's kids' last name from her dead husband. There were 3 of them: Robert, Roena, and another girl slightly younger, I recalled. All of them had to be in their twenties by now, but here was Mr. Icicle still playing Santa Claus for them.

Well, that explained why he felt the need to 'get up' some big-money games in L.A. while the Tour was winding down on the East Coast, yet gosh, he certainly didn't realize the harm involved -- that was obvious. I tried to be gentle about this danger at first.

"That's real nice of you to want to take care of everyone," I began …

"But what," Lloyd had shot back in his frosty tone.

"Let me draw you a mental picture," I countered. "Let's think of each little bit of stress in our lives as an emotional bullet. Okay, when some of those bullets strike our minds, our mind can deflect them at first. However, if too many hit us at once, or too many of them packing greater emotion join the smaller ones in hitting us in the head in rapid order, our ability to defend ourselves is weakened. You with me so far?"

"Sounds like I should be dead," he grumbled.

"No, no," I assured him, "the mind is a pretty tough hombre; yours sure is! Still, here's what may be happening in your case: For a month-and-a half now – you said you've been involved in 2 to 3 money matches a week since early November -- you've been 'taking' a lot of stress bullets nearly every day. I mean, it's not just during the golf matches that there's a lot of tension involved. Your mind has been going 'on alert' in anticipation as soon as one of these money-games gets scheduled as well. So, at night your stressed-out mind no longer has as much strength left to combat the most worrisome memories you own, your war visions."

Mr. Icicle wasn't 'buying' my image of things though. Full of pride, he'd said, "Now wait a second, Bobby. You should know me well enough by now to understand that I mean it when I say that playing golf for money is like a 'walk in the park' for me, having seen what real horror is. I don't want to say you're talking out of your ass but … You're off the mark!"

"Okay, let's probe farther though, Lloyd. Those stress bullets that are striking into you these days. They're coming in effect from a machine gun strafing your whole body – your chest, your gut, your groin …"

"Ouch," he had punned back. "That's a low blow, Dr. Shout."

Losing patience, I'd stressed, "It's your long-term health we're talking about here, Lloyd. No joke. Those night terrors can lead to bodily damage where a man is weakest! I've seen it!"

In response, he did turn serious and assured me that he'd gotten the picture. He understood that the wise thing for him to do might be to 'take it easy' between tour seasons to 'recharge his battery'. "But Bobby," he concluded. "I 'live' now for the fucking 'action.' Without the 'high' those games give me to balance my crappy nights, I'd just as soon be gone. Thanks for the advice though." And then Mr. Icicle wished me a good holiday season and hung up.

Alone again, I realized that I'd been way off on my initial premise. Lloyd probably felt little about Pearl Harbor Day. That wasn't his war. December was the anniversary of his hellish time in the frozen forests of Belgium. Stupid me!

That December 7th had begun with some other bad news on the golf front. The morning paper included coverage of the first round of the Miami 4-ball tournament and let me know that Jimmy Demaret along with his 'little brother' Jackie were already 'out' of the 5-round match-play event the very first day.

Worse, they had been upset by an obscure pairing, John Barnum and Jack Shields. Barnum was winless in his career on the PGA Tour at the time, though he was roughly Jimmy's age. (Strangely though, the great Barnum did win an event, the Cajun Classic on Tour 12 years later, to become the only pro ever to get their first PGA circuit victory after the age of 50.)

I wondered how Jimmy had weathered this embarrassing defeat. Had he been the one to drag their team down, or had it been Jackie Burke? And where was Demaret 'licking his wounds' now after another blow to his golfing ego?

It wouldn't have surprised me if he was about to take the boat to Havana, where I knew he was playing in the last official event of the year, starting on December 14th. The Wardrobe had once told me that he loved Miami nightlife but that nowhere could compare with the hospitality offered to Tour professionals by the ladies of Cuba. 'Dr Shout' never did probe into just what Jimmy meant by that, my feeling being that this state of affairs was best left between James Newton Demaret and his wife Idella.

Of course, Christmas season was starting to get in full swing and although I hardly expected to receive much joy through the mail – being a bachelor who'd changed towns just a few months earlier – still a card arrived on December 11th that I'll never forget. It was from Byron and Louise Nelson. Accompanying the printed greeting was the following handwritten text, penned by the former Mr. Golf:

Howdy, Bobby,

Louise and I want to invite you and Cheryl Lynn to the 5:00 Christmas Eve service at our church along with a holiday supper at our place after that. I suggest you arrive here around 4 o'clock.

We know you probably want to visit with your own families later that night, so dinner will be prompt upon our return to the ranch, the wife assures me. Hope you both can come. My best, JBN

The 1st thing I remember thinking, much amazed, was *Well don't that beat all?* I mean this invitation was so unexpected on so many counts. For one, I didn't think that I'd ever even mentioned Cheryl to him. And though maybe Byron had heard about our dating – through the Dallas 'grapevine'? – how could he have known that my mother was still not ready to recognize my girl at a family affair?

So here was Mr. Golf and Louise giving Cheryl Lynn and me a bona fide excuse for enjoying each other's company on that special night and Margo Shout couldn't say "Boo" against an invite from the great Byron Nelson! I wanted to kiss the man, practically.

Really, I'd hardly done anything for him; he didn't need my friendship in the least, and yet he wanted to do this kind thing for us. I would be giving his wife Louise a good 'smack' on the cheek, you could bet your prize steer on that! And, when I told my Miss Highsome about this Christmas Eve offer at work that day, she said the same about Byron. It was a wonderful surprise.

A week later, that is on Monday December 18th, the results from the Havana Pro-Am tournament were in the paper. The previous day Jim Turnesa had completed his conquest of the Havana Country Club with a 7-under 65 giving him a 4-round total of 21-under. That was a great score but I was more interested in how Jimmy had done.

He'd finished in 11th place with a 279 score, 12 back of the winner. That mediocre result was hardly a Christmas present for my 'patient' and I continued to worry, waiting for his next call. It came on Wednesday the 20th.

I could hardly believe how ebullient Mr. Wardrobe was when he first came on the line, remarkably early for him! Was Demaret masking how crummy he felt? Of course I knew that he was heading to the Concord Hotel with his family in a day or two and that Jimmy had been psyched about that vacation and potential business opportunity, but gosh, the man was sounding like he was some Yellow-breasted Chat singing -- one of my favorite Texas birds.

It turned out that the presence of amateurs in the Havana field had given Mr. Wardrobe a super chance to strut his stuff, sartorially speaking. As he explained, "You know that clothing outfit 'Palm Beach' – they sponsor our New York City tournament in June – well, my partner was one of their senior V.P.s. He was real interested in me working with them on a line of golfing duds. It looks like a sure thing, just the kind of deal I wanted."

This was great, just what Jimmy needed to see himself as: a champion gracefully transitioning into a life with many roles rewarding him for his golfing fame. We wished each other the best over the holidays and then he was gone. I smiled a lot the rest of that day, even through a minor fracas at work.

Dallas was in the midst of quite a dry spell that December, also featuring a comfortable high temperature of around 60 degrees, and it continued like that on Christmas Eve day and right through the holidays. When I picked up Cheryl

Lynn at her parents' home at 3 o'clock on that Sunday to head out to Byron's place, I was pleased to see how sensibly she'd dressed.

Her suit ensemble was not exactly somber but seemed certainly dignified with its rich blue hue. By contrast, at work Cheryl usually had 'something on' that spoke more of a "come hither" aspect – a flouncy skirt with a tight blouse for example. Now don't get me wrong: I liked her glamorous style, but at the Nelson's Church of Christ my honey-haired sweetie would have stood out like a 2-headed hen if she'd dressed typically.

Anyway, the warm and gracious way Cheryl carried herself throughout our time with the Nelsons that evening made me all the more confident that she was the girl for me. As I kissed her long and hard in my car before walking Miss Highsome to her parents' front door, it took a lot of will power for me not to propose to her right then and there.

However, there was still the matter of my family's approval – foremost Margo's – to deal with lest I inflict an awkward family future on my prospective bride-to-be. At my mother's mansion that night it gave me some hope to note that mom wasn't making a single 'dig' at Cheryl to my brother and his wife while we enjoyed eggnog and carols. Could this be a sign that Margo was 'coming around'? I prayed that my prayer at the Nelson's church was being answered.

Christmas 1950 was no doubt my most memorable – in a fantastic way – out of the hundred I've known. And brand me a shallow materialist but yes, this number-1 rating is based on the presents I received that day!

To start with, when I walked into mom's living room on the 25th, there was a leather MacGregor golf bag waiting for me, stuffed with a brand-new bunch of top-notch 'Tourneys.' "Margo," I'd cried out, "How did you know I've been lusting after this very set."

"Well actually honey, that's a gift from Byron Nelson. He tried 'em out he said and they should suit you fine, according to him," she finished with a smile.

Naturally I was astounded. *What the heck?* Then my mother resumed speaking as though she'd read my mind.

"Mr. Nelson also told me to say that you've more than earned a nice gift from him. On account of your inviting Byron to compete in the Sharpshooters Invitational, the MacGregor Company has informed him that they'll be able to set up a 'Mr. Golf Exhibition Tour' in 1951 after all. It seems that his performance back in October impressed a lot of folks who read about it. So dear, enjoy!" mom concluded, waving a hand toward the bag.

As I hefted the persimmon driver which wound up working magic for me for the next 20 years, my accompanying thought was *I hope the people who wrote to MacGregor were equally impressed by Byron's sterling actions at the Invitational. He deserves to know how decent people felt about his departure – not just the gamblers.* And then I felt a thrill, just at the thought that he had struck balls with this very set.

A minute later, my attention was drawn back to the golf bag. On its hand-grip was hanging a bronzed bag tag. I assumed that Byron must have forgotten to remove it because the word "Colonial" on top, then 3 Cs in a triangle, was followed below by the phrase "Country Club" and "Member." My ever-observant mother called out to me, "No honey, that's no mistake. Allow me to congratulate you, Colonial's newest member!"

What? First off, although I was making good money now, working for the family business, my income was still shy of the kind of initiation fee and dues that Colonial demanded. On top of that, there was a considerable waiting list to get into the club and I hadn't even asked to join those hoping to join.

But the real shocker was this: To get into a golf club as elite as this, you needed to get sponsored by a member and approved by their board which meant multiple interviews. No one from Colonial had even called me. So what was going on?

Margo was ready to explain some of the details that had culminated in my getting in. "Shout Petroleum Company has paid your initiation fee, dear. As I see it, we'll get our money's worth with you schmoozing some of our biggest business contacts there. And don't worry – you'll still have time to work on your vets personnel-projects. However, as I said when we welcomed you 'on board,' Bobby, we do need your type as an ambassador for us, too."

Hmmm. Should I tell her I don't want to play lots of rounds down there in Fort Worth if it's about business? Heck, no! I thanked Margo from the bottom of my heart for using her influence and the company's cash to vault me over many others on Colonial's wait list.

Then though, when it occurred to me to ask a few more questions about all this, mom shushed me by putting a small, wrapped box into my hand, as she cooed, "This is really from me, son. Wait 'til we've opened all the other gifts, okay?"

20 minutes later, all the stockings emptied, and the presents to and from mom, my brother Leroy, his wife Betty, their daughter Susan, and me having been opened, it was time for the 1 last gift. I recollect Leroy smirking when Margo gave me the 'go ahead' to rip off the wrapping.

Well I did, and boy what a surprise! There greeting me was another layer of Christmas paper around the little box. But it was the gift tag that floored me. "To Cheryl Lynn. Best wishes, Margaret Shout. P.S. I hope you can wear it to our New Year's Eve party!"

I looked at my mother. No doubt 'Dr. Shout' was grinning from side to side. "Does this mean what I think?" I asked.

She gave a theatrical sigh before saying, "Yes. I've gotten some very good character references for that girl of yours recently. So who am I to 'throw a monkey wrench' into the works."

Leroy spoke up. "I did some checking, too. It seems some guys in our company aren't above spoiling a girl's reputation if she doesn't favor them. That won't be happening again," he concluded with emphasis.

Those 2 people who I loved and respected more than any other -- excepting Cheryl of course – were back 'on my side'! Could a guy get any luckier? Of all the Christmas Day turkeys I ever savored, that particular bird seemed forever the tastiest. And late that evening, when I gave my girl the gift from mom in private and she read the tag, her face had never looked sweeter.

After I'd fastened Cheryl's new necklace 'on' for her, she was ready to rush to a mirror, but I put my arm about her waist and whispered, "Hold on." Then pulling out an engagement ring box from my pocket, I opened it while stammering, "Miss Highsome, will you marry me?"

We agreed to keep our nuptial plan secret – for all of 6 days. On New Year's Eve, Cheryl brought the ring out of hiding, and everyone at the Shouts' annual party was soon buzzing with the news. I took my spouse-to-be home that night at 1 o'clock, the year 1950 now gone.

Returning to mom's house to help her tidy up, I shouldn't have had a complaint in the world, but there was 1 thing bothering me: Ben Hogan. He'd written that he'd be in touch during the holidays. My 'patient' was known for doing what he said. Yet I'd heard nothing from him, and if the Hawk was making the trip from Fort Worth to Dallas this January 1st, it was 10 times more likely to see our Longhorns 'take on' Tennessee' in the Cotton Bowl than to visit with me.

When I shared this lament with Margo though, my mom had an unexpected 'comeback.' "But didn't you get his message, dear?" In response to my dumbfounded look, she gushed, "Why Bobby, did you really reckon that me, a mere woman, could push you to the 'front of the line' to get into Colonial? There's only 1 member there that could make such a thing happen – a friend of yours!"

The blast of gratitude and relief that rushed through my soul was as though a Texas twister had decided to spare me and mine. Ben had really forgiven 'Dr. Shout'! This news capped a year that I doubted would ever be matched in my life, and though I've now almost lived a century, no annum has nearly compared with 1950 for being a time chock-full of God's blessings on me, though the renewal of war did stain my joys.

CHAPTER 13

Lloyd afterwards

L LOYD EUGENE MANGRUM'S battle with his stressed heart ended at age 59 in November 1973 when wife Eleta laid him to rest in a high-desert community some hundred miles northeast of Los Angeles. True to form, Mr. Icicle had coolly combated serious illness for a very long time.

In fact, he'd withstood eleven heart attacks before the twelfth killed him. Yes, 12 attacks! And the early discomforts of arterial disease had been with him all the way back to the middle 1950s. Mangrum's golfing record reflects this fact; we'll 'dip' into that in a bit.

As I've noted, you'll find his grave site in a California desert town. Its name is Apple Valley. And Lloyd chose to make that out-of-the-way location his home base from 1955 'til his demise 18 years later. Surprising? Well read on.

Back when Mr. Icicle had moved into a custom-designed house by the 18th tee of the town's sole country club, little Apple Valley's money men were doing a good job of attracting 'stars' from California's biggest cities.

Singing cowboy Roy Rogers and Dale Evans -- his wife and partner in movies and shows -- were among Lloyd's gaudy new neighbors there. Of course as this book has made clear, socializing for the hell of it was hardly ever high on Lloyd's list. On the other hand, where there were moneyed folks, his gambling side could sometimes prompt him to 'play nice.'

On top of that, since the little town did have an airport, both San Diego and Vegas, along with L.A., could be easily reached when the itch for extra 'action' grabbed him. Yet there was a more fundamental reason why ole Lloyd 'took up' the resident pro's job at the Apple Valley Country Club in '55 when barely 41. He was hoping to 'find a cure' for his escalating ills through the aid of the sweet dry desert air there -- a far cry from L.A.'s smog -- though the apple orchards once in town by the river were 3 decades gone.

Or to quote ex-Staff Sergeant Mangrum's grumbling report around then, "I'm doing a fucking delaying action against a superior force -- my health enemies. You get that, Shout?" I guess I had sounded somewhat incredulous when he'd first mentioned Apple Valley. My bad.

Mr. Icicle never admitted to me the exact date of his first heart attack. Was it in 1955, hushed up but prompting his move to Apple Valley, I always wondered? In September of that year President Dwight D. Eisenhower happened to suffer his first of many such attacks (after playing 36 holes earlier in the day). Against most odds, ten years later both he and Lloyd suffered heart attacks on the same Thursday, November 11th 1965.

However, while that incident counted as only the President's second myocardial infarction, Mangrum could boast of having survived 7 of them. So what did Dr. Shout's most rascally 'patient' do? He boasted to me that he had sent the perfect telegram from one golfing gambler to another: "Dear Ike, I'm 5 up on you." Cool Lloyd having fun though his life was 'in the balance.'

It was not lost on me of course that with the Viet Nam conflict raging, the Veterans Day remembrances taking place that November 11th were particularly powerful. Perhaps this military-shaded holiday had triggered major internal stress in these 2 formidable ex-warriors, leading to their attacks, but I was not going to probe Lloyd about it – and didn't – when next we spoke. Why not? 'Cause that would have been like asking him to scratch at a snake bite and lick his fingers to boot, mentally speaking.

Three years earlier in 1962, Lloyd had suffered another attack around the same time. It was the afternoon after Veterans Day on this occasion that he was admitted to Apple Valley's St. Mary's hospital. And Mr. Icicle was less than 4 months' clear of his heart seizing up in July, so this repeat incident was especially worrisome.

Sure enough that 48-year-old's ticker took another turn toward crisis just 2 weeks later on November 25th. Yet rather than 'letting go,' he managed to last till 1973. You had to reckon that Mangrum was truly one 'tough bird.'

Oh yeah and it's worth noting that George S. May, Lloyd's long-time benefactor at the Tam O' Shanter club, had died of a heart attack in March of '62. George like Lloyd was a hell of a man who'd risen from little – he'd started out by selling Bibles. But by the 1950s May had become one of professional golf's greatest promoters, funding those yearly 'world championships' at his course as well as being the first powerbroker to get golf televised.

When I read about this strong man's passing, my hand reached for the phone. It seemed to me that although May was an older man than Lloyd – George died at 72 – still his death due to a heart problem might be shaking Mr. Icicle's grip regarding his own mortality.

"No, boy," I remember Mangrum replying. "George had a belly on him; not fit like me. Don't worry yourself. I'm not going anywhere for quite a while. Case closed." Yet I was concerned about the power of suggestion embodied in May's passing, and would have liked to have talked Lloyd through it more. Well there you go: All those attacks later the same year …

Barely over 40, Lloyd Mangrum the golfer was just about 'out of gas' when he felt forced to move to the quiet and clean air of Apple Valley in '55. However some might say the golf gods felt their riverboat gambler deserved 1 last supernova moment in response to this retirement admission. Or if you think such sentiment is 'bunk,' maybe it was the extra doses of oxygen percolating through Mr. Icicle at his new desert home which gave him the energy to begin 1956 'with a bang.'

What I Bobby Shout am referring to is Mangrum's wondrous, out-of-nowhere performance at that year's Los Angeles Open. He had won only a single tournament over the previous 2 seasons, yet not only did he beat all comers at '56's opening L.A. tournament – he did so in record fashion!

Why, ole Lloyd was so far ahead after 3 rounds that his 72 on the last day was still good enough to give him a 3-shot victory and the greatest 4-round total in the history of the event, that score being 272.

No, I wasn't there to witness this ending. But back in Dallas I made sure to have my radio 'on' that January 9th evening. When the sports report included this news about how Mr. Icicle had fared that Sunday, I don't mind saying that I let out a cry of joy. 'Cause if there was 1 championship that had to mean the most to Lloyd at this juncture – beyond the Majors now seemingly out of his reach – it had to be the L.A. Open, his hometown event – and more!

You see my irascible 'patient's win there in 1956 was his 4th, which now tied him with Ben's record for most victories at Riviera. And although the press had long since dubbed the course as "Hogan's Alley" due to his winning both the L.A. and U.S. Open there in '48, the best total Hogan had ever shot was 275.

Did Lloyd send his despised rival a 'bragging rights' telegram of the sort he'd later 'lay on' Dwight Eisenhower? Had Hogan in any way congratulated the 'traitor' on his sparkling 272 – while icily noting the greater difficulty of Major championship conditions? I never asked either man, afraid it might shake the fragile trust that both of them had in me. Yet I sure as heck would have liked to know.

Mr. Icicle also 'made a run' at his elusive second Major that year, finishing tied for 4th in the Masters but then ... well that was the end of his contending. When the 1956 U.S. Open 'rolled around' in June, Lloyd was 'back on the shelf.' It was his second straight 'missing in action' from our national championship. In '55 he'd qualified and been 'penned in' to tee off at 9:36 on the Open's first day but felt too unwell to play.

In 1957 the riverboat gambler was back competing but missed the cut; tied for 37th in '58; didn't make the championship in '59; and in what would be his final attempt at a 2nd Open, tied for 23rd in 1960. Somehow Lloyd did manage to drag his body around the hills of Augusta National every year through 1962. However his Masters record after 1956 was likewise anemic: Three missed cuts and no better finish than a tie for 28th.

As for the British Open and PGA, he'd abandoned both events long before due to his lack of endurance: Mangrum's final PGA appearance being 1952; his 1 try at the Open 'across the pond,' 1953. When I'd asked Lloyd if he was 'going over' that year only because Ben Hogan was figuring on being the first man to 'hold' 3 of the current Majors in a single season by conquering Carnoustie, Mr. Icicle had chuckled over the phone before growling, "Damn fucking right. Europe war demons or not!"

And when Ben did win there, Lloyd 'back in the pack' at 24th, I reckon I felt about as happy for one as I did sad for the other, both of these burning rivals having gotten deeply 'under my skin.' Need I add that Lloyd Mangrum never won another tournament, on the Tour or off, after his '56 L.A. win? Well let's return to happier times for him, primarily the stretch from 1951 through 1953 when there still remained plenty of golfing highlights for the condemned ex-Texan to savor.

Over that 3-year period, Mr. Icicle notched an additional 10 wins on Tour including a couple of L.A. Opens, Phoenix Opens, a Western Open, and his 2nd All American Open at Mr. May's Tam O'Shanter. This haul brought his PGA total up to 34 victories (with 2 more to come) and what should have been a certain ticket into our sport's Hall Of Fame. However, that honor came surprisingly late considering his career. Lloyd finally was voted 'in' in 1998, a full quarter-century after his death!

Well I could understand his major contemporaries -- Nelson, Hogan, and Snead – being part of the Hall's inaugural class in '74 while Mangrum was not among the 13 first chosen. But by the early 1990s when men like Gene Littler, with but one Major like Lloyd and 7 fewer PGA wins, and Harry Cooper who lacked any Majors among his 36 wins, were getting picked while my 'patient' wasn't, I'd begun to get riled, 'cause it appeared like there was a 'personality contest' going on.

Yes ole Lloyd had often been a pain in the ass to both his fellow competitors and the media alike, but the man COULD play, and oh was he clutch! His record as an individual in 4 Ryder Cups (1947-53): 6 wins out of 8 matches played, with 3-1 records in both the singles and foursomes portions of those Cups.

The PGA picked him to captain that '53 squad and Mr. Icicle, though his heart was battered by then, brought home a winning side. Unfortunately, this Cup went down to the very last match and putt. I feared what that strain might do to Lloyd's insides even before the quote he gave the press. "I'll never, never captain an American team again because of the 9,000 deaths I suffered in the last hour."

Yet the riverboat gambler took another chance with his health by allowing himself to be convinced to serve as a vice-captain ("honorary" back then) for the '55 U.S. squad, in a year when he'd won zero tournaments worldwide. The fact that the contest was being held not far from Apple Valley (in Palm Springs) probably was the key factor allowing him to take part ... Respect – he had it from his peers in spades, but not from some short-sighted World Golf Hall of Fame voters!

Anyway, with these thoughts in mind, late in 1992 I'd decided to lobby again as delicately as I could on Lloyd's behalf for the World Hall, starting with his, I hoped by now, mellowed major competitors – Ben, Byron, and Sam. Not surprisingly, it was Lord Nelson who gave me the most hope when he said that in his upcoming autobiography the toughness of Lloyd as a competitor would 'come through' loud and clear. I'll follow up on this promise in Byron's own "Afterwards" chapter.

However there's still more to praise about Lloyd Mangrum the golfer here and now. You see, during the 1990s when I was touting Mr. Icicle for the Hall, sometimes I'd get the response that after all he did win only 1 Major. True. But I Bobby Shout would retort to them, "You show me any other player who has 1 or 2 or even 3 Majors to their credit who can match the sustained excellence of Lloyd in the Open and Masters."

Let's start with Augusta. Ole Lloyd played there 13 times between 1940 and 1956, finishing no worse than 9th on an astounding 12 occasions! His record at the Masters includes two 2nds, two 3rds, three 4ths, and two 6ths. Add to that a 7th, 8th, and 9th place – one of each – and I reckon that Fate owed the riverboat gambler at least 1 title at Bobby Jones' place.

As for our Open, along with his triumph in the first one played after WWII, Mr. Icicle notched 2 top-10s as a pre-war youngster, then went on a streak from 1950 through '54 where he finished 2nd – the bug-penalty Open! – 4th, 10th, 3rd, and 3rd again! I rest my case.

No, wait – there's this too. From 1951 to '53 when Lloyd was looking in top form with those ten Tour wins, 1952 looks 'leaner' with only 2 such victories, though the Western Open was a huge title back then. However that same year he'd invested considerable time and energy in a trip to Australia, grabbing first places in both that country's richest event at the time (the Ampol) as well as at Adelaide, while also outplaying the field in Asia's oldest championship, the Philippine Open.

With these triumphs to go along with Mr. Icicle's 1946 Argentine Open win and his earlier European post-war victories, Lloyd had certainly proved himself to be an international 'great.' Yet you wouldn't believe how many World Hall Of Fame voters I had to educate in this regard. Some of them had dismissed Mangrum from consideration solely because they'd heard 'the stories' about his surliness. It was very frustrating, trying to combat that, especially considering that the American PGA had awarded my 'patient' a place in their own Hall way back in '64 before Lloyd had even turned 50!

Through the final decades of Lloyd's life, he allowed me to stay in touch. It sounds silly but I felt honored. Most of our communication was in the form of lengthy phone conversations, though long-distance calls were darn expensive back then.

I'd always phone him on our shared birthday, August 1st, also around Christmas time, and sometimes when I was watching a Major on T.V., knowing that he'd be 'tuned in' too. His commentaries about the play were often brutally perceptive, quite a contrast from the more polite announcing that ruled back then.

You may remember Arnold Palmer's classic collapse against Billy Casper on the Olympic course in the '66 Open? How Arnie was well ahead both late in the Sunday round and during the following day's playoff? Well as 'the king' was walking off the 15th green on Sunday with 3 strokes still in hand with 3 to play, my telephone rang and it was Mr. Icicle. "Arnie's fucking done," Lloyd had growled. "Too bad."

"What?" I'd shot back. "Are you saying he's not going to win this thing?" And though I'd protested, a shiver of dread had zapped through me at Mr. Icicle's prediction.

After all, his voice of doom didn't stem from enmity. Lloyd liked Arnold a lot. The fact that Palmer and Hogan were frigid with each other was reason enough, I guess.

It didn't seem to matter that Arnie had found a way to stay stateside during war – like Ben and Sam had done. The fact was that Arn had chosen to enlist in the Coast Guard in '51 rather than risk being drafted for the fight in Korea, after he'd dropped out of college that year.

And strangely, the riverboat gambler – who'd never 'tipped his hand' emotion-wise on the course -- also had informed me that he enjoyed the way the super-transparent Palmer conducted himself while playing. In response to my surprise back then, Lloyd had barked with impatience, "No, Shout, I mean the man's fearlessness: his gutsy 'go for it' style! He 'gets it' – that golf's just a game, whatever the stakes."

Well what Mangrum had called to share with me on that '66 Open Sunday was that he'd just observed an Arnie who'd finally lost his golfing courage. The veteran cardplayer went on to explain that moments earlier, Palmer had exhibited a poker-like 'tell' so powerful on the 15th green that Mr. Icicle could only conclude that Arnold, besides being destined to lose to Casper, would probably never win another Major. I of course found that hard to believe and pressed him about what he'd seen.

"Bobby, you watched what I saw, didn't you?" Lloyd had snarled at me. "There's Arnold facing a mere 10-footer for par, and after he settles into that knees-locked putting stance of his, he looks up at 'the line' not once, not twice, but 4 times before being able to 'pull the trigger'! That was the act of a man scared to fail. The 'old' Palmer would have stroked that 'baby' without a damn 2nd glance."

Then my long-time 'patient' continued with his soothsaying: "Don't be surprised to see our boy leave a not-very-long putt or two short of the cup soon. When a player's bluffing his state of mind but his small muscles 'feel the panic,' that will happen. Likewise, expect Palmer 'to pull' some fucking 'funny clubs' now that he's unsure whether being fearless still works for him. He'll hit an iron off some tee at some point, rather than the driver he'd usually use without a thought."

Decades later, when a highlights reel of ABC's coverage of that Open became available through YouTube, I was able to review the '4-peeks' moment at 15 that Lloyd had described, as well as reminding myself of how accurate his pre-depictions of Palmer's later mistakes at Olympic proved to be. Study Arnie's body language – full of head shakes – even after he sinks his last short putt on Sunday to get into a playoff with Casper.

Some big names have written that Arn made a heroic 6-footer, but no, it was only about half that length. How do I know? Byron Nelson was there for ABC and made 'the call': "3-and-a-half feet," he drawls, and that's just how it looked.

There was another side to Lloyd Mangrum few people got to see. He had softened a bit in his later years, his sleep having quieted somewhat after he'd stepped back from the pressures of big-time golf. Anyway, at times on the phone I'd go so far as to 'rib' him, and generally he 'took it' in good humor.

One of my favorite jabs was to read Lloyd quotes from his second venture into golf authorship, a book titled HOW TO BREAK 90 AT GOLF. This time – scorning the philosophy of his maiden attempt, GOLF: A NEW APPROACH – Mr. Icicle had indulged in lengthy descriptions of how to play various shots. Or, I should say, his muddle-headed collaborator did, a 'ghost writer' by the name of Otis Dvpwick.

Here's what Mangrum/Dvpwick had to say on page 52 of that 1952 work in reference to blasting from the sand: "Your arms should be straight and *stay* straight throughout the entire stroke."

Aping Lloyd's own colorful language, I'd sputtered to him over the phone, "What kind of fucking contortionist can keep *both* his arms straight through the entire backswing, boy, and not wind up either pulling a shoulder muscle or chopping straight down on the sand – by following your advice, you damn fraud?"

He'd replied, "Don't you worry, Shout. That crappy book sold so well it was 'brought out' again at the start of '54 -- with the title HOW TO PLAY BETTER GOLF. And I can tell you that some of the suckers who bought the book you're quoting went ahead and paid for its twin, too, thinking I'd written different stuff So, little man, don't argue with success!"

'Cause of personal reasons I'm certain that one of the later times I visited Apple Valley was in 1967 during the "Summer of Love." The journey to Lloyd's place was something I did to make my West Coast swing at least a little worthwhile, after 'striking out' in my efforts to convince Cheryl Lynn to leave the streets of San Francisco. Yes, my 40-year-old wife had abandoned us in Texas to become a free-love 'flower child.' What a shame that was! Stay tuned for more on this 'far out' interlude in *my* Afterwards chapter.

At that stage, though Mr. Icicle had started to need periods of rest each day, his competitive fire was still plenty alive. Almost the first thing he said when I joined him out on his porch was "How 'bout that fucking Nicklaus – shooting 275 in our Open. There's another record ole Bennie Hogan can't call his own anymore."

I Bobby Shout just shook my head. You should have seen that gambler's evil grin!

Well it must have been about 100 degrees out there – low humidity or not! – and Lloyd's skin looked as leathery and wrinkled as a long-used golf glove, but he wouldn't take my hints that maybe we should adjourn to his air-conditioned abode. I think he wanted to outlast somebody at something, and so Mr. Icicle kept us both frying for a while.

Toward dusk, the "Squire of Apple Valley" as some local wags had dubbed him, took me out for a quick 9 holes. I hadn't brought clubs and Mr. Icicle did me no favors in handing over a none-too-fancy set for my use.

Naturally this had to do with a bet as to who was going to shoot the better score: He the shitty, 'broken-down' old pro – his words – or me the "young whippersnapper." I was a soon-to-be 47-year-old at that juncture; he still 52, but I 'played along' gladly, just to see this master 'paint another picture' on grass.

And despite the addition of an oxygen tank for Lloyd to take a swallow from once in a while, he still cut a dapper figure on the course, both in attire and golfing style. I Bobby Shout loved it as he 'drew the ball' in a light arc just where it needed to land to get close to most of the holes on his way to taking $300 'off me.'

He birdied 5 of those 9 holes – making a sweet mockery of our match – his feet-together putting style as casually elegant as ever. I'll admit that I'd been dreading the first appearance of twitching nerves during his stroke after so many heart seizures, but his movements of the putter that afternoon were silky.

Eleta and Lloyd took me out to dinner that night and most of what he'd 'taken off me' went into providing us with deluxe 'dishes' and plentiful 'booze,' though she made a point of cautioning him to chew more slowly and to sip his drinks. Mr. Icicle loved her 'to death' still – his longtime traveling partner and business manager -- that was obvious. Anyone else trying to corral him the way Eleta did would get a punch in the nose for their trouble, I reckoned as this merry night continued on.

About 4 years later, in mid-July of 1971, I was delighted to find that the Associated Press had assigned a reporter to profile the now veteran of *ten* heart attacks, Lloyd Eugene Mangrum, and that the *New York Times* had even 'picked up' the story.

It pleased me right off that the lead paragraph had presented Lloyd along with Ben and Sam as members of a "Big 3" on Tour around 1950 just as Palmer, Player, and Nicklaus had been called in recent years. And although the reporter muddied up the nature of Mr. Icicle's wartime injuries, I reckoned the article was 'right on' for the most part.

Here's an early sentence by the writer that's pure Lloyd: "Mangrum has retained some of his soft Texas accent and has lost none of his acidity. A friend once said he would like to write a book about him but was afraid it would be so full of bleep-bleeps it wouldn't make sense." That friend obviously wasn't me!

The most telling quotes in this article not surprisingly came from the riverboat gambler himself. In regard to still getting in a round at his Apple Valley course now and then, Lloyd continued, "I never liked to play with just anybody. Fact is, I never did like too many people." The reporter tried to soften this truth by adding that his subject really didn't mean that. But I knew better.

Reading this blunt confession from Lloyd brought back to me the decades-long irony involving him and Hogan. The 2 men shared eerily similar mental make-ups, yet rather than being attracted to each other, they'd been repulsed by what they saw. I actually teared up, thinking what a more humane pair they might have become if comrades rather than foes.

There were other allusions in this story harking back to 1950. Lloyd was asked about the Open at Merion that year. His anti-USGA reply began, [It was] "a bleep-bleep bowling alley … They make the rough so high you could put a man and a monkey in it and the monkey would do as well as the man."

And then there was Lloyd's dislike of the nickname given to him as the "Squire of Apple Valley." It turned out his aversion to that title stemmed from his – yes – dislike of Gene Sarazen who'd been dubbed a "squire" years earlier for having bought a New York farming estate. This mention made me recall with a grin that Mr. Icicle had threatened Sarazen with a putter in the locker room at Augusta in '50, if Jimmy Demaret's account was to be believed. I did!

I *was* disappointed in one respect by this article in that there wasn't a single word written about Lloyd's folks. Not that I was surprised. He'd always deflected my questions on that subject.

Still, I reckoned that his parents were a key piece to the puzzle of the man's dark side. You want an example of how peevish any mention of them made him: The 1 time I asked Mr. Icicle what his father had done for a living, he'd blurted back, "Not much," and that was that. In fact, I didn't learn their names, Jim and Louetta, 'til 3 months before the riverboat gambler's death in '73.

Lloyd had divulged those names after a typically livid string of oaths ending with, "Oh what the fucking hell. Seeing how I'll soon be 'cashing in my chips,' Dr. Shout, you might as well know at least that. But no more damn questions about them." At this point he'd picked up an old service revolver and pointed it my way. "Or you're going first."

Well I didn't ask him if the thing was loaded. I didn't ask him a 'damn thing' more that August afternoon in Apple Valley. From then on we spent the precious time reminiscing about the Tour 'til I had to get to the town's airport, and when the following Veteran's Day heart attack 'did Lloyd in for good,' I Bobby Shout swore like I never had before – in his honor – at the newspaper obituary, bringing a look of horror to the face of my flabbergasted wife.

CHAPTER 14

Byron afterwards

WHILE COMBATIVE LLOYD Mangrum died the earliest (1973) of the Texas Quartet and endured the shortest life span (dead at 59), John Byron Nelson Jr. lived an extra 35 years to the ripe old age of 94, expiring gracefully on his front porch in Roanoke, Texas in 2006. Ben (1997) and Jimmy (1983) had both been gone quite a while.

It was a bright fall morning on September 26th that Byron departed this earth for heaven, an exit which seemed perfectly fitting to me, seeing how that Christian man deserved sainthood when compared with many of his rough-hewn golfing peers. However, even saints have sinful moments and 'Lord Byron' – or 'Mr. Golf' if you prefer – was no exception. In due time, I Bobby Shout will 'flesh out' this charge, though regretfully.

I reckon you recall that Nelson's impressive performance in the inaugural Texas Sharpshooters Invitational had led to a surge in demand for him to appear after all in exhibitions sponsored by his club company MacGregor. Well before the new year 1951 had hardly commenced, Mr. Golf reminded the world in the best way how he'd gotten that moniker, leading to even more requests for Byron to 'show his stuff' in the Northwest on a spring tour. Ultimately he was booked to provide 26 exhibitions over a single month's time there.

In early January of '51, Lord Byron had made the trip from Texas to California to participate in Bing Crosby's annual 'clambake,' which along with the Masters were by then the only 2 competitive events he was sure to be at. (And have I mentioned? I always hated that nickname "Lord Byron," considering what a scoundrel the poet Byron was.)

Anyway, during this era the Crosby tournament consisted of only 3 rounds instead of 4, with the now-lost Cypress Point being one of the 'tracks' in play. What *was* the same then as now was the event's unusual approach to its pro-am teams.

Bing did not allow his amateur buddies to be 'cast aside' during the tournament proper. Instead, every amateur could hope to raise a pro-am trophy on Sunday, with a glory no less coveted than the individual pro who'd outshot his peers over the long weekend.

Well at this particular Crosby, Mr. Golf had been partnered with the iconic Eddie Lowery of Francis Ouimet caddying fame, but their pro-am performance had earned no hardware. 4 teams bested them, and their score of 202 trailed the leaders by 6 strokes.

On his own ball though, no one beat Byron! Despite bad weather, his 5-under 67 on Saturday the 13th, bookended by two 71s, was good enough to win by 3 strokes, earning him both a $2,000 first prize plus an extra dose of publicity to stoke the public's interest in his golfing wisdom.

I'd recognized right off that this win would benefit Nelson in those ways. Yet I Bobby Shout had no clue how Byron's being out in the Northwest later that year would result in a new role in the world of golf for him, kick-started by none other than his Crosby partner Eddie Lowery, once a pint-sized caddy but by 1951 a millionaire car dealer in San Francisco with oodles of golfing connections.

Upon Byron's return home from Pebble Beach I'd invited him to lunch at the Golden Roadrunner restaurant. Hearing him tell how he'd finally made it to the victor's circle again was a conversation I was raring to have.

After we'd settled in to wait for our orders to arrive, I Bobby Shout -- with all the delicacy of a saloon gal seeking a drink – fired some questions right off at Mr. Golf: "So how did you do it, Byron? Did you have some special 'game plan.' Were you feeling as confident as you were when on top in '45? How about your nerves? Did they jolt your stomach some on the way in?" And so on …

John Byron Nelson just gave me that wry look of his before drawling, "Now Bobby it really wasn't me as much as the other fellows. You know how Bing's tournament week is one big party any year. Well with all the bad weather this time around, the boys were stuck inside with nothing to do but chat up them starlets and show the Hollywood folks how us pros can 'hold our liquor,' too."

I should of reckoned that Byron would find some way to be modest about his triumph! He'd continued on about how most of the field were battling a lack of sleep and 'hangovers' all 3 rounds while he the teetotaler was 'fresh as a daisy.' "If I was ever gonna win another time on the PGA circuit, Bobby, this was it."

And then the former Mr. Golf let his amiable mask slip for a bit. With eyes hardened, he added, "Of course I'd practiced extra this time before heading West, seeing how it seemed folks needed some reminding that I was still a player worth seeing in an exhibition. Come March I'll be working on my game even harder, right up 'til it's time to go to Augusta."

So powerful was the determination in his voice that I exclaimed back, "I bet you will win a 3rd Masters!" to which Byron had replied that he neither expected victory nor deserved it considering all the blessings he'd already received, but who knew what the good Lord might ordain.

If this sounds somewhat egotistical on that good Christian's part, let me remind you that he'd finished tied for 4th there just 9 months earlier, back in 1950. And heck, the man wasn't yet even 40, his 39th birthday still a couple of weeks away on that January day we'd dined.

Well come that April, Ben Hogan mounted a campaign at Augusta that involved 3 weeks of preparation on site and it paid off in a win. Worse for Byron, the leaders who'd bested him at the 1951 Masters through the second and third rounds were not just the Hawk and Slamming Sammy – the 3rd member of that temporary triumvirate was one Skee Riegel, who hadn't 'taken up' golf 'til age 23 and was on his way to a winless career on the PGA Tour.

Though Byron never voiced his frustration over this shocking turn of events at that tournament, it had to gall him that Riegel held on to second at the end while the best that Mr. Golf could do that year was tie for 8th! And worse would follow: With 1 exception, Nelson never cracked the top 10 again at Augusta, nor did he win any other tournament in the U.S. – on or off the Tour – after 1951. However, like many of the golfing greats, my 'patient' was treated to 1 last golden year of sorts; that was 1955.

Soon to turn 43 years old, Byron had once again partnered with Eddie Lowery at the Crosby in January, and this time that pair did win the pro-am. As usual, the weather had turned rotten.

In recounting this victory to me, Mr. Golf gave the lion's share of the credit to his friend and benefactor Eddie. According to Byron, Lowery had had to make use of every one of his 8 allotted handicap strokes to get the team 'over the finish line' in 1st with a final-round net score of 63. And though I assumed that this story was partly fiction -- Nelson being his usual humble self -- I soon learned otherwise.

How? Well several days later I got another call from the Roanoke rancher giving me the news that Eddie had felt so good about his performance at Bing's event that he felt ready to play in the '55 Open at St. Andrews. Oh and he'd urged Byron to come along and compete as well.

"Are you going to do that?" I'd asked in disbelief, knowing that Mr. Golf's wife Louise would not take kindly to Byron over-stressing himself by playing overseas, especially after seeing him return from California totally drained by the Crosby event. It was one thing to make some extra cash for the ranch doing exhibitions and 'good-old-boy' tournaments; another to risk an ulcer at a foreign Major.

Byron knew right off what I was 'getting at.' Mr. Nelson had chuckled before replying how Louise had demanded a follow-up week in Paris for sightseeing, which would also serve as a winding-down period for Byron before the brutal return flight. Back then, a TWA sleeper plane could take up to 24 hours – fighting headwinds -- just to return to New York from 'Gay Paree.' But there was the added understanding that Eddie would pick up most of the tab for the entire trip.

Little Lowry, the San Francisco wheeler dealer, knew his new bride would be apt to stay in a better humor if provided with some female company while he and Byron trod the Old Course, and so the deal was struck just as Louise desired. I'd found that Nelson often put forth his wife as the hard bargainer in the family, but he too did not disdain a good deal.

Thus in June this mixed foursome flew by way of 2 North Atlantic airfields (for refueling) in order to reach Scotland, a mere 14-to-16-hour journey back then, during which Mr. Golf was made retched both by his claustrophobia and the tension produced by a rocky storm during the flight. Byron hadn't shared this part with me, but it 'came out' later in his book.

And though Eddie had arranged to 'get the goods' on how to play that devilish Old Course by convincing the British sportsman and journalist Leonard Crawley to 'talk them through' their practice rounds, Eddie failed to qualify for the championship while Byron 'made it through.'

In fact, when Nelson got back home he told me that he'd felt great about his ball-striking during the Open and it had only been the super-slow greens which had doomed him to a 5th-place finish. I mention this because of the likely part this fact played in what happened next while the Nelsons prepared to relax in Paris.

According to Mr. Golf's autobiography HOW I PLAYED THE GAME, which didn't 'come out' till almost 40 years later, his buddy Eddie had happened to 'run into' one of his cronies on the Old Course during the Open and this gent was the current president of the French Golf Federation. The upshot of that 'chance meeting' was both Eddie and Byron being offered the chance to compete in the French Open, which was scheduled to begin the week following the British.

In his 1993 book, my 'patient' paints a picture of the invite having occurred without his knowledge and heck, what could he do but politely play, though the prospect of being a 'golf widow' for a second straight week in Europe had made Louise mad at *Lowery*. Well when Byron told me this tale upon his return to America in '55, I couldn't help lifting my eyebrows at him, 'cause I reckoned he was more than strong-willed enough to say "No" to the French if he'd felt like it – and his wife would have loved him for it – but when a golfer is 'striping it,' he wants to play! (Oh, and Eddie Lowery failed to qualify for the final field again.)

Fortunately Mr. Golf's competitive instincts were "right on," culminating on July 14th, Bastille Day, when he did win the darn thing, the first American since Hagen in 1920 (not '22 like in the book) to take this French prize. And further negating the Nelsons' potential marital breach was the fact that Eddie did finally make good on his talk about Parisian sightseeing, banking the Nelsons for a third week in Europe.

However I knew better than to talk to Louise back home about the 10,000 franc winnings that resulted from Byron's 17-under effort. Why? 'Cause I'd heard how he'd pledged anything won in Paris to help pay their hotel bill. And since the foursome had stayed at the Ritz, this meant that 100% of the purse was fated to Eddie, leaving not even a penny gained to feed one of the Nelsons' hens.

Nor did I dare ask her about the bawdy French dance reviews that Eddie had 'dragged' the Nelsons to a couple of times, though it wasn't like Louise didn't know 'which end of the horse was what.' No, at heart the first Mrs. Nelson was a proper lady as well as a friendly one and I admired her for that.

While this French tournament triumph would prove to be Byron's 'swan song' in big time events, that didn't mean his clubs were never involved again in making golf history. In fact a notable example of this sort occurred the very next year. That was 1956.

Have you ever heard of "The Match," probably the most famous better-ball round in American golfing history? Well once again it was Eddie Lowery 'pulling the strings' that led to Mr. Golf's involvement, but to fully appreciate the 'back story" to "The Match," we need to reverse to the year 1952.

In August of '52, Byron had been back out in the Northwest doing another round of exhibitions. It happened that the U.S. Amateur was being held at the Seattle Golf Club and one of Eddie's San Francisco protégés had made the match-play portion. Always 'in debt' to Eddie – for his ongoing generosity – Byron was quite ready to do his friend the favor of taking a look at the young stud in action. You've probably heard of him – Ken Venturi?

Well Kenny lost early in that Amateur but Nelson did see promise and soon thereafter started working with Venturi on his game in the Bay City. Later Byron had grinned while describing to me the young man's face when first told there were 6 things in his game that needed urgent attention, Mr. Golf's pronouncement having come on the heels of Kenny shooting a 66 at the San Francisco Golf Club in Nelson's company. That exceptional score had been accomplished mostly through a good day's pitching and putting Byron had added.

And it wasn't too long before my 'patient' 'got roped' into acting as a golf mentor/coach for another of Lowery's part-time car sellers. Harvie Ward could beat Venturi as often as not, and went on to win both the U.S. and British Amateurs. Unfortunately, Eddie's loose financial ways would eventually 'come home to roost,' costing Harvie his amateur status among other casualties, but that's another story ...

Suffice it to say, Byron was a pioneer in offering his golfing wisdom without charge to promising amateurs and struggling pros, 'racking up' his greatest fame in this regard by taking Tom Watson 'under his wing' after the young star's game had regressed during '76. What a contrast this was to Ben and Lloyd, who were apt to snarl a "No" if asked to give a *single* lesson, even if bribed mightily! Yes, Byron was blessed with a freely-giving spirit.

Anyway in January of '56 the usual mix of pros, stars, and big-money folks had gathered again for Bing's annual "clambake" and the Nelsons found themselves dining with their host George Coleman and the Lowerys on Monday night of tournament week. As they chatted, the conversation turned to just how good were young Kenny and Harvey.

Eddie Lowery had 'jumped in' – not Byron! – to claim that his 2 employees could in fact beat any other twosome at this point. George – a long-time buddy of Ben Hogan's – countered, "Is that so? Even pros!?"

When Eddie wouldn't 'back down' in the face of Coleman's skepticism, a $5,000 wager was soon on the table, though George had chosen both Byron and Ben for his team. And though Hogan was not present at that moment, a quick phone call from George got him 'on board,' with the match scheduled for the very next morning at Cypress Point, on Tuesday, January 10th.

Let me remind you of 2 things: First off, that five grand was a hell of a lot of money back then; and secondly, though Byron felt it best to recall the bet being lowered significantly by the time they teed off, I still don't believe it.

So here you had 2 golfing legends taking on a pair of young studs, mere amateurs whose very own swing guru was now out to outplay them, on the most magical course in the country. How could a gallery of a thousand then, not turn up to see 'the fun' though 'mum had been the word'? Nor how could a skilled writer like Mark Frost not produce a bestseller out of the wondrous golf played that day!

I won't spoil the ending by revealing who won, except to say that on the 18th, Hogan was left with a reasonable birdie try which would put the 4 players collectively 26-under-par. Before stroking that putt he was reported to have said that he'd be damned if he was going to be tied by a couple of amateurs. And yes I later asked the Hawk if he'd indeed muttered those words. In reply I got only one of his famous icy stares. That was good enough for me. If I was truly a betting man, I reckon I'd 'back' the answer "Yes."

By the way, there was a sort of 'The Match II' involving Byron again, 12 years later in '68 when Mr. Golf was more than old enough to play on today's 'Senior Tour.' No one's written a book around that number II, but it is mentioned by Nelson himself in his 1993 autobiography.

You may recall that during World War II, Byron's golfing success in the U.S. was only approached by 1 other pro, Harold "Jug" McSpaden, who earned that pair the moniker the "Gold Dust Twins." During 1945, Jug set a record by finishing 2nd in Tour events 13 times – while Byron was winning nearly all of them!

Jug did win once in '45, but not by besting Mr. Golf. The two were partners that year while winning the Miami International 4-Ball. Forty years later Harold McSpaden summed it up by telling Byron that "If you wouldn't have been born, I'd have been known as a pretty good player."

Anyhow, McSpaden had designed a course outside Kansas City, Kansas called Drub's Dread which had premiered in 1966 as the longest and toughest track in the world at 8,101 yards! And 2 years later, for publicity purposes Jug 'got up' a better-ball match pairing him with Byron versus Arnie and Jack. This time Mr. Golf made no mention to me about bets having been made, but he did mention that 'the old-timers' would be playing the course at 6,700 yards while Palmer and Nicklaus had a 7,600 yard layout 'on their hands,' and that's what the papers later reported.

It sorrows me to say this, but Byron's recollection of this match as told in his book 25 years later 'gets things wrong' and is one of a surprising number of memory lapses on the author's part. In his defense though, professional 'fact checkers' were hardly standard at that time.

Reading what the by then octogenarian Mr. Golf wrote (lots of excuses actually) you would think that he and Jug got clobbered that day in '68. But the fact is – and I kept the AP report of this contest – the older pair only lost 1-down, beaten by an Arnie birdie on the monstrous par-5 17th hole!

Conversely, Byron recalls playing the 17th 'for kicks' with the match already concluded, and being proud to have 'hit' the green with driver on a long par-3. A confused fiction alas.

However, one thing that is for sure about that day, August 12th 1968, was the ages of those 4 combatants: Byron (56) and Jug (60) combining for 116 years; Jack (28) and Arnie (38), 66 years. In fact, the 50 year's difference in combined ages was used to figure the distance handicap that the older men would have, that is,

50 yards less per hole, amounting to the aforementioned 900-yard disparity in the teeing grounds to be used, should the match make it to the 18th.

By this stage of his life, John Byron Nelson Jr. was already a veteran of 11 years in the golf-television business, and would go on to 'log' another decade's worth of 'calling putts' both at the men's and women's Tour events. It was in 1975 that Mr. Golf 'had had enough' of the travel and various network fooleries. He told me that it had been over his strong objections that ABC had made him try to draw diagrams 'live' to supplement his words about what the players faced, and the whole thing had embarrassed him 'on air.'

At this point, I reckon it behooves me to give my assessment of Byron's intelligence, lest you think that the episode noted above was typical of his cognitive abilities. Many folks have concluded that Ben Hogan was a genius. I'm here to let you know that if Nelson possessed a lesser brain, it wasn't by much. The fact that he was the man who first figured out the necessary bodily actions needed to play well with steel shafts should be evidence enough. However, allow me to cite a couple of other telling examples of both the man's smarts and his heart.

In 1965 the former Mr. Golf had finally been given the chance to captain the American side in the Ryder Cup, naturally a non-playing leader at age 53 with a sore back that had required surgery several years before. That year the U.S. again won 'easily' as they seemed to every 2 years – 11 triumphs over the past 12 Cups -- but upon his return home Captain Nelson had some news for me.

"Bobby Shout," he'd begun, using my full name as he did when something important was 'in the air,' "I don't want you spreading this about, but I gave 'the enemy' some aid and comfort after our matches was over at Royal Birkdale."

A twinkle in his kind eyes told me that what was coming was far from scandalous, yet still I was intrigued. Byron could be much more of an 'out of the box' thinker than most folks imagined.

"Some of them British big shots did me the honor of asking why us American players were playing a better game than their guys these days – and a different-style game – higher, curving shots. Well I was honest with them." (*As if he wouldn't be*, I'd gushed inwardly.)

Mr. Golf had pointed out to our foes that because our larger ball produced more backspin when struck than their "British balls' did, American players could 'hit down' on the ball – confident that the resulting shot would fly up. By contrast, the smaller British ball demanded more of a wristy flick for height, which effectively increased each club's loft, but also elevated the potential for 'fatted shots.' The Americans 'hit-down' method in turn made recovering from long grass more dependable, since a steeper arc meant contacting less of a plant barrier on the way to contact.

Byron went on to say, "What really 'opened their eyes' though, Bobby, was when I pointed out these additional advantages of our higher-spinning ball. They had thought their lower-flying, straighter-by-nature British balls were best for combating the high winds and severe rough of links golf. Well I told 'em 'Yes' for some of the time, but not always – that's the problem with a ball like theirs which resists curving. It's too one-dimensional."

What he had meant was that an expert player with the American ball could offer more resistance to a sideways gale by intentionally spinning his shot into the wind, and in that way keeping his ball from being pushed off the fairways. Nor was our ball apt to be stymied when a big curve was needed to slide a shot around an obstacle, like the trees on 'dogleg holes' faced by the Brits during most Cups played here.

Well you might think – couldn't any other American Ryder Cupper of that time have made the same argument? No, not quite so convincingly.

You see, Byron may have been the straightest-hitting champion of all time, as Jack Nicklaus once said, and as his British rivals had surely seen for themselves. So for him who could hit the bigger American ball just as accurately as the masters of the smaller British one to say that he needed the help of a larger ball's greater spin at times had to be eye-opening!

Four years later, the 1969 Ryder Cup returned to Royal Birkdale and on this occasion ended in a 16-16 tie. I wasn't there to see how many of the British side had converted to our ball, but I did find that Byron was somewhat pleased rather than disappointed by that matches' outcome.

The British ball was banned from the "British Open" 5 years later, forcing the United Kingdom's finest to 'go American.' In 1990 the R&A outlawed their former trusty ball totally. In his final book, Mr. Golf recalls this process happening much more quickly, contrary to these facts. Yet a botched timeline does not diminish Nelson's good intentions in the least.

My second example of Byron's exceptional intelligence and awareness of others' needs has to do with the PGA tournament that still bears his name. This story started back in 1967 with the Dallas Open's struggles to attract good fields. Ticket sales were lagging once again and the sponsoring group, a civic organization called the Salesmanship Club, had expressed their worries to Byron who was scheduled to provide radio commentary for the event.

In short, Mr. Golf got Arnold Palmer to 'sign on' and it made a huge difference in the galleries that year. The Salesmanship Club, having seen the power of a celebrity golfer to up their 'take,' then turned around and asked Byron if he would lend his name to their golf fundraiser from then on.

Well Nelson accepted but not with the notion of just being some figurehead. He'd already toured the civic club's facilities for helping troubled youths and been impressed enough that when he was asked to get involved, Byron was 'all in." So, ahead of the inaugural "Byron Nelson Invitational" in '68, its namesake spoke up on the subject of what would attract a great field to the new venue Preston Trails, and the 'Salesmen' listened.

"Bobby," he'd told me. "Preston Trails was a fine new course but it was a men-only club with little thought to women or children for heaven's sake! I explained to the "Salesmen" that many of the pros liked to travel with their wives and needed to bring their young kids along, too. That being so, my 'pitch' was if we let them know that we're providing a staffed nursery – no other events on Tour were doing this – and a relaxing spot for the women, they'd be begging their husbands to play in Dallas. And well, it worked!"

Talk about a man who possessed strong emotional intelligence as well as the more traditional kind. That was Byron 'to a tee.' Yet he was human and I must include in this account the dispute that strained our relations for many years after, my having taken Mr. Golf to task for what he did *not* include in his 1993 book.

My trouble with the rancher-turned-author's text centered around his 'treatment' of Lloyd Mangrum. You may recollect that Mr. Icicle won the 1946 U.S. Open. Well Byron was 1 of the 2 opponents who Lloyd beat in a playoff for the championship that year, and on page 161 Mr. Golf dwells on an "80-foot putt" made by the winner *on the 9th hole* of the 18-hole 3-man duel as being the lucky, decisive 'blow' in Mangrum's 1-stroke victory.

Further strengthening the impression that there was something shaky about Mr. Icicle's triumph were the loser's words which say one thing then reverse course -- simultaneously providing Byron with a sort of excuse. "I'd have to say it was the best I played to lose a tournament in my whole life. My concentration was probably not as good as it should have been, because I'd made up my mind … that if I won I would announce my retirement …"

It's still hard for me to cotton how much covering-up Mr. Golf did in his scarce account of that historic Sunday play-off at the Canterbury Golf Club on June 16th – both as to his own failings and Lloyd's courageous comeback. And I saw the action first-hand, having made the 7-hour drive from my University of Chicago 'digs' to northern Ohio on Friday, the long drive seeming like a lark, me being only in my mid-20s at the time.

First off, there was a playoff needed only because Byron had finished 'like a dog' during Saturday's 36-hole presumed finale. 15 feet from birdie with 1 hole to play, he missed then missed again from 3-feet for bogey. And on the 36th, a pair of bad hooks left Mr. Golf with a 30-yard pitch to the home green. When he didn't get up and down for par, it was that lapse which allowed Mangrum to tie, he having finished with 3 pars.

So, some 20,000 of us showed up for the Sunday playoff, though I Bobby Shout would be one of a mere four grand who'd stay till the bitter end. You see, the Sabbath proved to be a double-round affair as well, all parties having tied with 72s in the morning. Later, the weather got very bad while the players were still out battling in the afternoon, causing a mass exodus, as they say. More on this climax shortly.

Byron's book skates past the morning round except to note that Mangrum and Ghezzi both made long 'bombs' for bird on the 4th while the author missed a much shorter attempt. I'd been prepared to see Byron's envy of Lloyd's putting wizardry appear in print, 'cause I'd heard groans from him even back then. For example, after the 2nd round of that same championship, Mr. Golf had been quoted by the reporters that if he could have putted like Mangrum did that day, he – Byron – would have shot a 57, not the 69 he recorded.

Anyway, it would be 4 years later that I met either of these men for the 1st time, but I was there and like many was sucked into rooting for the underdog who was a decorated veteran. I'm sure that this was another aspect of that playoff which stung forever for Byron, seeing how he *was* Mr. Golf at the time, with his 18 victories the previous year. Still, that 80-footer he laments in his bio – that was only 45-feet, as it was reported the next day in the press, and more a testament to Lloyd's prowess than luck, I thought.

More so -- luck aside, Nelson led by 2 strokes over Mangrum with 6 holes to play on that Sunday, when as I've said, the weather turned nasty! Amid the rumbling and distant lightning that the players had to ignore over the next 3 holes, it was Lloyd who performed like a hero, birdying both the course's 13th and 15th holes with putts of 12 feet. And during this stretch a shaky Byron again suffered the ignominy of 3 putts from 15 feet, thus falling a stroke behind.

Back to Nelson's book ... When I got further down that page 161 of the autobiography, I did feel a bit better upon reading Byron's statement that Lloyd Mangrum "was the most underrated player of my time." However, the rest of that paragraph brought to mind the story of a cowpoke who shot an Indian in the chest 'cause he wanted to see if Redskins were as hardy as he'd heard.

Mr. Golf continued, "He won twenty-one tournaments, including the '46 Open. He was a fine player, but he had kind of an unusual, funny sarcasm ... it made him sound kind of tough."

Well first off, I practically gagged at the immensity of Byron's slight. How had Lloyd's 36 Tour wins been pruned to a modest 21? The mistake looked nothing like an innocent typo. No, an exact number of victories is what Byron provided as fact -- not some approximation like "more than twenty." I had to wonder whether my good Christian friend was subconsciously wishing away the degree of Mangrum's success. Or worse, was there a conscious falsehood at play?

That Byron went on to provide no praise of Lloyd's playing, in particular regarding his fabulous scrambling and putting, beyond the stock phrase "fine player," while devoting a full 3 lines to 'damning with faint praise' Mangrum's sense of humor seemed hardly charitable to me. After all, Byron had begun this section like he was going to explain how underappreciated Mr. Icicle was as a golfer – not as a person.

The balance of this paragraph did nothing to soothe me either. In fact it only made me feel worse for both Lloyd and Byron! You see, Mr. Golf tells of an interview he'd done at a tournament years earlier which seems to 'rub in' Mr. Icicle's anonymity more than dispute it. That is, the questioner asked Nelson if he could name the 7 pros who'd won more than twenty events on Tour in their careers. Byron writes, *"I'd been doing a little studying* for my own broadcast work and got through all of them, including Lloyd, and she said I was the only one who'd remembered Mangrum ..."

I was left with this daunting question: Having studied players' career records for his work, how could even an older Byron have authored a book which 'pegged' Lloyd for merely 21 wins? I Bobby Shout had 1 remaining hope. This autobiography's table of contents listed a second-to-last chapter called "Golfers I've Known Over The Years." Maybe Lloyd Mangrum's golf would be better highlighted there, re-fanning his fame?

It turned out the answer was a big fat "No!" While Hogan and Demaret appeared among the cast of "my favorites" who received a half page or more of Byron's reminiscences, Lloyd was excluded from the chapter. Okay, I realized that Slammin' Sammy also didn't get a capsule in this part of the book, *but darn it*, I swore inside, *he didn't need the ink like Mangrum did to get his golfing-due from posterity!*

At that point, I Bobby Shout should have taken a walk and counted to a thousand, I suppose, but instead I phoned the author immediately and 'let him have it.' I can't recall every word I threw at Byron, being so 'heated up,' but I do know I questioned his worth as a Christian if he couldn't forgive someone who'd been dead for 20 years!

And yes, I may even have hurled the slur "hypocrite" at him – which of course was going too far. Anyways, Byron 'took it' like the classy man he was, saying only that he was sorry I saw things that way.

What I do know is this: Though the next several years after the book's publication saw Byron and I lesser friends, we did 'make up' long before his death. Guess what, too? After the reaming I gave him, I heard that Mr. Golf in '94 started asking the younger pros each year at the Masters as to whether they'd heard of Lloyd, and if not, he told them how good Mangrum really was. Did all of this help lead to Lloyd's finally making the Hall of Fame in 1998? I reckon so ... and hope so, seeing what it cost me.

About our eventual reconciling, it happened in 2000 a week before that year's Masters. Byron was 88 by then while I was no 'spring chicken' either, set to turn 80 that August. I reckon you'll recall that our estrangement had begun in 1993 when his autobiography prompted an angry outburst from me. So we'd been 'on the outs' for about 7 years.

It behooves me to say that I Bobby Shout owe a great deal to Mr. Golf's second wife, Peggy, for her role that day. She and her rancher-husband had been married for 14 years by then, having wed about a year after Louise Nelson's death due to her 3rd or 4th brain-stroke, in 1985. In his choice of a 2nd mate, Byron had once again been blessed. The current Mrs. Nelson had been very good for him and he both adored and trusted her.

On that March 31st, I'd gotten 'a game' in the morning at Colonial, the temperature around 58 degrees when we teed off and expected to climb into the mid-60s by 3 p.m. The breeze was light with no rain expected. My left hip was bothering me again but I managed to 'scratch out' a 39 on the front and so was feeling a little better as we walked from number 9 across toward 10 and the clubhouse with our caddies.

Why, I don't know, but I happened to glance toward the practice green, and there were Byron and Peggy having some sort of contest with another couple. One could guess that this putting activity was foreplay to a lunch date only. Because by that time, though Mr. Golf was still scheduled to hit an honorary opening shot at the Masters, I'd heard that his playing days were over.

Anyway he looked toward me with either a scowl on his face or maybe just with his eyes squinting against the light – I couldn't tell which. Still, my knee-jerk action was to face away and keep walking.

After we'd waited a bit for the group in front to hit their seconds, with me anxious to move on, it was my honor to tee off. As though shooing away the presence of a ghost I flashed a 2nd glance toward the practice green but Nelson was no longer there. Instead, Peggy was guiding him over toward us, it appeared.

Like a raw kid I told myself to stop shaking and just hit the darn ball. Luckily, I smacked it good! By then, the Nelsons were close enough to us that I could hear Byron drawl with some obvious wistfulness, "Wish I could still hit 'em like that."

His compliment brought tears to my eyes, which I slapped at as I turned to him in order to say properly. "Thank you, Byron."

"I was thinking," he responded, and then paused – during which moment Peggy's arm could be seen to squeeze his in encouragement. "Bobby, it's about time we had you out to the ranch again. Call me soon and we'll fix that up."

My answer was vigorous nodding; I was too choked up to speak, overwhelmed by our past histories. Seconds later, Byron had given us a weak wave and Peggy had turned him back toward the clubhouse. Mr. Golf, he who had given Bobby Shout a set of hand-picked clubs so many Christmases ago, was ready to return his friendship to me. Such a valuable gift! I couldn't concentrate properly on the back 9 and shot a crummy 47 that day, yet I was still glowing on the way home.

CHAPTER 15

Jimmy afterwards

JAMES NEWTON DEMARET'S colorful life continued for a decade after Mangrum's death in 1973, though Jimmy was the 1st-born member of the Texas Quartet. To review, his birth year was 1910 while Ben and Byron arrived during 1912; Lloyd in 1914. With 1983 nearing its end, the Wardrobe's life span was sputtering as well, though he didn't know it.

In fact on the late December day which saw Demaret's death at 73 he was trying to do at least a morning's worth of 'paper-shuffling' at his beloved Champions Golf Club in Houston before lapsing back into 'the holiday mood' and the daytime boozing that went along with it.

I Bobby Shout never found out exactly what it was which called for Jimmy's attention outside on that chilly 28th day of the month, but we Texans all heard how his attempt to swing himself into a waiting golf cart resulted in him collapsing then and there instead. Another victim of a heart attack, 'laughing boy' never even had time for a final quip before expiring. That fact saddened me even more, as I reckoned that Jimmy would have liked to 'go out' in comic style in his 73rd year on this earth.

Still he'd set a fine example for the rest of us during his days, showing a sunny, caring side to others – whatever their station – on the course and off. Mr. Wardrobe's warm style had always returned quickly too, after those rare bouts of peevishness which surfaced in him, stemming largely I always reckoned from the self-image insecurity that haunted his core. And yes, Demaret could sulk if provoked. Witness his 6-year Masters boycott from '68 on. But Jimmy also managed to cloak his wounded feelings in first-class humor sometimes.

Did you ever hear his 'line' after the dedication of the Hogan and Nelson bridges at Augusta National in '58? Well a bit of background first …

Those 2 memorials spanning Rae's Creek on the 12th hole had joined another celebratory bridge, this one on the par-5 15th, built in 1955 to commemorate Gene Sarazen's immortal double-eagle shot during the second Masters twenty years earlier. If you'll recall how Demaret felt dishonored by his ranking in Sarazen's book published during 1950, and here Jimmy was now – the only 3-time Masters winner to date – having been given zero on-course recognition, let alone bridges built for him, then you should be able to imagine the hurt behind his quip to the effect that, 'I don't even have a damn outhouse with my name on it there!'

Even as late as 1982, the year before 'laughing boy's' demise, Jimmy had not outgrown occasional sour outbursts. I kept the May 9th Washington Post clipping in which he responded with some very rough words to a reporter's question about the current crop of professionals. "They're all out here for the almighty dollar … They come out of college and say, 'Where's my agent, my make-up man, my lawyer, and my golf course.' Something's got to be done … Most of us came out of the caddy ranks. We learned how to say 'yes sir' and 'no sir.'"

Farther down in that article, Demaret's nemesis Sarazen is quoted as saying the reason that pros had become so robotic on the course was "Too much pressure, too much money," but Jimmy wouldn't buy that excuse. His follow-up remark was, "There are an awful lot of spoiled brats on the tour …"

It seemed to me that Jimmy was being overly harsh, fueled by envy of the way young players by then got both an advanced education and were eased into pro golf by the current setup. His own scant schooling had to be part of what was prodding him to be so critical too, I reckoned – another of Demaret's insecurities at work.

On the other hand, I realized, maybe it was me playing the psychologist too much in this case. After all, Jimmy was just one of several senior pros who had panned the younger guys in that article. And what practical concern lay behind their combined scorn? Well the old guys in '82 had only gotten a Tour of their own going for 3 years, and bashing the conduct of the players on the regular circuit – e.g. during pro-am's – was surely seen as a crafty ploy to herd more dollars their lovable way.

When I phoned the Wardrobe not long after to gauge how authentic his wrath toward the younger guys was, he answered me by saying, "You know, partner, when I hosted the Legends of Golf event at my Onion Creek course (back in '78) I saw the glow on the guys' faces at being real competitors again and I swore we'd have a Tour of our own. You can't always play nice, Bobby. To get oil, you gotta pump the well as you well know. But yeah, some of those kids are money-hungry bastards, just like we were when young," he'd chuckled. So there was my answer.

Anyway lest you think I Bobby Shout am about to portray Jimmy's life after 1950 as one long slog into bitterness, let me declare that the truth was anything but that, fortunately, for a generally kind, friendly, and witty man!

By the time I'd met Jimmy in '50 he'd already made his share of appearances on national radio shows. Among the Texas Quartet each had his boosters as to who actually was the best golfer, but there was never any doubt that 'laughing boy' could do handstands over the other 3 in terms of being a media host, entertainer, and salesman!

That Palm Beach clothing deal which came the Wardrobe's way late in the featured year of this book – well, that was just the beginning of Demaret's career as a hawker of shirts, slacks, and of course golfing headwear. A few years later, Jimmy was being given credit for designing golf shirts as well as modeling them under the Demaret trade-name. According to ad-copy appearing in '54, Jimmy had found both the new acrylic fiber Orlon, and its interweaving with a natural fiber Thalspun, to be great for golf clothes. Never heard of Thalspun? Why it "looks like wool and wears like iron," according to the printed puffery back then.

In addition to his ads for First Flight golf balls, the Wardrobe as spokesman was all over our Texas airwaves and print media during the 1950s and 60s for products that had nothing to do with his profession. Jimmy's endorsements ranged from automobiles to dart games to dictation equipment to medicinal cures.

On television, 'laughing boy' got to play himself in an "I Love Lucy" episode, broadcast on May 17, 1954, and later on the "Jim Backus Show." His radio-commentating grew to include such notable events as the "World Championship of Golf" and the Masters. Also, he'd ventured into film-production, making Bobby Jones' style instructional shorts in which the pro used banter with celebrity-pupils to make his golfing points. Some theaters rented these to show.

Of course he'd already appeared in a motion picture, Ben Hogan's bio movie "Follow the Sun," shot during 1950. And, using Hogan's spectacular 1953 season to his advantage, Jimmy came out with his one-and-only book the next year, MY PARTNER, BEN HOGAN. You won't find any "ghost writers" given credit on the title page of that work, but 'the author' was not shy about crowing to me that it had taken two of them to 'clean up' his language – Jimmy making fun of himself for the laughs he craved.

Toward the end of the '50s, a development related to golf – though *not* related to Jimmy's own game – seemed to be like 'the cherry on top' to his coping with a lesser role on Tour during that decade. Never mind that the Wardrobe did have a playing revival in '57 – challenging in 2 Majors and winning 3 minor events on Tour -- after only garnering 2 small titles the previous 4 years. (There would be no more victories, thanks to a dismal miss of a 2-plus footer on the final hole at the '64 Palm Springs Classic.)

No, what really re-stoked the Demaret ego in 1957 was finally getting the Champions Golf Club project 'off the ground' with his former 'little brother' Jackie Burke Jr. Of course Jimmy had a joke about that development. He told me how he and Jackie had been talking about starting a club for 15 years, but Jimmy wanted to call it "Champions Golf Club" and felt that they 'couldn't get away with it' till his younger partner-to-be could boast of a Major triumph as well.

Finishing the '53 season Jackie had won 10 Tour events but also had reached his 30s with no Major yet. For the next 2 years Burke Jr. won nothing, while all the time according to the Wardrobe *he* was getting itchier to start the Champions project. Demaret in fact swore to me that his lambasting Jackie over that stretch about his lack of credentials, plus hinting how maybe Hogan would make a good substitute partner, was what got young Burke going! "Yep," Jimmy had concluded. "Jackie went out and won those 2 Majors – the Masters and PGA – in '56 'cause of how 'hot' I'd made him."

It didn't matter that I knew the "Champions" name had been suggested by a PR hack hired to create publicity which would attract members – after development of the club was underway! The way "laughing boy" told his tale was so entertaining, all I could do was laugh.

But Champions Golf Club has been no joke. With a grand opening in April of '59, the Cypress course – the original 18 holes built there– was selected to host both a Ryder Cup (1967) and the men's U.S. Open (1969) within its first decade. This is a happenstance which should perk the interest of even the casual golf fan, and I don't mean as a testament to Demaret's friendly 'pull' on others! What I Bobby Shout *am* implying is that it's as rare as a 3-horned steer for a club in the true South to get either of those events, let alone both, over any period of time.

And according to Jackie Burke Jr., it was Jimmy between the two of them who had by far the most to do with the creation of the Cypress Course as a layout worthy of golf's biggest events. That only made sense since the younger Burke was still competing regularly on Tour, while by then the Wardrobe's time was more his own.

Don't get me wrong though: Jimmy in spite of his long experience playing great golf courses had neither the patience nor the desire yet to really 'play' golf architect. He and Jackie got a pro designer Ralph Plummer to flesh out their thoughts about holes at the site, and to do the 'nuts and bolts' stuff involving irrigation and such. However, the Wardrobe was always ready to jump on a bulldozer or to hit plenty of golf shots toward prospective bunkers, greens, and creek hazards that existed there.

In the mid-60s, the Demaret and Burke twosome repeated their roles in the creation of Champions' second 18, this time hiring former-pro George Fazio to perform the formal architectural duties for the envisioned design of their Jackrabbit course. Still, we do need to back up a few years and then go forward again in order to do full justice to 'laughing boy's' career as a golf course developer.

Let me begin by admitting that my apprehensions were misplaced about Jimmy trying to mesh with a northern Jewish crowd at the Concord Hotel in the Catskills of New York state. He came to love the place, hanging out as its resident pro for stints equaling several months each year, well into the 1960s.

Part of his enthusiasm stemmed from the chance to be a consultant at the birth of another notable golf course, just a year after Cypress opened. When I asked Jimmy in '59 what he and the folks at the Concord had in mind, he'd grinned. "Well pard, nobody brags about how easy their course is, now do they?"

Accordingly, the Wardrobe brought in an esteemed designer, Houston friend Joe Finger, to do the taxing stuff, while the Jimmy and Jackie duo set about envisioning a 'track' that they could claim to be as tough as any in the country! The "Monster" opened in 1963 and did not fail to meet its birthright, torturing the average golfer with more than 7,000 yards of tight alleyways between lakes and trees. In an ironic twist, it was Jimmy's old 'pal' Gene Sarazen who'd coined the "Monster" term for the course at first sight, playing before the press prior to its formal opening.

It was 6 years later in '69 that the public learned that 'laughing boy' was not yet done with golf course architecture in Texas. An Austin insurance company owner (and crack amateur) Jimmie Connolly had lured Jimmy with the idea of building a new course as part of a housing development in that city's southeastern suburbs. The property they went on to amass included 3 miles along a little stream called Onion Creek.

When my 'patient' tipped me off that he was fixing to go into partnership with Connolly, he was excited to be the true designer this time but had more than a little trepidation. "Bobby, when I heard the project would be in Austin I was hoping for some hilly terrain to work with – different than what we had for Champions -- but nope, most of the land we've got ain't no hillier than a Tomboy. Plus, I'm supposed to squeeze the front 9 between a mess of housing on 1 side and Onion Creek on the other. The routing on the back 9 – same thing. In fact, it's gonna be even tighter. Well, this *is* supposed to be a neighborhood course, not a tournament track," he'd concluded with that wistful smile of his.

Unfortunately, it took 5 stressful years to get to the grand opening of Onion Creek Golf Club (in '74), but I Bobby Shout am happy to report that my 'patient' did do a fine job with what he'd been given. It's a tight course with small greens and more par-3s than '5s' but that's not to say that Jimmy didn't produce a good test, which included using massive lengths of rope to 'lay out' his desired bunker designs.

On top of that, the necessarily short length of the Onion Creek Golf Club happened to play a key role in the success of Demaret's last major contribution to the world of golf. How so? I'll explain, but we'll need to curve around quite a bit, just like Onion Creek flows around Jimmy's last golf course.

Back in '59, when not contributing to the design of the Concord Hotel's envisioned "Monster" course, Jimmy was beginning yet another role on television, that of a 'play-by-play' announcer for a weekly golf-match program. You older folks I reckon are probably the only ones with any memories of "All Star Golf" but that entry was the pioneering show of this type, preceding the likes of Arnold Palmer's "Challenge Golf," "Big Three Golf," and the most successful, "Shell's Wonderful World Of Golf."

"All Star Golf" had actually surfaced on TV 2 years earlier in 1957, but after trying out 1st one host and then another, the producers turned to the Wardrobe. Jimmy with his glibness and wit proved to be a perfect fit, and he left on his own terms after the '61 season, with thoughts of creating a 2nd course at his Champions Golf Club, (the previously noted "Jackrabbit" course).

As soon as my 'patient' told me he'd been hired to do the show, I told him they'd never want to let him go, so perfect was his bubbly personality and vocal talent for this still young medium. Yet, Demaret did admit to having some nerves about his new venture.

"I don't just get to say my own words all the time," he pointed out. "There's stuff about the match rules and prizes and so on that they say I'll be reading off of big cue cards. Well Bobby, I ain't no professional actor. If I'm focusing on the words on paper it's not gonna sound natural, let alone witty," he fussed.

Yes, there was Jim Demaret fretting that he might come across as a bore, even if briefly. And he was not ready to step out of his verbal 'armor' which had served him so well from boyhood on – even at age 49. We had a good talk about that.

Then he went ahead and did as the show's director expected, reading 'on air' as required, with somewhat 'wooden' results at first, but the rest of his expert banter during the actual matches more than made up for those slow beginnings. I Bobby Shout was proud of the Wardrobe's willingness to risk and grow, he who now like Ben Hogan was a certified airplane pilot, though Jimmy had stalled in the process for over a decade.

Anyway, one of the aspects of "All Star Golf" which sticks in my mind – probably 'cause of my own involvement in creating the Texas Sharpshooters event a decade earlier – was a hokey special event apart from the show's normal format. That is, it was decided during the 1960 season to have 4 players, not 2, compete in a twosome round-robin of 54 holes to determine a cumulative-total, stroke-play winner. In other words, this 'match' was really no different than your average 3-round tournament.

So Jimmy (who was pardoned from his announcer role for this extravaganza) played 18 holes first with Sam Snead; then alongside Jackie Burke Jr.; and lastly, on the course with Cary Middlecoff to compile a 54-hole score, as did the other contestants. The 'kicker' was that this mundane affair was labeled by the TV show as "The Match of the Century"! Kind of a joke when compared to Hogan and Nelson versus Venturi and Ward at Cypress Point in better-ball match-play 4 years earlier!

Moreover, with no offense intended to today's Yorba Linda championship golf course in the California desert, if one were seeking a setting for a true "Match of the Century" … well, you know … Plus, that track, having opened only 3 years earlier, lacked its current mature foliage, and thus looked very similar to a Texas wasteland on our black-and-white television sets.

When paired with Slammin' Sammy, Demaret shot a 67, one lower than Sam. But Snead got the last laugh, and the hefty 1st prize of $10,000, by following up his initial 68 with another one and then a 67 of his own for a 203 total.

Meanwhile Jimmy had to make a 4-footer his last round on 18 to tie Cary for second at 209. That clutch putt had to feel good, but it carried also a certain sting with it for the Wardrobe, seeing how he'd carelessly missed a 6-incher the very first day which cost him both a record-tying 66 at the young Yorba Linda course, as well as the $7,500 he would have won for finishing second on his own.

Later I'd asked Jimmy about his breezy reply when told that the tiny missed putt had cost him a share of the course record; his televised words in effect being, "I'll just have to shoot 66 here next time." In person, he'd stared at me with a surprisingly grim look.

"Missing bothered me – sure. But if you're smart, you never show it out there. Some pros aren't as nice as me," Jim continued with a quick laugh before darkening again. "They'll 'go for your throat' if they sense an insecurity; it's always been like that. Sam in particular. He's good at messing with the mind, and I'm not ready to retire from competition, Bobby, so no more talk of whiffs or chokes or shanks or any other golfing unpleasantness," these final words laced with a gleam of humor once more.

Anyhow, 5 years later – with the Jackrabbit course at Champions a done deal – Jimmy was fixing to latch onto another commercial opportunity when a big one 'fell into his lap.' He was asked to play in a match against Sam Snead on television, to be aired in 1966 on "Shell's Wonderful World of Golf," and though he'd declined to appear on the popular show earlier, this time Jim had accepted.

I Bobby Shout had asked the Wardrobe what had changed his mind? Was it his currently lighter work schedule, or the chance to beat Sam again, or, I'd joked, perhaps because TV programs like this one were now in color, giving him the chance to re-wow home audiences with his fashion sense.

Laughing boy had quipped back that he missed seeing Gene Sarazen, the show's color commentator, so much that he hoped an appearance on the show might 'open some eyes' and get him hired as a co-host, so the two of them could 'make up.' We'd both guffawed at that notion, guessing that Sarazen would probably 'walk' if asked to work with Jimmy.

However, 'money always talks,' and after 4 seasons of production, the Shell programs were losing steam with audiences. The smooth-talking George Rogers was excellent in setting the scene for the international courses the show now favored, but he had no punch as a golfing commentator. And perhaps the cantankerous "Squire," as Gene was known, at age 63 was feeling a bit tired of the amount of talking he had to do each episode – to give each match a feeling of golfing drama.

In any case, quicker than a roadrunner can cross the street, Jimmy was elevated by Shell's producer Fred Raphael from golfer to play-by-play commentator for the show. And, it proved a good hire, extending the original program's run another 5 years into 1970.

As for the Sarazen/Demaret relationship 'off the set' when they weren't acting chummy for the camera, Jimmy put it this way. "Bobby, I never brought my clubs no matter where we traveled. That way there was no chance of Gene getting me out on any course. I swear that wop played every damn day! Instead, for public consumption I claimed to be a big fan of sightseeing."

Then he'd paused and winked before continuing. "Oh yeah, I saw some pretty interesting sights at a 'watering hole' or two each trip in my spare time as a tourist."

And now we get to the payoff of how Demaret and his Onion Creek course changed the history of golf in America. You see, it was Jimmy's Shell producer Fred Raphael who was finally able in the mid-1970s to sell a TV network on the idea of a golf show starring senior players. This seed morphed into a legitimate 72-hole event for 2-man teams playing better ball.

Well, Fred of course wanted the 'old guys' to look good on television so he naturally turned to the Wardrobe for advice. No surprise there, nor the fact that Jimmy had chortled back in effect, "Look no further, partner, than my little Austin track. I can still 'go low' there on a good day, so those younger bucks are bound to." (Laughing boy, by then in his late 60s, was referring to the age 50-plus pros who'd be competing.)

Anyhow, Onion Creek thus became not only the initial host site for the Liberty Mutual Legends of Golf event in '78, it held that honor all the way till 1990. You older folks no doubt remember the impact which that Texan tournament had.

Everyone gave the "Legends" credit for being the single greatest factor leading to the formation of an American Senior Tour in 1980. I've always been glad that Jimmy got to see this happen, only 3 years before his sudden demise.

Oh yes, and thank heaven the powers-that-be finally had the sense to elect 'laughing boy' into the World Golf Hall of Fame while he lived -- an overdue honor that materialized only months before his death, that December in '83. There's a video out on the Internet which was done at Onion Creek earlier in the year and captures the wounding of Jimmy's pride from this long slight.

When the interviewer mentions how Demaret was to be inducted along with Bob Hope, come May, the Wardrobe responded by both listing his previous 'hall of fame' honors, all given well in the past, along with the comments that he hadn't thought much of the 'World Hall' till recently, and that his favorite Hall admittance would continue to be the "Texas Sports Hall of Fame."

I Bobby Shout am here to tell you that Jimmy was full of 'sour grapes' about the newest Hall, right up till the day he did 'get in.' But who could blame him?

Unfortunately, there was a deeper blow to Jim's secretly fragile ego that didn't get resolved before his passing. I can name this lingering upset in 2 words – Ben Hogan – but the bitter tale of their later relationship takes a great more telling.

You see, from the time James Demaret first met the Hawk in 1932, and over the next 20-some years, Jimmy Demaret thought he'd become someone special to the loner Ben. And, why wouldn't he, considering their habitual partnerships in 2-man events, and moments like the June day in '48 at Riviera when Hogan bettered Jim's record-score of 278 'in the house' at the U.S. Open by completing his own final round for 276?

I've mentioned Jimmy's sole book, "My Partner, Ben Hogan," which 'came out' 6 years later in '54. Well it offers as good a summary as any about how the Wardrobe felt things were back then between him and his pard:

"When I hear a lot of misinformed people talk about Hogan's disregard for others and his cold ruthlessness, I always think of that day. After he had won, Ben walked up to me and said serious-like (he still knows no other way), 'Jimmy, I'm glad I won, but I'm sorry I had to beat you.' That kind of talk and sentiment I've always heard from Ben. He meant every word of it. Hogan and I are close friends …"

What a terrible irony! You see, it was Jimmy's doing this book -- with only the best of intentions as is said – which cost him the Hawk's oh-so-reluctant trust. In later years, every time I'd seek to spark a reconciliation for both their sakes, Ben was adamant in the most indirect ways – the cutoff, the glare, and the return to silence. But I got the message: Demaret had both betrayed the Wee Ice Mon's privacy, and used *Ben's* achievements and fame to make money for himself. End of story; Hogan was not the forgiving type, in spades!

I Bobby Shout sigh at my pride now, ever reckoning that I had the clinical skill to get that man to see what he didn't want to. Hennie Bogan was alive and well even as the Hawk aged.

Except ... Well, there was this belated pronouncement in Ben's later days. Like Byron giving Lloyd *his* golfing due after the man's death, Hogan did memorialize Jimmy with words not kind but simply true: "He was the most underrated golfer in history ... This man played shots I hadn't dreamed of. I learned them. But it was Jimmy who showed them to me first. He was the best wind player I've ever seen in my life."

Yet there was this maddening part about being outside of Hogan's good graces which both I and Jimmy suffered; me for months at a time; Demaret, all the way from the mid-1950s to the '80s! Pardon another cattle analogy but it was like the bony steer that will casually kick dirt toward your face while he eats on your land, never deigning to swing his horns at you.

Here's 1 instance: It was never any trouble for Ben to accept Jimmy's invitations to play in events at Demaret's classy Champions club after their unspoken 'split.' After all, Ben just had to act like Ben – cool and reserved.

But after the Hawk began to play less at Colonial in favor of his friend Marvin Leonard's new Forth Worth club in the late '50s, he never once asked Jimmy to go out on that Shady Oaks course with him, though the layout was a wonder in terms of bulldozing an unpromising hilly tract into a 1st-class track. Poor Jim. He couldn't get Hogan to admit a damn thing was wrong, and so he fixed on using a 'cutting wit' in response, although I'd warned him of its futility with Ben, and the further possible damage to his own-by-nature sunny psyche.

Thus among the array of publicized Demaret witticisms, some of the later ones probably sound downright mean to uninformed folks. For example, there was Jimmy in a group, upon seeing the Hawk eating at a club by himself, chirping, "Hey, there's Ben Hogan sitting with all his friends." And another time, feeling not so funny, Jimmy admitted with bitterness that "Nobody gets close to Ben Hogan."

Still, I Bobby Shout have always preferred to dwell on the Wardrobe's sunny side, which was the essence of him in spite of his having grown up poor. Did I mention how he'd been cut-off from schooling in order to earn food money for the other 8 kids in his family?

Well make no mistake! When Jimmy had to 'drop out' as a junior high-schooler, it wasn't half-welcomed because formal learning came hard for him. No, James Demaret was blessed with a powerful ability to retain information – he never forgot names -- along with all the other aspects of a high I.Q. Born to better circumstances, he might well have wound up as the most popular professor on a college campus!

Laughing boy was also savvy about money, though not many of us friends realized it. In fact I once warned him that he was generous to a fault, but guess what? Jimmy died with plenty of dough to spare. And while the Great Depression made plenty of folks into future penny-pinchers, Demaret stayed gloriously immune.

I'm closing with what I hope is now obvious to you: That so many of us golfers and the game of golf itself would have been much poorer if Jimmy had not chosen the little white ball as his life. I mean, who else has ever won the Masters and stepped up to receive his trophy while crooning the song "Do You Know How Lucky You Are?" The year he did that was the red-letter year I met him through Ben. 1950.

CHAPTER 16

Ben afterwards

BEN … HENNIE Bogan. He was the 3rd of my Texas Quartet 'to go.' The end was swift for William Benjamin Hogan but not really, alas. Before the Hawk entered the All Saints Hospital in Fort Worth on Thursday morning, July 24th 1997, due to a fall caused by a stroke, he'd been in a major decline for roughly 2 years. After being operated on for colon cancer in 1995, lung troubles had followed for the "Wee Ice Mon," who'd never been able to quit smoking totally.

The Hawk wasn't in shape for visitors at All Saints, Valerie had said. It pains me that I and so many others who would have wanted to, didn't get to say farewell to him, as he died there the next day – Friday, July 25th 1997.

But what a 'run' the "Little Man" (I hated that newspaper tag he'd worn so long) had made during his 84-plus years on this earth. Even after he'd almost died from a ruptured appendix ten years before his total demise, the then 74-year-old Hogan clung on for 2 months in Fort Worth's Harris Hospital, unwilling to 'give up' while his beloved golf-club business needed him alive. And he'd survived once more, the man who'd been flattened by a Greyhound bus in 1949, 38 years earlier.

Hogan had outlived another heavy smoker, Lloyd Mangrum, by 34 years. "Bantam Ben" had gone on for 14 years after his good-time, one-time buddy Jimmy Demaret had expired. Only Byron Nelson, who'd irritated the Hawk plenty by besting him early and often, did it again in the race for survival – living

9 years beyond '97. I reckon the two of them don't talk about that in heaven; it wouldn't be Lord Byron's way to taunt Ben on such grounds. Anyway, let's get back to the Hogan legacy, awesome yet as thorny as our honey locust trees.

You may know that his greatest stretch of Majors came in the first 3 years after his U.S. Open win at Merion in '50. To recap, in 1951 the Hawk had followed his first victory at the Masters by famously bringing the Oakland Hills "monster" to its knees in that year's Open, then grabbing the season's biggest financial prize by winning George May's World Golf Championship in August. Three wins in 4 times out, not bad!

Yet 2 years later, he'd smashed that peerless percentage with what was called the greatest season ever enjoyed by a professional (up 'til then) when Bantam Ben 'took' the Masters and both Opens, while also winning 2 of his other 3 events played in '53.

Can you imagine the willpower required to achieve such results, seeing how agonizing aches, cramps, and spasms were a fact of life for 'my patient' during that entire period? How Ben required countless hot baths, rub-downs, and leg-wrapping to even allow him out on the course. Oh yes, and an increasing reliance on alcohol post-round to 'get him through' the harder throbbing caused by the walking demands of golf rounds. (Ben despised taking pain pills – a 'control issue' of course.)

As amazing as these facts are, Hogan biographers tend to skim over his Major-winless year of 1952, but they shouldn't! 'Cause Bantam Ben might have easily won both the Masters and Open that year, too, giving him a run of 8 straight Majors entered and won – hard for me to fathom even now, though I was there to see that he was in more than sufficient 'form' to get job done. So what caused the Hawk to fall short? Bad luck with the weather!

I Bobby Shout can assure you that Ben was always competing while on a 'razor's edge' of fragility during the '50s, considering his mangled legs, bad knees, shoulder problems, declining vision, and so on. On top of that, he was routinely in danger of his energy reserves running dry. If you'd ever seen the look of total exhaustion and pain on his face during unguarded moments just after each tournament effort, I wouldn't have to tell you this. Forget his beaming smiles for the cameramen; the Hawk was hurting every minute during that era.

Well at the Masters, in '51 and '53, the golf gods had smiled on 'my patient' by providing pleasant afternoons for him to clinch these Majors. When Ben needed his best round of the week to win in '51 -- and got it with a 68 -- he'd been given an afternoon that hovered on either side of 70 degrees, the warmest day of that week. And, in '53, following a Thursday and Friday which had been on the warm side (rather than overly-cool), the temperatures had moderated by Sunday into the low 70s, to which the Hawk had responded with a magnificent weekend of scoring, 66 and 69.

By contrast, the Masters weekend in '52 was a recipe for a stiff-limbed Hogan, suffering already from poor circulation in his legs. Temperatures in the mid- to low-50s dominated. Winds between 15- and 25-miles-per-hour increased Ben's chill. The consecutive 70s shot in rounds 1 and 2 during '70s weather,' and a decent 74 on Saturday considering the colder conditions, had gotten him a tie for 1st with Snead, but the Hawk's 'goose was cooked.'

That Sunday, he soared to a 79 which included five 3-putt greens. Ben made excuses to no one, but believe me, the grip of tension on his cold body surely upped his level of leg spasms, making it hard to focus and execute with a putter on slick surfaces.

Likewise, a pattern of good-weather wins and a bad loss was the pattern for Hogan in the U.S. Open over that 3-year stretch, with '52 again being the stinker, and a highly ironic one at that. There was Ben with a 'home field' advantage that June, the championship being held at the Northwood Club in Dallas, and he'd responded in the first 2 rounds with an unprecedented low total of 138.

However, the low-90s temperatures on Thursday and Friday had taken their toll on the Hawk's inner hydration, and when Saturday saw a high of 96 degrees, Ben wilted in that heat, posting two 74s to finish 5 shots behind a young and cool Julius Boros.

After Ben's magnificent campaign in 1953, you could have gotten odds of 1,000-to-1 from any Texan that Hogan would not be 'shut out' in the victory column over the next 2 seasons – let alone 5! Yet that is what happened on Tour. In fact, it wasn't till '59 that the Hawk's next (and final) win came, not surprisingly 'in his backyard' at Colonial, his 5th triumph there.

At the same time Hogan had many a chance to prevail, most notably in the Majors of course. His closest finishes all came over the next 3 years ('54 to '56) with 2 second-places recorded at both the Masters and Open.

He lost a playoff in each, just as he had in 1950 in his 1st tournament 'back from the dead,' when he had to go a 5th round against Snead in L.A. You know my opinion about these losses; Ben was just too tuckered out to prevail. And, his loss in the '54 Masters was by 7 strokes to a 'hot' Cary Middlecoff's 279, so none of 'my patient's' many birdie misses were crucial.

But the way he fell to Middlecoff again, this time in the 1956 Open at Oak Hill captured in a nutshell why our Ben would not be a Major winner again. The 3-foot putt had become his nemesis. And at the Majors each course demanded the making of not just simple short putts. Devilish ones had to be mastered, and the Hawk's throbbing body was no longer 'up to it.' He'd missed one late against Snead in their '54 Masters' playoff; he'd done the same on number 12 when he was starting to rattle the Iowa club-pro Jack Fleck during their playoff at the '55 Open.

And at Oak Hill, the tiddler he missed was to stay tied with Cary through the next-to-last hole in regulation. Ben wound up 2nd in that Open by a stroke. I'd never reckon that the Wee Ice Mon's psyche was not up to facing another playoff, or was influenced by this demon in that key stroke. Still … could you blame him, exhausted and snake-bit as he was?

I Bobby Shout heard the theories from Ben's fellow pros and the public alike as to why he – once one of the game's best at holing putts inside ten feet – had become reduced to making jabs with his putter after seemingly unable to 'pull the trigger' for cringeworthy amounts of time. Some said the nerves in his hands and wrists were finally showing the fraying they'd received in the Greyhound crash.

Others claimed – some with relish – that Hogan was simply 'showing his age,' losing his touch on the greens in his 40s as many a champion before him had. "No, it's his eyes," was another refrain. "The Hawk can hardly see with his left one now, so his depth perception is poor, nor can he 'see' the line as well anymore."

Well maybe each of these explanations did play a part in the Wee Ice Mon's mostly continual putting decline through the 1950s. However the Hawk's pride did cause him to reveal something else to me.

"I'm not afraid to make my stroke," Ben had growled, utterly 'put out' at the thought. "It's my damaged legs. I challenge anybody to try to putt with fireworks of pain going on down there. When I seem to be hesitant on the green it's me waiting for the spasms to cease for a second. Sometimes they will, you know, and then I putt. Too often, it's no use and I have to do the best I can in spite of that goddamn distracting shaking aching that won't let up in my legs!"

Was he unable to admit that his putting woes were largely a mental thing? I never even suggested such a weakness to him, fearing that Hogan might shut me out forever in response. Was this my bad – a therapist not talking out issues with a patient? Perhaps, but to quote my inner cowboy, "If you run at a bull and he gores you, then you sure as heck won't be around later to save him from a blizzard."

Anyway, I reckon there's another reason that accounts for the Hawk's fall from perennial tournament winner to habitual runner-upper after his climatic triumph at Carnoustie that July in '53. You see, it was around this time that Ben's up-till-then monomaniacal focus on beating every other golfer every time out began to splinter due to a serious rival.

I'm speaking of the Hawk's envisioned monument to the memory of his blacksmith father, the aforementioned suicide Chester Hogan. To wit, during that summer in 1953 Hennie Bogan in partnership with a local investor named A. Pollard Simons had purchased a vacant Fort Worth warehouse for the sole purpose of turning it into a golf clubs factory. And Ben had no intention of merely being a figurehead for the woods and forged irons to be produced there by the Ben Hogan Company.

You may recollect that his marriage with Valerie had yielded no children, for whatever reason, though many thought it was the Hawk who'd made that call. Well the company he founded was psychologically the baby Ben had never had, as I saw it. So like any good father, the 41-year-old Hogan was ready to do almost anything to give his child 'a good start in the world.'

What am I talking about? After spending for the space, the necessary machinery to make clubs, hiring numerous staff, making models and running through a major production cycle, when the Ben Hogan Company finally had its 1ˢᵗ sets of clubs ready to sell a year later, the Hawk had ordered, "No, scrap 'em. They're no good."

Not surprisingly, his biggest co-investor Mr. Simons had howled in dismay. Those clubs had cost $100,000 to make, Pollard had argued. Surely they were good enough to sell?

Hogan not only refused to budge about selling, he swore that he could not afford a partner like Simons whose zeal was not purely about the quality of their merchandise. So Ben being Ben, he 'marched down' to the bank and took out a loan of nearly half a million to 'buy out' Mr. A. Pollard Simons. And understand – even though my patient had 'done quite well' between the Greyhound bus settlement plus his 'take' from the movie *Follow the Sun*, (a somewhat sappy production, I cannot deny), on top of all his golf-related earnings, the size of that loan was still a huge deal for him.

Of course, later Ben's best buddy and backer Marvin Leonard did gather together a rich bunch to substitute their names for Hogan's on that financial obligation, but it wasn't because the Hawk had cried out for help, you can be sure of that! As the Wee Ice Mon told his workers at his factory in the early days when thoughts of joining a union were afoot, he'd started over before from scratch plenty of times, and would do so again if he needed to – an icy hint of firings matched by the coldest glare in Texas. You can imagine how that 1ˢᵗ union-vote went.

Over the 1ˢᵗ 7 years of its existence the Ben Hogan Company was a big success, even making its founder good money. Then came 1960. The Hawk was still only 47-years-old that summer. Bolstered by an improved brand of liniment, Ben and his golf game had been 'looking up' over the past 13 months, with a win at Colonial in May of '59 and a tie for 6ᵗʰ at the '60 Masters where he'd managed 3 rounds good enough to be 1 stroke back of the leader before fading with a final 76.

Unfortunately for the Hawk's psyche, it was Arnold Palmer who prevailed that day to grab his 2ⁿᵈ Masters in 3 years. It was no surprise to most of us that Arnie had won; he'd been the hottest player on Tour that spring with 4 victories already. But "Iceberg Hogan" as his detractors had labeled him long ago was not warmed by the feel-good story of the charismatic Palmer looking like golf's next superstar.

How could anyone not root for Arnie, you may ask? Well we'll have to delve into the previous history between these 2 studs, plus the perpetual mental gymnastics engaged in by the Hawk in his pursuit to win tournaments, as well as poor Hennie Bogan's hunger to remain the richest pro golfer around for as long as he lived. Let's begin with Hogan the monster-maker.

Starting with Byron Nelson, then Lloyd Mangrum, followed by Snead and at last Palmer, Ben had found it useful as a competitor to exaggerate what he saw as the weaknesses or less engaging characteristics of each man so that he might feel entitled to dislike each one in turn. This of course is only my theory; Ben never said so much to me, but it made sense.

Creating villains provided more fuel for the Hawk's already massive willpower, so that when Bantam Ben came up against his fiercest rivals in the big events, he could snarl with a sense of rightness, *I'm going to crush that son of a bitch!*

Thus he'd labeled Lord Byron as lazy and lily-livered, a player who could have won so much more if he'd 'hung on' – certainly not a man worthy of the title "Mr. Golf." In Ben's eyes, Mangrum was a pure jerk, with his holier-than-thou war record permitting sarcastic greetings to "Mr. Hogan" whenever the press was around.

Snead was pictured as just a crude, hillbilly ape, his hyper-flexibility giving him an unfair advantage over other swingers of the golf club, let alone the Hawk with his broken body. And Palmer, he was an insult to how golf was meant to be mastered, that is with rigid self control and a cocoon of concentration.

Ben bristled to see this "Arnie Palmer" lashing at the ball and sending it all 'over the lot' with a brutish swing -- while smiling at the gallery throughout! --only to wind up with pars or birdies by virtue of fortunate run-ups or long putts made. After Arnold's 1st successes on Tour, Ben had asked within the young man's earshot, "How the hell did he get in the Masters?"

And as Arnie later revealed, Hogan was so rude that he never even called Arnold by name when their paths crossed. Fast forward to 1967 when Palmer's glory years were 'in the books,' yet Ben (according to some sources) as Ryder Cup Captain that year upbraided Arnold for arriving 'late,' and kept 'the star' out of 1 match, another insult!

Sadly this hostile stance toward Palmer wound up eventually 'biting Ben in the butt,' with the seed of his misfortune planted by the Hawk's decision to sell a controlling interest in his company about 6 weeks after the '60 U.S. Open. The buyer was a behemoth firm, American Machine and Foundry, a manufacturer of products ranging from bowling alleys to nuclear reactors. I Bobby Shout had been caught totally off guard by the news of this transaction and couldn't help myself from calling Hogan to hear his thinking.

After all, the Ben Hogan Co. was his 'symbolic child' in my mind. I Bobby Shout couldn't understand how the Hawk, whose 'gut' craved absolute control, had now been willing to have others be in charge of his most precious project's fate -- with him powerless to stop unwanted change.

"No, no, Shout," he'd responded, obviously irritated by my concern. "They gave me everything I asked for. I'm still the chairman of the board. I get to run the company as I damn well please. That's in writing."

"But Ben," I'd asked. "What if AMF sells the Hogan Company to someone else?" He paused to puff on a cigarette then spoke with what I could sense was his trademark glare, "There is no Ben Hogan Company without Ben Hogan."

For the next quarter century – up 'til the mid-1980s – it looked like the Hawk had been smarter than me or any other doubters, until … but we'll get to that later.

When Ben did sign that contract in 1960, he'd gotten a whole lot more than continued company control and a great new distribution network through AMF's sporting goods division. What had sealed the deal for my patient was the size of the check involved!

Some said it was for as much as $3,000,000, making Hogan suddenly one of the wealthiest men in Texas. More vital to the Hawk, it gave him the capital to try and stay a step ahead of Arnold Palmer in the financial power game amongst pro golfers.

You see, Arnie had taken that year's U.S. Open on top of the Masters, leading the 'smart money' to predict that his role – already robust as a pitchman – would soon blast off like one of our country's new rockets. Ben hated to believe them but he did. And although he scorned Palmer's willingness to 'cast integrity aside' in order to hawk a hundred products, while Hogan had stuck largely to ads for golf, liquor, and tobacco, Hennie Bogan could not let the young muscleman out-net-worth him without a tussle.

So what was Ben's master strategy to compete? He'd planned on doing it the old-fashioned Texan way by dealing in oil and cattle, which happened to be good for me. I probably would never have been invited as one of the Hawk's rare luncheon guests at Shady Oaks if I didn't have 'insider info' about what to look for in oil-leases. Hogan in fact got rather skillful at scouting out already used properties that still might have a good 'strike' in them.

As for cattle ranching, the Shout Petroleum Company had gotten into that field in fact at my urging. I'd preached the benefits of diversification, but I probably wouldn't have pushed so hard if I Bobby Shout hadn't seen another angle which intrigued me. That is, there were war veterans who didn't have the skill-set or make-up to be of use to us in the oil business. Yet some of them would be 'born cowboys' I figured. And I was still out to aid as many vets as possible with good jobs on their return home from duty.

Anyway, I had this ranch-buying and operational experience, too, to offer Hogan, and he took advantage to 'pick my brains,' his pride put aside in his determination to make oodles more cash.

It always seemed to me as well that Ben suffered from the instinct that he could never have enough wealth itself. This was not an uncommon mindset among those who grew up poor. On top of that, the Hawk had known the desperation and humiliation of being broke or near-broke all the way into his late 20s, so how could anyone blame him for craving super financial security later?

One last thing about Ben's state of mind following the U.S. Open that summer in '60 … I reckon he might have seen the futility of trying to compete with Arnie on and off the course from then on – and lived out his life happier -- if only he hadn't played so darn well in that championship at the Broadmoor in Colorado!

Nobody else 'hit' 34 straight greens during that Open's 2-round Saturday finish. Had anyone ever, other than Hogan? Yet, due to too many birdie-chances missed that day, Ben had opted to hit 'the perfect pitch' to a front pin protected by a moat below on the par-5 17th. He wanted a tap-in for the bird that would put him 1 ahead of Palmer for the win with 1 to play.

Instead the Hawk's shot had tumbled back down the bank and into the water leading to bogey and defeat. Ben never changed his opinion in public that he had chosen wisely and *had* hit a shot which could have easily bounced forward, stiff to the cup – whenever any brave soul dared to ask whether he'd miscalculated slightly. To me privately, he gave the exact same message … but added that the memory of that shot was going to always "cut my guts out."

In the locker room after that fateful round, Ben coming off a triple bogey on number 18 that dropped him to 9th place -- after being inches away from a singular triumph -- was in no mood to be gracious. He did what he could to snipe at Palmer's good fortune, remarking that "I played 36 holes today with a kid [Nicklaus] who should have won this thing by 10 strokes."

The Hawk didn't contend at Augusta or in our Open the next year, and after that, he didn't tee it up in the U.S. Open from '62 through '65, his body and outlook too broken, most folks reckoned. However, after playing better again at the Masters in 1964 (a tie for 9th), Hogan opted to play in the PGA Championship that July after passing on our Open a month earlier! And it wasn't like this was the initial PGA to be played as a standard 72-hole stroke-play event rather than the bruising match-play marathon it had been. The switch to medal play had taken effect back in 1959. So what was the Wee Ice Mon up to, repeating this pattern again in 1965?

Had Ben concluded that Opens were no longer winnable for him, due to the utter mental and physical strain that an 'Open course' annually demanded? If so, okay, yet I wondered how the heck he thought he could cope with the heat of mid-July in Columbus, Ohio (the '64 PGA site), and mid-August in western PA the next year.

I Bobby Shout reckoned I'd found the answer to this riddle once I realized that the PGA was scheduled to be contested at Laurel Valley, a course in Palmer's 'backyard' in '65. You see, by then Arnie lacked only the PGA crown keeping him from joining Sarazen and Hogan as winners of the professional 'career grand slam,' that is, being victorious in all 4 Majors. And so Ben was fixing to do his best to keep the upstart Palmer from joining that exclusive club.

When I broached these thoughts to the Hawk sitting at his table in the Shady Oaks dining room, I wondered whether he would throw his food my way before ordering me out. Instead, with a steely grin he'd replied, "Damn right, Dr. Shout – good diagnosis," before returning to his meal.

However the plan didn't work, Hogan finishing 9th and 15th respectively in those championships after failing to make any sort of charge in the final round. How could my 'patient,' a sweated-out, limping 'little man' of 53 years summon the level of will needed at those junctures? Of course he couldn't! Nevertheless Arnie failed to win, too, and never did capture a PGA

If you find it hard to believe that Ben's animosity toward Arnold Palmer extended to the degree described above, allow me to add a note about the 1967 Ryder Cup to come. I've mentioned that the Hawk apparently 'balled out' 'the King" upon his arrival and sat him for a session. Well there is this about the way Arnie announced his presence to the 2 teams practicing on Champions' Cypress course.

Piloting his private plane into Houston, Arnold went out of his way to 'buzz' the Champions fairways at a ridiculously low height before heading to the airport. I could see how Ben might take that as a personal gesture of disdain, 'cause whereas Palmer was already known as a man who flew planes like he attacked a golf course – bold and fearless – by that time word had also spread that Hogan was no longer comfortable with flying, even as a passenger!

Poor Hennie Bogan, all the willpower he'd exerted back in the 1940s to banish his fear of heights and become an aviation instructor during the war meant nothing to upstarts like Palmer. *Well has Arnie ever crash-landed a plane with loved ones on board?* I could just imagine Hogan spitting out these words inside, almost as a curse, on that October day in '67.

Perhaps the poisonous psychic divide between these 2 super-strong-willed men was nowhere better illustrated than in their best-known instruction books: Ben's FIVE LESSONS (1957) and Arnie's MY GOLF AND YOURS (1963).

Hogan the perfectionist took months and months to hammer out a book totally devoted to *his* way of swinging, aided in this task by an illustrator who drew like Michelangelo, and the finest wordsmith in golf at that time. Whereas Palmer talks of golf being a simple game, and spends more than half his text on club-choice, course decision-making and other mental topics. The few chapters focused on swing mechanics are bolstered by simple line sketches and photographs, with Arnie not averse to mentioning other pros' grips, stances, and swings that differ from his approach.

Heh. I suddenly feel like a calf that's strayed from his mama and winds up stuck in a barbed wire fence. Let's get back to William Ben Hogan's sunset years as a playing pro.

Following his 2 unsuccessful tries for a PGA crown in 1964 and '65, the Hawk had to make a choice due to his limited tournament endurance. Should he continue to try to block Arnold from victory in that event, or go back to going after a recognized record fifth U.S. Open? (He'd won the so-called Hale America National Open way back in '42, a title the USGA had co-sponsored, but most folks thought it shouldn't be counted as a "U.S. Open," due to war-time irregularities.)

With the Professional Golfers Association Championship being held again in Ohio, but even later in July than it had been 2 years earlier, Ben knew the prospects of wilting heat were high. On the other hand, the 1966 U.S. Open site was the Olympic Club out in San Francisco near the foggy, cool shores of the Pacific. Hogan chose Olympic and the weather didn't disappoint, but to no avail.

While 2 men were tied at 2-under after 4 rounds, the best Bantam Ben could do was 11-over after rounds of 72-73-76-70. It had been a dry tournament with daily highs ranging from 67 to 74 degrees, ideal golfing weather. Hogan didn't wilt, shooting his best score on the final day, but this made the major gap between him and the leaders all the more bitter, especially since one of them was Arnold Palmer, now a play-off away from capturing a 2nd U.S. Open.

However, there was a lot more to this story of Ben versus Arnie. You see, on Sunday with but 6 holes left to play, Palmer had a huge lead, so much so that he 'forgot' about winning the tournament in his zeal to best Hogan's Open record of 276. Instead, with Billy Casper applying pressure, the King failed to protect his 6-shot advantage, thus forcing an extra 18-hole affair on Monday which Arnold lost.

Next time I saw Ben I said, "That was a tough way for Palmer to lose" – my way of baiting the Hawk into a response. He'd replied, "Yeah, too bad," spoken grimly as usual, but his blue-grey eyes shone in the manner of a man holding back a joyous yell.

Ironically the very next June did see Hogan's Open scoring record beaten, by big Jack who shot 275 at Baltusrol with Arnie 4 strokes back in 2nd. This time Ben finished even farther behind, 17 strokes to be exact. The 'writing on the wall' now was branded so large that even a 1-eyed jack back in Texas could read it. At age 55, 4-time Open winner William Ben Hogan was done with entering major championships, a retreat he'd announced on other occasions but now in 1967 finally meant for good.

That decision left him with little in the way of an annual golf schedule. Still another shoulder operation caused him to stay on the tournament sidelines for all of '68 and '69, but once 'fit' again, he could always play in the Colonial.

And then there was Jimmy Demaret's place in Houston. Ben couldn't count on less than hot weather there even during its spring dates, but the Champions' 2 layouts were darn flat and that made it easier on his legs. Plus he reckoned that the owners of the place, Demaret and Burke Jr., could see to it that the Hawk's well-known demands for a bubble-like existence would be respected.

So I wasn't shocked when an "out of nowhere" Ben showed up to compete in the 1970 Champions event. Nor did it surprise me when -- just as Hogan had done in 1950 -- he astounded pro golf with his ability to go forward under tournament pressure after a serious-injury layoff and still perform as a world-class ball-striker!

Not that I Bobby Shout expected the 1-eyed Hawk to win. The reports I'd gotten on his putting-state indicated that no miracle cure had been found. Yet to see him 'hang in there' once again well into the final day of a tournament … heck, it was so gutty on his part that I felt the urge to hug him at the end, though God help me if I'd ever moved to do so!

Alas, that was pretty much his last hurrah. When he tried to compete at Colonial the next week, his knee freshly strained, the results were predictably poor. I reckoned that this was it then for the Wee Ice Mon in 1970 as far as tournament golf … maybe forever.

But in late July I got a call from – of all people – Valerie Hogan. Hearing from her was a rare thing, even rarer than receiving a 'ring' from the Hawk. On top of that, she who was usually so reserved and reticent jumped right into a lengthy monologue -- by her standards.

She'd begun, "Hello, Bobby. This is Valerie Hogan. How are you?"

As soon as I'd responded with the usual pleasantries, I asked her how I could help, sure that this was the only reason we were on the phone. Then she jumped right in.

"You are always so smart. Yes I do need your help. It's Ben. He's itching to compete again, but you both know that I travel reluctantly if at all anymore. And the Tour is up in the Northeast now. I won't fly but I would be willing to do a long train trip. He doesn't believe me. Thinks I'd be a nervous wreck – even after

I told him that I'm hankering to get some new dresses and there's no place like New York City for shopping – so the travel would be worth it."

Valerie plowed on, "You know me; I can't fool anybody. When I tried to say casually that I'd heard the Tour would be playing at Westchester in August, just outside the City, and wouldn't it be nice for him to take his clubs while I did the shopping and then we could dine with old friends each night at wonderful restaurants … Well he 'saw right through me.' That's my Ben. What should I try now? Or, would you …?" She hesitated at this point, and I knew what Val wanted me to do. Still, I had to conform to a certain formal way of doing things with that woman.

Thus I replied, "Would you like me to speak with him? I could do that if you really want me to."

"Oh yes," she'd said primly. "You seem able to persuade my husband about things like no one else. I would be ever so grateful."

"All right then," I answered. "I'll think on this for a couple of days and then contact him."

After a swift goodbye as though exhausted by our exchange, Valerie Hogan hung up, leaving me 'kicking myself' for being drawn into her intrigue. I really didn't want to disappoint her. Yet no good could come from Hogan trying tournament golf anymore this year was my current opinion.

I Bobby Shout spent the better part of 2 days thinking and then writing a note to Ben which I sent to his office at the Ben Hogan Company in Fort Worth. My choice of that address went with the hope that this way Valerie would never get a glimpse at my effort. You see, after scratching my brain, the best approach I could come up with was the use of 'negative psychology,' an approach which Val Hogan might not understand.

To wit, in that little letter I started off by telling the Hawk about his wife's request to me, followed by the sentiment that "But no one can persuade you about anything, I know. You always make up your own mind." Then my message continued on to how her request made me feel sort of twisted, because although I wanted to do as Mrs. Hogan had asked, it seemed to me a terrible idea for Ben to try a comeback near 'the Big Apple.'

"You may be feeling pretty good now, but sitting cramped up during a multi-day train ride to New York is apt to take a harsh toll on your body. Plus, once you're out on the course the weather's going to be hot and humid there, it being August – and you know how badly your muscles can spasm when dehydrated. So why put yourself through another public display of poor golf? Heck, you can do that by going out in the heat right here in Texas and wilt walking a course!"

A letter arrived a week later in my mailbox from Bantam Ben. I must confess that my hand shook while I opened it. The unfolded sheet revealed a single phrase however. "Thanks for the advice, Kid!" I was a man soon-to-turn 50 years of age that August. Yet he'd used "Kid." That was a 'handle' he hadn't chosen in addressing me for a long, long time. I breathed out in relief, believing that whatever decision he would make, he hadn't condemned me for my part in it.

Well, Ben and Valerie did make the trip with plenty of time for Mrs. Hogan to "buy out" several ladies' stores since the Hawk got to the Westchester course almost a week early to practice. Unfortunately, the weather projected for the start of the tournament on July 30th, and the next day as well, was for temperatures to rise to the mid-80s with very heavy air, so stagnant that some pros made jokes after the event about not having seen anything of New York City (due to smog).

The Westchester Classic's tee times were made by a modified sort of draw but suspicions were that some accommodation might be made for William Ben Hogan, out of respect for the extraordinary amount of prep time he needed each morning to be fit to play. After the fact, my own guess was that the Hawk had been out to outsmart the warmer weather and hinted to the committee that he wouldn't mind teeing off before mid-morning.

However, when the Wee Ice Mon's tee time for the opening round was announced as 7:24 rather than 9 a.m. or so, he was not shy about stating his displeasure. Could you blame him, considering that this start time meant either he had to get up by 4:00 a.m. or sacrifice some of his essential pre-round rituals?

Anyway, Ben stumbled to a 78 that Thursday and promptly withdrew. I feel obliged to include the fact that the tournament authorities did offer to 'bend the rules' for him, hearing his dismay about the 7:24 time, but Hogan said "No thanks." Then – in a fit of delusion I have to say – he made news 2 days later by telling the head of the PGA that he *would* be competing in their Championship, scheduled to begin out in Tulsa at Southern Hills a mere 12 days hence on August 13th 1970.

Another equally bruising rail journey, searing Oklahoma heat, a gimpy knee worked too hard already in preparing for Westchester … no, Ben didn't make it to Southern Hills, though he'd said how much he was looking forward to competing on a course that featured Texas-type grasses, particularly on the greens!

In 1971 he tried 1 last time to remain a tournament golfer but after a 1-2 punch of withdrawals at Champions and Colonial – in a 1st round and practice round respectively – even the 58-year-old Hawk knew that he was 'down for the count.' The question had become, how would Ben pass the time in his 60s, 70s, and 80s if he were to live that long?

In September of that year, at the Hawk's request I took him out to Hopkins County east of Dallas to tour our Shout Double Rig Ranch, a 3,000-acre spread dedicated to raising nearly 1,400 beef cattle. Ben had talked of getting into ranching and I reckoned that now that he'd come to terms with the fact that tournament golf was in his past, he was ready to get serious about a purchase. Yet I had my doubts …

During our day at the ranch which featured a mini round-up to move some of our stock to a different pasture and even the branding of some calves I'd had the boys save for this visit, Mr. Hogan could not have been kinder or more considerate to the Double Rig's 'hands,' several of them being Korean and/or Viet Nam vets. Not surprisingly, he asked some sharp questions about the work, but more than that, Ben showed real interest in their past and present lives. You could tell that he liked these cowboys and felt some connection to their independent ways.

But knowing the Hawk as well as I did by this time, his subtle reactions to various aspects of ranching were not lost on me. No.

Recollect that Ben was always a meticulous dresser, his custom-made clothes pressed and creased to a tee. Then picture him encountering the heavy dust thrown up by hoofs, and the cow-pies minefield on the ground. His nose, mouth and eyes could not totally hide his distaste. Nor, I could tell, was he – a man of quiet solitude – thrilled with the racket made by yelling men and mooing beasts out there.

Did Hennie Bogan cringe a trifle when we witnessed the roped-down calves having a red-hot branding iron pressed to their hides? I reckoned so, but whether that was due to memories perhaps of his father's scars from blacksmithing, or a reaction stemming from the colossal pain he'd been made to suffer since his accident, who could say? It would be foolish to try to pry such a thing from Ben. I did know that much.

Well Hogan never did buy a ranch, though he mused on the idea – usually to the press – from time to time. You need to remember this: Ben had always felt it less than honest for someone to 'put their name to' something they weren't really connected to – like Arnold Palmer's ridiculous number of endorsements. So the Hawk couldn't in good conscience put his name to a ranch, seeing how, much of its operation would repulse him. Many folks might think this stance of his bordered on plumb crazy for an investor. Yet I Bobby Shout had to admire this ultra-proud man once again being true to himself.

Through the next 12 years -- as the 1970s morphed into the 1980s – I could see Ben inching his way through his 60s and beyond. During this stretch, it seemed his life as a less public figure granted him more peace but he'd also begun to get more whiffs of mortality. He saw Bobby Jones 'go,' then his trusted mentor Marvin Leonard, and the Hawk's sister Princess followed them to the grave, leaving my 'patient' shaken.

Ben also suffered some business disappointments along the way. In 1973 he'd taken the role of consultant for a massive piece of property north of Fort Worth. The Hawk was supposed to help the architect Joe Lee craft a pair of superb courses as the hub of a full-blown community project. But money problems surfaced early and the single track when finished never reached anywhere near to Hogan's initial hopes.

Bantam Ben's input on the ultimately scaled-back course was quite visible however. He'd convinced Lee to bulldoze titanic avenues of open land for the Trophy Club's holes-to-be, having stated that trees were an unfair hazard. Surprised by this stance, I quizzed the Wee Ice Mon. Seeing how he could curve his ball at will, what was the problem? "I hate trees," was all he'd say.

What was the Hawk? Almost forty years 'ahead of his time' in preaching this approach to golf architecture? I've chuckled seeing today's renovations by hot-shot architects hailed as revolutionary because they've reverted to tree-cleared, bare tracks.

Unfortunately the Ben Hogan Golf Company had also begun to 'feel the pinch' during this decade. As most golfers know, Karsten Solheim and a following herd had begun casting clubs rather than forging them which allowed perimeter-weighting for a kinder response to 'off-hits.' But inflexible Ben, who'd always crafted clubs 'for better players,' would not readily 'turn his back' on his late father's blacksmithing method. When I asked him whether he'd tried hitting the new Ping irons, he just scoffed. "Those clubheads are hard as rocks. Pure junk."

Nevertheless that "junk" was grabbing market share from the Hawk, and his company's hold on the ball sector, at one time supreme, was shrinking as well due to the rise of Surlyn covers. That material too was too darn hard for Ben's taste.

If you wonder how the Hawk felt he could afford to be so stubborn while sales dropped, I reckoned the answer lay in the state of his competition for greater wealth than Palmer. You see Arnie had won, 'the king' making so much cash by the early 1970s that Ben could see no worth anymore in maximizing his own profits.

Thus – and this seemed a healthy thing at first – for the 1st time in his life the Hawk had found that less competition had its benefits. In his case, this meant doing what the heck he felt like doing, say relaxing, rather than grinding out each day's existence. So my 'patient' began a habitual routine along these lines.

He continued to arrive at his Fort Worth factory office at 10 a.m. and leave at noon, just as he'd done during the company's 'best times.' And now his door was often open, an invitation to his sales reps and other employees to 'shoot the bull' for a while. Then it was off to the Shady Oaks Club for the afternoon. He'd usually eat there by himself – by choice -- followed by either serious practice, or serious play with the members he liked.

As Ben aged, he'd go fewer and fewer holes, opting instead to set up somewhere alone on the Club's 'short course' to bang ball after ball. Later in the day came card-playing and drinks. That's when the Hawk would 'let his hair down' – telling spicy stories and joking with the rest of the guys. Eventually he'd head home to Valerie, only a 5-minute drive in his Cadillac, yet a constant worry for Val, due to her husband's blatant tipsiness.

Offers to travel were almost always declined, likewise any public display of his golfing skills. In 1978 when Jimmy Demaret urged Ben to be part of the first Legends tournament 'right in his backyard,' the Hawk turned him down flat. It appeared to me that Hogan was on course to become yet another monumental figure turned recluse.

The former Texas Iceberg now needed the cozy sanctuary-feeling provided by Shady Oaks so badly that it became a 7-days-a-week ritual for him. He'd go to watch televised football, even golf, with buddies on weekends there, before or after practicing. Nor was Ben above 'sneaking' into the closed Club on Mondays to eat in its eerily empty grill room. I Bobby Shout know this for a fact since I was one of the outsiders he'd ask to bring lunch. However, 2 developments in the 1980s arrived to at least delay this trend toward greater isolation.

Before I talk though about that decade which took Ben through his 70s, it wouldn't surprise me if you've been wondering, "And what was Shout doing for Hogan's peace of mind during the 1970s?" Well I wasn't just 'sitting on my horse' the whole time!

First off, I was quite aware that he had lost his identity as 'the great golfer' who could defend his claim at any golf course in the world. The poor Hawk had become like a long-horned steer that has broken off one of its magnificent pair of menacing points all the way back to its skull, leaving the beast puzzled, insecure, and uncertain how to act.

We had plenty of talks throughout that decade, me gently urging him toward new goals and Ben being Ben. When I tried to get him to express something he'd still like to achieve, the reply was "win more tournaments" and there was no trace of a grin as the Texas Iceberg announced this.

Changing tack, I suggested that now might be the time to see more of the world. Naturally, given his and Val's travel phobias, the Hawk looked at me like 'I could go fly a kite.' But I countered with, "But wait, Ben, I'm not talking about flying anywhere. Right down in Galveston there are cruise ships that sail to lots of places."

I continued, "You two could take a short cruise to Mexico, just to see how you like being on the boat. It's not like being cooped up on a train or plane. Plenty of room onboard for taking walks. They've got swimming pools and even mini-driving ranges so you could still hit as many balls each day as you like."

In response he'd growled, "I've been on big fucking ships out in the Atlantic on the way to and from Ryder Cups and when a storm hits, you get tossed around like you're in a dinghy. Val would die of fright."

"But I'm not talking about crossing oceans, Ben. Some of those cruise ships out of Galveston hover near our coast all the way past Florida and then you've practically reached the tropical islands. At that point, you're on land for day excursions more than you're at sea, and once again never far from another island. You know, you might just see something down there that would inspire you in a new direction ..."

He stopped me there. "So you think I'd enjoy smacking balls off a damn mat in front of a crowd of gawking strangers like I'm a carnival attraction on the boat?" The Hawk had a point – if he wasn't able to leave his darned sticks behind for a week. Renting a private yacht? I knew that Ben would blow that thought 'out of the water' too. This discussion had gone nowhere but I wasn't done ...

The suggestion that he start some charity venture was met by, "I already give plenty as I see fit. Don't need other people to get involved."

Another time I offered that perhaps he'd be interested in funding a public service project – and I Bobby Shout paused to cringe before saying – "like a suicide-prevention phone line." The Hawk didn't throw me out right then and there but the depth of his glare said that this topic was closed. I'd gambled and lost by presenting a choice where his core emotions lay.

So I 'went after' his cerebral side. The Texas Iceberg was warmed occasionally by the sight of fine art, according to Valerie. Could Ben find some satisfaction in becoming a collector, I posed to him? When he growled immediately about the travel involved, I had a counter. "You can hire someone to scout for the works you'd be interested in ... a certain artist, a certain theme. And this person can oversee getting the art delivered to you for viewing; galleries would be willing to do this for a famous person who has real money." He said he'd think about it.

In my mind there probably wasn't much point in bringing up the idea of the Hawk mentoring young golfers, but I tried. His ornery response was, "It's all in my instruction books. Can't they read?!"

It burned me a bit to hear this deceit from him, considering that Life Magazine had paid him big bucks to share a swing "secret" which supposedly he hadn't told before – and more recently there he was again, negotiating with golf magazines to reveal his "real secret."

Heck, the Hawk had never shown anything but scorn for member-hackers when he'd been paid by country clubs to represent them on Tour. Nor was he known for giving tips to even the finest golfers who sought him out, unless they used Hogan equipment. Ask Gary Player; ask Nick Faldo. So I quickly gave up trying to sell Ben on any version of him becoming a beloved figure to promising players in the future. Well doggone it! That was before she came to town.

It was the summer of 1983 when this miss appeared at the Shady Oaks Club, she a newly-minted junior member down from the North, all of 18 years old and about to begin her college golf career at my old job-site Texas Christian University. The girl was raw enough to have no idea how famous the Hawk was. And although she'd been told not to disturb Mr. Hogan, that outgoing gal soon broke through the taboo and before long became his driving-range buddy. But was that all?

Unfortunately, her girl-next-door good looks were just the 'tip of the iceberg.' She had what we gentlemen used to term politely a "nice body," so nice that she later was paid to wear certain clothes companies' outfits on the ladies Tour. It was only natural that Ben's detractors and all those members who'd been disappointed by his response to their pleas for swing-help were happy to add to the whispers that the Hawk had turned into a 'dirty old man.'

Nor did Bantam Ben do much to defuse these rumors over time. During his young female friend's 4 years in Fort Worth he was not shy about touching her, and not always for the sake of instructing. Worse he seemed unconscious of the fact that throwing a candy bar her way on the course as he buzzed by in his golf cart constituted a suggestive act to some folks.

I think it was in the spring of 1985 that Valerie Hogan finally called me. She, for one, would never get anywhere near to uttering the word "phallic," I knew. The closest Val could come to indicating her distress – probably due to beauty-parlor rumors – was to ask, "Bobby, do you think I should worry … about Ben practicing so much?"

My response was to speak openly. "Valerie, I don't think you have a thing to worry about involving that TCU player he's coaching." And here I was sorry but it had to be said: "She's a granddaughter substitute, that's all. The girl is 20 years old, just about the right age if you and Ben had had kids and one of them in turn had birthed a female. Heck, she even acts like she's got the Hawk's genes: loves to hit balls, likes to learn every sort of new shot by figuring it out on the range, and she's good! That gal was all-conference last year and I reckon she'll 'make it' on the LPGA Tour right out of school. That's what has attracted your husband to her."

Really I thought I was right. I hoped I was right and I hoped that Val believed that I was right too, even though Ben had begun to spend the night elsewhere if the two of them had had an evening spat.

Oddly, it was a new spate of rumors in the spring of '87 that helped both of us to see the absurdity of the charge that the old Hogan was obsessed with a college kid. Namely, the wags pointed to the news that the usually reclusive Hawk had just made a television commercial which showed him hitting the company's new clubs, and this was proof that the Hawk still wanted to 'show off' to the young lady who was soon to graduate and leave Fort Worth.

Well the truth of the matter was that the new president of the Ben Hogan Company -- Ben had been sold again, this time by AMF to Minstar – back in '84 had shown the Wee Ice Mon some dismal sales projections. This data indicated that his namesake company would be out of business in a few years if they did not adapt.

So Hogan had agreed to the design of a new iron, still forged mind you, but now featuring the popular cavity-back. And later 'the brass' had to practically beg the by-then 74-year-old Ben to film the TV commercial – all the way out in L.A.! -- which showed him hitting those Apex irons while speaking of their superior 'feel.' No gal had anything to do with it! And yes, that ad did boost the company's sales dramatically.

Maybe Ben had been right to stubbornly oppose a flight to the West Coast when he hadn't been on a plane in years, not to mention the added stress of being adulated by a crowd of hundreds during the filming of the Apex ad. 'Cause not too long after he returned home his appendix burst, which nearly 'did him in.'

Moreover, after 6-plus weeks in the hospital, the weakened Hawk's clarity had begun to unravel at a more rapid pace. Valerie reported to me that he was both forgetting things said by others sooner and experiencing bouts of confusion more dramatically. She hated the idea of the guys at Shady Oaks seeing her husband grown so feeble, but for a while he continued to go.

It didn't help his state of mind that Minstar turned around in '88 and sold the Hogan Company soon after Ben's effort had gotten it back 'in the black.' Nor was the identity of the new owner a calming development for the Hawk.

You younger folks will have to understand that some of us who'd been involved in a war against Japan were still having trouble trusting the Japanese even by then, and Ben was little trustful to begin with. So when the head of the Tokyo-based firm that now 'called the shots' came to call at Shady Oaks, the Hawk was in no mood to be polite. "Mr. Isutani, you've bought the family jewels," the Wee Ice Mon stated in a loud and slow -- foreigners can't really know English -- tone of voice. "Don't fuck it up."

Alas, Minoru Isutani did just that. He 'threw money' at starting up a "Ben Hogan Tour" for up-and-coming players, then spent a disastrously large amount for Pebble Beach in 1990. With his Cosmo World Corp. overextended, the Japanese whirlwind had to turn around and sell off Pebble at a huge loss soon thereafter. In addition, his various mistakes forced him to dump the Ben Hogan Company in 1992 as well, though by this time, a simpler face-to-face commercial with Ben just sitting in his Fort Worth office had already proved magic in the marketplace again.

The new owner of the Hogan Company didn't hesitate to announce that he was closing down the Fort Worth factory and moving all assets to Virginia. You see, this 'bean-counter' named William H. Goodman had previously purchased AMF's bowling divisions headquartered in that state and reckoned that he could save money by combining operations as well as restarting the Hogan company as a non-union shop.

Ben's now figurehead status with the company did him no good when he protested the loss of local employment which would result from the move. And so the Hawk's final years would be spent feeling major remorse that he'd ever given away his symbolic child.

There's not much left to tell. The Hawk had ambiguous feelings about doing a memoir during the later stages of his life. He'd say that no one was going to give a damn about him a few years after he was gone. Yet Ben did have serious talks with a buddy, the great Texan sportswriter Dan Jenkins, about 'getting his life down on paper.' Jenkins later said that the 'bottom line' was that the little man couldn't 'open up' enough.

His dementia of course only increased as Ben slid toward colon cancer in '95 and his stroke-related death in 1997 at age 84. Valerie became very much his gatekeeper, perhaps too good a one. She'd stopped him from driving, smoking, or seeing his Shady Grove buddies pretty much – the only things the Hawk really had left to enjoy.

I didn't blame Valerie for wanting to keep the world from ever seeing her husband 'fall on his face' or even hear rumors to that effect, just as Ben himself had wanted no cameras shooting him when he made his return to golf at L.A. in 1950 – in case he toppled during a swing. But I couldn't deny that Mrs. Hogan might be getting some perverse satisfaction out of being the controller finally, rather than the controlee.

Ironically, the college girl who'd kind of rekindled Ben's golfing spirit in the 1980s became somewhat close to Valerie during his last years, partly because the gal was safely married and an out-of-state resident by this time, I reckoned. Anyway, she got access to the Hawk far more readily when she was in Texas than any of us locals did.

Actually, access to Ben had dried up like a Texas ditch in August. Every time I called Val to suggest a visit, she seemed to have some excuse ready at hand as to why I shouldn't. So it was that I fixed on taking matters into my own hands, not having seen Ben in several months, starting since the fall of 1996.

In March of '97 I Bobby Shout began to play amateur 'private eye.' I'd hang out at a distance on the Hogan's road and watch through binoculars at the comings-and-goings at their house. It seems I've forgotten to mention that when Ben had the thing built, he'd ordered that there be no guest bedroom included, so I knew that there were never any relatives staying over – it was just Ben, Valerie, and a black woman who was serving as the Hawk's daytime caregiver.

Over the next week, Valerie was picked up twice -- to go out to lunch, I reckoned -- and then a strange, touching thing happened each time. Ben's aide, who I'd heard was also assigned to drive him places, led the Hawk out to his Cadillac in the driveway, put him in the driver's seat, and after seating herself beside him, lit up a smoke for Bantam Ben to enjoy. Not just 1 cigarette either; she and he would chat like a couple of buddies for 20 minutes or more. *This is a brave woman*, I reckoned, giving me hope that *she'd* let me in to see my 'patient.'

Anyway, having witnessed this routine for a third time, I was fixing to make my move. After they went inside, I waited for 15 minutes in case Ben had to use the toilet or something, then walked up and rang the bell. The woman answered the door promptly.

As soon as I'd said "Howdy ..." though, she interrupted me.

"I know who you be, Mr. Shout. I's real sorry but Mrs. Hogan's instructions is that no one be allowed in to see Mr. Hogan, especially if the missus ain't home." Belying this rejection was a sideways motion of her thumb. I figured she was telling me that Ben was out on the back patio, so I headed around the side of the house, and there he was, huddled up in an outdoor rocker.

The pangs that hit me upon being up close to him again were stunning. He had on the same French-style beret he'd been wearing at our 1st meeting on the Hulen Street bench. And though it was a pleasant spring day, Ben was clutching a blanket over his legs. I could see that they were now just as scrawny as they'd been back in January of '50 when he was still reeling from the crash.

I could only bring myself to half-whisper, "Hey there, Hawk."

He opened his eyes – those blue-gray diamonds – and after a pause murmured, "Dr. Shout." Then in a tone of accusation more like Ben he added, "Where you been? And what about my Shady Oaks guys? I knew I'd be forgotten, but not this fast!"

Should I have told him the truth – how his wife was responsible for this lonesomeness he was feeling? I couldn't. Betraying Valerie in that way would have only made the Hawk's misery deeper, I reckoned, by torturing him with a sense of alienation from even the woman he'd so long loved.

Instead, I tried to assure him that we all were real concerned about him and only staying away so as not to tax the strength he needed to recover his health. He didn't reply except to hum an old tune. Then this man I'd known for 47 years baffled me for the umpteenth time.

His voice now dreamy-like, he mused, "Bobby, I still want to buy that ranch. It's got to be 3 or 4 times bigger though than Nelson's little place. And no pigs or chickens like Byron's resorted to! I'm raising long-horned cattle, period. Is that understood?"

While humoring him, I didn't know whether to laugh or cry as the saying goes. Most of Ben now was surely gone. But his ferocious competitive spirit was still alive, and probably would be till his final breath, at which point I Bobby Shout could hear his Hennie Bogan persona uttering an exhausted lament, "Why, Daddy? Why did you do it?" Hogan had pretty much stopped going to church in his later years.

It struck me as kind of fitting though sad that a similar harsh mindset had seemed at work in Valerie through her choices for Ben's funeral. Byron Nelson could have given a wonderful eulogy, I reckoned, but he had been snubbed – not offered any part in the service. Byron being Byron, he came to pay his respects anyway. And he of all men by then probably understood and forgave.

CHAPTER 17

Sam afterwards

SAMUEL JACKSON SNEAD outlasted Ben Hogan by nearly 5 years, Slamming Sammy's death coming shortly after a stroke in May of 2002. The man missed making it to age 90 by 4 days.

I only met the Slammer a couple of times, so you may want to take my opinion of him 'with a grain of salt' but here it is: I didn't cotton much to Sam at all. First off, he was known to tell filthy stories with glee even if there were ladies present. Nor was Snead a respecter of matrimony, cheating with countless women. Worse he treated those lovers like they were facial tissues – using then discarding them almost immediately.

If any money were on the line in a social match – and he always wanted to play for cash from what I heard – Samuel's dark side often surfaced. He'd do most anything, especially in the gamesmanship area, not to lose. And on those rare occasions when he didn't win, Slammin' Sammy was a sore loser, grumpy and slow to settle the bet.

Anyway this book is not about him. For that reason you will find this chapter to be brief. In fact, I've included this section with his name on it largely to report more about Sam's perspective on my Texas Quartet, and also 'cause I reckon it's time to 'clear the air' about who was the greater player, him or Hogan?

Okay I'm a Texan, so I won't blame you for looking for some kind of bias in my claim that it's no contest – Ben was best – but here are the facts. The Majors 'make the man' in my book, and the deeper a body 'dives in,' the greater Hogan's superiority speaks out. The bottom line is this: Ben captured 9 Majors; Sam, 7. Well during the Wee Ice Mon's career trying to win them (from the 1930s through 1967) he was 'only' able to tee it up 58 times.

Whereas during the same stretch, Slammin' Sammy had 24 more chances to 'rack up' these titles. Yet Ben won more. (And we aren't even counting the 30 extra entries into Majors that Snead made after the Hawk retired from those competitions.)

On top of that, there's the fact that when both did tee it up in the same Major, Ben won 8 of his 9 titles while besting Sam, but by contrast, Snead only ever beat Bantam Ben 3 times when the two were contesting for the same Major win. I Bobby Shout dare any denizen of the Virginias to 'take this bull by the horn' and flip my verdict about who was the better player!

Moreover, out of Samuel Jackson Snead's own mouth came the finest evidence I can cite for who thought who was the 'top dog' between them. In 1952, Sam started the Masters not having won a Major with Hogan in the field since 1942. And during Snead's PGA win that year he hadn't topped Ben directly. It was Jim Turnesa who 'took out' the Hawk in the quarterfinals.

After 3 rounds in the '52 championship at Augusta, the 2 men were tied. But the 'smart money' favored Hogan, seeing how the previous year Sam had led after 54 holes, only to shoot 80 on the final day while Ben's 68 'sealed the deal' for a Masters victory.

Well in this finale Samuel J. Snead at least matched par with his 72 but was that good enough to be the 1952 Masters winner? This time it was, seeing how Ben couldn't 'get the ball in the hole' all day, skying to a 79.

With victory secure, Sam had been asked to play radio commentator as Hogan limped in. And before all the world the Slammer pronounced 'in public' this verdict, "I guess Hogan is human after all," as in, 'He's always seemed to me to be super human on the course.' At least, that's my 'take' on Snead's confession. Later the Slammer would back that thought up with, "the three things I fear most in golf are lightning, Ben Hogan, and a downhill putt."

Just as Hogan's favorite guy to team up with was Jimmy Demaret, Snead liked having Lloyd Mangrum as his partner. The two played together in 4 consecutive Ryder Cups from '47 through '53, thrashing the Brits to the tune of 6-and-5, 5-and-4, and 8-and-7 (!) in 3 of the matches.

However this didn't signify that these two were the best of buddies, even though I reckon that Lloyd's foul mouth and Sam's dirty stories got along all right. I ask you to recollect how Mangrum whilst delivering his victory speech at the Motor City Open on July 4th in 1950 had taunted Snead for missing a short putt to tie him on the final hole.

And wasn't the Slammer just another of those pros who'd turned 'tin soldier' and stayed safely stateside during the war -- in the eyes of combat vets like Mr. Icicle?

Well Sam waited until after Lloyd had died to deliver a certain story which to me had a whiff of revenge about it. Yet I also wondered whether the Slammer had been afraid to share it while Mangrum's fists were still alive.

You see, according to Snead, 1 time on the road he and Mr. Icicle were having a pleasant time at the table in a café when Lloyd's foot accidently tripped a fellow walking by them. The man got up protesting, but he didn't get much out of his mouth before Mangrum picked up the sugar bowl on that table and rammed it into the aggrieved guy's nose with such force that it knocked him to the ground. Then Lloyd stood over his bleeding victim ready to 'whale the tar' out of him if he made any move to get up.

Sam said he had to pull Mangrum away and out of the place, and then concluded with "Some of us weren't sure Lloyd was quite right mentally because of what he went through in the war."

In its retellings, either Snead or his listeners offered some different details like Mr. Icicle had apologized but the man kept bugging him, the weapon that came to Lloyd's hand was an ashtray, it was Mangrum who told Snead that they were getting out of there after Mr. Icicle had coolly thrown a 10-dollar bill on the table. But 1 thing is certain.

When Samuel Jackson Snead had finished this part of the narrative he added the observation that he'd known some bad hombres but not a one who was any tougher than slim Lloyd. And furthermore, Lloyd Mangrum was who Sam wanted at his back if he ever got in a barroom brawl. It did make sense that a man who could swing a golf club at world-class speed might well have lightning-quick hands, and if you ever saw the killer-look that came at times into Mr. Icicle's eyes, you wouldn't have doubted ole Sam's sincerity for a moment.

Sam and Jimmy Demaret would have been legendary boozing buddies, except the Slammer didn't drink. Both looked for a 'good time' whenever off the golf course and usually found it. Each had been snubbed by the moral 'high horses' at Augusta, though it was the 2 'bad boys' and not Ben or Byron who were the only 3-time Masters winners of their era. So S&J shared that bond of disgruntlement.

And thus their barbs at each other were for the sake of wit rather than looking to wound – and each knew it. Jimmy compared Sam's side-saddle putting stroke to somebody basting a turkey. Snead countered by snorting that Demaret looked like a 'pansy' majorette, the way his pre-shot routine included taking several short mincing steps from in back of the ball while twirling his club in those huge hands he had.

Then the Wardrobe would focus on 1 of Samuel's hairpieces, expressing his wonder that a guy with some much 'dough' couldn't find better-fitting 'rugs' and the Slammer would 'make a face,' pretending to be insulted. It was all in fun between them – mostly.

As you might expect, the relationship between Snead and Nelson was a whole other matter. That good Christian man could in no way condone Sam's antics with the ladies, and Sam for his part couldn't be blamed for labeling Byron as a boring 'stuffed shirt' though this charge was unjust, considering Lord Byron's true piety.

Not surprisingly, Sam Snead like Lloyd Mangrum was missing among the golfers featured in the 'profiles chapter' of Nelson's 1993 autobiography. And elsewhere in the text Byron opted to describe a less-than-flattering quirk of the Slammer's – he feared cameras on the course. I reckon probably that Sam's hearing – like many of his other physical traits -- was superior to the average man's, and so he could detect the clicking sound of a camera shutter even from a distance, and it distracted him during his swing.

However I Bobby Shout do not want to give the impression that Lord Byron refused to give the ultra-talented Snead his due as a player. For example, Nelson once said that Sam "did to the tee shot what Roger Bannister did to the 4-minute mile."

What Byron meant – especially for you younger folks who may never have heard of Roger and his 1954 feat – was that just as Bannister showed that a man could run a faster mile on the track than what was previously considered possible, no one before Snead had ever hit the ball consistently so far yet also straight. High praise indeed!

In closing this chapter, I too would like to recognize at least 1 positive aspect of Samuel Jackson Snead's make-up. Although he sometimes spoke out of 'both sides of his mouth' – to some folks saying that Byron was the best he'd played against, while telling others that there'd been no one better than Ben – the Slammer did show a lot of heart at times.

He was known, for instance, to have saved several of his brethren on the Tour from getting roughed up by their bookies, Sam having lent each of those gambling fools a large amount to 'clear' their accounts. We're talking several-thousand-dollar loans, a lot of 'cabbage' back in those days! And this 'soft touch' side of the Slammer extended to giving money to many who needed it wherever he 'hung his hat,' with no fanfare about his generosity at all.

Yet for the life of me I couldn't forgive Snead for being so cheap when it came to little stuff like picking up a tab or paying off a small bet he'd lost. Yes, I'd been introduced to this confounding type of person in my psychological studies. If someone grows up poor then becomes wealthy, it's in 'the literature' that there can be cross-currents of money-guilt yet also an obsessive fear of somehow winding up in poverty again. Maybe Sam did harbor at his core this combination of behavior-generation? But darn it, I still didn't like the man, and that's that.

CHAPTER 18

Bobby afterwards

THIS BOOK WAS not intended to be about me, Robert Nickel Jefferson Shout. So I'm fixing to keep this chapter short like the one you just read about Samuel Jackson Snead. Besides, I've lived a fairly unspectacular life, no outstanding accomplishments to my credit.

Yet I Bobby Shout feel obliged to say a few words pertaining to myself, starting with a major confession. As you know, I was involved in an oil-rig explosion back in 1941, which caused damage to my right eye and ear among other 'breaks' and bruises. Well after I'd gotten fully mobile again, it was time to visit our local Draft Board. And on the day I went, my daddy said not to worry. That things would be fine.

The first discordant note I discovered at the Selective Service office was the guy handing out the registration forms asking me, "You're Tom Shout's son, right?"

Well I replied "Yes," filled out the paperwork which included a place to list injuries, and after a brisk physical, waited to see the interviewers, all the time 'chewing on' that first question I'd been asked.

When called into the interview room -- rather than being asked anything -- I was told right off that I was probably 4-F due to my limited eyesight but that was mute anyway since my work as an employee of Shout Petroleum gave me the deferment classification II-A, "Men necessary in their civilian activity."

At that point I was upset. Yes the oil industry was vital to keeping our war machines running in Europe and Japan, but my work at Shout Petroleum … Well let's just say I wasn't a key cog in making the company function. It seemed to me that I could be more valuable to the war effort doing paperwork 'behind the front.' "Couldn't I be a I-B maybe?" I asked them. (That was the classification for limited military service.)

But they replied that it would be best for me to stay at Shout, and I Bobby Shout didn't make any further fuss, though it was evident to me that my dad had influenced things. The bottom line was that I didn't even need to get used to sleeping anywhere but in my own bed the entire course of that war! And as time went on, my guilt grew over how I hadn't fought harder to sacrifice like others.

It was thus for my own sense of self-worth that I turned post-war to the task of aiding veterans through finding them jobs. And the effort did make me feel less guilty. So now you know. My 'good deeds' were very much tainted!

Having gotten this avowal 'off my chest,' I feel a bit better about describing the rest of 'my days.' However, in describing my life starting in the early 1950s, there is the path of the Korean War to be reckoned with, as the painful background to all our individual goings-on back then.

Peace talks began in February of '51, but they dragged and dragged and dragged, while the stalemate between our side concentrated in South Korea and the enemy up in the North remained a potential powder keg of renewed all-out fighting.

It wasn't until more than 2 years later that terms were reached to formalize the end of active combat, in July 1953. And at last many more of 'our boys' were allowed to return home.

By then Cheryl Lynn and I were young married folk with a son Tom born in '52 and Cheryl already pregnant with our second who proved to be a girl, born in February 1954. We named her Donna Margo Shout (after our 2 moms) and she was as boisterous a child as Tom was taciturn.

Anyway for the rest of that decade and through much of the '60s, this family of mine -- along with work -- took most of my energy. It was a happy period though I'd hoped to have more children. Cheryl had said "No," however, after number 2. She wanted to have 'some life' besides being tied down with kids and I couldn't blame her. So my wife when not mothering had gotten involved in social clubs and do-gooding efforts, which seemed to make her happy enough.

Meanwhile, outside of hosting customers who wanted to play Colonial and getting in an occasional weekend round at Northwood in Dallas, I wasn't playing enough to keep my golf game sharp and so had to be content with reading about the Texas amateur circuit rather than being part of it. Jimmy and Lloyd urged me at times to 'keep up' my game while I was still in my 30s and 40s but it was hard.

By nature I'd never been terribly disciplined about time management. Guys who'd get up at the crack of dawn to practice or play before heading into work – well, that just wasn't me. Still, I felt good about life through that whole period.

Then came Viet Nam, war protests, civil-rights agitation, rock music, recreational drugs, and *our* teenage children, not to mention 'free love,' culminating out on the West Coast in the "Summer of Love," 1967. I was nearing my 47th birthday at that point, pretty conservative, and wanting no part of any of those crazes.

Whereas my 13- and 15-year-old had begun to be seduced by peer pressure into championing those same things, right to my face! I tried to explain the dangers of such pursuits to them but Cheryl Lynn – just on the verge of her 40s -- was no help, mostly telling me that really "I should get with the times." And suddenly she was gone!

The mother of my children, it turned out, had flown to San Francisco without telling a soul in advance, wanting to see for herself the amazing hippie scene happening there – she told me in a long-distance call a day later. Of course I blurted out to Cheryl, "Well when are you coming back?" Her reply was that she would be careful and call home each night. Then my wife hung up, leaving me to concoct a story about her having to go out West to visit an ill aunt.

Cheryl made good on her promise for the first week or two. I asked whether she was 'fine' for money and she snorted at me before replying that a credit card and checkbook had accompanied her West. Then she'd said, "There are plenty of people living out here happily with not much 'bread' – that's cash, dear." I started to worry more after that.

When my 7-years-younger mate didn't 'make' our regularly scheduled evening phone call for the 1st time, I had to stop myself from 'jumping' on a plane. Next night my wife did call, with a lukewarm apology about having been tied up with some protest meeting – and that was it! I told her I was coming out on Saturday and that she should meet me for dinner at the Hilton where I'd be staying. Cheryl Lynn said okay and was there at the appointed time, but our meal turned stormy when I pretty much demanded that she fly back with me. "I'm not ready," she insisted while tears began to fall. So I 'backed off.'

It was darn hard to leave the woman I still very much loved – hippie clothes or not – back in San Francisco, but I did it. A month and a half later, early in the evening, Cheryl's Buick pulled into our driveway. She was home. Tom and Donna raced to her and almost toppled her over with their hugs. To me my wife gave a look that pleaded *Please forgive me.* I did, and am so glad of it. Nor did I ever pry about any 'free love' or drug-taking that might have transpired.

One silver lining of this jolting experience was that Cheryl Lynn seemed somehow a kinder and wiser person following her 'vacation,' and that included a more supportive stance toward my golfing. In fact she downright encouraged me to "self-actualize" my talent for the game, as though she'd finally found golf to be a worthy pursuit in life.

Well "self-actualization" wasn't a new concept to me – I'd studied Maslow's "hierarchy of needs" pyramid back in the 1940s -- but I got Cheryl's message and rejoiced. She'd 'signed off' on my getting out on the course more often.

So I did. And this development led to what I called in retrospect my Hogan era, though I really was no better than a "Chicken Hawk" as Ben's disciple Gardner Dickinson had been dubbed.

Finishing off my 40s over the next 2 years, I played and practiced like I hadn't since my college days, even entered some state amateur events to refresh my competitive edge. However the real prize in my mind was to win a Senior Club Championship at either Colonial or my Dallas club, Northwood, and so at age 51 in September of 1971 'my legend' began.

That year – to my surprise – I prevailed at both clubs! I Bobby Shout had never thought of match play as a strength of mine, but somehow the Hawk's cool competitive composure had leaked into me, I reckoned. In neither tournament that go-around did I ever feel any 'tightness.' My driving, my approaching, my putting – all seemed straight-forward. I just 'let it happen' and the victories in match after match came easy.

Not so in '72. I was lucky to repeat at Colonial, thanks to some weak holes by opponents at the right times. At Northwood, my game turned erratic and only a 'hot putter' got me to the final match. I didn't putt well on that occasion and got trounced, 4-down with 3-to-play.

In 1973 though, my golf was superb if I do say so myself. It would be false humility to phrase it any other way! The sense of looseness in my movements was back and a new putter worked like magic for me. A 4th and 5th Senior Club Championship followed, won with relative ease. Some reporter wrote in a Texas paper that Bobby Shout had become a highly-feared competitor among his Dallas-area rivals. Well I never would have 'gone that far' but there was no local opponent who scared me right then either.

As we all know, golf is more fickle than a Texas winter. I tweaked my back early in 1974 and by compensating for the injury did something bad to my swing. It took me 'til August to start playing decently again. Then I realized I had no 'fire' in me anymore about the upcoming club championships. Bobby Shout retired from those competitions while still 'on top' and I've never looked back at that decision with regret, though Ben pronounced me a first-class fool.

The next dozen years seemed to pass by in a wink. My kids Tom and Donna graduated high school, then college. He went off for an M.B.A. and much to my surprise so did she. They both joined Shout Petroleum right out of school and mom made them 'work their way up' toward senior management positions. All was well at home too till 1986, when Cheryl Lynn detected a lump in her left breast.

1987 was a nightmare. Although my wife underwent painful, humiliating procedures, there was no stopping the cancer and she died in July of '87. My mother Margo Scott followed her 2 months later, the victim of a massive stroke during the course of a routine work day. She'd stayed at the helm of our company, seemingly invincible, right up to the end. Naturally all of this (along with Ben's recent decline) sent me reeling but I could have reacted better.

Instead of helping my older brother Leroy to fill the leadership void left by my mom's demise, I became a pretty average employee at Shout, doing just enough to 'coast' toward my retirement, while my kids were learning to 'grow up fast' at the company. Part of my lack of energy at work during that key time was due to my after-hours activities, it shames me to say.

Not long after mom's death, I who at 67 was now single, well off, and cowpoke fit, had a brigade of Texas widows and divorcees bidding for my attention and I Bobby Shout did not let them down. Like Jimmy Demaret reborn, I spent night after night 'on the town' carousing. During my first 67 years on this earth I'd only known 2 women in the Biblical sense, so somehow I reckoned it was fair to taste as much female flesh as was offered to me, in an effort to keep my grief and loneliness tamped down.

This lewd conduct went on for several years until I began to tire of the ladies. And to tell the truth, the best of them had already given up on my ability to commit. It was then at the age of 74 in the fall of 1994 that a notion came to me which gave some sense to my finally retiring. And so I did, effective on December 31.

In February of '95 I booked my first cruise. I was going to 'see the world' at last – by boat – just as I'd advised Ben those many years earlier. But I had more on my mind than just sightseeing. A la Lloyd Mangrum, I Bobby Shout was fixing to play the role of 'riverboat gambler' on ship.

You see, while "Texas hold 'em" poker was just starting to get popular country-wide and didn't fully flourish 'til several years later, I'd already had plenty of experience at the game in various clubhouses around Dallas, plus Lloyd had 'let me in' on some of his secrets. So I always found my way to the card tables on board during the several cruises I took annually over the next several years, and it didn't surprise me that I did all right.

I got to see a lot of Europe that way as well as parts of Asia and most of the major islands in the Caribbean. To soothe my guilt for being out of contact with Hogan during those voyages, I would send him a postcard nearly every day, hoping to stimulate his floundering mind.

My last cruise was a return voyage from Southampton, England, to New York on the *Queen Elizabeth 2* in early August of 1998, the round trip having been a birthday present to myself for turning 78 on the 1st of that month. I Bobby Shout was now a 4-year veteran of the floating-poker-game circuit and who knows how much longer I would have followed this route but for the captain of that great ship.

A few of us players had been invited to dine at his table on the 2nd night out and 1 guy couldn't resist asking the captain whether he did any gambling. The man, who really looked his part – with a distinguished gray mustache and regal bearing – growled back that in his 5 years thus far at the helm of the *QE2* they'd lost half a dozen men overboard, fools who had lost big earlier in the evening then jumped. "So no, I don't take part in your *games*, gentleman." And he'd uttered this 'put-down' like we were robbing folks and pulling the trigger at them too!

After the rest of a subdued meal, I went back to my cabin to soul-search. I could recall 'cleaning out' at least 4 fellows who'd groaned at the time that they'd lost their last penny. Lloyd had warned me never to feel sorry for a sucker. I'd thrown a bit of cash back to each of them and thought no more about it, but now …

I could feel guilt closing in. No matter the amount of my losses any given session at the table, it had always just been fun for me.

Back in Texas, I reckoned that some time out at the company ranch might restore my spirits – just doing honest work handling cows and steers. Though I was retired from Shout Petroleum, no one had ever seemed to mind my 'lending a hand' there. But on my 3rd day as a 'bunkhouse boy' the horse got spooked and threw me into a fence. Both my left hip and leg got broken. At my age this meant the end of my cowboy days, I knew deep inside, though I told the guys I'd return.

So what was left for me – once I'd mended – with a new century and my 80th birthday on the horizon? I thanked God that I was able to return to the golf course and still make good swings. That was a bonus! Yet I felt a post-round emptiness that socializing in the clubhouse didn't 'fill' any more than a cube of sugar would a steer.

On March 31st of 2000, as you may recall, I 'ran across' Byron Nelson at Colonial and he officially forgave me for my virulent protests regarding his book's treatment of Lloyd some 7 years earlier.

Moreover, that good Christian helped me find purpose again, he the only one left of my Texas Quartet. It started with dinner at his place. Somehow Byron knew that I'd lapsed in my church attendance since the double-death year of '87, and he urged me to come to theirs the next Sunday. I went.

And though their congregation gathered a 40-minute drive from where I was then living in Dallas, I Bobby Shout became a habitual attendee. The dynamic energy of what's come to be the largest Church of Christ in the country appealed to me. The folks there were warm and welcoming, but not in the conniving way that the widows and divorcees had treated me a decade earlier.

It turned out too that I craved the pleasant feeling that comes from doing good works in a hands-on way, like driving supplies to folks who were ailing, or raking leaves to keep someone's yard looking neat and trim. With a congregation in the thousands, there were always good deeds to be done locally. Yet no one was looking for me to just throw money their way.

Church expanded to being a multi-day-per-week lifestyle for me from then on, including Wednesday night Bible study. I'd become an early-to-bed, early-to-rise do-gooder of humble spirit – at least I tried -- and wouldn't take any guff from my country club friends about it!

Then Byron Nelson died in 2006, but I didn't sever my connection with his church. To this day – and I'm writing this final chapter in 2015 at age 95 – my life still involves praying, helping, and sharing fun at the (formerly Richland) Hills Church of Christ, south of Roanoke and north of Fort Worth.

Well I reckon we've reached the last stage of my saga. Me the author of this manuscript. It was in late October of '06, a few weeks after Lord Byron's 'passing' that I got up the gumption to begin, on the first real cold day that fall. I didn't expect 9 years to pass before I'd get to the point of writing this last section, but that's life.

There were illnesses of course that slowed me, along with the need for more and more napping, I'm not ashamed to say. Anyway my slumbers often included dreams of the past, which proved useful.

Maybe this notion wasn't wise for an old coot like me, but I was determined to do the whole project myself. No researchers or fact-checkers were hired. Heck, I didn't even work with an editor. Instead I took suggestions – or not -- from my kin who were willing to read parts of the story. So I can honestly say that all the credit for the good stuff in this book, and all the blame for where I 'got it wrong,' are solely my affair.

In my final will and testament, this manuscript is headed to the 1 grandkid of mine who 'went literary.' That's right – this memoir will be published after I'm gone. After all I wouldn't want to see Ben blocking me from the Pearly Gates due to my 'big mouth.' To you folks who have read this thing entire, I say "Bless you, and thank God for his many mercies. Amen."

....

Hold on. I'm now past 98 years of age and had my annual checkup today. Doc says there's nothing wrong and I might just live to 110. That doesn't thrill me and I've had a change of mind about publishing the book. If I'm still around to reach 100, that's it – I'll be showing it to my grandkid and telling him to 'get it out' right quick. Publishing independently is fine by me. I'll just need to revise my introduction a tad is all. Okay then, now you know sure'nuff how I'm going to proceed, so I'll say no more except "Go, Mustangs!"

The End

ACKNOWLEDGMENTS

Gladly given

IN THE SPIRIT of full disclosure, allow me to begin by stating that I am not *that* Randy Smith, the native son who hangs his hat at the Royal Oaks club in Dallas, grooming pros' games. No moonlighting novelist he.

Actually, I am not even a Texan. My experience of being in Texas amounts to one occasion changing planes in the Dallas airport. Life for me has taken place more than a thousand miles from the Lone Star State with the exception of a few years in a Missouri college town. I've also never had any Texan friends. So, I must beg the forgiveness of any 'son of Texas' who wishes to 'string me up' for the hopefully few cultural *faux pas* in this book.

Also, if this initial admission prompts some curiosity as to why I dedicated two-plus years to researching and writing such a novel in the twilight of my career as a golf author, you are not alone.

What, I've asked myself, would Bobby Shout say? "Why that's like asking a blue-eyed steer who his sire was?" In other words, who knows why? But for those who find such an explanation unsatisfying, I add these details.

Above my workstation at home there's a framed trio of old black-and-white photos showing three golfers competing in Scotland. From left to right those heroic figures following through on wood shots are Bobby Jones, Ben Hogan, and Arnold Palmer. (I'd already written a long piece involving Bobby years ago, so he was 'out' as 'novel' material.)

On the wall to my left as I type this, one larger photo dominates. It's a classic color shot of Ben and Arnie at the '66 Masters. They are standing side by side on the tee – both puffing, both with their left arms outstretched, leaning on their tiny drivers -- but there is no sense of companionship beyond their shared pose. Both men look grave and utterly detached. So, which of these two greats was I to choose as the central figure in perhaps my final book? The King or the Hawk?

Ladies and gentleman, I had a tiebreaker. Thirty years ago I'd dared to send the manuscript copy of my first short-story anthology to Mr. Hogan for his birthday, excusing my impertinence by mentioning that he'd played a part in one of the tales. I shivered at the thought of receiving any reply, but one did come and promptly, dated August 13, the day after his celebration!

Here is the text of that brief note: "Thank you for sending me the manuscript copy of your book, *Golf In A Nutshell*, for my birthday. I haven't had a chance to read it as yet, but it certainly does look interesting. I appreciate your thinking of me, and with all good wishes, I am … Sincerely," [signed] Ben Hogan.

Thus, I'd been hooked on the Hawk for a long time. (Nor had I ignored the literary potential of Arnold Palmer up till then. You'll find him to be a bit player in my previous novel GOLF'S PRICE.)

As for the state of Ben's mind when he signed that letter to me, yes we all know now that it was well into the dementia phase of his life. If you told me that a secretary had written the text probably and placed it before Ben for his wobbly signature, I couldn't deny such a scenario. Yet I still feel wonder at having connected with the Hawk at all. Perhaps between my gift's receipt in '92 and his death in '97, Hogan listened to my stories sometimes, read to him by Valerie or his care-giver. We'll never know, will we?

One further thought: Seeing how the first short story I ever attempted did involve Ben (though I failed to complete that one) perhaps a psychologist might submit that I was 'closing the circle' of my writing career by returning to Hogan with this novel.

In any case, let's move on to those individuals whom I wish to acknowledge for their assistance in helping me take QUADRUPLE BIRDIE from notion to reality. (By the way, the novel's 'working title' was TEXAS QUARTET.)

At the top of this list is Maggie Lagle, Historian, USGA, who got me going on this project by promptly providing a detailed 1950 PGA Tour schedule. Following her are the biographers and memoirists who provided me with the facts to build many of the bones of this story.

To begin, I am indebted to James Dodd for his thorough account of Hogan's life as well as his fine follow-up volume which sought to 'dig out' the relationships between Ben, Byron, and Sam while telling their life stories. I also thank Curt Simpson for revealing gritty truths in his biography of the Hawk. Byron Nelson's and Gene Sarazen's autobiographies were of course essential reading, as was Jimmy Demaret's '53 book about the friendship he thought he shared with Hogan.

Speaking of Jimmy, I found John Companiotte's work about the Wardrobe to be invaluable. And Kris Tschetter's look-back at her relationship with the Hogans illuminated another aspect of the puzzle that was William Benjamin Hogan.

Another category of books which enabled me to include accurate details in the novel were the historical accounts of great golfing events, including Tom Flaherty's year-by-year summaries of the Masters, ditto Robert Sommers on the U.S. Open, and Al Barkow's masterful volumes about the PGA Tour in general. (His 'take' on Sam Snead is another good read.) Nick Callow's guide to all the Ryder Cup competitions proved quite useful as well.

My Texas Quartet's own instruction manuals yielded some good material, particularly in the case of Lloyd Mangrum who has yet to have a full-length biography devoted to him. Arnold Palmer's early work in this genre also deserves a read, or re-read. For the record, Cornish/Whitten's golf-architectural compendium, along with golf atlases and record books, came in handy in consort with the other sources.

Next in line are those institutions also deserving of my gratitude. I could never have gotten a good handle on the 1950 PGA season and beyond without the contemporaneous coverage provided by the Associated Press, New York Times, Washington Post, Baltimore Sun and Los Angeles Times.

All of these sources were available to me in one electronic, highly searchable database called Proquest Historical Newspapers. Kudos to my Baltimore County Public Library for providing free access to this invaluable resource.

As a career librarian from the early '80s on, I've had a ringside seat to the rise of the World Wide Web from mere curiosity to fabulous research tool. For a writer these days needing a lightning-fast education on a hundred different topics in the course of doing a book, websites are a godsend (so long as one uses them wisely).

Ditto to finding trustworthy assistance right down to the level of a single word: Spelling, meanings, usage, origin – they're all there on the Web. So hallelujah for Tim Berners-Lee who invented the WWW, and gratitude to the few of his ilk who've perfected it.

Having praised humans and their creations, I must turn to the gods before ending this particular paean. Thanks be to the Golfing Gods for the unseen guidance they provided to this project. To the God of Bobby Shout, I salute you for the good and great you inspire. And to a personal goddess – wife LouAnne – I reserve my final words of awe. You edit my rough prose so faithfully that the angels must smile over your shoulder. Dear, may your prayers be answered. Amen.

ABOUT THE AUTHOR

Randolph "R.N.A." Smith

R.N.A. SMITH HAS written and published nearly a million words related to golf. Residing now near Baltimore, he and his Quaker wife are celebrating forty-six years of marriage this year. Their son is a Nordic scholar, currently employed at a Midwestern college. The family has been and will forever be corgi-lovers!

Made in United States
North Haven, CT
22 April 2022

18453893R10136